PRAISE FOR THE PROMISE BETWEEN US

"If you leave your newborn child because you have unstoppable thoughts of harming her, are you a good mother or a terrible one? This dilemma is at the heart of Barbara Claypole White's novel, a wrenching story of how one woman's OCD has a ripple effect on those around her—including the people she tried hardest to protect. This is an eye-opening and realistic exploration of mental illness—a topic that greatly deserves to be front and center."

—Jodi Picoult, *New York Times* bestselling author of *Small Great Things*

"Barbara Claypole White does not merely write about people with mental illness—she inhabits them; she IS Katelyn, the young mother overcome with images of killing her new baby, the mother who leaves her baby to keep her safe . . . Later White IS that same child, Maisie, now beginning to struggle with OCD herself—and all Maisie's worries, all her thoughts and the details of her pre-teen life are precisely, exactly right. Perfect. White knows how to tell a story, too, how to fully create each additional realistic and fascinating character, and also how to increase suspense as the family drama unfolds. This brilliant novel about obsessive-compulsive disorder is compulsively readable."

—Lee Smith, *New York Times* bestselling author of *The Last Girls*

"In *The Promise Between Us*, bestselling author Barbara Claypole White explores survival, shame, and above all, compassion. With the deft hand of a true artist, she creates complex characters, whose lives have been ravaged by mental illness—when it goes unchecked and through its tumultuous effect on generations of women from one family. Readers will be drawn into Katie Mack's world, they'll root for her and her daughter, Maisie. *The Promise Between Us* redefines motherhood and sacrifice, delivering a heartfelt story with a powerful message."

—Laura Spinella, bestselling author of the
Ghost Gifts trilogy and *Unstrung*

"Barbara Claypole White knocks it out of the park with her latest family saga, *The Promise Between Us*. In this riveting page-turner, Claypole White digs deep into the intricacies of her characters' lives and the devastating effects of a mental illness when left unchecked. It can easily be classified as a story about motherhood, family, and sacrifice. But mostly, it's a tale of love, redemption, and renewal. *The Promise Between Us* has something for everyone: suspense, romance, and even a hint of mystery. A fast-paced read that captivates from the first word until the last. A definite book club selection that I highly recommend."

—Kerry Lonsdale, *Wall Street Journal* and Amazon Kindle bestselling
author of *Everything We Keep*

"In *The Promise Between Us*, Barbara Claypole White masters the art of bringing a reader up close and personal to the influences and forces of a mental illness. In this powerhouse of a story, Katelyn MacDonald's decision to give up the precious gift of raising her baby, Maisie, in order to protect her, makes for a compelling page-turner. This is an in-depth portrayal of what it means to live in a world where every single thought or action comes into question; it is a story for the times, a story filled with stark realities; but most important of all, it is a story about hope, healing, and the strength of a mother's love."

—Donna Everhart, *USA Today* bestselling author of
The Education of Dixie Dupree

The
Promise
Between
Us

OTHER BOOKS BY
BARBARA CLAYPOLE WHITE

The Unfinished Garden
The In-Between Hour
The Perfect Son
Echoes of Family

The Promise Between Us

BARBARA CLAYPOLE WHITE

LAKE UNION
PUBLISHING

Text copyright © 2018 by Barbara Claypole White
All rights reserved.

Published by Lake Union Publishing, Seattle

www.apub.com

Amazon, the Amazon logo, and Lake Union Publishing are trademarks of Amazon.com, Inc., or its affiliates.

ISBN-13: 9781542048989
ISBN-10: 1542048982

Cover design by Shasti O'Leary Soudant

Printed in the United States of America

For my two Christmas stars,
fearless in their compassion:

Zachariah Claypole White
Stephen Whitney (1987–2016)

Every thought is just a thought until you assign it meaning.

—*Angie Alexander, founder of Friends with OCD*

When the world says, "Give up," Hope whispers, "Try it one more time."

—*Author unknown*

Raleigh, North Carolina

Crouched in the corner of my baby girl's bedroom, we both shake: the three-legged mutt and the mother with a colony of fire ants multiplying in her brain. Hardly a five-star protection squad, but we would die to keep Maisie safe.

Ringo nudges my arm and wriggles closer. His circle of trust is small, namely me, but then I rescued him after he collapsed in our driveway, deprived of food and love. Neither of us has eaten. I can't, and Ringo won't leave my side. Not tonight.

Across the room, the blinds are open. The sky is cast-iron black, no stars. In the red metal crib with polka-dot bedding, under the soft light of her Winnie-the-Pooh lamp, 'Mazing Maisie makes suckling noises. I don't have to see her to know she's sleeping with arms flung above her head, mouth blowing pretend kisses.

What goes through her mind at seven months? I know it's more than instinct. I know the smile that greets her daddy or her aunt—even her godfather the one time he deigned to visit—is pure joy. You can't fake joy. Is she dreaming under the gaze of the cow jumping over the moon? I was six months pregnant and screeching along to Bruce Springsteen when I painted that mural. Although, let's be honest, I traced the outline. Cheated, the way I'm cheating at motherhood.

The sound machine hums fake waves. Harmless waves. Gentle waves that bring memories of our weekend at Ocean Isle when Maisie was six weeks old. Cal saying, "My girls," as if he'd won Best Family and couldn't believe his luck. Will that change when he comes home from his conference and sees the trash can full of sharp objects: the kitchen scissors, the butcher knife, the pruning shears?

Anything that could be used to hurt Maisie.

Who am I kidding? Anything I could use to hurt Maisie.

"If you have to take me down, buddy," I tell Ringo, "do it. No hesitation."

He licks my face.

All I want is to be a good mother to my baby girl. Stopped bathing her unless Cal was in the house, because what if I slipped and she fell out of my hands? Unplugged the kitchen appliances, because you never know when one's going to short out and start a fire, right? Stop, avoid; stop, avoid—my new pattern, but it isn't enough. Nothing I do is enough.

I'm a middle school teacher, not the next Susan Smith. She strapped her babies into car seats, watched them drown, and lied about it on national TV. I wouldn't have lied. I would have killed myself. Slowly, painfully, with a dirty knife from the garbage.

A car door slams in the street. I sit up and listen, but no key turns in the lock. I slump back against the bedroom wall and rub my hands down my thighs. Try to erase the sweat. Ridiculous to crank the heat up to eighty, but Maisie must never feel the February cold. Purgatory is cold, not warm. I should know. I shivered through my childhood.

Has Cal finally been able to get a break? I've made him twitchy. Anxious. He fusses over what I eat and when I sleep. What sleep, Cal, what sleep? He's found a sitter for next weekend, one of his grad students. I know he wants to help, but how can I trust our baby to a stranger? And what if, what if we were in a car wreck and something happened to both of us?

2

I grab my head, dig in what's left of my fingernails. I wasn't this way before that news report. A mother had drowned her baby in the bathtub. I cried as I sliced up raw chicken for dinner and wondered how a mother could do that. Then my mind showed me. Showed me, Katelyn MacDonald, as Norman Bates in unwashed yoga pants.

That's when they started: the images.

I haven't told anyone about my private horror movie. Not Cal, not the doctors. They would take Maisie away. I'd lose her forever. Baby blues, the pediatrician said when I told him I worried all the time. Depression and PTSD, the shrink said. Easy fixes—swallow these pills and think happy thoughts. Apparently seeing my mother stab my father at the kitchen table was enough to send any future adult loco. According to the professionals, we never escape our childhoods. Mine was short-lived after the kitchen incident. Dad ran off, and Mom prayed and drank, prayed and drank, while I raised my baby sister.

Twelve years old and anointed mother of the house.

Another image pounces, then hammers and pounds. An image so perverted I want to puke or open the window and toss myself out like an unwanted spider. I shove my hand across my mouth and bite down. Hard. I am not this person. I am not.

Are you still listening, God?

I need sleep; I need Cal to come home.

He doesn't believe in therapy, but he urged me to take the pills. Doesn't know I flush them down the toilet. When I filled the prescription, I was still nursing. How could I risk drugs entering her system, contaminating her little body? And now that she's weaned, I can't take the meds, because what if they erase my fear, but not the images? I need that fear. It's all I have left to protect Maisie.

Turning, I check she's still in the crib. Still safe.

On top of her bookcase, the Winnie-the-Pooh lamp glows. Embers glow, the embers of a fire. Fire. Fire maims, fire kills. The lamp flickers. Is it a fire hazard? Yes! Terror steals the world's favorite teddy bear, labels him a threat.

Winnie-the-Pooh waits for my next move.

My heart booms in my ears. The world slants as if trying to shove me off. Wobbling, I stand up. Tap the wall four times—four to keep Maisie safe. Has to be four. I need to unplug that lamp; I need to dump it, but I can't risk moving, because what if? What if I pick up Maisie instead of the lamp? What if I drop her? What if I want to drop her?

What if I'm the one weapon I can't toss in the trash can?

The floor shimmers, seems to pitch and roll. I shake my head. Can't pass out, not if there's a fire. One spark, that's all it would take.

One spark.

My mind cracks open. Why, why is this happening again? New images hit like buckshot. A fire flaring, Maisie trapped in the crib, me picking her up, me dropping her on the stairs. The fire claiming her. What if I want the lamp to short out and burn the house down? What if I want her to die?

The image plays again and again. Always again. No pause to reload. Legs can't support my weight. Kicked in the gut, I'm on my knees. Powerless, I curl up and scream silently.

More images attack in a fresh assault. Over and over. Over and over.

A twisted thought—loud, clear—shouts, then roars. Lunges and jabs, sharper and sharper. An ice pick in my brain: I'm going to kill my baby.

That's not true! I love you, Maisie. I promise I will protect you from danger.

But what if I can't? What if I'm not strong enough to be her mother? What if I'm not who I thought I was? What if the danger is me?

The front door clicks; fear keeps me paralyzed.

The hall light goes on. Ringo wags his tail—thump-thump, thump-thump against my ribs—and Maisie starts to howl. From silence to screams in less than two seconds. Must go to her, must comfort her. Can't, because what if? What if?

Cal rushes through the doorway and lifts Maisie from her crib. He kisses her pink cheeks. I want to hold my baby girl. I want to kiss her. But it's not safe. I'm not safe.

I know how bad I look: dirty hair, unwashed clothes. I probably smell. Can you smell evil?

"Why are you on the floor? Why didn't you pick her up?" He frowns at me. "Why's the house hot?" He looks around the room. "Where's your sister?"

So many questions, but then again, I'm not the mother either of us expected. Took me three years to talk him into having a baby. Welcome to hell, honey.

The Winnie-the-Pooh lamp flickers again, and he leans toward it. Words smash together in my throat, dry as kindling: Don't touch it! Don't touch it! Too late. He mutters about a new bulb and turns back to me.

"Why are you crying?"

His girls are sobbing a duet. Cal looks from one of us to the other, but he doesn't step closer to me. Good, he's putting her first, as he should. He sways and rocks and pats and cradles. Maisie begins to settle. He's finally learning how to soothe her, but he needs to keep practicing, because I can't touch her anymore. I can't pick up my own baby.

I could drop her down the stairs. I could throw her down the stairs.

I sniff, swipe my hand under my nose. Sit up.

The image still plays. Never-ending background static. Or is it the theme song of a psycho?

"My sis—she got the flu," I say. "I . . . I didn't want her near Maisie."

"Why didn't you tell me? All those texts I sent to check in, and you didn't tell me? Mom would have helped out."

But that's the reason I kept quiet. The perfect mother-in-law who sees only the perfect son. Doesn't he understand the weight of shame?

Cal's beautiful blue eyes stare. On our wedding night, he murmured I'd saved his life. I trust him, he trusts me, and I haven't been honest. I glance at the Winnie-the-Pooh lamp, stand up, and swallow. He waits for my explanation, follows my lead as always. Ringo waits too, head resting on his paws. I'm a deer trapped in the headlights of insanity.

"I need help," I mumble.

"I know." He keeps rocking Maisie. "I've been reading up about childhood trauma, and we need to talk, but not tonight. Let's bring Maisie in with us so we can all sleep, and we'll tackle this in the morning." He tries to give me a smile, but it won't stay in place.

"I don't think this has anything to do with my childhood. I think this is worse."

He stops moving. "Worse how?"

"Something happened to me after Ocean Isle. I keep picturing these awful things—in my mind. And they feel so real. I can't get rid of them, Cal. Can't make them stop."

I inhale, exhale; he watches.

"I see myself hurting Maisie, even though I would never do that. Never. But what if the house burns down with Maisie trapped in her crib and it's my fault? What if I start a fire and don't even realize it and . . . I think I'm going mad."

"You need to go to the ER. Now." His voice is cold steel. "I'm calling your sister."

"What? No! No, they'll take Maisie away and lock me up in a cell with no light and no air and—" I grab my arms, scratch my skin. Want to claw it off. Want to rip myself into pieces. Want to tear out these images. "Please. I love you, I love you both."

Eyes darting in every direction, he starts to cry. "You admitted that you want to set our house on . . ." He waves it away, doesn't want the visuals. Neither do I, but I have no choice. My mind has no "Off" switch.

"I didn't! That's not what I said, I—"

I start to reach for him, but he holds up his palm in the universal sign for "Stop." Shaking, he takes a breath. His fear sucks the air out of my lungs.

"Callum, please . . ."

He reels to one side and then staggers past me.

My family has left me. Or maybe I left them first. The lock on our bedroom door clicks, and Ringo whines. A new thought settles, one I don't dispute. One I know is the truth. After months of uncertainty, of dread, of fear over who—or what—I've become, I have my answer.

My husband is terrified of me. I am a monster.

ONE

CALLUM

Star Wars goggles perched on top of her head, Maisie glared at the life-guard and cleared her throat loudly. The pimply teen finally turned his attention to the young girl waiting to intercept him as he approached the ladder chair for his shift.

Callum, slathered in SPF50 and sitting under the shade of a huge umbrella, grinned. There was much to regret and second-guess in life, but not the last decade of fatherhood. Raising a confident, fearless child might be his greatest achievement. Might be his only achievement if he didn't finish the manuscript before the school year started.

"This is my friend Ellie's first time at our pool." Maisie reached behind for Ellie, who continued to stare at her toes. "And she'd like to take the eleven-foot test, please."

"You need to take it, too?" the lifeguard said.

With a low laugh, Callum sat back to enjoy. For once he was the spectator in this chafing against every rule deemed unfair by a child flexing her newly acquired ten-year-old muscles. The lifeguard had no idea that he'd met his match.

"No offense"—Maisie flicked back the long red hair she refused to have cut—"but I take the test on the day the pool opens *evvvery* summer, and since I turned ten a *whole* week ago, when my dad let me see *Star Wars: The Force Awakens* even though it's PG-13, I don't think I'll need to take the test ever again." Her eyes opened wide as they always did when she was constructing her concluding argument. "Actually," Maisie continued, "I plan to start a petition to have it abolished for kids who have reached ten. We're quite old enough, thank you, to swim in the deep end without taking an annual test."

Even though your dad wishes you weren't. Callum swatted a mosquito on his thigh.

Maisie cleared her throat twice. That throat clearing had become persistent. Allergies? He'd add it to the growing list for her ten-year checkup at the pediatrician's.

With a splash, Maisie and Ellie jumped in the pool, and Callum craned his neck to make sure they both resurfaced. As two small heads—one red, one blond—bobbed up, his mind ran through the afternoon chores: drive Ellie home, stop at Whole Foods to replenish his stock of melatonin, take their elderly neighbor's dog for a walk, and hopefully squeeze in a couple of hours on the manuscript before relaxing into Saturday evening with his family. Relaxation wasn't a chore, but it didn't come instinctively. Other parents at the pool made it look effortless—by ignoring their kids. That was never going to be an option. He couldn't even take his eyes off Maisie long enough to glimpse the headlines on his unopened *New York Times*. And with Ellie he had double the responsibility.

Kids squealed, and across the blue water, so artificially happy, Jake made an entrance with the cooler that likely contained the usual supplies: two water bottles filled with screwdrivers—one weak, one strong—juice boxes, organic baby carrots, and slices of apple. Bathing-suit-clad moms followed his buddy's progress across the concrete.

"Morning, 'Mazing Maisie." Oblivious to his audience for once, Jake walked to the edge of the pool, hooked a finger over his sunglasses, and slid them down the bridge of his nose. He blew Maisie a kiss, then pushed his sunglasses back into place.

The woman on the chair one over sighed.

"Uncle J." Maisie scowled. "I'm actually quite busy helping Ellie prepare for the eleven-foot test."

"Which she will ace, as you always do, darlin'."

Callum swiped the towel off the chaise lounge he'd been saving in the sun. Two months into their Saturday mornings at the pool, and despite hiding in the shade, he was still a delicate shade of pink. Unlike Jake, who had a deep, even tan. "Hot enough for you?"

Jake dumped the cooler on the ground and kicked off his slides. "Not until I start sweatin' like a bug." He flopped down, folded his arms behind his head, and raised his face to the sun. "Bliss. I could almost be back in LA."

"You better have sunscreen on, otherwise Maisie'll give you hell."

"That she will. You realize my darlin' goddaughter is the only female on the planet who bosses me around?"

"Wait until the hormones kick in. You and I won't stand a chance."

Before long he and Jake would be the enemy, but Maisie still said "Daddy" as if it were the best-kept secret in the universe. Unless she was pestering him for a phone, with the logic that *everyone* going into fifth grade at her year-round school had one. Maisie, however, was not getting a phone.

"Talking of females, where's Lilah Rose?" Jake always used Lilah's full name, saying it was too pretty to shorten, but Callum knew the truth: Jake hadn't been won over by her. Not yet. Hell, neither had Maisie. Team MacDonald was about to expand to four. And Lilah and Maisie weren't wearing the same jerseys.

"The excitement of the pool proved exhausting. My lovely wife was imitating Sleeping Beauty when we tiptoed out."

"It's weird, man. Hearing you say 'wife' again."

"No weirder than when you slip back into that country accent after two decades of acting classes."

Jake shrugged. "Could be moving back here helped me find myself."

"Hopefully marriage the second time will do the same for me." Although, old and new had started blending into a nauseating assault of doubt. After all, if history were about to repeat itself, how would he know? Pregnancy the first time around had also been stunningly normal.

Jake rolled his head to the side. "You're not having second thoughts, are you?"

"Absolutely not. You know how I feel about Lilah. The universe merely gave us a big heave-ho in the right direction."

"Pregnancy's one almighty heave-ho," Jake said.

"It's just . . ."

"Been two men and one kid for a while?"

"Something like that. How was your week?"

"Outstanding. What's not to love about summer? Kids on Film pulls in good money, and this week's campers were rarin' to go. Don't even miss acting when I'm mentoring kids this fired up, and you're changing the subject." Jake lowered his voice. "Remember what I told you. Stay grounded, stay rooted in the present. It's a beautiful day, you're here with Maisie and me, and we've got vodka. Right there, that's three reasons to be grateful. And here's a fourth: you managed to drag Maisie away from organizing her new school supplies. Beats me how any kid can find back-to-school in July thrilling."

"She prefers the year-round model. You know how bored she gets if she's home all summer."

"That magnet school is something else. Imagine if we'd had Quidditch on the curriculum. I could've been a straight-A student instead of the class dumbass."

"You weren't a dumbass."

"You forgettin' I was repeating first grade when we met?"

"No, I'm remembering that your aunt was a useless guardian. She should have figured out you were dyslexic years before Mom did."

Jake's aunt, who had begrudgingly taken him in as a seven-year-old orphan with no other family, branded him stupid even before middle school. When Jake was accepted into one of the premier acting programs in the country, no one questioned why Callum's parents had hosted the party.

A whistle blew, and Callum sat up to check that Ellie and Maisie were still in his field of vision. Satisfied the whistle had nothing to do with either of his charges, he slumped back. The high dive vibrated with a loud crack as a young man bounced off the board, flew high, and sliced into the water headfirst without leaving a ripple.

"I dreamed about *her* last night," Callum said.

Jake's mirrored sunglasses failed to shield Callum from his glare.

"Katelyn's not coming back. Ever. And that is a blessing for you and Maisie." Jake swung his legs around and planted his bare feet on the hot concrete. Resting his arms across his thighs, he leaned toward Callum. "And I've told you a thousand times, what happened was not your fault, so stop beating yourself up. You might have been blinded by love and lust, but Katelyn was always wound tighter than a dollar store watch."

"She was a good mother, Jake. At least until the end."

"And what—you can be a good mama if you abandoned your baby? That makes as much sense as tits on a bull. You, on the other hand, did what any good parent would do."

Callum knew what was coming next. He always knew.

"You protected your daughter," Jake said.

"Which I couldn't have done without you."

Jake raised his head to smile at the busty brunette walking past in a bikini. And kept watching as she disappeared into the changing room. "Yeah, well, that promise I made when we were kids didn't come with an expiration date." Jake popped open the cooler, grabbed the red water bottle, and slugged. "Here." He handed over the blue water bottle.

12

"You're way too serious for someone who's about to toast this beautiful July day with vodka—watered down enough even for you."

"It's not beautiful, it's inhumanely hot." Callum took a sip and then another one. "I can't wait for the fall."

"Now that's plain sacrilegious. And for goodness' sake, stop nipping at that thing and take a man-drink."

Callum gulped diluted orange juice that tasted as flavorful as seltzer water. "The dream's got me thinking, that's all."

"And I know where that thinking leads, so let it go." Jake flashed the smile that a decade earlier had earned him $350,000 for one afternoon's work on a hemorrhoid cream commercial. "And now you get your happy ending with Lilah Rose, your cosmic reward for being the patron saint of fathers."

"She's the one in line for sainthood." Callum shook his head. "Inherited all my crap, and I didn't even give her a honeymoon."

Maisie clambered out of the pool and gave them a thumbs-up. What a treat to see those big hazel eyes minus the new black frames. He had worked hard to talk her into the green pair, but Maisie insisted on Harry Potter black, and he caved because it wasn't a battle worth fighting.

"She did it!" Holding up Ellie's hand, Maisie stood in front of him, dripping chlorinated water. She gave Callum the smile that for years had been the only thing worth living for.

"High fives all around, ladies," Jake said.

"I thought Lilah, I mean Mom"—Maisie shot Jake a look—"was going to join us?"

"Pregnancy's a tough job, sweetheart," Callum said. "Your mom gets wiped out, and she didn't sleep well last night."

"But everything's okay? She looked quite pale when we left. Do you think we should check on her?"

"Wake a sleep-deprived pregnant woman? Not without full body armor." Callum smiled; Maisie didn't.

Her constant concern for Lilah's health might have been endearing, if it wasn't coming on the tail of endless worry about middle school—a year away. Maisie had always been a serious child, but this nervousness was new. Maybe it was part of her sudden desire to be a mini grown-up. Or maybe his little empath was picking up on his mood. Because what he hadn't told Jake, had no intention of telling Jake, was that the insomnia and night sweats were back. And when he did manage to fall asleep, Callum shot awake, gulping through anxiety that clung like a low-grade fever.

Maisie chewed on the end of her hair. Another new habit. Had it begun before or after he told her about the baby? So much had happened so fast in their world. The real question, though, was whether it was too fast.

"Peanut," Callum said, "please don't do that."

"Yeah, it's *gross-oid*," Jake said.

Ellie giggled, and Maisie stopped chewing her hair, but a deep frown remained.

"How about you two splash Uncle J with a few cannonballs?"

"Dad." The frown vanished, and Maisie held up her arms as if they were exclamation points. "You know cannonballs are only allowed off the diving boards."

"Yeah, *Dad*." Jake stood up. "Get with the program."

They grinned at him, Maisie and Mad-Max-Mama, as Jake had called himself when Maisie was a kindergartner and other parents labeled them an alternative family thanks to Jake hamming up his role at school events. Pretense, according to Jake, was the cure for real life. Callum wasn't sure he agreed.

"Who's up for a game of 'Let's Sink the Unsinkable Jake'?" Jake held out both hands and glanced over his shoulder. "Let it go, man. All of it." And then he disappeared toward the shallow end with the girls in tow.

Let it go, but how? What if I fail Lilah as I failed Katelyn?

A hummingbird buzzed toward some huge red flower. Katelyn had loved hummingbirds. She used to make up sugar water for them and clean out the feeders every week with tiny brushes. Callum tried to give the brushes and the feeders to her sister, along with the boxes of books and clothes, but Delaney lived in a small apartment and insisted he keep everything in the attic. It was the first of their many arguments. Delaney came to hate him surprisingly quickly, and he could hardly blame her. Katelyn hadn't been of sound mind when she made her decision. He and Jake didn't have any such excuse.

Sweat dribbled down his spine, and Callum inhaled the scent of summers at the pool—fried food, sunscreen, and chlorine.

His old shadow reappeared: the question that had slunk back to plague him despite his April wedding in a church filled with dogwood blossoms.

Why, why me?

TWO

LILAH

Lilah snorted awake to paint fumes and recycled warm air blowing from the fan Callum had angled in her direction. August was roaring at them with Sahara heat, and their air-conditioning was on the fritz, turning her into a cranky caricature of pregnancy. Of course, she'd already become a cliché:

Former student falls in love with her thesis advisor and fails miserably to use her diaphragm or mother his daughter, who looks at her as if she's a very large cockroach.

Terrific. Now she was thinking of herself in the third person.

Wiping drool from the corner of her mouth, Lilah stared at the walls of primrose yellow she had regretted before the paint dried. After slipping silently into Callum's ready-made family that included the attack-dog best friend, she embarked on a redecorating binge as if nesting were an Olympic sport. Post-structuralism, however, made more sense than paint chips. And why had Callum not vetoed the white sofa? He stopped rubbing her feet.

"I was snoring again, wasn't I?" she said.

Callum grinned.

In the days before he woke her every morning with a mug of tea, she had been able to sleep through any alarm clock on the market. Now, pregnancy had dragged her into the subculture of the sleep obsessed. Lilah frowned. She should be working on her syllabi, not napping on the sofa.

"Pissed off and pregnant's a good look for you," Callum said.

The anger didn't even stay around for the two-second mark. It was Callum's deep-blue eyes that did it, along with the disheveled russet mane. Ditch the trendy glasses and put him in the family tartan, and half of America would mistake Professor Callum MacDonald for an extra on the set of *Outlander*. Her husband was, in one word, gorgeous. There it was again, the *h*-word. *Husband.* How did this happen? Two PhDs between them, and they couldn't figure out contraception.

She chewed her lip.

"In case you're interested, that's also a turn-on." Callum's soft brogue, topped up from a lifetime of summers in Scotland with his parents, became more pronounced when he talked sex.

"You're not so bad, either, my Hot Scot."

Dipping forward, he kissed her—slowly and gently. Lilah shivered and breathed in his scent: lemongrass and shaving cream. This life with Callum had been her fantasy, but not a year out from graduating and landing her dream job at Meredith College. Not before she wrangled her dissertation into publishable shape. Not before Callum finished the book that was his ticket to becoming a full professor. He had barely touched his manuscript all summer, spending every minute with Maisie, as if about to lose her forever.

Lilah rubbed her belly. "You're watching *Star Wars Rebels* without Maisie?"

He grabbed the remote, hit the "Mute" button, and tossed it back down on the coffee table. "There's nothing on, Maisie's in her room, and you were—"

"Snoring."

Callum eased her feet off his lap and turned with that quirk of a smile that was guaranteed to make her heart over-rev. "Did I ever mention my weakness for beautiful women who snore?" His index finger beckoned her, but after lumbering toward his end of the sofa, she toppled against him and groaned.

"What's wrong?"

"Other than me moving slower than a centenarian? Nothing." The morning sickness had long gone, but Callum still fussed over every twinge, every cramp, every groan. "What's Maisie up to?"

"Prepping for her quiz on Monday." He was decent enough not to add, *If you studied the kitchen calendar, you'd know.* She'd given up because the month-at-a-glance pages told her nothing about how to become Maisie's mother.

"Don't you find it strange that a fifth-grader's doing homework on a Saturday night and not painting her nails, demanding you buy her skinny jeans, or hankering after the member of a boy band?"

He sat up, leaving her no choice but to do the same.

"Maisie takes pride in being a good student. Besides, she still likes Jamberry nail stickers, has no interest in fashion trends, and thinks all boys are annoying. Jake and I, despite being a pair of overgrown boys, are exempt."

Callum stood, tugged up his sweat shorts, and began to clear the coffee table. His calf muscles, toned from the long bike rides with Jake, flexed. As he reached for her empty glass, he threw a smile over his shoulder. His conciliatory smile. After years of watching his face in undergraduate and graduate seminars, she could read every expression. What went on behind those expressions was another matter.

Lilah had never believed the student rumors that painted Callum as gay, but lacked empirical evidence until she turned up—here—with a thank-you bottle of bourbon after her graduate hooding ceremony. When she woke up naked in his bed, she couldn't decide whether she'd won the state lottery or should never again set foot in North Carolina.

But then Callum looked at her as if she were the eighth wonder of the world, and said, "When did you realize I was in love with you? I thought I hid it pretty well." Although, if Maisie hadn't been down at Pinehurst with the grandparents that weekend, if Callum hadn't been plastered, if not for the alcohol, would she have found the courage to make the first move Callum still teased her about? Not that she could remember. Bourbon—evil stuff.

One thing she did remember, could never forget, was the exact moment her teacher crush had exploded into love. It was at the beginning of her second year of grad school. Her period started while she was sitting in the front row of his class, wearing white pants. She pretended to gather her stuff as everyone shuffled out, but Callum lingered. Finally he walked over, squatted down, and said, "Is something wrong?" And then the warmth between her legs switched to a gush, and she was fresh out of options. After she explained she was having a female problem that didn't play nice with white jeans, something she would never have confessed to another professor, he fetched a sweater from his book bag. "I always carry an extra layer as protection against the library's air-conditioning," he said. "Wrap it around your waist and I'll walk ahead of you to the nearest bathroom. Then I'll give you a ride home so you can change." She'd slept with that sweater for a week, tucking it under her cheek and inhaling his scent each night before—

"Daddy?" Maisie appeared in the doorway, dangling a piece of paper and her loved-to-death stuffed rabbit, Lulabelle. With a red pencil slotted behind each ear, she was wearing a typical Maisie creation of polka-dot capri leggings and a psychedelic T-shirt. Lulabelle, who was hidden when friends came over, rarely left the bedroom, and Maisie was trying hard to drop *Daddy.* She had started referring to Callum as *my dad,* in a way that seemed to imply *You're not my mom.*

"Hey, peanut." Callum opened his arms.

Maisie launched herself at her father, and they clung to each other, forming the impenetrable unit that was Callum and Maisie. The youngest of five, Lilah had been lucky if either of her parents remembered her name. At Maisie's age or now, at thirty.

"Oof, thanks for knocking the stuffing out of me." Callum stroked the long red hair that announced Maisie as his daughter. What had she inherited from her mom? "Is something wrong?"

"My homework, Daddy. I can't do it, I simply can't."

Hefting herself onto her feet, Lilah glanced at the paper in Maisie's right hand. "Not surprising, sweetie. Math is an instrument of the devil and definitely not as much fun as making up stories." Lots of fantasy stories with mythical mothers who had superpowers. *No pressure there.*

"Your mom has a point." Callum winked at Lilah.

Maisie burrowed into her dad, and he made soothing noises. "Talk to me, peanut."

"Math is super annoying and I can't get it right." Maisie spoke in a rush and then held up her homework. A large hole obliterated the answer to the first question.

"Sweetheart—" When Callum spoke to Maisie it was as if nothing else mattered. "Come to me before you get this frustrated. What are parents for if not to share the misery of homework? Let's take this into the kitchen and gobble an entire pint of Phish Food!"

Maisie pulled back with knuckles on her hips, her homework hanging from one hand, Lulabelle from the other. "Really? *You* are going to eat half a tub of ice cream?"

"If you're going to force me to do math on a Saturday night, I'll need a vast intake of calories." He tickled her and she giggled.

They headed into the kitchen. Lilah picked up the sections of the paper Callum had gathered together for recycling and his two empty beer bottles, and followed.

Maisie sat at the table, legs tucked up and Lulabelle stretched across her lap. Callum had already pulled out the Ben & Jerry's and was rummaging in the drawer for spoons. He handed one to Maisie and offered one to Lilah. She shook her head and opened the stainless steel fridge in the high-tech kitchen that was nothing like her old galley kitchen. After grabbing a small bottle of Pellegrino, she leaned back across the counter to watch Callum do what he did so well: parent for two.

"And Ava Grace is going all crazy girlie girl on me." Maisie held up her palms in exasperated surrender. "She's started talking about hairstyles."

"Not *hairstyles*." Callum gave a mischievous grin.

"Actually, yes, Daddy. She thinks we should be wearing matching ponytails and you *know* how I don't like to have a ponytail. It hurts the back of my head! And I don't want to be a twin. I want to look like me. But if I don't start wearing my hair in a ponytail, she might think we're not best friends anymore. It's the causation of much stress."

"Causation?" Lilah laughed.

Eyes wide, Maisie gave her the look that said, *Oh, yeah. Giant cockroach.*

"Well, that's super annoying." Callum did his impression of a pre-teen pout. "So you had a falling-out with your best friend, and homework's stinky."

"Affirmative." Maisie picked at her toes.

"Anything else to add to the list?"

"Lilah's right. Math is evil." Maisie bolted up and dug into the ice cream.

"And?"

The fridge made the fizzing noise that still caught Lilah by surprise.

"I think I was rude to Ms. Black. I didn't mean to be, but I—"

"Did you apologize?" Callum said.

"Yes! Multiple times. But now I'm worried she hates me and she'll be super glad when I leave for middle school. And I don't want to leave her ever, and I don't want her to hate me. Do you think she does? Hate me?"

"Your teachers love you," Callum said. "No one could hate you."

Maisie glanced at Lilah. Wow, that was so not fair.

"I'm sure it's fine, sweetheart. Ms. Black would have reprimanded you if you'd crossed a line, and as for Ava Grace, talk to her. You guys have been best friends since forever. I hate to think of you arguing."

"Oh, no, Daddy. We would never argue. *Nev-errrr.* But what if she decides she likes Ellie better than me because I won't wear a ponytail? After all, three is a very difficult number."

"Friendships are tough, but you're not responsible for other people's feelings, and you have to be true to yourself." Callum paused. "Never blindly follow what someone else wants you to do. There's a word for that, when a person tries to make you do things—*manipulation.*"

Hmm. Overkill for a comment on ponytails.

"Talk to her," Callum said. "Anything else going on in school?"

"Actually, *yyyes.* I had to be on Parker's team for 'capture the flag' yesterday, and he is such a cheater. He cheated so much that everyone was looking down on our team, and I had to say to Ava Grace and Ellie, 'Please don't blame my team for all these things.' Cheaters are super stinky."

"Amen," Lilah said.

The kitchen clock ticked; Maisie looked at her dad, her gorgeous hazel eyes hidden by those horrendous black frames; the overhead fan hummed as the blades turned.

"Did Parker get caught?" Callum said.

"Oh, yes. Ms. Black never lets cheating go unpunished. It's a carnation of lying."

"Incarnation," Callum said.

Maisie attacked the ice cream, digging out the marshmallow. "I like the word *manipulation.* I'm going to remember it."

"Hey, stop eating all the good bits." Callum snatched up the pint of Phish Food and clasped it to his chest.

Maisie stuck out her chocolate-covered tongue, and Callum laughed.

"Okay," he said. "Shall we try this together, see if we can knock the homework out of the ballpark and then watch a movie on pay-per-view?"

"I can stay up late?" Maisie grinned.

"Sure. Saturday night with my girls? Sounds perfect."

"PG-13?"

Callum peered over his glasses, and Maisie sighed dramatically. "Ellie's dad lets her."

"One more word about PG-13, and there won't be a movie."

"Fine."

"You know what, guys? Party on without me. I'm off for a long soak in the tub and an early night. And if either of you gets sick from gorging on ice cream, I'm not rubbing any tummies." Lilah kissed the top of Maisie's head and moved toward Callum.

He circled an arm around her waist and pulled her in for a chaste kiss. "Sweet dreams, my darling." Then he leaned in to whisper. "Wake you later?"

"People! Child present?" Maisie made a slashing motion across her throat.

As Lilah climbed the stairs, her family giggled in the kitchen below. Halfway up, she paused to catch her breath by the stained glass window Callum's first wife had chosen. The garish purple-and-green iris design was on Lilah's to-be-replaced list, but even so, it was unlikely she could exorcise the whiff of mold. No one had noticed that the porthole window leaked after it was fitted, allowing rain to seep into the frame of the house, undetected. The smell, a rotting memory of Katelyn MacDonald, lingered.

Lilah started chewing her thumbnail and then stopped. Maisie had an unpleasant habit of gnawing on her fingernails as if trying to chew herself raw. Lilah had always prided herself on not being a nail-biter, and now, thanks to a dead woman, she was.

What did it mean to be obsessed with a ghost?

THREE

KATIE

Manipulating six thousand degrees of heat never lost its novelty. Neither did controlling power tools that spun and whirred and sparked. Through Katie's auto-darkening helmet, her world was black except for the dot of green light, silent but for the sound that always reminded her of sausages sizzling or sparklers crackling. She released the trigger, and the green burst became an orange glow. Her MIG welder cut out with a satisfied *puff*.

Katie flipped up her mask and slid out her earplugs, leaving them to dangle from the orange connector cord around her neck. Grinders and chop saws screeched and whined in the old tobacco warehouse with the leaking roof and occasional rodent. Other artists in the Durham Sculpture Workshop banged things together and apart as they turned scrap metal into treasure. Green Day's cover of "Like a Rolling Stone" started blasting.

Smiling, Katie leaned in to examine the tack welds on the backside of the frame. Four, one in each corner. Three was the easiest, but four was better. Next, she prepared for the weld bead, which would fill the space between the joined pieces of metal. She marked up the iron with soapstone, rested her left foot on the shelf under her worktable, and angled her body to be perpendicular to the weld.

The helmet came back down, the earplugs went back into place, and sparks flew. Katie lost herself in the simplicity of the process: she pushed the trigger, electricity traveled down the copper-coated steel wire, electrons jumped from the tip of the welder to the metal, and the shielding gas sprayed out to push away the oxygen. Electrons, gas, wire, and heat all worked together to create a simple bind that, if done right, held.

Damn. She couldn't see properly. Ben, the star of the studio, who had taken her on as his personal project, taught her the two cardinal rules of welding: comfort and clear vision. When you couldn't see what you were doing, it was time to stop. The welder clicked, and Katie tugged off her helmet.

A baby cloud of smoke hovered over her work. She made fresh marks with the soapstone and kept her leather-covered fingers away from the weld. It might have turned to the consistency of silver putty, but it was still nine hundred degrees of burn. In the early days, before Ben had taught her about protection and safety, she made the mistake of wearing a cropped T-shirt to a welding class and came home with a burn across her stomach.

Katie inhaled, her sense of smell the best early warning system against sparks landing somewhere they shouldn't. She detected nothing worse than a burning residue reminiscent of a dentist drilling.

At the back of her workbench lay *That Perfect Moment*, the piece for the frame she was welding. She had treated the old brass kickplate with various patinas: the splash of red was applied with heat, the blue waves came from a chemical reaction. The two dark shapes under the light of the mystical moon were the hallmarks of a Katie Mack piece. No one but Katie and her sister, Delaney, knew the secret: the shapes represented a mother and a daughter. But how to attach the ragged sliver of copper without losing the slight shadow it threw toward the figures? The problem niggled, threatened to become a delay. A cause for alarm. Katie tapped the worktop and stopped. If she slipped a washer underneath the copper, then bolted it, that would raise it enough to keep the shadow.

A large hand pressed down on her shoulder, and Katie smiled. Even with his infrequent girlfriends, Ben wasn't a toucher, but he knew never to surprise her during reentry to the real world. How had he learned so much when she'd given him so little to work with?

She pulled off her gloves, removed her earplugs, and turned to the huge figure in a black sleeveless T-shirt and a tie-dye skullcap. His gray eyes were hidden behind red-framed safety glasses. As usual, they needed a good wipe. She almost reached for them, saying, *Here, let me.*

"You missed another school group," he said. "What's the excuse this time?"

"Kids in a place where a thousand things can cause danger isn't my scene." Katie lowered her safety glasses, turned off the gases on her welder, and undid the ground clamp.

"Nor mine. One spark on a kid's jeans, and—"

"Can we not go there? Stuff of nightmares for me."

"Jesus, Katie. We keep having this conversation. I don't want kids in here, either, but someone has to be the safety patrol, and you're a natural with kids. I'm not. You should be the one in charge of the school groups."

"I can't." She didn't mean to snap.

With a sigh, Ben pulled off his glasses and skullcap.

Katie glanced at her clock. She'd lost four hours to her art. "Sorry, I'm running late. Need to get back to the day job and write those fourth-grade items." Ben had never expressed curiosity about why she wrote and scored standardized tests, but then he never asked the tough questions. Not even when, five years ago, she moved back to central North Carolina to become his intern with a determination that had surprised her and Delaney. And Ben.

"I need five minutes of your time," Ben said. "Don't make me beg."

Trent wandered over. He hadn't been around in days, thanks to the demands of his paid welding job. Ben never understood how anyone could work a mindless nine-to-five in welding and then find the energy to use the same process to create art. But Ben was earning his living as an artist; he could afford to be rigid. Or was it, quite simply, that he always knew what he wanted? Certainty—the one thing she craved, the one thing life could never provide.

"What's up?" Trent said.

"Safety glasses?" Ben pointed at the box of glasses inside the door. Part of his new "safety first" campaign—implemented after Trent's ophthalmologist had removed several shards of metal from his right eye—the box was mostly ignored.

Trent replied with an impish grin. "Did you guys see the FireFest video on YouTube? I think they got my good side."

"You won't have a good side if you don't wear safety glasses," Ben said.

"Come on, man. Lighten up."

"I don't do light. Katie—" Ben held up a hand. Two fresh cuts sliced his palm. "Wait two minutes."

And then he asked Trent about an upcoming class they had agreed to co-teach. They made a good team in the classroom, despite their different styles—and physiques. Thanks to all the lifting and hauling of steel, Ben was a Viking built for battle; Trent was a mix of scrappy street fighter and Dudley Moore in *Santa Claus: The Movie*.

Katie finished clearing up and let her mind drift back to FireFest. The three of them had slept in Ben's truck to save money. He insisted she and Trent take the back—the small woman and the small gay man—while he squashed his six-foot-four frame between the steering wheel and their crap on the passenger seat. Ben was quiet and distracted all weekend. Iron pours could bewitch with their primal, unchoreographed ballet of fire, but casting wasn't Ben's thing. He was strictly a large-sheets-of-steel guy and grew restless when he was away from his art for too long. No, he'd gone to watch over her in true mother-hen fashion. And in the snap of a millisecond, her mind bounced back to the place it shouldn't go. But the annual photo of Maisie could arrive in Delaney's PO box any day, and this waiting was always a time of atonement and, worse, hope. Cal was later than usual. Why? Why hadn't he mailed the photo right after Maisie's birthday? Had something happened, happened to Maisie?

Katie pulled her phone from the flapped pocket of her leather apron. She needed to leave, get some air.

"Coffee break in an hour?" Trent called out as he ambled toward his area.

"You just got here!" Ben called back and then turned his gray eyes on her. "Don't even think about leaving."

Katie glanced at the clock again.

"Come on, you know it won't hurt if you're five minutes late." He frowned at her.

Yes, it will. I'll be off schedule, and off schedule is a bad place for me.

"The director of the Contemporary Art Museum emailed me last night. Everything's going ahead as planned for our September show," Ben continued. "And they've chosen the kids who are going to be our docents, or public guides."

She stretched out the fingers of her left hand and then curled them, one by one, into a fist. "Good for them. Irrelevant for me."

"Yes and no. Whitmore would like one of us to meet with the kids. He's requested you, and I second that."

A heavy tool hit the concrete with a clang, and the goldfinch that had managed to get trapped inside the building flapped up near the ceiling. Her heart pounded as her phone buzzed with a text. Delaney.

I'm waiting by your truck.

Come in, Katie typed and hit "Send."

"I never do public events, Ben. Never."

"I know and respect that. But this is different."

"Different how?"

Why does Ben put up with me? What if he's been faking all these years? He only took me on because I forced him to. What if he hates me?

"The director wants to make your piece the focus of the exhibit. He's into your concept of recycling fear to create art. In fact, Whitmore wants to talk to you about doing your own show." Ben smiled.

"Who's Whitmore?"

His smile slipped into a sigh. "You weren't listening, were you? I've told you already, he's the director of CAM."

Ben looked tired. Was he getting enough sleep?

I did that to him; I'm a shit person. Wait, that's correct. A blend of truth and OCD. Damnit, Katie. Don't agree with the OCD. See? This is why I can't go to Raleigh. My mind's going to become a mushroom field again. OCD popping up everywhere like fungus, a scattershot of obsessions, of intrusive images, and—

"It's hard to commit to anything right now."

"But this is huge. You're branching out and leaving me behind."

"What if I don't want to leave the nest?"

"Hey, stop picking at your skin and pay attention." His chimney sweep hand grazed her forearm. "I'm proud of you."

"But I—"

"Don't do Raleigh, I know."

An old image pounced. One she hadn't seen in a while. Her hands picking up Maisie . . . and throwing her down the stairs. The images of harming Maisie had long vanished because Maisie was no longer part of her life. But what if they were back in the same city? What if?

That's OCD trying to scare me, trying to hold me hostage with old fears. An unwanted thought is just a thought; it has no power. Did I hurt Maisie? No, that's why I left. To keep her safe.

Katie glanced down at Ben's steel-toed work shoes. No laces and easy to remove if a stray spark landed where it shouldn't.

"What if I came with you?" he said.

"Went where with my sister?" Delaney sauntered toward them in a skin-tight denim skirt, her cropped T-shirt hanging off one shoulder to reveal a turquoise bra strap. With heavy black eyeliner and that slight sway of her full hips, she was more groupie than bookkeeper.

Ben stared at her flip-flops and shook his head. "You're not—"

"Wearing safety glasses or sensible footwear, I know." Delaney turned to Katie. "Hard day playing with fire?"

"Hard day poring over people's accounts?"

Delaney's laugh competed with the angle grinder whirring on the old loading dock. "Hope I'm not interrupting, but we need to plan a visit to see our mom before my sister finds another hundred excuses to get out of making the trip to Greensboro. For our mother's birthday."

"Would you at least think about it? Please?" Ben raked his hands through his dirty-blond hair. He kept trying to sculpt it up, but the front continued to flop forward into a cowlick that made him look younger than thirty-five.

"Think about what?" Delaney said.

"Stop being nosy, honey."

"Can't. I have a very boring life and thrive on gossip. Ben? What am I missing?"

"The director of the Contemporary Art Museum is your sister's latest fan, but she refuses to meet with him and the sixth-graders who are going to be our public mouthpieces for the show's opening night. Plus he's interested in doing a Katie Mack show. Which is—"

"Huge." Delaney nodded. "But we're talking Raleigh, right?"

"Yes."

"Raleigh," Delaney repeated as if she hadn't heard him. "You know what? You should go, Sis. This is one of those subliminal messages from the universe. Same as when you wandered into that art show in Asheville and met Ben."

"Excuse me?" Katie shot her sister a warning look.

"Think of it as a big-ass exposure."

"That's what I'm trying to tell her," Ben said. "You can't have too much exposure as a young artist."

"I'm hardly a young anything, and that's not what she meant." Katie glared at her baby sister. Delaney raised her eyebrows, and a slow smile spread like a dare. They were back to being teenagers: Katie struggling to keep Delaney out of juvie; Delaney sneaking in after curfew, stinking of weed.

"One of you care to explain?" Ben folded his arms.

"Oh, for goodness' sake, tell him," Delaney snapped. Katie didn't answer. "Fine, I'll do it. An exposure is—"

"A method of confronting irrational fear," Katie said.

Ben scrunched his lips together, the way he did when he was concentrating. "That's how you got into welding, to confront your fear of fire, yes? This is something similar?"

"I guess, only this is a fear of driving." The lie slid out easily, covered in the powdered sugar of truth. Ben still believed she hated highway driving, but she didn't. Not anymore. It was an excuse used to cover up a multitude of things she didn't care to explain. Driving on the highway was an old fear, confronted years earlier at excruciating cost. Learning to handle fire had been far less painful.

Liar. I'm a liar.

No, thinking I'm a liar doesn't make me one. I'm telling a half-truth to protect him. From me.

"Sis, it's time," Delaney said quietly. What she really meant was *You're in a holding pattern.* Staying away from Raleigh was no different from dumping all the knives in the trash nine years earlier. It was avoidance, and avoidance was a one-way ticket back to hell.

"I'll drive," Ben said. "We can grab dinner afterward."

"Nice," Delaney said. "It can double as a date."

"Maybe that wasn't a date." Ben frowned.

31

"See?" Delaney said. "Even your seriously cute welding guru has given up making the moves on you."

"At the risk of repeating myself, that wasn't—"

"This from the person who has turned down two marriage proposals from her live-in boyfriend," Katie said.

"Three, if you count the time we were drunk and—" Delaney flashed her green eyes at Katie. "Never mind. Come on, get back on the dating wagon before you become a wizened old crone. I hear Ben's single again."

"Don't mind me, guys," Ben said. "Really."

"What happened to—" Katie gestured as if attempting to sign, but it didn't help her remember the young woman's name.

"Olivia." Ben glowered. "She dumped me. Apparently I spend my life in the studio."

"I heard you stood her up. Again."

"Lost track of time working on a piece," he mumbled. "How the hell do you know this, Delaney?"

In the opposite corner Trent snickered.

"Really bad idea to confide in the studio giggler," her sister said.

Wait. Had Ben mentioned the breakup? What if he told her when she was zoning out? What kind of person didn't realize her friend might be suffering? Should she apologize to him? Was she a bad person if she didn't apologize? But Ben and Olivia had only been on a handful of dates. Hadn't they?

Delaney linked her arm through Ben's. Ben stiffened. "Okay, forget dating this hunk o' love, but please, Sis. Think about going to Raleigh. Don't do it because we're asking. Do it for yourself. When we left the mountains to come back to the Triangle, you said it was time. Well, ditto."

Was it, was it time? The cracks were opening up again, almost imperceptibly, but that was the monster's MO. A year ago Katie had finally qualified for health insurance with access to a bona fide mental health professional, not a student in training, and he'd known less about OCD than she did. And now she had a $4,000 deductible, which meant therapy appointments were out of pocket, and her pockets weren't that deep. So she was off meds and flying solo, using self-taught techniques to tackle fear. Except for the biggest fear of all.

What if I drive past her? What if I hit her? I could kill her, run her over in my truck, the perfect killing machine.

A thought is just a thought; it has no power. Have I ever hit anyone? No. I'm a good driver. Could I get in an accident? Maybe, but that doesn't mean anyone would get hurt.

Delaney cleared her throat. "An answer sometime this century might be good."

"I'm weighing my options," Katie said, but her sister kept grinning.

"I don't want to push you into something that makes you uncomfortable," Ben said.

I control fire; I am strong. I'm a welder who works in a helmet decorated with Power Girl stickers.

"Yes." Katie took off her apron and hung it up. "Yes. I'll do it."

Delaney stared, openmouthed.

"Didn't think I was up for the challenge? I'll go, but only by myself. And if I have a panic attack on I-40, crash, and die, I'll come back to haunt you both. Consider that fair warning."

"Stop right there," Ben said. "You make the arrangements, and I'll drive." He removed a scrap of paper from his jeans pocket and handed it to Katie. "Whitmore's contact numbers."

Delaney looked at him. "Love it when a plan comes together, don't you?"

An image pounced, of bashing in Ben's head against the MIG welder. Katie slowed her breathing.

A thought is just a thought, not an action. It can't hurt anyone; it has no power.

The thought passed, but unease twittered.

Delaney was right. Going back to Raleigh was the ultimate test, the ultimate exposure. Keeping OCD chained when it latched on to Ben—a friend kept at arm's length—was one thing. Taking it on a field trip into the city where the two people she loved most lived, worked, played, and laughed? That was in a different league.

Katie picked at a torn piece of skin on her fourth finger until it came free with a sharp sting. *A different league.*

FOUR
KATIE

Katie dropped to her knees in front of the Videri Chocolate Factory. She might have arrived forty-five minutes early—less time than it had taken to get from downtown Durham to Raleigh driving well below the speed limit—but it could take her that long to find her keys. And now she was kneeling in a city parking lot. Kneeling in a parking lot, reaching under the truck, and—*Aha!* Found them. But that didn't stop the shaking. A full-body shake. Why had she done this without Ben? On what side of stupid did that belong?

As she stood up, an image of a dead child flashed. A child she had killed. With her truck. Her OCD, the voice, whispered to go back and check. But she hadn't run over a child, had she?

The cab's so high, how would I know if I'd hit a child? What about that car stopped on the shoulder? I'm sure I spotted an empty booster seat in the back. Suppose I ran over a child and left the scene of an accident? Oh, God, heart's racing. Pulse all over the place. Need to go back and check, but there's not enough time. Late is never an option. I'm freaking out, I'm freaking out. Can't breathe. I'm having a heart attack. I'm going to die, here, in a parking lot. Alone.

No, this is anxiety, Katie. Focus on your breathing. Breathe. One, two, three, four; one, two, three, four. It's just anxiety. You'll be fine.

I control fire; I am strong.

The parking lot attendant limped over, a guy who looked as if he should be whooping it up in a retirement community, not collecting parking fees in ninety-degree heat.

"You picked up a leaf, ma'am." He pointed to her knee.

"A leaf?" Katie brushed it off her jeans.

"Yup. I'm guessin' fall is on its way. How about that?"

"Yeah. How about that."

She took a deep breath, exhaled, and paid him. Then she blew out another breath, and another, and another. Released each one into the Carolina-blue sky, let them float away with the toxic thoughts.

A thought is just a thought; it has no power. And OCD lies. I've never hit anyone. I'm a good driver, a safe driver.

With a backward glance at the Chocolate Factory, she left the parking lot and headed up the street toward the Contemporary Art Museum. Anxiety hovered like a swarm of no-see-ums, her heart thumped in her throat, but adrenaline powered her legs. Kept her moving. To her right, a jackhammer drilled, decimating concrete as a work crew destroyed to rebuild. The warehouse district was reinventing itself.

A glass office door opened, and a group of arty types tumbled out, laughing. Katie sidestepped their energy. Had she ever had such enthusiasm for life? A serious child, she realized her life plan without missing a step: watch over Delaney, get into UNC, complete a master's in teaching, become a beloved teacher and a devoted wife. She was a good everything until she had become a mother.

CAM greeted her from under a geometric canopy that zoomed down low as if captured mid-flight. The glass wall of the museum was decorated with white shapes: a fish, a moray eel, a basketball, the words "The Nothing That Is."

The Nothing That Is. Nice.

Katie pushed open the large yellow door and entered the museum. Above her, tubes of light hung down between one-dimensional blobs that resembled painters' palettes or flat clouds. Clouds . . . a quiet, distant idea for a piece. Less than an idea, more of a tingle. And a huge departure from the metal panels that hinted at darkness lit only by a blood-red moon.

She walked in circles, eyes up, listening to creativity spark.

"Don't get dizzy," a young woman with blue hair said from behind the information desk.

"It's speaking to me as all art should." Smiling, Katie walked over. "Katie Mack. I'm here to meet with the docents, but I'm ridiculously early."

"No worries," the young woman said. "Once the kids arrive, there's a cyclone of chaos. If I were you, I'd look around while it's quiet. I'll tell Whitmore you're here."

"Thanks." Katie wandered into the lofted space where an installation was going up behind huge sheets of opaque plastic.

The white expanse calmed. Silence, glorious silence, descended in her brain as she walked down the concrete ramp and through a glass-walled space, empty but for a long table. She kept going, onto the lower level, stopping by a black-and-white photograph positioned under its title: *Failure of the American Dream.* A man draped in an American flag stood in front of a village of tents, staring into the camera.

At the edge of her sight, a tent was displayed in a cordoned-off area. Not a tent for family camping trips, but a tent for permanent shelter. It could have been her tent, the one she had lived in until the day Ringo died. She should walk away. Shouldn't go into the exhibit, shouldn't.

She went inside.

A list of rules for the homeless community hung on the wall. One column said *do*, one said *don't.* The last line was a reminder that you might not have a home, but you were free. Living in a tent hadn't helped her understand the concept of freedom. And neither did life in a four-bedroom colonial. No, the power to act without boundaries, without restraint had come from salvaging discarded, broken scrap.

What might have been was another unwanted thought. Better for Maisie to grow up believing her mother was dead rather than worrying about a parent who had considered suicide. But to be so close after nine years . . . What time did Maisie get home from school? Had Cal found someone else? Was he with her today, on what should have been their fourteenth wedding anniversary?

What if I get lost driving home and end up on my old street and run her over? I could kill her. Katie stared at the stained sleeping bag on the floor. *I did the right thing when I gave her up. I saved her from the trauma of being my daughter. I kept her safe.*

"Katie Mack? Thank you for agreeing to do this." A man with short gray hair, octagonal glasses, and garnet studs in both ears walked toward her, hand extended. Dressed head to toe in dark gray, he was cute in a precise way. As she shook his hand, Katie checked his fourth finger. "Get back on the dating wagon," her sister had said. How was she supposed to do that when no relationship survived the three-week mark? When she still loved the man she'd married? No wedding ring—she looked into Whitmore's face—no chemistry.

The clamor of recess surged above them, a sound no teacher could forget.

"The excitement level is always high when the kids arrive, but they'll settle down soon. And their visual arts teacher will be around for crowd control."

"I'm used to kids." Katie paused. "I mean, I taught middle school briefly. In another life."

Did I lie? I think I lied. I'm a shit person. Was that a lie? No, that was the truth.

Her stomach did somersaults to the pulse of *what if.*

"Let's give them a few minutes to put their stuff in the cubbies, shall we?"

Pinpricks of sweat dribbled down her chest. "Tell me more about the docents."

"Such a smart, quirky bunch. Quite outspoken, too." Whitmore smiled as if remembering something. "We have twenty right now. Mostly kids who don't quite fit. True individuals. And I should probably show you how to do the CAM high five. They take it seriously."

He led Katie in an elaborate dance of hand movements.

"Which schools do they come from?" she said.

"Two magnet schools in the downtown."

What if I ran over that kid when I turned off the highway? I could have, I could have run over that kid and not realized. I need to go back and check. Go back and check.

Whitmore kept talking; the private soundtrack in her brain kept playing.

A thought is just a thought; it has no power. I would know if I'd run over a kid.

"The program uses art as a vehicle for leadership, critical thinking, creativity, public speaking, and teamwork," Whitmore said. "The changes we see in the kids throughout the six weeks are amazing. It makes young people fearless."

"Fearless." She nodded.

"The kids choose a specific piece to work with and become experts on it. The voice of the artist, if you will. On opening night, they introduce themselves, give a brief overview of their piece, and take questions." He glanced up at the ceiling. "I think our fearless leaders might be ready. Shall we go meet them?"

No. I'd like to go home now, please.

"Lead the way," she said.

They walked up the concrete ramp, Katie gripping the steel railing. Could he hear her heart pounding? Could he smell her fear?

I control fire; I am strong.

In the space with the wall of glass, a group of kids now sat at the long table, sketchbooks and pencils in front of them. They looked up as one, in silent reverence. Everything around Katie sharpened: a slight antiseptic smell, a chair scraping across the floor, the intensity of the sun beyond the glass. Her ears started to ring, her throat tightened.

Whitmore walked toward the corner, where he leaned against the wall in an effortlessly casual stance, and a middle-aged African-American woman moved forward. She gave Katie a warm smile.

"I'm Lynn, the teacher."

"I'm Katie, the artist." Katie shook hands and held on tight.

Lynn leaned in, the bangles on her wrist tinkling. "You'll be fine," she whispered. Katie almost believed her.

As Lynn read the official Katie Mack bio to her students, she glanced occasionally at Katie. When Lynn announced, "And now, I'd like to welcome Ms. Katie," Katie pictured herself running for the door.

Lynn clapped, the kids clapped, Katie's stomach roiled.

Who can tell me what the verb roil *means?*

I'm back in a classroom and they have no idea. I could pick up one of these kids and throw him or her through the glass. What if I picked up one of those kids, and—

That's the voice. A thought is just a thought; it has no power. Besides, I might be a girlie welder, but I don't have the strength to throw anyone through that glass.

Tell them about my work with Ben.

And she did. As Katie talked about taking her first welding class to prove she was stronger than her fear of fire, and about meeting Ben at an art show and falling under the spell of his sculptures, her pulse began to slow.

The OCD curled up in silence.

She was hitting her stride when a girl joined the group. Her style said, *I do it my way,* and Katie smiled at the mismatched Keds worn with capri leggings, a striped T-shirt, and a French beret that gave her a beatnik style. Her hair seemed to be pulled back in a ponytail that was caught under a cropped cardigan, and her eyes were hidden behind black-framed glasses too big for her face. Why hadn't the child's mother talked her out of such a terrible choice?

"I'm very sorry for the disruption," the girl said. "My stomach's been feeling a bit bubbly."

One of the boys giggled, and Katie grimaced at him until he blushed.

"Should I call your parents?" Lynn said.

"No, thank you." The girl cleared her throat several times and sat down.

The next two hours, which included a snack break, flew past. Energized, Katie couldn't wait to report back to Delaney. She had done it. Driven to Raleigh without causing an accident and taught a class of middle schoolers without hurting anyone.

Victory is mine, OCD.

Maybe, when she got back to Durham, she'd ask Ben if he wanted to grab dinner out.

Urged on by Lynn, a chorus of young voices sang, "Thank you, Ms. Katie!" and the kids bounded for their cubbies like caged rabbits set loose. The girl in the beret, however, packed her *Star Wars* backpack one item at a time. Her friend fidgeted and said, "Hurry up already."

"Please go on ahead, Ava Grace," the little girl said. "I need to ask Ms. Katie something."

Katie smiled, and the little girl in the beret walked over. She was smaller than the other kids. Petite.

"I was super excited to meet you today," the girl said. "Yours is the piece I've chosen to work with. I think it's awesome that you made it by firing guns."

"Well, I had help from my sister since I'm terrified of guns. But the idea was to create beauty out of fear. I like how the bullets left clear holes, but in the bottom right-hand corner, the buckshot warped the metal without breaking through. It made an impact, but the metal stayed strong. Refused to shatter."

"Gosh, yes." The little girl frowned. "That's super cool. Can I interview you?"

"Now?"

"Oh, no. I have to go home now. We would need to make a special arrangement, because I have lots of questions."

"I'm sure you do." Katie smiled. "You asked great questions in class. Very insightful."

"Thank you."

"Simon!" Lynn yelled as one of the boys dashed for the exit. "Wait!"

"How about you take the other kids to the lobby," Katie called over to Lynn, "and I'll escort this young lady out in a minute."

Lynn mouthed her thanks and left.

"Yes," the girl said, as if they were still mid-conversation. "And I love the blood-red moon. I'm writing a story to go with it." She smiled and it transformed her face. She had the most adorable freckles.

"By the way, we haven't been formally introduced. Obviously, you know that I'm Katie, and your name is . . . ?"

"Maisie MacDonald."

Air whooshed in Katie's ears, light sparked, pain ripped through her chest. She was going under. No oxygen. Legs buckled. She was sitting. Why was she sitting? Could she still breathe? She had to breathe, just breathe. No, it wasn't possible.

What are the chances? What are the chances? Maisie, lying in the red metal crib with arms flung over her head, mouth blowing pretend kisses. Maisie.

How could she not have recognized her own daughter?

"Oh my gosh!" Maisie said. "Are you sick? Do you have a headache, a fever? There's been a nasty virus going around school. I hope we didn't bring any germs. Do you think it's the flu?"

I was right to stay away. She grew up to be sweet and kind. Did all that without me ruining her life.

"I know it's a little early for flu, but I haven't had my flu shot yet. You look very pale. You're not going to throw up, are you?" Maisie took a step back and started scratching her arm. "Have you been exposed to anything contagious? What are your symptoms?"

She's checking. Compulsive checking, the telltale sign of . . .

Katie's heart raced to shutdown.

She's so small I could pick her up, carry her to the floor above, and throw her off the walkway.

"I'd better get Mr. Whitmore," Maisie said.

"No!" Katie grabbed Maisie's arm and then released it. "I mean, I'm fine. Bit light-headed. Skipped lunch, which was—"

"A very, very bad idea." Maisie's huge eyes grew wide in emphasis.

What if I picked up the pen on the table? I could take out her eye with it, I could—

"Pretty name, Maisie. I knew someone called Maisie once. Long time ago. What do your parents do?"

"My dad's a professor of English and comparative literature at NC State and quite famous in the field of the Scottish Enlightenment. His name is Dr. Callum MacDonald. Do you know him?"

Katie shook her head as another image flashed, but this one real. A memory: "Do you promise to love and honor her until death do you part?"

"I do," Cal had said. *I do until I lock her out.*

"And—" Katie swallowed. Acid burned her throat. "Your mother?"

Why did she ask that? Why was she making her daughter say the words "My mom is dead"? Because she was a terrible person, a terrible mother.

I could push her through that window. What if I pushed her through the glass?

"Oh, it's very sad. She died when I was a baby, but I didn't know her, so I'm not really, *really* sad. I mean, I'm sad that I never met her, but my dad's the best and I have Uncle Jake, who's Dad Point Two, and now I have . . ."

Katie clutched at her heart.

"Are you sure you're not sick? You look a bit funny. Oh, I didn't mean that to be rude. I hope you don't think I was rude. I wasn't rude, was I?"

"No," Katie squeaked. She was in a room with Maisie. Her daughter was kind and beautiful, had no dress sense, and was checking.

She has OCD. How? How can that be? From me, must be from me. But how? I had postpartum OCD. Nothing before then and . . . nothing. I ran away for nothing, I failed to keep her safe. Why didn't I reach out to Cal and warn him? Why did I blindly accept his no-contact rule? Why? I should have questioned where my illness came from, whether I could pass it on. I'm a failure, an aberration of motherhood. I didn't keep her safe.

"I *reeeally* think you should eat something," Maisie said. "I'm sure Ms. Lynn has leftover baguettes and Nutella from snack. I'll go find some and—"

"S-story, you're making up a story? Do you often write stories?"

"All the time," Maisie said. "I'm going to be a writer when I grow up. Well, I'm one already. A writer's someone who writes. That would be me." She gave a grin that accentuated her overbite. "I really like the Wings of Fire series. That's how I became best friends with Ava Grace. She saw me reading it one day, and she *lovvves* the series, too! We started our own book club. Actually, I'm a bit worried about Ava Grace. She's—"

"Wordsmith." It came out as a whisper. "You're a wordsmith."

"That's what my dad says. I love to collect words—especially long words."

I used to collect poems. For the cadence, for the sound of words.

"H-he must be very proud of you."

44

"Oh, yes. He is."

She hates me. I've ruined her life. Does she know, know she has OCD? What if she doesn't know? Oh, God, what if she doesn't know?

On the other side of the glass, a Honda Civic pulled up with flashing lights, and Lynn led Ava Grace toward the passenger door. "That's Lilah. My ride!" Maisie raised her hands. "I better go. She might get upset if I'm late, and I don't want to upset her. Are you sure you're not sick? I don't want to give Lilah any germs. She's in a very delicate way."

"No, I mean yes, I'm not sick."

"I'll find Mr. Whitmore on the way out and tell him you need food! I would love to come and see your studio. I'm sure my dad would bring me, and that way I could interview you."

"No."

Maisie screwed up her face.

"It would be much better, much better to meet here. I work with lots of dangerous power tools that . . . but I could come back. Here. To talk. With you." *No, stay away from me, Maisie. I'm not safe.* "Maybe we could meet after class next week. If you wanted. If you could stay late."

"That would be super awesome. I must go now. Goodbye, Ms. Katie."

Katie reached for her daughter, but she'd gone.

Slowly, Katie stood and staggered to the window. She stared at the woman in the Honda Civic. A babysitter? She looked too young to be a girlfriend, with those long blond ringlets. China doll ringlets; the opposite of Katie's black pixie haircut. With Ava Grace in the back, the young woman leaned toward the now-open passenger door. Both of them waited for Maisie to come into view. And there she was, in a flurry of movement.

For nine years—nine years—she had backed herself into a corner of certainty, played right into the hands of OCD. Convinced herself staying away was the right thing to do. The photos Cal mailed were her penance, her hair shirt, but she had made her decision. Stayed dead to both of them.

Did I do the wrong thing? All these years I thought she was better off without me, but what if I'd never left? If I'd stayed, I would be there for her, guiding her through. Helping her. Instead, I abandoned her. Abandoned her to fear and shame. Abandoned her to OCD.

Heat rushed to her face, burned from the inside out. Maisie wasn't living an idyllic childhood in a wooded subdivision of Raleigh. She was a child whose mind was about to eat her alive.

Katie grabbed her stomach. She was going to throw up. Maisie paused, glanced toward Katie, and waved.

She waved.

Get away from me, Maisie. I'm not your mother, I'm a monster. Stay away, stay away.

Come back, please come back. I love you. Don't leave, please.

Grief hooked Katie in the gut, threatened to knock her to the ground, kick her senseless. She pressed her forehead and palms against the glass while Maisie hauled her stuff inside the car. There was no kiss from the driver. Must be a babysitter, or Ava Grace's mom. Standing up straight, Katie turned her back on the future that should have been hers.

She walked toward a chair and collapsed onto it. New worries piled up like a highway wreck as Katie twisted her fingers through her hair. Over and over; over and over.

I want to yank it out by the roots. I want, I need, pain. This is all my fault. Why did I run away? Why did I stay away? What if I'd gone back?

"Maisie insists you need a snack," a male voice said. "Is everything okay?"

Katie stared at the table. "Sorry. I didn't mean to scare her. Did I?" She glanced up at Whitmore. "Scare her?"

"Heavens, no. Maisie was concerned you might be sick. Can I get you something? You're awfully pale."

"No, thank you. I have, I have anxiety issues. And today's been difficult. A difficult day. But I'm fine." She tried to smile. "I'm fine."

"Panic disorder or obsessive-compulsive disorder?"

She blew out a long breath. "How did you know?"

"Firsthand experience. My ex struggles with both. I think that's the reason I'm drawn to your piece. I'm well acquainted with the toll anxiety takes."

Ex made sense because anxiety annihilated families. Destroyed love.

"How can I help?" Whitmore said.

"Would you mind if I sat here for a while?"

"Stay as long as you need. Can I call someone for you?"

Katie shook her head. "I prefer to be alone. But, I would like to ask"—*Don't, Katie, don't*—"about Maisie. I gather she's going to be my docent?"

"Yes, she quickly became a favorite in the program. Not that we have them, you understand, but Maisie's quite special. Whip-smart, with an intellect beyond her years, and yet refreshingly innocent. Her fashion choices are a staff talking point."

Katie groaned, then covered it up with a cough.

Choking on leftovers of motherhood stolen from a stranger.

"And she's in sixth grade?" Had Maisie skipped a grade?

"Fifth. Apparently she's having trouble transitioning to the concept of that big life change called middle school, so her art teacher petitioned for Maisie and her best friend, Ava Grace, to join the program. We do often accept younger kids."

Maisie had been checking; she hated change. Her daughter definitely had OCD. Why? Why did OCD have to claim Maisie, too?

"She was very kind to me. Maisie. Very kind." Katie grabbed the pen one of the kids had left on the table, pushed the top up with her thumb, pushed it back down. Up, down; up, down.

"That's Maisie—fiercely compassionate. Last week she insisted we help a wounded squirrel the kids saw get run over. When one of the sixth-grade boys tried to tease her for helping a rodent, she gave him a talking-to. Lynn can't wait to get Maisie over at the middle school."

"Will you thank her, for helping me?"

"With pleasure, and I'll be in my office if you need me. The door's always open." He smiled and left.

Her phone announced a text from Ben.

You about to leave? Everything okay?

She put her phone down on the table, pushed it away, and stared at nothing. Five minutes later it rang. When she didn't pick up, it rang again, echoing around the space. Bouncing off the walls to the tune of memories. Echoes of her family. She reached out to put the phone on mute, but it rang again. Two buttons: one green, the other blood red. She hit the green circle.

"You do know I can tell when you've read a text," Ben said.

She didn't reply.

"Want to tell me why you're not answering?"

Holding the phone to her cheek, she closed her eyes and rested her head on the table. "I don't think I can drive home. Would you come get me? I know it's a pain, and it's rush hour and the traffic will be—"

"Katie. This is why I offered to take you."

I'm asking him to do something he hates: load his motorbike on my truck. I don't deserve his friendship. I'm a bad mother, a bad friend, a bad human being.

"It's fine. Forget I asked."

"No." He sighed. "Of course I'll come. Do you still have that heavy board from the last time so I can ride the bike up into the bed of your truck?"

"Yes."

"Give me half an hour to clean up and find my tie-down straps."

She nodded.

"Katie? Does that sound like a plan?"

"Okay," she whispered.

Ben hung up, and she stared through the wall of glass. Hell rose on the horizon as surely as if a tsunami were building and she could do nothing but watch.

One thought kept playing, and she refused to boss it back:

When can I see my daughter again?

FIVE

MAISIE

Maisie clicked her seat belt into place and twisted around to see if Ms. Katie was still watching, but she'd gone.

I really, really hope she isn't sick. I really, really hope I don't get it.

Gosh. What a selfish thought. Am I a bad person?

She should be worrying about Ms. Katie, not herself. Did Ms. Katie have Zika? Not many people in America did, but Ava Grace's dad, a doctor at Raleigh Regional, had explained Zika in great detail. Lilah should be especially worried since she was pregnant. Would Lilah get Zika? Get Zika because of her, because she'd been in contact with Ms. Katie and now she'd contaminated Lilah? *But hold on there a cotton-picking second.* What exactly had Ms. Katie said? Had she said she did or didn't feel sick? She was or she wasn't sick?

Concentrate, Maisie, remember the conversation. The exact words.

"How was your day, girls?" Lilah said.

"Very long." Ava Grace yawned and fell asleep. That was Ava Grace! Put her in the back of a car, and she was asleep within two seconds. It was quite an accomplishment.

"Today was super awesome, Lilah!" Maisie said. "I mean, Mom. Sorry, Mom."

Maisie scratched her arm, and kept scratching. Even though it stung, it didn't feel right. She had to keep doing it.

"Bug bite?" Lilah pulled out onto the road.

A FedEx truck honked, and Lilah slammed on the brakes.

I'm a bad kid, the worst. What if I distract Lilah and we crash? And what if she dies? What if it's my fault? I have to keep apologizing. If I don't, Lilah will die.

Why couldn't she stop thinking about being a bad kid? Why couldn't she stop worrying about Lilah dying? Why were these horrid thoughts taking up a whole room in her brain? No, multiple rooms! Maisie closed her eyes as tight as she could and willed the very weird thoughts to vanish. But when she opened her eyes, those thoughts were worse. Stronger. Bigger. And she didn't want any of them.

I'm a good person. I do random acts of kindness in school and tell Daddy, and it makes him so proud. I'm a good person. But what if I'm not?

"I'm sorry. I don't mean to be a bad kid."

"Where's this coming from?" Lilah watched extra hard as she pulled back onto the road. "You haven't done anything wrong."

"Are you sure I haven't?"

I'm a bad kid. The worst. If I don't keep apologizing, Lilah will die.

"Maisie, sweetie, you're a great kid. You want to know about bad, remind me to tell you stories about my two oldest sisters. My mom blames them for turning her hair gray."

Those stinky thoughts went quiet. *Fantabulously quiet.* She wasn't a bad kid! Lilah had said so. And she would try extra hard from now on to use the *mom* word, even though it felt itchy. Her real mom lived in sunlight and daydreams. Her dad would never talk about her, but Uncle J said that was because it was too painful. Uncle J told her lots about her mom, about how kind and beautiful she was, with her long black hair. It was the reason Maisie kept her hair long. There were no pictures, because her dad had destroyed them all in his grief. So said Uncle J, the *Wikipedia* of her mom.

Lilah messed with her seat belt. Like it was hurting the baby.

She's going to die because of me. I'm a bad kid, the worst. Lilah's going to die, and I'll be to blame.

No! Those horrid thoughts were back. Why wouldn't they stay gone? They had started at the wedding, when the minister said the bit about till death do us part. And she started thinking about death because her mom had died and it wasn't like she could lose another parent. What if Lilah died? Maisie checked her own seat belt twice. Had to be twice.

"Are you okay?" Maisie said.

"Define 'okay.' I had no idea it was so hard becoming a mother."

"Sorry." Maisie glanced down and back up. "Sorry I make things hard for you. Mom."

"No, sweetie. I didn't mean you, I meant Baby MacD." Lilah pointed at her rather huge tummy. Not that there was anything wrong with being fat. Gosh, no, but Lilah used to be so skinny, and now she was quite the opposite. "Let's drop the mom thing. Until you feel ready."

"But my dad said—"

"I'll talk to your dad. We've thrown a lot at you recently, and I have no doubt that over time, we'll come up with our own mother-daughter name. Something more organic."

"Sorry."

"Sweetie, stop apologizing. You've done nothing wrong."

"Okay." But what if she had? Would Lilah die if she stopped apologizing? That didn't make sense, so why was she thinking it did? Her mind had become an *extreeemely* confusing place.

"Tell me about your after-school program. Did you meet any future Picassos?"

"It's a docent program, not after-school." Maisie pinched her fingers together and held them up to emphasize her point. Poor Lilah. She might have a PhD, but she didn't always get family things right. "And

Ava Grace and I were very lucky to be accepted. It's a big deal to be with the sixth-graders."

Not that she wanted to be with the sixth-graders, because that meant leaving elementary school, and middle school was so big and so scary and she loved her teachers and she really, *really* didn't want to leave them. And she really, *really* didn't want to go to middle school next year. Why couldn't everything stay the same? Why did things have to keep changing? Maisie tugged on her seat belt. She could hardly breathe, it was so tight.

Lilah smiled. "Guess it's my turn to apologize. Sorry. I'm a bit behind on the parental learning curve."

"Oh, I didn't mean to make you feel bad."

"You didn't. You called me out on something I got wrong. Quite right, too."

They drove by the park where they'd collected acorns on the walk to CAM. Maisie leaned down to make doubly sure hers were still in the outside pocket of her backpack.

"I met an artist today. A real one, and I'm going to be her docent. She's super nice and she wears these earrings that make this great noise like wind chimes, and I'm going to ask her where she got them so I can ask for a pair the *moment* my dad lets me get my ears pierced."

"Uh-huh." Lilah looked up in the rearview mirror.

Lilah drove very slowly, while everyone shot past. And they had no music. Uncle J always turned the radio up full volume so they could sing along. They were going through a My Chemical Romance phase, which was very progressive for a ten-year-old. So Uncle J said. He'd also threatened to tickle her to death if she ever started listening to Justin Bieber, but he had agreed to give Taylor Swift a go. What music did Ms. Katie like?

"And she's *super* pretty, the artist lady. Her name's Katie Mack, and she's a metal artist. We might need to spend extra time together so I can learn everything there is to learn about her piece. She said maybe next week I could stay late. Do you think I can?"

"We'll have to ask your dad, but I don't see why not."

"Awesome! We have lots to discuss, Ms. Katie and me." She paused. "Ms. Katie and I. I wanted to go to her studio, where she works with other metal artists, but she said they use dangerous tools so that's why we have to meet at CAM, and I'm hoping she brings her sketchbook, because she told us she draws out her ideas first."

"Good plan, since you're not crazy about loud noises, and I'm pretty sure a metal artist works with fire, which—"

"I'm scared of, I know."

Why did Lilah have to focus on things that gave her a stomachache? Maisie hugged her tummy. "Oh my gosh. I really like Ms. Katie, did I tell you that already?"

Lilah waited a super long time to answer. "Yes. I figured out that part."

SIX
KATIE

After vomiting in the gutter, Katie headed straight and left CAM behind. She crossed endless side streets lined up like graves. Stepped down off one curb, stepped back over another. Kept walking, kept heading nowhere. Cold—she rubbed her arms. It was pushing ninety degrees, and she was cold.

OCD and regret joined forces in a never-ending loop. *I should've gone back. Cal would've taken me in, wouldn't he? Maybe not, but I could have at least tried. The divorce was all for Maisie, and it achieved nothing. Nothing. What if she's already in hell? Does Cal know? Would he listen if she tried to explain? What have I done?*

When a car screeched and a driver honked, she glanced up and mouthed apologies. On the edge of a small city park opposite, sunlight the color of molten iron lit up a bench under a giant, twisted tree, its exposed roots spilling over the lip of the sidewalk. Soon it would be the gloaming, the in-between hour that was neither day nor night. Looking both ways, Katie crossed the main road, headed for the bench, and sat. City crows cawed, and a motorbike revved.

Vehicles rumbled past, all heading one way. People with brief-cases and phones walked by with purpose. Everyone had a destination, including Ben, who strode toward her with a deep frown and his helmet tucked under one arm.

He stopped in front of her. "I thought *stay put* was a straightforward direction."

Katie looked away. Across the square of green, a woman chatted into her phone, ignoring the little girl who bounced up and down, saying, "Mommy, Mommy, look what I found!" The woman leaned down to speak to her child in a sharp rebuke. Katie chewed on a sore spot inside her mouth and turned back toward Ben.

"Sorry, sorry. I shouldn't have asked you to come. I'm sorry."

He ducked his chin and gave her that look, the one she knew meant *Stop already.*

"Hey, we're good. You don't need to keep apologizing."

Ben joined her on the weather-beaten bench and placed his dented black helmet between them. Each nick represented a fall off the 1970s BMW that was one hundred percent original. She didn't know the story behind each ding, each scuff mark, because she had set the ground rules: *Let's keep our friendship in the here and now.* No backstory, nothing too personal. And yet, she was about to change that. She had known it the moment the words "come get me" left her mouth.

He shook his hair from his face; it tumbled back within seconds. "Since you didn't cover your tracks, I assume this isn't a 'Get lost, Ben' statement. Want to talk or just sit? I'm good either way." He paused. "Why're you smiling?"

"Sometimes when you run away, you want to be found. And, as Delaney said, sometimes the universe sends a message. Like meeting you in Asheville and you saying, 'If you move to Durham, I'll take you on as my intern.'"

"I offered because you were feeding my ego. I never expected you to follow through." Ben stretched out his legs.

A cyclist pedaled frantically along the road, weaving and dodging.

What if he hates me? What if I deserve his hate? What if I've been using him for his art? What if we have an accident on the drive home and he dies because of me?

"I want to tell you who I really am," Katie said. "But it might change what you think about me, and I'm regretting that already."

"Katie, I know who you are."

"What if I'm not the person you thought I was?"

"How about you let me be the judge." Ben reached over and covered her hand with his. His rough, blackened, warm hand. "Spill."

"I was born and raised in Boston. Irish on one side, southern on the other. And I'm forty."

"You look years younger."

"And I have a chronic illness, but it's not physical. It's an illness of the mind."

What if I pushed him into the road, pushed him under a car?

"Mental illness is still an illness." He curled his fingers over hers. "My youngest sister, the one out in Seattle? She had an eating disorder in high school. Then went off to college and became an addict. Now she manages a silk-screen printing business and runs a support group."

"Why didn't you ever tell me?"

"This from the person who vanishes whenever my parents come for a visit."

"I'm not good with families."

He grinned. "Tell me something I don't know."

The sun had begun its descent behind the buildings opposite. Shade crept across Katie's end of the bench, and on the other side of the square a car alarm blared.

"Did she ever try to kill herself, your sister?"

"No. She overdosed as a freshman, but it was accidental."

"Mine wasn't an overdose." Katie paused. "And it wasn't accidental."

A young couple ambled by, arms entwined, laughing. Lost in a moment of happiness and love. Did they realize how lucky they were?

After all—she stared back down at Ben's hand, still covering her own—happiness and love weren't codependents.

That FedEx truck? I could push him underneath, watch him bleed.

A thought is just a thought; it has no power. Thinking something doesn't make it true.

"Have you heard of the anxiety disorder, OCD?" she said.

"You have OCD? That's why you can't drive home?"

"Yes." She tried to pull back her hand, but he flipped it over and wove their fingers together. "My mind has a nasty habit of getting stuck on violent thoughts. Like hurting people with my truck. Which is ludicrous, right?"

"Wait, in the studio you talked about irrational fear, and I've witnessed enough tears during movies to know you can't tolerate violence." He squeezed her hand. "All this is about irrational fear?"

"Except it doesn't end there. OCD goes after what matters most. Tortures you with your worst-case scenario. For me that means hurting someone I would die to protect." She swallowed. "My real name is Katelyn MacDonald, and nine years ago I lived here in Raleigh. With my baby girl"—she glanced up; a muscle twitched under his left eye—"and my husband."

"Nah, you're a Katie. Katelyn doesn't suit you."

She wiggled her hand free and slotted it between her thighs. With her other palm, she rubbed her arm. "You really want to hear this?"

"I've spent years playing twenty guesses with your secrets. I'm not moving."

"The simple version is that my mind snapped after our baby girl was born."

"And the not-so-simple version?"

"Images came from nowhere. Violent images. A never-ending horror movie with me in the starring role." She rocked back and forth. "I saw myself pick up a vegetable knife to stab her. I saw myself hold her under the bathwater. I saw myself throw her down the stairs."

Ben sat up slowly and turned to face her. "If this is painful, you don't have to tell me."

"No, I do. I need to say these things out loud. I need you to understand why I ran. I need you to know that even though I'm a mother who did the unimaginable, I abandoned her because I thought I was a monster. I mean, a normal person doesn't have perverted thoughts, right? I threw out all the knives and stopped bathing her, but the noise in my head got so loud. I didn't know how else to protect her. From me. That's why I ran. Do you"—she watched him—"think I'm a monster? No. Don't answer that. That's OCD asking. But I don't want you to think I'm—"

"Remarkable, Katie. What you've overcome is remarkable. How did you get well?"

"I'm not well. I'm a high-functioning faker." She stared into her lap.

He leaned down so he could look up into her eyes. "Let's stop that one right now. No more faking around me. Nothing but the truth."

Then he sat back and so did Katie.

"The truth? Well, it gets worse. I lived in a tent with my dog, apparently for seventeen months. When he died, I gave up. Wanted to go home, but I couldn't do that to my baby girl. Suicide seemed the only option. So I mailed her a suicide letter, and once you've mailed your child a suicide letter, life isn't worth living. You can't go any lower. But still, I couldn't take that final step. It was a week before I attempted to throw myself off an overpass. I think the letter was a test, a prayer that my husband would come rescue me. I wanted him to follow my trail, and he did. Tracked me through the return address on my letter, but by then it was too late. A Good Samaritan had already saved my life, if you call knocking me unconscious saving me. Cal called every ER in the area and learned I was in a psych crisis unit. He handed the information over to Delaney, and she moved up to Asheville to take care of me. Without her and my social worker I would never have coped. No health insurance and a long way to crawl. But I had a diagnosis, or rather two, and neither one was psychopath. So yay me."

"Yay you." He gave a lopsided smile that stretched into a dimple. "And the second diagnosis?"

"Depression. I'm a thousand percent better than I was, but I still have days when it takes all my energy to function. Any hint of stress can get me spinning in my own little distortion. Being around me full-time isn't easy. I have lapses when I slip back into old habits."

"How does that look on the outside?"

"I can't process uncertainty, so I check. I seek reassurance. Find ten different ways to ask you when the fire marshal's coming to replace the fire extinguishers."

His smile was back. "And after the ninth time, I pretend I haven't heard you."

"Admit it, that annoys you."

"A bit, but I've accepted that you and I approach life differently. That doesn't make your way wrong or mine right. It means you've got more nervous quirks than I have, and I can be too stubborn for my own good." He paused. "How the hell did you guys manage before you moved down here?"

"Delaney started freelance bookkeeping so she could work from home, which is a nice way of saying she wanted to keep an eye on me. But that's the happy part of our story, since it's how she discovered her talent for saving small businesses."

"And what were you up to?"

"Surviving. I got cheap meds through a community health clinic, but they didn't have a mental health specialist on staff. We had no money to hire a therapist, and you need serious therapy for serious OCD. Things called CBT—cognitive behavioral therapy—and ERP, if you're interested. That's where exposures come in—ERP stands for exposure response prevention. At one point I was a guinea pig for a few psychology students. Other than that, I did my own therapy. Sometimes it worked, sometimes it didn't." She sighed. "Self-directed therapy is only for the desperate, but I did one thing right. I decided to tackle my fear of fire. Figured I had nothing to lose at that point.

"The first welding class was my idea of an exposure. Who knew I'd get hooked? When I'm welding there's no room in my mind for anything else." Katie rolled her neck and something crunched. "There you have it. Therapy, Katie Mack style."

"What happened to your family?" Ben said quietly.

"I never saw them again." A male cardinal flew by, all handsome and red. "And we made a deal, the right deal for Maisie. At least, I thought it was. At the time."

"Maisie, that's a sweet name."

She smiled, and they fell into silence as the traffic dwindled. Rush hour was long gone.

"I didn't want her to need for anything, especially love. I grew up with an unfit mother. I didn't want that for Maisie, so I let her go. I had to let them both go."

"He didn't come to see you, your husband?"

Katie shook her head. "I was in bad shape. Couldn't even talk to him on the phone. He funded Delaney's move to Asheville and paid my hospital bill. In return, I agreed to a divorce and Cal's demand for full custody, but his lowlife lawyer decided it wasn't enough. Insisted the mentally unstable mother surrender her parental rights. At first I didn't want to take that final step, but my lawyer was young and didn't know how to fight. And then Delaney asked what my heart told me was best for Maisie, so I signed away my life.

"But it was tough on Delaney. She'd become Maisie's full-time babysitter, even though she and Cal didn't have the best relationship. I guess she had to blame one of us for my leaving, so she picked him. Delaney and I agreed to stay dead to Maisie, and Cal's best friend agreed to step in as our replacement. The four of us did what we thought was best for

Maisie. I hated that Delaney had to give her up, too, but Maisie was better off without me. I always believed that. I had to."

I could hurt Maisie, even now. What if I still want to hurt her? No, no, I would never do that. I love her. But what if I don't? I wasn't a mother to her. Running away isn't love.

"Hey, I understand." Ben moved his helmet and scooted over until their thighs touched. He put his arm around her, and Katie leaned against his chest.

"That's an unusual arrangement," he said. "Two men raising a little girl."

"Cal and Jake have an unusual bond. Have since they met in first grade. Cal had just moved to the States, Jake had just moved to Chapel Hill to live with an older aunt after he was orphaned. Jake was taking first grade for the second time, and Cal was new to the American classroom. Guess they bonded early as outsiders." She shrugged. "Jake and I never figured out how to trust each other or share Cal. After our wedding, Jake's aunt died and he ran off to LA to make it big. When I left he was still out there. A washed-up actor by day and a nanny to an autistic boy by night. Jake was always good with kids. It's grown women he can't handle. Delaney was one of his casualties."

"Right, then. I'm putting him at the top of my shit list."

"You have a shit list?"

"Not until today. Did you ever tell your husband about the OCD?"

"No, because I didn't know. The night I ran away, I asked for help, but he locked me out."

"Bastard," Ben said in a voice she didn't recognize.

"I don't mean from the house, from our bedroom. Things had been bad between us for months. I was already seeing a therapist. A useless one who only focused on my childhood trauma, which brings us to the fun part. My parents."

Cars crawled up to the light. Stopped, idled, went.

"When I was twelve, my mother snatched a steak knife out of my hand and stabbed my father."

"In front of you?" To his credit, Ben didn't flinch.

"Not, you know—" Katie mimicked Norman Bates slashing at the shower curtain. "It was pretty minor as stabbings go, but my father, being a stand-up guy, ran off, never to be seen again. Mom moved us back to Greensboro, her hometown, and became an alcoholic shut-in. She'd never been the most emotionally balanced person, but the move was meant to be our do-over. After that I pretty much raised Delaney, and then she raised me."

"What was wrong with your mother?"

"Who knows? Once we moved she upped the Hail Marys and drank herself into la-la land."

"You're Catholic?"

"Lapsed."

Katie looked up at the sky. It wasn't dark, not yet, but the outline of the moon was visible. "Cal has an even harder time processing violence than I do. He knew about my mom, but we both pretended it didn't happen. We were good at that. Pretending things hadn't happened. When I finally tried to explain what was going on in my head, he probably assumed I'd become my mother. Easy mistake."

"You're making excuses for him?" Ben's arm slid from her shoulder.

"That's why Delaney suggested I come to Raleigh today. She thought it might help me stop wearing this." She pulled up the long chain that hung around her neck and showed him her gold wedding band.

"He didn't stand by you, Katie. That's shit behavior however you look at it."

She re-hid the chain under her T-shirt. "I believe marriage is for life, and I understand why he acted as he did. We both put our daughter first."

"I'm sorry your husband failed you." Ben laid his hand, briefly, across his mouth before resting his knuckle under his chin. "And that your daughter doesn't know her mother's an incredible human being."

"You're biased because I worked for you for free. But wait, there's more!" she said in a late-night infomercial voice. "Not all the docents are middle schoolers. Two of them are fifth-graders, and one of them is Maisie. Maisie is my docent."

"Jesus."

"And I think she might have OCD, and if I'm right, I need to talk to Cal, need to warn him there's a time bomb ticking in her head. But what if I'm wrong and I charge back into their world for no good reason? I stayed away to keep her safe, Ben. But what if the OCD's doing everything to her it did to me? What if Cal doesn't understand the danger?"

What if I see her again and hurt her accidentally?

"Is it genetic?"

"I guess, but faulty brain wiring isn't that simple. My OCD was triggered by postpartum overdrive, an obsessive need to protect my baby. I might have wondered about Maisie once she reached puberty or adulthood, but at ten? And yet why *didn't* I think about that? While I was walking here, I started remembering weird shit Mom used to do and weird shit I did as a child. What if our OCD is genetic? What if I had it at Maisie's age and didn't realize? What if by running away, I didn't protect her from anything? What if I simply hung her out to dry with a man who sees intrusive thoughts as a threat?"

"That's a ton of what-ifs. Where's this insecurity coming from? You're not insecure, Katie. It's one of the many things I admire about you."

"It's doubt, not insecurity."

"Huh. That's pretty interesting."

"Not if you have the doubting disease, I can assure you. Why, Ben, why did I have to be so convinced staying away was the right thing?

Certainty isn't real, it's an OCD con." The ringing in her ears reached a crescendo until she could hear nothing but the memory of waking every morning to the promise of forever. "I love you today and forever," Cal used to say. Forever was another con. Another certainty that didn't exist.

Ben slapped his thighs and stood. "We need a plan."

"You don't want to run back to Ohio, never to return?"

"Wouldn't be able to take the winters. My blood thinned after I moved south." He assessed her with those huge gray eyes. "I always knew you were resilient, but this? You, Katie Mack, are a constant wonder." Ben offered her his elbow. "Come on. We're going out for dinner."

"Why?"

"That's what friends do, knucklehead."

She stretched, stood up, and rubbed life into her buttocks, numb from sitting on a hard bench. "I haven't scared you off?"

"Your story's inspiring, not scary. Is there a local support group around here? If not, you should start one, spread the hope."

"I was in one a while back, but no one else had violent thoughts. A roomful of people with obsessions and compulsions, and they found my fears bizarre. Harm OCD is the dirty underwear of the OCD world. The only thing worse is pedophile OCD."

"Pedophile OCD?" His chin jerked back.

"Yeah. And people think we're neat freaks and hand washers."

"Definitely start your own group. You'd be terrific."

"Maybe one day. Right now I have a hard enough time helping myself."

"This from the woman who sat up with me all night after a sculpture fell on my head."

"Someone had to." She slotted her arm through his, and they started walking. "Where are we going?"

"Wherever we want. How do you feel, now that you've told me the truth?"

"Exhausted, but okay. I think. I still have to figure out what happens next, though."

"That's easy." Ben nodded at a green neon sign advertising beer. "I suggest a drink."

"I want to hate Cal so bad. Why, why do I still love him?"

"You're asking me to explain love? Have you paid any attention to the disaster that's my dating history?" He shook his head. "You're a mom. I should have known."

"I was a middle school English teacher, too. In my old life."

"And you let me deal with the school groups?"

"I struggle around kids. So many potential targets for the OCD beast."

He stopped and pushed open the door to the bar. The smell of hops welcomed them inside, along with raised voices and a whoosh of air-conditioning. "What else do I need to know about OCD?"

"Everything," she said. "I'm going to tell you everything."

SEVEN
KATIE

Moths danced under the outside lights, and Delaney finally stopped choking on her vanilla bean iced tea. Farther down the street from Cocoa Cinnamon, beautiful people drifted around the food trucks parked outside Motorco, the music hall. The crisscross of white lights strung overhead added to the street carnival atmosphere. A green katy-did, a bush cricket, landed on their trestle table and sang its song: *Katy-did, Katy-didn't, Katie did, Katie didn't.*

"Have you lost your ever-lovin' mind?" Delaney's voice came out hoarse. "You can't see Maisie again."

"Why? I'm not breaking the deal if she doesn't know who I am."

Liar. What if I accidentally tell Maisie I'm her mom? I could trigger a serious OCD episode for her. What if I'm lying? Am I—lying?

"I'm only going to see her once. That's all," Katie said. "To make sure. I need to make sure."

"That's checking."

"It's not. I'm ninety percent sure she has OCD. Or eighty percent, but definitely above sixty. Her body language screams anxiety. And she checks worse than I do."

I ran away because I didn't love her enough to stay, because I could have harmed her.

No, I do love her, and I didn't hurt her yesterday. Have I ever been a threat to Maisie?

No, but what if . . .

A mosquito buzzed by Katie's ear, and OCD droned worse than a trapped hornet.

Delaney snatched up a wad of paper napkins and swiped at the tea stain across her chest. The guy with two full sleeves of tattoos at the next table watched. "Hey"—she glanced up—"stop looking at my boobs. I'm not some peep show."

The guy blushed, and Katie gave him a sympathetic smile, which was ridiculous. Maybe she didn't know what was best for anyone. Maybe she never had.

"I'll spend another hour with Maisie, maybe two," Katie said, "and if I'm sure, Ben can take my suspicions to Whitmore, who'll listen because he has firsthand experience with OCD."

"And what happens on the show's opening night?" Delaney said.

"Ben will stand in for me after I come down with a nasty case of food poisoning."

What if Maisie doesn't have OCD, and I'm making all this up because I want to see her again? How do I know I have OCD? What if I don't? What if I'm using that as an excuse because I don't want to admit I'm a child killer? How do I know I'm not a monster?

A thought is just a thought, and I control fire. I am strong.

Katie's left foot tapped the ground. *Tap, tap; tap, tap.*

"I don't care what cockamamie plan you and Ben cooked up." Delaney fixed her green eyes on Katie. "And yes, he's getting the same pep talk. Dealing with a life of worry before you've been measured for your first bra? I can't imagine, but—"

"You were measured for your first bra?"

68

"Mom, in one of her saner moments," Delaney said. "Sis—I love you. I know what this means to you, but no good ever comes from kicking over big rocks. Not unless you're hunting for a nest of copperheads. That part of your life is over. Done. *Finito.* End of story."

Katie stirred the white chocolate latte topped with ginger that Delaney had told her was a crazy choice for a sweltering August evening. Crazy choices—she peeled her sweaty thighs apart—another Katie Mack specialty.

"Are we talking about me and Cal, or you and Jake?"

"Cheap shot. You know I don't think about Jake anymore."

"The same way I never think about Cal?"

Delaney scanned the night sky. Was she searching for shooting stars, as they'd done when they were kids? Katie followed her sister's gaze, but couldn't make out anything beyond the Big Dipper. A band started up inside Motorco, playing with the beat of a dirge. Did Maisie have a favorite band? Did she play an instrument? Maybe something big and bold and twice her size, like a trombone?

"Do you think he's still in her life?" Delaney said.

"Jake? Undoubtedly. She referenced an Uncle Jake."

"There can be only one." Delaney got that distant look again. Was she remembering Jake napping with Maisie on his chest at the christening? After flying back from LA for the service, he had slipped effortlessly into the role of human pacifier. Cal was grateful for the break from Maisie's crying jags and so was Katie, until the spouse of one of her teacher friends mistook Jake for Maisie's dad. Or maybe Delaney was thinking about how she and Jake disappeared later that night. As they had after the wedding.

"Honey, please tell me Jake isn't the reason you keep putting off all those marriage proposals from Patrick."

Delaney laughed, and the tattooed guy risked another glance. "That's so preposterous I'm not even going to answer it." She picked at the back of her amber ring, one of the many non-engagement rings

Patrick kept giving her. "You think she's a bookworm or a gamer? Most kids are either-or. And physically is she a Sullivan or a MacDonald? It was hard to tell in last year's photo. Is she small like you?"

"Yeah." Katie grinned. "And she has my ex-mother-in-law's overbite."

"I need more, more details." Delaney slid a finger up and down the condensation on her glass.

"She's eager and inquisitive, talks with exaggerated mannerisms, and dresses as if raised by wolves. There's an innocence about her, but also a seriousness. Oh, and she's a writer. How perfect is that?"

And I could ruin it all, couldn't I?

"English major mom, librarian grandmother, professor dad. Makes sense. But we can't interfere."

Katie's tongue rubbed the sore inside her mouth. It would never heal unless she left it alone. "And why is that?"

A dog walker strolled by, texting despite the small troop of dogs on leashes attached to the back of his belt. Confident in his ability to remain in control. Katie combed her fingers through her hair and began twisting. Even after five years, the short hair still surprised her as much as her reflection in the bathroom mirror: the multiple ear piercings, the heavy black eyeliner copied from Delaney, the boho chic that had started as disguise and now felt right. Non-OCD right. Music pulsed louder as Katie turned back to her sister.

"Please, Sis. Don't do this. Callum shut you out when you needed him. Not once, but twice. In my book, no one gets a third chance. If you do anything—*anything*—that risks contacting that asshole, you might as well hand him a baseball bat and say, 'Here, have another swing and finish me off.' On the other hand, if you want to take up voodoo and stick a red-haired male doll full of pins, I'm game. Don't think for one second that I'll ever forgive him, either for what he did to you or for drop-kicking me out of my niece's life."

"And Jake?"

"What about Jake?"

"Come on. You don't think Jake had a hand in stripping me of my parental rights? That's a move with Jake's signature all over it."

"Why do you hate him so much?" Delaney reached for her purse and riffled through its contents.

"I don't, but more to the point, why don't you?"

"Can we forget about Jake? He also belongs in our past, and you can't reinsert yourself into Maisie's life because of this." Delaney slid an envelope across the table as if it were rigged to explode. Then she leaned over and fished Katie's drugstore reading glasses out of the messenger bag discarded in the middle of the table.

"Here, you'll need these." Delaney held out the glasses. Katie hesitated before taking them.

Someone laughed, a dog barked, a new song started playing in Motorco, and the tsunami roared closer. Shaking, Katie touched the handwriting, ran her fingers over the return address: Cal's office. He'd relegated her to campus mail. And the postmark was . . . *July 9?*

"You've had this since Maisie's birthday?" Katie said.

"I couldn't figure out how or when to tell you."

The envelope was torn open. Katie reached inside, but there was no photograph. She pulled out a folded piece of paper—a letter—and took off her glasses. "Will you read it to me?"

Delaney nodded and began.

"Dear Delaney, How are you? I think of you often, and I hope things worked out for you and Katelyn. Every day I look back on our lives together with such sadness and regret. How did it all go so wrong? I loved Katelyn with such passion. I will never forget that, and together we created Maisie, the best of both of us.

"I'm sorry that I didn't have the strength to bring Katelyn home from Asheville. I'm sorry that I dumped everything on you. I knew, however, that you would do a better job than I ever could. You forget you watched me look after Maisie and your mother.

"I had always planned to tell Maisie the truth, when she was old enough to handle the fact that her mother had abandoned her and her father had lied to give her the illusion of a happy childhood. No, not an illusion. Thanks to Jake, she's had a childhood of love and giggles."

Delaney paused to look up. Katie had no words.

"When she first asked about her mother, Maisie was four. Kids in preschool can be so cruel. One of them taunted her about having two dads. I told her that Katelyn had been swept away in a rip current when we were visiting Ocean Isle, because that trip was the last happy memory I had of us. Lies often conceal the truth, don't they?

"What I did back then, I did for Maisie. I had to put her first, as I know Katelyn did when she agreed to my terms. I was barely holding things together even before her suicide letter arrived, and what little strength I had left belonged to Maisie. Please tell Katelyn it was the lawyer's idea to go after her parental rights. He convinced me it was the logical—safe—decision, and given the events of the last year, I agree. I'm happy again, Delaney, finally happy. I fell in love with an amazing young woman, an ex-student, and we got married in April. We're expecting our first child in November."

Katie grabbed the chain around her neck. *The young woman in the car.*

Delaney reached over and touched her hand. "You want me to stop? I can give you the précis."

Katie blew out a breath and shook her head. She kept breathing, just breathing.

"I know that Katelyn loved us before things went so terribly wrong. I hope she received the help she needed; I hope she also found her second chance.

"As I try and figure out the best way forward for my new family, I know it's time to cut the last remaining tie. There will be no more photographs of Maisie. Ten is such a milestone. It was huge for me. The year I left childhood behind. I know this will be hard for Katelyn, and I'm sorry to cause her more pain. As always, I'm doing what I feel is in Maisie's best interests.

He sends his regards, blah, blah, blah." Delaney folded the letter and eased it back into the envelope.

Using the hem of her T-shirt, Katie polished the gold ring dangling between her breasts.

"Talk to me," Delaney said. "You okay?"

"No. No, I'm not. I feel as if one of those Clydesdale horses kicked me in the gut."

"I guess you'll back out of the Raleigh thing now."

Katie slapped both her hands on the table. "And why would I do that?"

"The ground rules have changed. He has a new family, and he's pulling the plug."

"I'm happy his life turned out well, but—"

"Bullshit. Like hell you are. I'm certainly not."

"He's asking me to stay away for his sake and for wife number two. Not for Maisie. What's going to happen when the baby arrives? Who's going to put Maisie's interests first?" Katie snatched the letter back from her sister. "All these years I've been working on the assumption she's better off without me. Now I know she's not. This letter"—Katie held it up—"is a red flag. Maisie's about to hit a crisis point."

"Aren't you being a little melodramatic?"

"The director of the art museum told me she's in the docent program because she's anxious about starting middle school. And now we're adding a new mom and a new baby? Do you need a reminder of the hell OCD put us through after we moved back here? And that was a decision I controlled. This is like throwing dynamite on a bonfire. With that much change, Maisie's OCD will think Christmas has come four months early."

"Sis, I hear you. But we can't pop back up in Maisie's life. We both know about abandonment issues. You think Maisie's going to roll out the welcome mat? And while you're talking about anxiety, learning your dead mother's alive is one cataclysmic trigger for stress."

"You think I would do that to Maisie? She'll only know I'm alive if Cal tells her. It won't ever come from me." Katie tasted vomit and swallowed. "Maisie knows me as an artist who had a funny turn when we met. I can explain I had an anxiety attack. I can reach out, talk to her about the noise in my head. What if I can get her to open up?"

"What if you can't?"

"What if I can? What if New Mom isn't up to the job of mothering a child with a broken mind, because she's too busy with a baby? Who's going to be Maisie's guide, her support? The man who doesn't believe in therapy, the man who failed to understand the same problem once before?" Katie thumped the table; the guys next to them stopped talking. "With the journey Maisie's about to take, it might be easier coming from a stranger."

"Stop right there. You're not a stranger."

"And you're missing the point. I might not be an actor of Jake's caliber, but I've been in rehearsal for nine years. I can do this."

"And how are you going to get close to her without Callum or Jake recognizing you?" Delaney said.

"I've checked Cal's teaching schedule, and chances are high New Mom will be handling the pickup. I'm pretty sure that was her yesterday. She certainly looked young enough to be an *ex*-student."

"And what if Callum sees you and thinks you've come to kidnap Maisie? What if he calls the cops or gets a judge to issue a restraining order? Have you thought about what all of this could mean for you?"

"I gave up my life to keep my baby safe, and then I agreed to a ridiculous deal when I was barely functional because I thought it was in my daughter's best interests. That's no longer the case."

"*Shhh.* People are looking."

"You think I care?"

Delaney leaned across the table. "Why don't I get word to Callum that we think Maisie might have OCD, based on your medical history?"

"He won't believe you. He didn't listen when I tried to tell him what was going on in my head. What if he reacts that way with Maisie? Who will she turn to?"

"Jake, she'll go to Jake."

"You don't know that."

Delaney looked away. "I would give my right eye for another chance with Maisie, but please, don't do this. I can't go through full-blown OCD again."

Katie stared into the night. "I won't let that happen."

"Can you promise me? Can you?"

"I have an agreement with Ben. If it gets bad, if I see the precipice coming, I'll call him."

"That's your backup plan? A guy who gets so lost in work he forgets he has a hot date? A guy whose only experience with anxiety is fretting over me wearing flip-flops to the studio?"

"He's a fast learner, and I'm pulling big sister rank. This conversation is at an end." Katie finished her latte. "Cal's remarried and he's expecting a second child? Whoopee for him. But I'm Maisie's mother, and I will be until the day I die. And you know what? Cal sent that letter because part of him is worrying about my intentions. Good, great. Let him worry. I'm taking action, and Cal can go to hell."

As Katie stood up, the OCD crawled back in. Wrapped around her heart, squeezed tight. Told her she was a phony, a fake mother.

I'm angry. I could use that anger to hurt someone.

Katie closed her eyes, breathed in through her nose, and imagined a thin black line floating around her head like a halo. Exhaling slowly, she pushed the line down over her eyes, her nose, her lips, and let it rest on her chin. Another inhale and she pushed the line down her neck to her shoulders. *What about the homicidal anger? I'm not dealing with you right now, OCD.* She pushed the line slowly down across her torso and arms, down her wrists and hands, and out through her fingertips.

Katie opened her eyes and, ignoring Delaney, snatched up her bag. Anger didn't make her homicidal, but it was a legitimate response. She would go back to her apartment and sit with her rage. Embrace it and then toss it in the garbage along with that last—ridiculous—molecule of hope. There would be no second chance for her marriage, but Delaney was wrong. This was not the end of the story. This was the beginning.

She ripped Cal's letter into a hundred fragments.

And put them in her bag to take home and recycle.

EIGHT
CALLUM

As they swung back and forth on Jake's porch swing, Maisie chattered away about some artist she'd met through the docent program. A living wall of holly and mature trees, swaddled in something Jake insisted was not poison ivy, concealed them from the quiet residential street in historic Hillsborough. The shoe-box house on the shady lot had been split into two apartments and modernized, but the yard was snake heaven, as evidenced by an elderly neighbor's recent copperhead bite. Imagining Maisie on the lawn was enough to bring Callum out in hives.

Maisie kept talking; he kept struggling to pay attention. The disturbed nights were beginning to exact a hefty toll. Focus was an issue right now, whether listening to Maisie, his students, or Lilah. Picking up coffee from Cup-A-Joe before he hit the highway might be wise if he didn't want to nod off at the dean's dinner table.

Callum squinted at the abstract metal sculpture of circles and spikes in the far corner of the porch. No matter how many times he looked at it, he saw severed heads on spears. When he had shared this observation with Jake, Jake commented, in a wry tone, it might be time to consider therapy.

"Daddy," Maisie said, "you are *not* paying attention."

"Sorry, sweetheart. I was lost in the moment with my daughter."

Maisie combed her hair with her fingers and thumb held in an odd way. She'd never done that before, but it seemed familiar. "Are you worrying about Uncle J, too?"

"Worrying about Jake? No. Should I be?"

She tapped her watch. "He's ten minutes late."

"Friday traffic." Callum tried to smile. "Which I will also hit on the drive back to Raleigh. I liked it better when your Uncle Jake lived closer."

"But, *Daaaddy*! This cottage is super awesome."

Maisie stretched her arms wide as if to say, *Look at this kingdom.* A small, well-trimmed patch of lawn disappeared over a steep slope with the bamboo railing and stone steps that Jake had constructed one weekend. The flower bed of hostas—the only plants Callum could identify, because Katelyn had labeled them deer food—circled the huge magnolia tree, the only tree he could identify, because of Jake.

On the other side of the yard, Jake's bottle tree lit up a dark corner with glass in every color imaginable. Jake, the master set builder, had created a grotto that welcomed you into his hidden world. Except for the doormat that said "Leave."

And then there was the snake problem, which was why Callum insisted Maisie play inside. She even had her own reading nook in the main room, created from netting, strings of white lights, and the old baby lamp he'd attempted to donate to a thrift store. Maisie had a hard time accepting change. She clung to the past, when all he wanted was to dash for the future.

"This place is perfect for a ghost story," Maisie said. "I think I'll start writing one this weekend."

Callum gave a mock shiver. "I love that you write ghost stories. I've always been too much of a wuss for anything spooky. A good bump in the night and I'll be hiding under the bed while you'll be investigating with a flashlight and a poker. Thank goodness I've got you to protect me."

"Oh, I will always do that, but you're not a wuss, Daddy. You're super sensitive, and that is very cool. But this place is really, *really* old."

"Nineteen thirties isn't that old. Not when you come from Scotland."

"Older than Grammy."

"Let's not share that with your grandmother, okay?"

The blue Honda Fit with the bike roof rack pulled up to the curb, music blaring through the open windows.

"Uncle J!" Maisie pushed off the porch swing and flew toward the car.

Thunder rumbled, and Callum's gut twisted up the way it always did when he thought about leaving Maisie. The music died, the driver's door slammed, and Jake stepped into view wearing strategically ripped jeans—was the fashionable term *distressed?*—and a crumpled blue linen shirt. Not exactly Jake's typical working attire.

Jake caught his eye and winked. "Lunch date ran late, sorry. Darlin'!" He lifted Maisie and swung her around. "I got you that present your daddy okayed." He put Maisie down and held up a plastic bag.

Maisie clapped her hands and squealed. "My very own phone. Thank you, Uncle J! You're the best."

Callum hadn't actually *okayed* the purchase of a phone. He merely gave up trying to out-argue Jake and Lilah, who teamed up to insist it was a necessary evil after Maisie and Ava Grace went missing in the forest behind their house for twenty minutes. Twenty minutes that had eviscerated him.

Jake took Maisie's hand, and together they walked across the front yard and up the steps of the porch. "Split, man. Get on I-40 before the traffic backs up. You and Lilah Rose enjoy your night out."

"At the dean's house," Callum said.

"Maybe he's grooming you for chair."

"Can't think of anything worse. Less family time."

"Got me there. Who would ever want to be apart from our number-one girl?"

"Uncle J." Maisie made the slashing motion across her throat that signaled *Cut the crap*.

"Getting too big for compliments, are we? Or do we keep those for the cute boy who watches you at school pickup?"

"What boy?" Callum frowned.

A bright white grin lit up Jake's tanned face. "I'll extract a full confession before you and Lilah Rose get home."

"Daddy, Uncle J." Red-faced, Maisie put her hands on her hips and rolled her eyes. "You both know the boys spy on us at recess because they are very immature and don't use their time wisely. All they know how to do is post silly videos of pillow fights on YouTube."

Thunder rumbled again, but the sky directly above was cerulean.

"Storm's pulling north," Jake said. "Go. Have fun and forget about us. We have our own Friday-night plans, starting with the Riverwalk and dinner at Hillsborough BBQ, and ending with a movie back at home if there's time." He turned to Maisie. "No more vomit-icious Disney fairy tales. I vote for *The LEGO Movie*. And yes, Dad. I'll make sure her light's out by nine."

"Can we do a PG-13?" Maisie's eyes grew wide.

"No," he and Jake said in a chorus of dissent.

"That's not fair." Maisie pouted. "Ellie's allowed to."

Because her father wants to antagonize his ex-wife. "Movie ratings exist for a reason," Callum said. "To protect you from exposure to things that are not age appropriate."

"I'm old enough for smushy bits, and *Star Wars*—"

"Was a birthday exception." Callum sighed. "Can we not do this now? Please, peanut? I have to leave. Come here and give me a Maisie hug. I love you."

Maisie threw her arms around his waist. "Love you, too, Daddy, even if—"

"Nah-ah, you know my main rule. Neither of us can walk away if one of us is angry." He held on and swayed from side to side.

"I'm not angry."

"Glad to hear it." He smacked a kiss on top of her head and turned to Jake. "I doubt we'll be home before eleven, but I'll have my phone on vibrate."

"Stop fussing and get your ass off m' porch."

"Yeah, Daddy." Maisie grinned up at Jake. "Get your—"

"Language, you two." Callum tried to sound stern, although part of him wanted to say, *Go for it, act out.* Maisie loved to argue her point, but she never broke a rule without permission.

As Callum headed back to the car, his mind imitated a gerbil scrambling on an exercise wheel. Every day, he saw more of Katelyn in Maisie. In her behavior, not in her appearance, since Maisie's hair announced her as a MacDonald. *Oh, God. The hair.*

His mind spun faster, this time remembering Katelyn. Remembering wrapping his fingers in her long black hair while he thrust deep inside her. The sex, until Maisie was born, had been intense. The fantasies troubled him for years. But there was another memory underneath: Katelyn twisting her own hair. Twisting it on one side, and then the other. Katelyn twisted, Maisie straightened, but the two habits were startlingly similar.

NINE
JAKE

Cicadas were singing his favorite song, and some bird farther up the Riverwalk chimed in with a chirp as sweet as honey. A horn blared in the parking lot behind them, and distant traffic rumbled. Could be it was heading into downtown Hillsborough on Old 86; could be it was speeding along the interstate that followed the historic Occaneechi trading path.

Jake inhaled the toe-curling southern heat with a slow smile and took in his surroundings. The tall yellow flowers on the riverbank glowed, and the wooden boards of the bridge bounced as a cyclist shot past. Beneath them, the Eno moseyed along in a lazy ebb, reflecting the sky. The orange light—the one that flattered every skin tone—was perfect for filming.

A raggedy group of red-faced high school kids jogged past. Some sadistic coach must be putting them through their paces. If he were a parent, he'd sure have problems with his kid running in this heat. He glanced at Maisie, arms flung through the railing of the bridge as if reaching for the reflection of the sun. She'd been kinda quiet since leaving the cottage. Lost in her own world wasn't a strange state of being for 'Mazing Maisie, but this amount of silence meant something was brewing in her supercomputer brain.

"That docent program still floatin' your boat, darlin'?"

"Oh, yes." Maisie stared down at the river. Tiny ripples broke the smooth surface. "I met this super awesome artist called Katie Mack."

"Cool name." Although K. M. as a pair of initials stood for nothing good. "Shoot, I nearly forgot." Jake reached into his pocket and pulled out the folded-up one-dollar bills. He counted nine and handed them over.

"Here you go. Nine dollars for the Wings of Fire book you're missing. To complete the series. I thought we could stop at Purple Crow Books and pick up a copy. Didn't you tell me it was eight dollars?"

Maisie stared at the money but didn't take it. "That's super kind of you, Uncle J, but can you give me eight?"

"You'll need a dollar for the sales tax."

"Oh, I can't take nine. It has to be eight."

Maisie and her moral compass. "Put the change toward something else."

But Maisie shook her head and ran off, leaving him alone on the bridge with a handful of money.

"Hey, Maisie," he called. "Wait up."

She sprinted to the right and continued along the riverbank. Jake took chase, stopping when she disappeared inside the large stick sculpture that could have grown from the forest floor. A natural observatory, the structure was woven out of saplings of elm, sugar maple, and sweet gum. Jake and Maisie had watched its installation: Maisie with horror because it had a limited life expectancy, Jake in awe because it was a thing of temporary beauty. One day it would break down and disappear back into the trees.

Late-afternoon sunlight and a crazy-ass squirrel kept him company while Jake stood guard. Maisie was by herself, but he glimpsed red hair as she dashed around in circles. Could be she just needed to burn off her mood. Maisie might be a chatterbox, but she couldn't be rushed if something was chewing at her. When she finally emerged, Maisie reached for his hand, and they started walking along the trail.

"Wanna tell me what happened back there?" he said.

"I'm very sorry, Uncle J. But I don't like odd numbers. They feel scratchy."

By three Maisie had developed her own expressions, but that seemed off, even for her. "How about I pay for the book? Would that work?"

She nodded. "Thank you, Uncle J. I'm sorry."

"Hey, nothing to apologize for."

They kept walking as the cicadas continued their music and the air grew still and gray. Jake glanced up to check for storm clouds.

"Maisie, you know I don't expect you to talk if you're not feeling the vibe."

"I know."

"But anything you tell me stays in confidence. I don't squeal to your daddy."

"I know."

He raised her hand and tucked it under his arm. "You know a lot, 'Mazing Maisie."

A couple came toward them, dragging a puppy on a leash. The woman smiled at him, blushed, but the man didn't make eye contact. Their body language screamed, *We're in the post-argument phase.* Given the guy's slumped shoulders, all bets were on him as the culprit. When they were out of earshot, Jake leaned in to Maisie.

"What d'you think their story is? Guy messed up big time, woman let him have it?"

"Whose story?" Maisie said.

"Darlin', you're slipping. Writers and actors never switch off their people radar. Observe, observe, observe."

"And observe."

He nodded at a bench that overlooked the Eno. "Let's sit and talk. Catch up on our week."

Maisie sat and examined the hem of her oversized T-shirt.

"You and Lilah Rose gettin' along?"

Maisie shrugged. A bird gave a solitary whistle that sounded mighty ticked off.

"I'm finding it hard, sharing your dad," he said. "How about you?"

"It's getting easier. Although I hope the baby's a girl. I don't think I want a brother."

"Sorry, but you won't have any control over that one. Is it still bothering you, the whole idea of calling Lilah Rose Mom? Want me to talk with your daddy some more?"

"No. Thank you. It's very important to him, and I'm trying super hard to cooperate." Maisie pulled up her legs and hugged them. She'd always been able to tuck herself up like a hermit crab. Oh, to be young and flexible. Every day he had more aches and pains. Gray hairs would be next. Well, would be if he stopped dyeing his hair, but that was a tough step for someone who'd always gotten by on his looks. Although, they'd also been the cause of so many bad decisions it was hard to know where to begin.

"Tell me something about my real mom again," Maisie said.

"Not much you don't know. Your mama was beautiful and smart, kind and funny. Real good at math, too. C'mon, baby," he said. "What aren't you telling me?"

A crow cawed, and they both looked up at the dead tree in front of them, its skeletal fork pointing into the now cloud-covered sky.

"Do you ever worry about bad stuff happening to me?" Maisie chewed on her lip.

"Only since the second I moved in with you and your dad. It was a huge responsibility being your babysitter. Bigger than huge." Jake measured out *huge* with his arms spread wide, and Maisie giggled. "'Cause I love you more than anyone, and I didn't want to mess up."

The birds fell silent.

"Do you ever think about starting a family, Uncle J?"

"Now what nonsense is that? I have a family. You and your daddy."

Maisie heaved out a mighty big sigh for a small person. "Don't you miss Los Angeles?"

"My heart was always here, you know that. Besides, I never cared too much about the fame. That kind of drive can wreck a life. Since I was younger than you, all I wanted was to act, and that part wasn't working out so well. After I got fired off that god-awf—not very nice soap opera, I was jobless. When your daddy suggested I visit for your birthday, seemed like the perfect time to check out the movie scene down south. But it didn't take more than half a day to decide your daddy needed my help more. Once I moved in with you guys, life got real simple real fast, and simple's pretty darn good." He paused. "Is that how you feel, that life's good?"

She rested her cheek on her knees. "Actually, I find there's quite a lot to worry about."

"Wanna be more specific?"

"One of our teachers had to take time off because her sister died having a baby."

"*Ahhh*, I get it." Jake wrapped his arm around her. "Childbirth can turn dangerous, but the doctors know ahead of time if there's a problem brewing. Your stepmama's in great shape, and everything's as normal as normal can be with her pregnancy. Nothing bad's gonna happen." He paused. "Is this why you've been wound a little tight recently?"

Maisie shrugged.

For a moment he wondered if she had inherited something nasty from her mama. If only he could remember what Delaney said about her sister. Not that they'd ever done a whole lotta talking.

"But what if I'm the problem?"

"Darlin'. You've never been a problem a single day of your life. Except when you got thrown out of preschool 'cause all you did was cry for your daddy." *And started sleeping so poorly that I became nuttier than a squirrel turd.*

The Eno had stopped moving. A frog croaked, and humidity bore down on his shoulders.

"But I keep worrying I am." Maisie sat up. "I keep worrying that I'm a bad kid and Lilah's going to die because of me."

"Whoa. Back up. You and I might have active imaginations, but there's no relationship between your behavior and Lilah Rose's pregnancy. Flat-out ain't possible."

Maisie gave him that adoring look with her huge hazel eyes. How come she never saw him as others did: a screwup with above-average acting skills?

"But what if I'm the causation of stress? Stress is very bad for pregnancy, and Ava Grace once said I can get on her last nerve like no one's business."

"That's Ava Grace's mama talking, and she's got less sense than a flamingo lawn ornament."

"Uncle J!"

"Well, I'm just statin' fact." Any guy could figure out that woman's greatest assets had nothing to do with her brain. "If you're going to start worrying as much as your daddy, you've got to come clean with me. Because I know you, 'Mazing Maisie. You'll keep it all to yourself so as not to upset anyone. Next thing, you'll start building up those walls, and you know what I always say about walls."

"You have to tear them down," Maisie said slowly.

"That you do. And you and me? We tell it like it is with each other and stay positive, because your daddy worries enough for all three of us, right?"

She puckered her lips.

"Know what I think?" he said. "When a brilliant young mind has something tough to process, it gets way too creative. Is this all about what happened with your real mama?"

Maisie cleared her throat several times.

"Please tell me, baby."

"Promise you won't tell my dad?"

"Jake-Maisie pinkie swear."

"Sometimes I see Lilah dying. And I worry that if I thought it, it'll come true. She's not, is she? Going to die?"

"That's the storyteller in you looking for the dark side of life."

"But my brain fills up with stuff I don't want to think about, and even my absolute favorite things aren't fun anymore." She scratched her leg like she had a mess of chigger bites. "It's very frightening, Uncle J."

Jake pulled her closer. "I don't know what's going on, but I promise I'll do all I can to help. And you know how seriously I take my promises."

An ugly thought crept in: the one person he wanted—needed—to discuss this with was the one person he couldn't contact. She had made that clear when she met Patrick. "I want more," Delaney said. "And you're never going to be that guy, are you?" And he'd answered no.

TEN
KATIE

Katie's empty stomach growled. Not just from hunger, but from lack of bedtime stories and snuggles, lack of wiped tears and kissed boo-boos. Lack of motherhood. Maisie, head down, continued to ooh and aah over the sketch for the buckshot piece. Weren't mothers meant to praise their kids' artwork and not vice versa? Katie straightened the corner of her sketchbook. Smoothed out the page, shifted in her seat. Chewed off a hangnail.

Am I making a good impression? Does she like me? Does she want to know me better? Why didn't I eat lunch? I never deal well on an empty stomach. Why didn't I eat something?

What if I never see her again? What if I get up and run away from her—again?

What if the six-week CAM program, already half-over, was her once-in-a-lifetime shot at mothering her own child? How could she destroy it with talk of monsters?

I don't love her. But I do, I do love her, don't I? Didn't I promise to protect her, keep her safe? Isn't that what I'm trying to do?

Another stomach growl echoed through the huge white-and-glass meeting space, empty except for her and Maisie.

Maisie stared up with big owl eyes. "Did you skip lunch *again*, Ms. Katie? My dad always says it's super important to eat three nutritious meals a day."

"Guilty as charged." Katie focused on a car moving slowly down the street. "I make incredibly bad decisions for an adult."

"I'm sure we could ask Mr. Whitmore if he has any more baguettes and Nutella."

"You know what I'm in the mood for? A huge hunk of real chocolate. Preferably white."

"Which is super hard to find." Maisie sighed. "I know because white chocolate is my favorite."

Katie sat on her hands so she wouldn't grab her daughter's face and smother it with kisses. "I think I know where to look." She stood up and pushed her chair back under the table; Maisie did the same. "Let's go on a chocolate hunt."

Did your dad ever read We're Going on a Bear Hunt *to you? I would have; I would have read it until you had your first book hangover.*

"Unfortunately," Maisie said with the sweetest frown in the history of frowns, "I think the chances of finding chocolate in an art museum are—" She held up her hand, her thumb and index finger curled together to form a perfect zero.

"Exactly. Have you ever been to the Chocolate Factory down the street?"

"*Nooo*, but I don't think that's an option."

"Because I don't have your father's permission?" Katie winced as if a splinter had driven itself into her eye.

Maisie nodded.

"What if another adult in a position of responsibility could grant us a chocolate pass? I bet Whitmore would let us sneak out if we built an airtight case."

Maisie scratched at the skin on the back of her wrist. "But I don't have any money," she said, blushing.

"Good, because I wouldn't let you pay under any circumstances. This would be my treat."

"Thank you. Thank you, that's super generous." Maisie continued to scratch.

"I feel as if there's another *but* coming."

"We would also have to watch the time really, *really* carefully."

"We can do that."

Maisie glanced up. Her eyes said, *More, I need more.* OCD always wanted more. Muffled voices moved through the exhibition space above, real voices from the real world.

"We're not breaking any rules if we have the director's permission," Katie said.

Was she feeding Maisie's OCD? *No.* That was a statement of fact, not reassurance, but did Cal or New Mom know the difference? When she told Delaney she could help Maisie, Katie hadn't believed it. Not one hundred percent. Not even seventy-four. But as she watched Maisie, feet pointed inward, mouth closed in a tight line, fingers dancing to a soundtrack only she could hear, it was as if Katie were looking into a mirror. And then Maisie straightened her hair twice on one side, twice on the other, with her thumb folded under her fingers, creating a makeshift flat iron.

I used to do something similar—twice on one side, twice on the other.

"What do you think, Maisie?" Katie swallowed. "Are you up for the chocolate challenge?" *Say yes, please say yes.*

Maisie hesitated. "I *am* very good at debating."

"In that case, we're off to Whitmore's office." Shoving her hands into her back pockets, Katie led the way.

She knocked on the open door, and Whitmore glanced up from his keyboard. "Good afternoon, ladies. Can I help with something?"

Katie ushered Maisie inside. "We have a problem and a solution."

He raised a perfectly arched eyebrow. "I'm all ears."

"We're trying to have a serious discussion about art. And we've been stumped by a desperate, clawing need for chocolate."

"That is quite a problem. What's your solution?"

"A quick visit to the Chocolate Factory," Katie said. "I'm appalled to learn Maisie's never visited this fine establishment. To be honest, neither have I."

Maisie nodded. "Ms. Katie's quite right. I've never been, but I don't have my dad's permission, which"—she glanced at Katie—"we realize would be a very good thing."

"I see. But you came to the right place, since I'm the king of the CAM universe." He smiled. "Well, Trudy, who mans the information desk, is the real boss, but I do have executive veto. How long until you get picked up, Maisie?"

Maisie looked at the clock. "Forty-two minutes."

Forty-two was a perfect, round number. A sign, a good sign.

"And do you share this desperate need for chocolate?"

"Oh, yes, I concur," Maisie said. "Plus Ms. Katie skipped lunch because she didn't want to be late for me, so indirectly it's my fault that she's in need of—"

Katie's stomach rumbled as if on cue.

"I hear your problem." Whitmore studied the abstract painting on his wall. "However, I can't let you leave the building without parental permission. On the other hand"—he gestured at the landslide of papers across his desk—"I am drowning in admin and can't help but feel a change of scene might help. What if I came with you and sat at a different table? Maybe by working off-site I could find the bottom of the black hole formerly known as my Gmail inbox."

"Black holes don't have bottoms," Maisie said.

"Exactly," Whitmore said. "Which proves that my short-circuiting brain needs cocoa."

"Thank you," Katie said in a breathy whisper.

A supervised visit, but the Newbery Medal of progress. Not only a mother-daughter outing, but a shared first that involved chocolate. And walking along a road. With moving vehicles. What if she pushed Maisie under a car? *What if, what if . . .*

"Give me two minutes, and I'll meet you in the lobby." Whitmore unplugged his laptop from a large monitor.

Katie walked out of the office and down into the lobby, Maisie by her side.

I could push Maisie under a car; I could kill her. No, no. That's OCD talking. I would never do that. I'm her mother. But what if I'm a monster? What if I don't love her? What if I never did? But that's not true . . .

Maisie glanced at her bright plastic watch. "We only have forty minutes left, Ms. Katie."

"I can set a timer on my phone, if you'd like."

"That would be awesome! Uncle J does get in a fluster if I'm not where I'm supposed to be when I'm supposed to be there. After Ava Grace and I spent a bit too long in the woods, he—"

"Uncle . . . J?"

"Yes! He's my favorite person on the planet. After my dad, of course. My dad always says Uncle Jake needs a girlfriend. Are you married?"

Katie grabbed the gold chain around her neck and held on as the links dug into her flesh.

"Ready, ladies." Whitmore appeared with his laptop and phone, and pushed open the big yellow door. A blast of August heat smacked Katie in the face, along with the sounds of construction: drilling, crashing, a yell of "Look out!"

Look out, Maisie. You're not safe around me.

She's so small, so defenseless; I could hurt her so easily. Push her under a car.

An image played, a depraved image. Katie sucked in her breath and briefly closed her eyes. Blocked out the sun, her daughter, the street, the passing car.

A thought is just a thought. It has no power.

"Ms. Katie and I are hoping for white chocolate. What's your preference, Mr. Whitmore?" Maisie had skipped through the open door and was on the sidewalk.

Katie shot between Maisie and the road. Whitmore turned with a puzzled look, and Katie forced her mouth into an overly bright smile. "A little overexcited at the prospect of good chocolate."

He nodded and spoke to Maisie. "I hate to break rank, but dark chocolate always gets my vote. High in antioxidants and good for cognitive function, which is exactly what I need."

As they walked up the street, Maisie chatted with Whitmore and Katie's flip-flops slapped against the pavement.

What if Jake recognizes me and calls the cops? What if the cops lock me up for child abandonment, child endangerment, being a psycho?

A thought is just a thought; it has no power.

Avoiding Jake was simple. *He's a slack-ass. Always runs late.*

She would set the timer on her phone, as promised, but five minutes early. And when they were close to the museum, she would pretend she'd left something behind and ask Whitmore to see Maisie safely back.

That's a stupid plan. Jake'll recognize me. I should leave, go home before I hurt Maisie. See that car? What if I . . .

Maisie grabbed Katie's arm. "This is so much fun! Thank you, Ms. Katie."

She was touching her. Maisie was touching her. "You're welcome."

"I like hanging out with you."

"I like hanging out with you, too. And how about we drop the 'Ms.'? Call me Katie."

"Oh." Maisie's eyes grew wide. "I don't know if that would be appropriate, since you're, like, a teacher."

I'm not, I'm your mother. No, no, I'm not. I abandoned you; I'm the worst mother. Jake hates me, and Whitmore would, too, if he knew what

I'd done. Susan Smith was a beloved kindergarten teacher compared to me. See that car? I could push you underneath it.

A thought is just a thought; it has no power. I control fire; I am strong. I want this next half hour with my daughter. This is my real thought, the one I want to keep.

"I'm super excited you get to meet Uncle J," Maisie said. "Maybe you'll fall in love with him. Women always do."

"Tell me about your dad," Katie said. *No, no!*

"He's super smart and the best dad in the world. Although . . ." She sighed. "I have a lot more rules than most of my friends. And a lot less electronic time. And he refuses to let me watch PG-13 movies when my friend Ellie's dad lets her watch them. It's super embarrassing because he even called up Ellie's dad *spec-iiifically* to tell him what I was and was not allowed to watch." Maisie rolled her eyes.

As they crossed the road, Katie glanced both ways and her heartbeat picked up speed, galloped for some imaginary finishing line she could never reach. But she kept her right arm raised and steady. Prepared to push Maisie behind her if a car came from any direction. They reached the curb, and her daughter continued to describe the man Katie had once promised, before God, to love until her last breath. A man with another wife, another family. Silently, Katie counted backward from one hundred and brushed sweat from above her lips.

I am calm; I am calm.

Stepping into the Chocolate Factory, they entered a cavernous world of industrial architecture, brick walls, steel and wooden beams, and light. Unexpected light, from a bank of windows, contemporary white fixtures, and strings of globe lights that illuminated the decorative squares of tin above them—renovated and polished to a contemporary shine. The ceiling had to be original. As original as the battered tin shutter she'd salvaged from a historic tobacco warehouse in downtown Durham and reimagined as *That Perfect Moment*. To their right, under a huge "Buy Chocolate Here" sign, shelves were stacked with bars of chocolate. Ahead, a brick opening led to the factory; on their left, the café beckoned. Smiling, Katie inhaled warm cocoa with a hint of spices.

"Hmm," she said.

"Hmm," Maisie said, and they both giggled.

After picking out a bar of peppermint milk chocolate to share—no white chocolate—they headed to the café counter and ordered an iced Americano and a frozen hot chocolate. Whitmore, who was clearly a more efficient decision maker than either of the two of them, was already sitting at a table, laptop open, with an espresso and a bar of dark chocolate.

Katie chose a table for two tucked against the brick wall, under a window.

"Do you think we'll have time to tour the factory?" Maisie said.

Katie shook her head as she set the timer on her phone. "Sadly, no. We don't want to keep your uncle waiting."

"He's not really my uncle. He's my godfather."

I know.

"Tell me about yourself, Maisie. What do you do for fun?"

"Mostly I write. When I'm not super busy with homework. I start middle school next year, you know." Maisie brushed her hair again. Twice on the left side, twice on the right.

"What do you do when you're not writing?"

Katie snapped the bar of chocolate in half, put one half on a paper napkin, and pushed it toward Maisie. Maisie thanked her profusely and then chatted away about Ava Grace and their friend Ellie. About the neighborhood pool and playing softball. And Jake. Unfortunately Maisie had a great deal to say about him.

"And sometimes Uncle J tells me stories about my real mom," Maisie says. "My dad can't talk about her. It's too painful for him, but Uncle J says she was beautiful and funny and kind."

Katie started choking.

"Are you alright, Ms. Katie?"

"Yup. Sorry." Katie smacked her chest. "Went down the wrong pipe."

Maisie started talking again, but thankfully not about Jake. "And now that I've turned ten, my dad lets me have sleepovers with Ava Grace and Ellie." Maisie popped the last piece of chocolate into her mouth.

Ten seemed awfully young for sleepovers. Katie didn't have them until she was at least fourteen. But that wasn't because of a parental embargo. Katie scratched her forearm again and again. It was because she couldn't handle disruption to her routines. Was OCD festering in her brain, even then? Had she always been wired for OCD until postpartum craziness pushed her over the precipice? When had Maisie's OCD started? Did she also have a trigger?

What if I'm the trigger for her OCD? What if the thought of my death was her trigger? What if leaving her created all this? What if staying away was the worst thing to do?

Katie picked at the edge of her paper napkin. "I couldn't do sleepovers at your age."

"Why?" Maisie bobbed around in her seat.

"I had trouble with spontaneity. I needed things to be familiar."

Maisie frowned and nodded.

Katie glanced at Whitmore, who was typing on his laptop. "You remember when we met and I had that funny turn?"

"Oh, yes. Are you quite well now?"

"Um, yes and no?" Katie's voice rose ridiculously high. She cleared her throat and started again. "I have an ongoing illness. It's not contagious or anything, but I was struggling. You see, I get very anxious."

"Why?" Maisie drew out the word, tiptoed around it.

"I'm allergic to change. Have a hard time with new things. Coming here, that first day, gave me lots to worry about, and I had a big panic."

Maisie's mouth twitched. "Is it still hard? To come here?"

"I'm afraid it is."

"How do you make yourself do it?" Maisie's voice was hushed.

"I have to be extremely bossy with the anxiety—tell it I'm in charge."

Maisie balled up her napkin. "Does that make it go away?"

"Not entirely. It's still there, but I don't listen to it, because I've bossed it back into place." She longed to reach across the table and tell Maisie everything would be okay. Except family history could prove her wrong. "It's like I have brain farts."

Maisie giggled; Whitmore looked up and smiled at them.

"I'm the only one who can hear the brain farts, but when they're very loud, they try to convince me that bad things will happen to people I love. Sometimes I even worry I caused the bad things, which is bogus because thoughts can't hurt anyone. They're not real."

Maisie stared at the table.

"Do you have brain farts?"

Maisie didn't answer.

"There's nothing to be embarrassed about, if you do."

Maisie rubbed her forearm.

"And if you do have these brain farts, you should tell your parents, so they can take you to a special doctor."

"I don't like doctors. And I'm not ill. I'm my dad's right hand *and* his left. He needs me to be strong."

"You can be strong and have an illness."

"Could you please take me back to the museum now? Thank you."

"I'm sorry, Maisie. I stepped over a line." Katie tried to stop her voice from shaking in tandem with her right leg. "I didn't mean to upset you. Are we still friends, 'Mazing Maisie?"

Maisie looked up with her beautiful hazel eyes. How could Cal deal with OCD if he couldn't even help her choose glasses?

"What did you call me?"

Shit, shit.

"'Mazing Maisie?"

"Only Uncle J calls me that."

No, he doesn't. He stole it from me.

"Well, it's a great name."

"Are you sure you don't know Uncle Jake? He's an actor and very handsome. He has black hair and his eyes are really, *really* blue."

Katie's timer went off.

"Oh, fudge!" Maisie shot up. "We should go!"

Whitmore got up from his table, too.

"Let's get you back. Don't want to keep Uncle Jake waiting, do we?"

They cleared off the table and headed back outside into the thick, warm soup of an August afternoon. And as they rounded the corner, there was Jake. Leaning against a neon-blue Honda Fit parked curbside, with ankles and arms crossed loosely, and face raised toward heaven. A vampire who loved the sun, who wore self-confidence as if it were a gift from a fallen angel. Ready for a date, no doubt, in his black jeans and white shirt that had to be linen, given the wrinkles. Still gorgeous, still a weasel she wouldn't trust even if she were trapped in a burning vehicle and he was her only chance of escape. She dug into her messenger bag and pulled out her sunglasses.

"Uncle J!" Maisie squealed.

Jake pushed off the side of the car.

"Oops! Gotta make a phone call." Katie ducked into a doorway. "Bye, Maisie! See you next week." She yanked out her phone and pretended to talk. Whitmore walked past, and she said a cheerful "Bye!"

Behind her, Jake's drawl filled the street, the air, the universe. Katie huddled farther into the shade of the doorway and held her phone tight. *Inhale one, two, three, four; hold your breath; exhale one, two, three, four. Repeat, repeat.*

When she glanced over her shoulder, Jake was watching. "'Mazing Maisie," he said, "why don't you wait for me in the car while I thank your teacher."

"She's not my teacher," Maisie said. "She's a metal artist."

"Is she now?" Jake said. "Hop in, darlin'. I'll be right back."

The sun had sunk low enough to hit that blinding spot. Moving out from the shade of the doorway, Katie stepped into the glare. Jake, sunglasses perched on top of his head, closed in on her. His piercing blue eyes were bluer than she remembered; his tan was deep and even. So was his hair color. Not peppered with gray, then? He probably dyed it. After all, Jake's vanity was an indelible truth. Along with the fact that you never showed him weakness.

He didn't blink, smile, or hesitate until he stopped in front of her. She nearly gagged on his aftershave. Some smells were impossible to forget.

"If that don't beat all." He gave a lazy smirk. "You're back, then?"

"Hello, Jake. Yes, yes, I am. And I'm here to stay."

ELEVEN
KATIE

Humidity sealed her in the moment; her heartbeat drowned out the city sounds. Jake leaned in, peppermint on his breath. Was he going to threaten her again? "Make him happy or else," Jake had said on her wedding day. Rather than specify *or else*, he'd moved on to seduce her sister.

"I don't know what your game is"—he kept his voice low—"but you come within spitting distance of Maisie again, and I'll call the cops faster than you can say, 'Well, hey there, handsome.'"

"Still as predictable as ever. Takes a small pair of balls to intimidate a small woman."

He pulled back, his face unreadable. "I'd like to say I've missed you, too, but we both know that would be a lie. I'm guessin' your reappearance has something to do with that letter Callum sent, but don't go worrying your pretty little head about it. 'Cause I'm on you like stink on shit, which means you won't be seeing Maisie again. Ever."

Above them a jet powered silently away from Raleigh. The white trail from its exhaust slashed another vapor trail already hanging in the sky.

"That's going to be hard, wouldn't you say? Since Maisie's my docent."

"Was your docent, darlin'. *Was.* Maisie loves this program a whole lot, and what matters to my girl matters to me, which makes the solution obvious: she gets to stay, you get to go, and we all live happily ever after. But since I'm a nice guy, I'll give you a choice."

"Yeah, you're a regular sweetheart. Still snorting cocaine, playing beer pong with tequila and rum, and screwing everything in a skirt?"

He laughed, but it was the cruel sound of a whip slicing through air. "You still nuttier than a pecan pie, and not one of the good ones with bourbon?" He sneered. "Back to your choice. You can take the easy way out and remove yourself from the program, or you can refuse, and I'll call the director first thing tomorrow and accuse you of saying something inappropriate. My guess is you'll never work with docents again."

This was the Jake she knew, not the one who'd told Maisie nice things about her birth mother. "You're a lowlife, Jake Vaughan. With less integrity than a sewer rat."

"Seriously?" Jake slipped his sunglasses back on. Reflective, of course. "The woman who broke her husband's heart and abandoned her baby is lecturing me on morals?"

"You know nothing about why I left, about what I went through."

"Uncle J!" Maisie called out.

"Comin', darlin'! Give me two secs." He paused. "I don't care why you left, Katelyn, but I'm sure glad you did. Crawl back under your rock and stay there. I've gotta split."

She grabbed his arm, and he turned to give her the evil eye over the top of his sunglasses.

"I didn't know she was in the docent program, Jake. I swear, I didn't know. She has no clue who I am, and I would never tell her otherwise. I would never put her through that trauma."

"And yet you're still here an' all. You could have backed out when you realized who she is. So what're you after?"

"You have to broker a meeting between me and Cal."

"Are you fucking kidding me?" he whispered.

"I wish I was. I have no desire to see my ex-husband, but in here"—she jabbed her fingers at her heart, and her voice vibrated—"nothing will ever matter more than Maisie's well-being, and after reconnecting with her, by mistake, I'm concerned that she's inherited something from me. An anxiety disorder that could make her life hell. I have to talk with Cal. I have information he needs. Information that can help Maisie."

"Maisie is not your responsibility. She's in a loving home, and Lilah Rose is a good woman. If Maisie has problems, which I'm not saying she does, Callum will deal with them."

"The same way he dealt with mine? I have obsessive-compulsive disorder."

"Sorry to hear that." He flicked away a hummingbird moth. "I'd be happy to hire a moving company to take you and your art back to Asheville."

"Do you have any idea how it feels to be tortured by violent thoughts that make you question everything you know about yourself? No? Welcome to my world, Jake. OCD can make you doubt your sexuality, hint you're capable of murdering a person you love, raping a child, or—"

"I have a good imagination." Jake glared. "You don't need to elaborate."

"Left untreated, it's an illness that gets worse and worse. In my case, it was nearly fatal. I've spent the last decade struggling to live with anxiety, and I'm telling you, Maisie is overly anxious. Without treatment she could end up living nightmares even an actor can't imagine. You want to risk that?"

Jake didn't pull away or ram her with another threat. He knew; he knew something was going on with Maisie.

"Her stressors are lining up," Katie continued. "Fear of middle school, uncertainty about a new mom and a new sibling, which means if her brain is wired the same way as mine, it's about to start launching grenades. And she told me she has to be strong for her father, which means she's not going to tell Cal. She's trying to deal with this by herself, and she can't."

"You sure are full of piss and vinegar these days. Got an opinion on everything, bless ya heart."

"For once in your life, listen to me, Jake. Do you know the reason that I was in a psych crisis unit in Asheville? Because of a botched suicide. So don't you dare dismiss what I have to say. I'm not asking for a second chance to be her mother. I'm pleading for the adults in her life to help her."

Jake dragged his hand over his chin. "What are you proposing?"

"Back there, in the Chocolate Factory, she was close to confiding in me."

"Now you're psychic, too?"

"Grow up, Jake."

"And you should stop acting ugly if you want me to listen."

"What can I say, you bring out the worst in me." She flashed a fake smile. "Look, what if you drive her over to my studio. I can show her more of my art and see if she opens up. You can listen and report back to Cal. Tell him what *you've* witnessed. If it comes from you, he'll listen."

Heat clung to the back of her neck, turning it damp and sticky.

"Fine. You can meet with Maisie once more, under my guidance. And if anything happens that suggests there's some validity to your *claim*, I'll go to Callum." Jake held out his hand. "Give me your card."

"You think I have the money to print up business cards?"

"You never heard of Kinko's?" The Jake smile. The one she'd seen on the hemorrhoid cream commercial ten years earlier. He'd sold his soul to advertise ass wipes. Hardly the leading man roles he was chasing when he left for LA. Left right after their wedding and didn't come back until Maisie's christening four years later.

Jake was a fine one to talk about running away.

TWELVE
KATIE

Income, it seemed to Katie, dictated choice in the treatment of both death and mental illness. Trowel in hand, she stared at the headstone her sister chose and her ex-husband financed. Apparently Delaney had requested a plot under the shade of one of the crepe myrtles currently glowing crimson, but their mother's remains lay here, baking in the sun.

In a plot no one else wanted.

Pigeons cooed, and sweat trickled along her spine. As she leaned forward, OCD ran the endless repeat episode that had started on the drive to Greensboro. *What if I hit that car? Go back and check, go back and check.* Maybe she should stretch out here on the clipped grass between graves, close her eyes, and admit defeat. Except then she would get chiggers. And at least one tick. And Lyme disease. Or Rocky Mountain spotted fever. Could you get both? Both would definitely be fatal, and while Cal and Jake might be happy if she really were to die, how would that help Maisie?

She ran a finger over the engraved dates. Fall 2007 was blank in her personal timeline—a season lost to tent living. Ma Sullivan's death had been one of many facts absorbed during recovery: my daughter is lost to me; my husband doesn't want me back; my mother is dead.

Katie finished digging up the dandelions and crabgrass, and sank back on her haunches. The lantana she'd planted two years ago, a hardy Miss Huff that could navigate winters and drought, glowed with tight balls of fire. The greenish bronze carex underneath seemed happy in the red clay.

"Am I like you, Mom?" she said. "Please tell me I'm not."

Finally she needed something from her mother. If only she could have realized that before Ma Sullivan had died—crushed by a tree falling on her car during an ice storm. Delaney's theory was the most plausible, since the accident happened a block from the local convenience center: their mother was heading out for a six-pack and a carton of Marlboro Lights. The real tragedy was that the convenience store had been closed that day. As any sane person would have figured out. And every idiot knew trees fell under the weight of ice.

Katie tossed her trowel aside. *I will be a better mom. Even if Maisie never knows who I am, I will be a better mom. I'll makes sure Cal understands what he's up against.*

A mob of crows rose, cawing and flapping, into the Carolina-blue sky, and several plots over, a family gathered around a fresh grave. A woman held hands with a little girl and a little boy. The children were squirming to break free, and the OCD hurled fresh images. Since bumping into Jake, new images had started amassing for an offensive. Once again, her mind was under siege. Katie closed her eyes and focused.

A thought is just a thought; it has no power.

When she opened her eyes, Delaney was strolling across the grass with hair, attitude, and confidence all bright and shiny in the sun. No wonder Patrick had fallen hard.

Delaney nodded at Katie's phone on the ground. "Never thought I'd see the day when you'd be waiting for a call from Jake."

Katie stood up and dusted red dirt from her knees, along with something small and black. A tick? Was she itchy? She was definitely itchy. Katie felt through her hair, checking for tiny lumps that might be ticks. When she lowered her hand, she accidentally brushed the side of her mother's headstone. And then she touched the other side, which didn't feel right, so she tapped the left side, and then the right. Four taps in total. Four, a number as soothing as the scent of lemon verbena or the sound of August rain.

"You just tapped Mom's grave four times," Delaney said.

"I know." Humidity reached down Katie's throat and coiled around her lungs. "I'm hunting for a new therapist."

"You might want to speed up the search."

Katie tapped once more. Five.

Live with it, Katie. Live with the prickliness of an odd number.

"Don't let Jake mess with your mind," Delaney said. "Trust me, he's not worth it."

"I'm not, and he'll call because in some dark recess of that egotistical brain, he knows I'm right."

"Did you forget his long history of losing women's phone numbers?"

"Projecting, are we?"

"Damn. No punches withheld today."

"By the way," Katie said. "I've had a revelation about Jake. I think his sluttish behavior is rooted in a deep hatred of women."

Delaney gave a *"Sheesh"* and rolled her eyes. For a flicker of a moment, Katie saw the resemblance to Maisie. "I can assure you that man doesn't hate women. Au contraire, he's something of an expert when it comes to fitting thing A into thing B."

"Oh, that's disgusting." Katie failed to spit out the image of Delaney's legs wrapped around Jake. "You ever wonder what makes him tick? He's forty-two years old, single, and runs a moviemaking school for kids."

"You checked him out?"

"Know thy enemy."

"Don't overthink Jake. He's a good actor who enjoys sex and being single. The end." Delaney flicked at something in the air. "How does he look?"

"Dangerous."

Delaney's smile belonged in another time and place.

"You're not going to gate-crash my next meeting with Jake, are you?"

"Are you questioning my devotion to Patrick? Because if you are, we're about to have a knock-down, drag-out fight like we haven't had since middle school. And I always won those."

Katie glanced at the phone again.

He's never going to call. What if he never calls? What if he's reported me to the police? What if he called Whitmore? What if there's a warrant out, even now, for my arrest? What if he told Whitmore I'm a pedophile? What if I am and I never realized?

"You okay, Sis?" Delaney touched her shoulder.

"The heat's making me sick to my stomach."

"You skipped lunch again, didn't you?"

"It's hard to eat right now. My stomach's too fluttery."

"I'm taking you out for lunch before we head back to Durham. Burger and fries." Cicadas buzzed, and Delaney stared at their mother's grave. "You ever wonder what would have happened if we'd stayed in Boston? The move down here really threw her off."

"Honey, she was always off, and *what if* is never a good path to follow. What matters are the concrete facts of family history: Dad was a loser, Mom needed a good psychiatrist and rehab, and somehow we survived. Although you did a better job than me."

"I survived because you set curfews and saved me from stupid decisions."

"Except for Jake."

"Yeah, well. I was old enough to own my screwups by the time our paths crossed. Besides, it was lust at first sight for me. When he finally noticed your baby sister and turned on that full-wattage charm, it was impossible to resist. Although you've never had that problem."

"Jake's never set his sights on me. Besides, I don't find physical beauty that appealing. I prefer a few nicks and dents in my guys."

"I'm calling BS on that one. Callum used to be eye candy." Delaney paused to examine a chip in her otherwise flawless turquoise nail polish. "And Ben's a total hottie."

"Not going there and you know it. I love him as a friend, and that means more."

"Your loss." Delaney nodded at the headstone. "Think Mom's eavesdropping?"

"If she is, she should be grateful that despite everything, we still have each other, and at least one of us found a good man, which is something she failed to do."

Behind them a mower started up, followed by a Weedwacker, even though the only weeds in the well-maintained cemetery grew on their mother's grave, one of the few with real plantings.

"Do me a favor," Katie said. "Never stick plastic flowers on top of my bones."

"Ditto." Delaney laughed, but stopped. "Do you ever wonder if we failed her?"

"How? We weren't equipped to take on insanity. We were kids."

"Yeah, but we didn't make it easy on her after Dad left, did we?"

"You mean I didn't. And you looked after her while I was off going psycho, which earned you karmic gold bullion."

"But I never forced her to change." Delaney splayed her fingers and appraised her amber ring. "Stereotypical enabler, that's me."

"We can't take responsibility for her failures. She chose to not seek help. Her choice, not ours, and if she'd been a better mother, she would have at least tried." Katie stared up at the heat haze shimmering over the downtown skyline. "But I'm a fine one to talk about seeking help. What a hypocrite."

"You did seek help—from the wrong person."

For the first time, Katie didn't defend Cal. Instead she made popping sounds with her lips, sounds not unlike welding. "I've been rethinking Mom and some of her habits. Remember how she used to flick light switches on and off multiple times?"

"Wow. I'd forgotten that. You think she had OCD?"

"I don't know. Maybe I'm grasping for connections. Or maybe I'm going around in circles. I've been rethinking myself, too. How when I used to play school with Dolly, secondhand Barbie, and that old sock puppet, they had to sit in a certain order. I keep wondering if OCD was building even then."

"Let it go, Sis. Wherever it came from, or why Maisie has it—if she does—is irrelevant." Delaney tugged a hairband off her wrist, grabbed her hair, and secured it in a messy ponytail. "So, other than the fact that you've started tapping inanimate objects again and you're micromanaging childhood memories, how's the anxiety?"

The two children Katie had watched earlier ran by, giggling.

What if I trip them up by mistake, and they fall and—

"Knocking around. But I intend to stay strong for Maisie."

"That didn't work out so well nine years ago, Sis."

"Because I didn't understand what I was dealing with. Now I do."

"And Callum and Jake?"

"Nine years ago I made the mistake of caring what they thought. That's no longer an issue."

"I admire the heck out of you." Delaney pulled up her fuchsia bra strap. "You know that. But this is a horribly gray area, and OCD doesn't do gray. Are you sure seeing Maisie again is a good idea?"

"Of course I'm not sure. I'm the world's most delinquent mother, and I have a screwed-up thought process. But if there's a chance, no matter how slim, that I can make a difference in her life, I don't care if I end up back in hell."

"You might not, but I do."

Katie's phone rang with her Dead Sara ringtone. *Jake.*

THIRTEEN
KATIE

"This dilapidated warehouse is living the dream?" Jake said.

As per her instructions, both he and Maisie were wearing safety glasses, jeans, and leather boots, and Maisie's long hair was restrained in Pippi Longstocking braids. But his snigger burst the bubble of joy that had kept Katie afloat since five o'clock that morning. Did Maisie hate the studio, too? Until today it had never mattered what anyone thought about the dank smell from roof leaks, the piles of rusty metal and fabricated steel, the jerry-rigged machines built by artists-turned-engineers, the growl of overused power tools past their prime. *Past their prime.* Was it time for Ben to call the fire marshal for another walk-through? Did the fire extinguishers need replacing? And that extension cord plugged into live electricity and raised off the ground in case of another flood, was it safe? Safe enough for Maisie?

Jake slung an arm across Maisie's shoulders in a proprietorial way, and Katie led them toward the back corner of the studio, away from her shearer, a machine designed to cut through sheets of metal. A machine that came with the warning sign hanging over Maisie's head: "Danger. Authorized personnel only."

Katie glanced from one artist's space to another. Was anyone welding? Was anyone using fire? There was a lull in studio noise, but how long before someone started using a grinder, with a head that could fly off and hit Maisie?

Maisie shouldn't be here. This is dangerous, too dangerous. I stayed out of her life for a reason. What if, just by being around me, she's at risk? What if I was wrong to bring her here? She's too close to the chop saw. What if I put her hand underneath, lowered the blade, and . . . An image. A bloody image.

A thought is just a thought, not an action. Katie kept walking. *It has no power.*

"Welcome to my office!" She swung around with an overly bright smile. At least her space was jammed into a corner. If she stayed here, with her back to the rest of the warehouse, she could act as a human shield against stray sparks.

"Oh, I love that poster, Ms. Katie." Maisie pointed at Rosie the Riveter. "Is she a cartoon character?"

"No, she's my inspiration. Rosie's a cultural icon. She represents all the women who worked in factories and shipyards during World War II."

"Awesome." Maisie wriggled out from under Jake's arm and dug through her backpack to retrieve a notebook and a pencil with a troll pencil topper. "I hope you don't mind if I make notes, but I'm on special assignment to write about the show for the school newsletter. The principal and all the staff are super excited about opening night. Everyone's coming."

"Including her daddy and her mama," Jake said.

Despite the large rusty fan attempting to cool down her work area, Katie's sweat glands were stuck on overdrive. Jake, however, wasn't sweating. He looked at home in her private space, but Jake seemed to belong wherever he landed. She reached up to twist her hair, and he watched. On the edge of her vision, Ben appeared.

"You must be Maisie." He held out his hand, and Maisie shook it. "I've heard a great deal about you."

"Really," Jake said.

Ben had a streak of dirt across his forehead from his helmet. Stretching up on tiptoe, Katie wiped it away with a finger, and he dipped down to kiss her cheek. Something he normally did only on her birthday. "And now for your annual kiss," he would say. Ben's familiar scent of fire, sweat, and Moroccan oil shampoo had always calmed her. Today it hypnotized. She beamed, he winked, and she turned around for the introductions.

"This is Jake Vaughan," Katie said. "Maisie's godfather, I believe?"

Jake gave a tight-lipped smile.

"Ben Holt." Ben and Jake shook hands.

"Let me guess," Jake said, "the boyfriend."

Ben's shrug seemed to say, *A gentleman never tells.*

"Wait a cotton-picking moment!" Maisie squealed. "You're *the* Ben Holt?"

Grinning, Ben flicked back his hair. "Last time I checked."

"Gosh, I am such a fan of your sculpture at CAM. I love the way the top part spins." Maisie twirled her pencil. "And those two sculptures outside must be yours. You have a very distinctive style."

"Why, thank you." Ben bowed.

"Would you mind very much if I interviewed you for the school newsletter?"

"I'd be honored." Stepping over Katie's drop cord without even looking, Ben pulled out her stool, wiped it off with his hand, and offered it to Maisie. She glanced at the seat before easing herself onto the edge. With her back ramrod straight, Maisie cracked open her notebook, placed it on her lap, and smoothed out a blank page. Then she raised her hand to her safety glasses and stopped. "Can I take these off to write?" She looked at Katie.

"I think your own glasses are big enough to protect your eyes. Ben, do you agree? I mean, if she puts them back on the moment she leaves my space?"

"I think it's fine, Katie." He touched her arm, then turned back to Maisie. "You know, Katie's way cooler than I am. She works with lots of different metals."

"You don't?"

"No. I'm strictly a steel guy. Steel makes sense to me." Ben stood with legs braced and arms crossed. He arched his back, and the movement accentuated his biceps. "I used to experiment with interesting metal shapes from the scrapyard. Collage them together and weld, cut, and invent on the fly, but then I decided nothing worked for me quite like steel. Steel's durable, yet malleable. Do you know what that means?"

"Actually, yes, I do. I am ten, you know." Maisie peered through her huge black glasses.

"And top of her class in everything," Jake said.

"Except for math," Maisie added.

"I hated math in school," Katie said.

"Gosh, me too," Maisie said, and Jake cleared his throat loudly.

"The rotation that spoke to you in my CAM piece?" Ben drew a circle in the air with his index finger. "That's what I'm searching for in my art. Artists have their own signatures. Katie, for example, has a unique ability to focus on flaws she discovers as she goes. And me? I'm focused on movement. Steel might be tough and heavy, but I want to make it dance in the wind." Ben's lips quivered in a barely suppressed smile. "That's how I met Katie. She asked me to teach her how to make steel dance."

"Is that so?" Jake said.

"Steel represents endless possibilities," Ben continued as if he were alone with Maisie. "It can be dark and earthy or polished to a radiant shine. I enjoy the conversations I have with steel. Working with it, however, can push me to the limits of sanity. Welding is intensely frustrating."

So's dealing with me. The only time Ben swears is when he's welding or dealing with me. What if I annoy him? What if he hates me? Does he—hate me?

A thought is just a thought. It has no power.

"Ms. Katie says welding calms her." Maisie frowned.

"Don't get me wrong. I'm passionate about my art, but welding for me means getting two huge pieces of metal to come together just right. That can try anyone's patience."

Maisie wrote and nodded.

"Welding's all about heat and leverage. How you apply them and in what order. Sounds simple, right? But think about the size of the sculptures you saw outside the studio. There's a lot of grunt work, dirt, and muscling it around to bring those babies to life. Plus it's ninety-five degrees in here all summer. That can make me snap."

"You never snap," Katie said. "Cuss, yes. Snap, no."

"Could it be he never snaps at you?" Jake said.

Katie ignored him.

"When she visited us at CAM, Ms. Katie talked a lot about her process. What's your process?" Maisie asked Ben.

"I have a basic idea, and then I throw flames on it."

Maisie gave a sharp intake of breath. "You don't plan it out in your sketchbook?"

"Like Katie?" Ben laughed. "No, I'm the opposite. I follow instinct. Big sheets of steel don't suggest anything. They're blank canvases. I start with a pattern and run it through the rollers. And then I begin contouring and figuring out what the shape wants to be. At that point it's talking to me, and hopefully I'm listening. At the end of the day, I want to be surprised by what I create. I want to watch it evolve."

"I see," Maisie said. "Ms. Katie also told us about casting. Do you cast?"

"No. Casting holds no appeal for me. You have to take all these steps to map out the process: make a model, then make a mold of that, then a wax of that, then a mold of the wax. Then you're melting out the wax, then you're pouring in the metal. And then you're finishing the metal. At that point I'm bored."

"That does sound quite tedious," Maisie said.

"Yup, and expensive. Look up Rodin. R-o-d-i-n. When he died most of his pieces were sitting in his studio as plaster models. He never saw them cast in bronze. No, I know what I like, and when I find it, I don't budge until the piece is finished. Working with steel is immediate and organic. I can cut up a piece, add another piece, and the creative conversation begins."

Listening to Ben talk about steel was one of the great pleasures of life. It almost allowed her to forget Maisie was surrounded by power tools that could slice off limbs, take out eyes, and crush skulls. Katie shifted, and Ben glanced at her.

"How did you start?" Maisie said.

"I didn't pick up welding until I was finishing my degree in studio art. And then I moved down here to Durham, got a little oxyacetylene set, and started messing around with sculpture. That's how I found my passion."

"Why did you move to Durham?" Maisie said.

"For a woman." Ben blushed.

I could kiss him. Where did that thought come from?

"Oh." Maisie blushed, too. "Would you please spell oxy-asset . . . ?"

"How about I write it down for you?"

Ben moved toward Maisie and stopped when she slapped her palm on her notebook. Jake's face was blank, but he cocked his head. Good, he was paying attention.

"I bet Maisie needs to write out everything herself," Katie said. "I know I would if I had a brand-new notebook." *And OCD.* A memory played. She must have been around Maisie's age, and she was standing in the kitchen in their old apartment in Boston, sobbing and screaming at her mother, who'd ripped half a page out of Katie's new sketchpad to make a shopping list. Her mother was laughing, but then again, she'd been drunk.

"No problem," Ben said and spelled *oxyacetylene* letter by letter. When Maisie spelled it back to him, he merely frowned as if listening extra hard.

"Do you have any more questions for Ben?" Jake asked Maisie. "We don't want to take too much of Ms. Katie's time, and I was hoping, Ben, that you might give me a studio tour."

Was it her imagination, or did Jake sound like a normal human being when he addressed anyone but her?

"Of course." Ben didn't move. "Maisie? Do you need to ask me anything else?"

"No! All done!" Maisie hopped off the stool, and Katie swallowed the scream of *Careful!* Maisie landed inches from the drop cord, one of many unseen hazards in the studio.

"If you think of anything else," Ben said, "you can always shoot Katie a text."

Jake narrowed his eyes.

"Oh, that is a *verrry* good idea." Maisie rummaged through her backpack. "I now have my own iPhone, thanks to Uncle J." She pulled out a phone that had been seriously bejeweled with plastic glitz, several rainbows, and a sticker of what appeared to be a lemur.

Ben recited Katie's number, and Maisie typed it in.

"All done?" Jake said. "Good. I'll be right back, darlin'." He blew Maisie a kiss.

She and Maisie were going to be alone again. In the closest thing she had to a home. The apartment didn't count, had never counted.

What if she trips? What if she falls? What if I push her? What if she doesn't have OCD, and I say the wrong thing and trigger it?

117

"Mr. Ben's very tall, isn't he? He's quite a lot taller than Uncle J." Maisie cleared her throat. "I'm sorry, Ms. Katie, very sorry, for what Uncle J said about the studio when we arrived. That was not acceptable, and I'll tell him when we drive home."

"He's simply being protective"—*as Ben is with me*—"and he wasn't rude." Actually, he was. "He loves you a great deal, doesn't he?"

Katie chewed on the spot inside her mouth.

"Oh, yes. Uncle J helped raise me." Maisie sighed dramatically. "But it's hard having a dad and a spare, which is how my dad puts it."

"That's going to get fun when you're old enough to date."

"Uncle J's already threatened to hog-tie the first boy I kiss. Yuck. Who wants to kiss a boy?"

"In a few years you won't think about much else. A first kiss is a rite of passage." Remorse—heavy and unyielding—sank to the bottom of Katie's stomach. She had missed so many firsts; she would miss so many more.

"*Ohhh*, what's that?" Maisie pointed with the neon-haired troll.

"It's called *That Perfect Moment*, and it's made of copper and brass."

"I like it very much."

"Me too. Remember what Ben said about flaws? You see the outline of the moon? That was a mistake. I had this aluminum circle I was going to put under the copper." Katie dove down to the shelf under her worktop, found the circle, and straightened up. She slotted it under the piece of copper she still hadn't decided how to attach. "But I accidentally held it in place too long and created so much heat that I ended up with this lovely shadow moon, which worked better than my original idea."

"Oh, yes," Maisie said. "The aluminum is too bright."

"Exactly! Which is the same problem I'm having with the rivets."

"What's a rivet?"

"It's a pin with a head on one side. The head is larger than the hole so that you can hammer it into place and it can't slip back through.

And then you grind it down to be level with the frame." Katie picked up a copper rivet. "Right now, I'm trying to decide whether to use copper rivets like this or"—she reached across the worktop for an iron rivet—"tone it down a bit with iron. What do you think? I'd love your opinion."

"The second one, the iron," Maisie said. "I mean, I guess. What do you think?"

"That you're right. The copper's too flashy."

Maisie grinned as if she'd won a medal, and a grinder fired up on the old loading dock. "It's quite noisy in here, isn't it?"

Katie pulled her protective earmuffs off the metal shelf behind Maisie. A rusty freestanding shelf that could easily tip over and rain sharp tools on her daughter's head. "Would you like to put these on?"

"No, thank you."

"I don't notice the noise anymore." Katie replaced the earmuffs and, with her right arm, coaxed Maisie toward the table. "When I'm working, it's almost as if I'm in a trance."

"I feel the same way when I'm writing a story, Ms. Katie."

"My mind can race in circles, except in here. My creative process is slow and demands absolute focus. That focus kicks out all the other thoughts. Before you came in, I was trying to decide how many holes to drill in *That Perfect Moment*, and where I should drill them. You see, I don't want them too close to the edge. Ultimately this will lie on top of the frame over there, the one I treated with a black patina."

"What's a patina?"

"A layer that forms on metal and changes or deepens its original color. That can happen over time or we can make it happen faster by creating our own patinas." Katie pointed at the piece of copper roofing that was lying on the table. "You see that lovely battered and weather-beaten piece behind you? The patinas were already there. All I did was rub them back in and polish them up. But I could have created the same effect with an acid that reacts with the metal as if it's been buried in the ground for a long time."

Maisie moved toward the drill press and pointed with the troll pencil topper again. "I *really* like all those metal curlicues. You could make jewelry with those."

"Del—my sister tells me the same thing."

"You have a sister? My stepmom's pregnant, and I'm hoping for one, too!"

"Is it hard"—a memory of the red metal crib flashed—"preparing for a new baby?"

Maisie shrugged and examined the sphere that was meant to be the earth, until it came out all wrong. Katie called it her WhatNot.

"I was experimenting with casting when I made that and messed up big time." Katie put her finger in the gaping mouth between the two halves she'd welded together. "I was trying to create two halves of a perfect sphere, but the wall was too thin and the metal cooled too quickly. This was the result—an imperfect cast. And then I went back in and made another one with the same mistake."

"Deliberately?" Maisie glanced up, her eyes huge.

"Art for me is about working through my need for perfection. I want it to be imperfect."

"But why?"

"Perfection stops you from enjoying the wonder of what is. It snares you with unrealistic expectations. Tells you constantly things can only be a certain way, and that's how you fall into the trap."

"What trap?" Maisie said.

"Of always wanting everything to feel just so."

Maisie combed her hair with her fingers, twice on one side, twice on the other. "Can I watch you work?"

"I'm a little uncomfortable with that idea." Katie put down the WhatNot. "A lot of my equipment is dangerous, and most of what I do involves sparks."

I could pick up the grinder and use it to bash in her head.

"See this little handheld grinder?" Katie picked it up, and her hand started to shake. She put the grinder down and scratched her thighs: back and forth, back and forth. "That could easily flip out of my hand and hurt you. Once, the circular blade shot off and narrowly missed my face."

"Oh." Maisie clasped her notebook to her chest. "Have you ever been badly hurt?"

"Nothing more than minor burns, but Ben had a sculpture fall on him." Katie tapped the top of her head. "It cut his head open, and he had to have fifty stitches."

Maisie gasped.

Maisie's going to trip over something and have an accident, and it'll be my fault because I scared her, made her careless.

Her stomach cramped. Was she going to retch?

A thought is just a thought; it has no power.

"Sometimes welding seems an impossible task, but then you change one thing, and everything clicks. Shall I tell you what the first step is in creating a Katie Mack piece?"

"Yes, please." Maisie opened up her notebook and smoothed out the page.

"I think about things that cause me worry."

With her pencil hovering above the paper, Maisie looked up. In the front of the studio, Ben laughed.

"My art," Katie continued, "is about more than salvaging junk or casting imperfect circles. It's also about crafting my worries into something I can touch, something tangible that makes them less scary."

Maisie began to write. Her script was strangely messy, her letters jerky as if written through jolts of pain.

Pain I caused? Katie swallowed.

"This is the first Katie Mack piece." Katie pulled the tarp off her knife sculpture. "Knives used to make me intensely uncomfortable. I mentioned it to Ben one day, and he suggested I explore that fear in a piece of art. This is how it all began."

"I don't like it." Maisie's hand shot to her mouth. "Gosh, I'm so sorry. Really, *really* sorry. What a horrid thing to say."

"No, I agree. I hate it. I wanted it jagged and ugly. This piece represents the thing I told you about at the Chocolate Factory. The echo in my head." Katie paused. "I call it *The Voice*."

Maisie glanced over her shoulder, then turned back. "Do you tell people, Ms. Katie, about your voice?"

"I didn't, but I'm trying to change. There's no shame in admitting your brain's a bit funky. It's like learning to read if you have dyslexia."

"Uncle Jake has that."

I know he does. "Well, in the same way that some people need to learn a different way of reading, people like me need to learn a different way of thinking. And it can be hard, but we have to teach ourselves how to manage our thoughts. Not let them manage us. Everyone has scary thoughts, but most people instinctively treat them as junk mail. We don't have that filter"—*you, me, and possibly your grandmother*—"so we listen to them, which makes them get louder until they slam us with an avalanche of fear. But the danger's not real. It just comes from a broken early warning system."

Maisie scowled and looked way too serious. Katie wanted to hug her. Hug her so tight that Cal and Jake could never pry them apart. An unbreakable mother-daughter weld.

"Lots of people have what I call *the voice*, but it's not the same for everyone, because we're all individual. For example, my voice shows me nasty images of doing violent things that I would never do, but other people are frightened of germs and diseases, or they have to pray a lot . . ." *Like my mother. Were her ritualized prayers scrupulosity at work?*

"Are you okay, Ms. Katie?"

"Yes, sorry. Sorry." She shook her head, but the memory stayed. "And some people do these rituals called compulsions. The voice tells them they have to do things in a certain way, otherwise there'll be bad consequences, maybe even for people they love. And while you know that doesn't make sense, it's not a risk you want to take. Right?"

Maisie touched her arm. "Ms. Katie? I have a voice, too," Maisie whispered.

"I know you do, sweetheart," Katie whispered back. "And I bet it's gotten a whole lot louder since you found out you were going to be a big sister." She squatted down in front of Maisie.

Maisie nodded and kept nodding. "I worry all the time that Lilah will die in childbirth. And the voice tells me it'll be my fault, but it also says that if I do certain things in a certain way, I can keep her safe."

"Honey, do you have a class bully?"

"*Yessss.* Parker, and he's a booger."

"And how do you deal with him?"

"I stand up to him." Maisie sounded indignant. "Especially when he's mean to Ava Grace and Ellie."

"That's exactly what you have to do with the voice. Treat it the way you'd treat a bully."

"I'm super glad I can talk to you about this. I can't tell my dad. He'll get upset and worry about me because he's super sensitive and can't cope with anything scary and I"—Maisie paused for a quick breath—"don't want to scare him."

"But he needs to know, honey. What if Uncle Jake could help with that?"

"You mean I wouldn't have to tell my dad?"

"I think you should let Uncle Jake handle that. And now that you have my number, you can call or text me whenever the voice gets loud."

"What's the worst thing the voice ever told you?"

"That I was capable of hurting the most important person in my life." Katie stared at the concrete floor. "But I didn't realize it was just a bully inside my brain, and I didn't get help. If you talk to Uncle Jake, you'll be streaks ahead of where I started."

"I think Uncle J will get it, but I'm not sure about Daddy," Maisie said.

"Then it's up to Uncle Jake to fix that."

"It's up to Uncle Jake to fix what?" Jake said.

FOURTEEN
CALLUM

The GPS told Callum his final destination was on the right. He'd programmed it to bring him here, to the last place he would ever choose to visit: the past. Lilah thought he was meeting with grad students. Had even asked which ones. Every day he laid out more lies, clung tighter to the fading illusion that he deserved a second chance. Across the double yellow lines, in a second-floor apartment, was proof that he didn't.

When Katelyn resurfaced after seventeen long months, Callum had taken advice from others. Today, he would handle things alone. Listen to the medical information that was, apparently, vital for Maisie—dear God, let it not be a predisposition for cancer—apologize, and get a credible explanation as to why Katelyn had upended his life. Jake's news that she was battling an anxiety disorder back then made sense; that she should reinvent herself as an artist did not. During four years of marriage, he never saw her so much as doodle. Maybe she was the master of disguise; maybe he had been in love with a mirage.

Would she threaten them again, as she had on the night she ran? He began to sweat. Hand shaking, he picked up his phone.

I love you so much, he texted.

Lilah replied immediately with a row of heart emojis. If he turned around now, he could catch her before she left to pick up Maisie. He could hold her and whisper, *Don't ever leave me.* Maybe add, *We need to talk,* and tell her everything. All the details even Jake didn't know. The details.

He swallowed a swell of nausea.

Callum parked on the road, alongside a chain-link fence topped with razor wire. He removed the key from the ignition and placed his hands back on the steering wheel. Sliding them into the noon position, he tightened his grip and stared through the windshield. If danger was coming, from which direction would it approach? He glanced into the overgrown lot with the boarded-up house. A terra-cotta pot sat disintegrating on the stoop. Earthenware shards lay where they had fallen.

The speech he'd prepared on the drive over fled his brain. It was, he supposed, what happened when you accepted the inevitable. *Dear firing squad, lock and load.* Or maybe he was having another out-of-body experience—spinning through space with a jet pack of shame. Dissociation and he were old friends. After all, that was his survival mechanism. Katelyn ran; he played possum.

He exhaled slowly and turned his gaze to the rambling house opposite with the huge front porch that leaned. It spoke of the old South, of heydays long past, of neglect.

Callum muted his phone and slipped it back into his pocket. Then he exited his car and hit "Lock" on his key fob, hesitated, and hit "Unlock." Reaching across to the passenger seat, he dragged his bag toward him. He might not be able to protect his family from the approaching storm, but he could keep his laptop safe.

A muscle car shot down the street, angry music blaring. The back of his neck prickled; the bag tugged on his right shoulder.

Callum never traveled light.

Looking both ways, he crossed the street and walked toward Katelyn's next move. All those years spent trying to erase their marriage, and what if Katelyn sparked something long buried? Even Jake didn't know that in his dreams, Callum still loved his ex-wife. It wasn't as if he had learned how to grieve or survive a breakup. They were in love and she vanished; she reappeared, and he had sacrificed her for their daughter.

Callum walked around to the side of the house, passed a dumpster, and stopped at the bottom of the metal stairs that led up to the second floor. At the top was a small landing with a collection of brightly colored plant pots. If Lilah were here, she would comment on the polished-steel wind chimes hanging from the eaves. She always homed in on people's details. After faculty social events, she would regale him with every nuance he'd missed. Lilah, his own personal translator.

He imagined her voice: "What do you think? Should we get some of those wind chimes?" Lilah turned everything into a joint decision. Once she figured out the truth, would there be any more *we*? How many times did his world have to shatter?

Grabbing the railing, he began his ascent, one step at a time. When he reached the top, he raised his clenched hand, avoided the hummingbird feeder attached to the glass with suction cups, and knocked. A surprisingly simple gesture that could cost him another marriage.

The door opened immediately, and there she was.

He blinked.

Yes, she was still there.

She stepped back. Heart hammering as if he were racing his bike, he narrowed the gap between them. Nine years of absence remained. She looked exactly the same and entirely different. She was everything he knew and nothing that was familiar. A stranger in sheep's clothing.

Behind him, the door closed, sealing off his exit. The place smelled of old age and damp. On the right was a small bathroom with a claw-foot tub and a plastic shower curtain pulled all the way around. Wooden floorboards creaked as she led him into a spacious room with a high ceiling, crown molding, and a breakfast bar. The furniture was sparse, but the bookcase was full. Strings of white lights had been hung over the double window. *Four strands of white lights on the Christmas tree, four strands in the huge fig tree in our bedroom. Always had to be four.* Strange fact to remember. Under the window, on what appeared to be an upturned plastic crate, sat a miniature garden with moss, tiny plants, and a pretend patio with a red table and four empty chairs. A perfectly orchestrated, abandoned scene. An old ceiling fan wobbled above them; a dreary metal picture watched him from the opposite wall.

"This is weird," she said, and he turned.

A hint of a smile played on the lips he'd once found irresistible. No lipstick, but thick lines of black gunk outlined her eyes. He'd never seen her hair short. Or with red highlights. Her toenails were painted blue—did she used to wear nail polish?—and she was dressed in denim cutoffs. A silver chain hung down her cleavage and disappeared under the black T-shirt that clung to her breasts. That was the first thing he'd noticed about her in college, her breasts.

His stomach lurched as if he were hurtling down an elevator shaft headfirst. Any second now, he could smash into concrete and split open.

"You look . . . different." Good, he could still speak.

"And yet you haven't changed one bit." She fiddled with the two earrings hanging from her left ear. When did she get the second piercing? "Can I get you something? Coffee? Tea? Vodka?"

He shook his head. "I'm married."

"Remarried."

"And my wife is pregnant."

"I know. I read your letter." Katelyn sat down in the fabric moon chair that belonged in a dorm room and gestured toward the futon opposite.

He sat. A herculean achievement since the futon wasn't on a frame. It was merely folded over to create a ridiculously low sofa. The coffee table between them was empty except for a vase of blue flowers, the blue of her eyes, and a white envelope. He glanced up from the envelope, its placement too obvious, too deliberate in a room devoid of clutter.

"Do you need money?" he said.

"Bit late to offer financial support, don't you think?"

"I don't know how to do this, Katelyn."

A ghost of a smile. "You think I do?"

She was eerily calm. Was this how she'd deceived him all those years ago, hidden her illness?

"How are your parents?" she said, and then started picking at her fingers. Maybe not so calm, then.

"In Australia on visiting professorships. A last hurrah before retirement." He took a breath. "Jake told me you want to talk about Maisie, but you have to know, I can't let you back into her life. She's trying to connect with Lilah, she's excited about the baby, she's—"

"Wonderful, Cal." Katelyn gave a real smile. "She's wonderful. Even her style is unique."

"Yeah," he said. "She's amazing."

"'Mazing Maisie. You did a great job raising her." Katelyn's smile disappeared. "I'm sorry you had to do it alone."

He nodded. "Jake helped."

Katelyn nodded. After nine years apart, they could only nod.

"Please tell me the *but* that's coming doesn't involve a court battle," he said.

"You think I would put Maisie through a custody trial?" Below them, a door slammed. "You might not believe this, but she's always been my priority. I left for her; I stayed away for her. Why do you think I agreed to a divorce?"

"You didn't love me anymore?" he said.

"I always loved you."

He stared at the pale-gray rug with the small brownish stain. "Before we talk about Maisie, I need to understand. Why, Katelyn? Why did you leave us?"

"I thought I was losing my mind. I thought I was dangerous. I thought I would hurt you both. I was sick, Cal, so sick. I didn't know I could get well. I didn't know there was a name for what I had. I didn't know that name wasn't *psychopath*."

"And now? Are you still sick?"

"You mean, am I a danger to you or Maisie?"

"Katelyn . . ." He sighed. "I'm asking how you are."

"I'm in a good place. My illness is under control, but seeing Maisie again has triggered"—she reached up to scratch her neck—"issues."

"Tell me what happened nine years ago," he said slowly, one word at a time. No different from climbing the stairs outside her door.

"I headed toward the mountains. Lived on the streets, moved through homeless communities where no one expected anything. Mostly I stayed in an old tent someone gave me, hoping I stank so bad that people would stay away. But when Ringo died, I didn't even care about surviving. I just wanted it to end."

"Ringo, he looked after you?"

"Until the day he died." She curled deeper into the chair, tucking up her legs in a way that mirrored Maisie. "After that, I moved into a shelter while I planned my suicide. Eventually I tried to throw myself off an overpass, but a Good Samaritan had other ideas. The next thing I knew, I was in the ER. Then they moved me to the psych crisis unit, and one of the psychiatrists diagnosed OCD and depression. All those violent images I had, the ones I tried to tell you about? Classic postpartum OCD."

She kept scratching her neck; he wanted to ask her to stop.

"My compulsions have always been mental. Pure obsessions locked away in my head. Easily hidden, which means you're off the hook, if you're worrying about missed warning signs."

"But, Katelyn, the night you left, you threatened to"—he swallowed—"torch the house."

"No, I didn't. I told you I had images of doing horrific things I would never do. My mind was stuck in a desperate need to protect Maisie. OCD is like, like, hyper-responsibility. It told me that lamp of hers was a fire hazard. I was trying to explain, and if you'd—"

"Been more sympathetic?"

She waved him off. "I'm not assigning blame. There is none, Cal. There's nothing but human tragedy."

"I'm sorry." Another wave of nausea hit. "What happened after Delaney moved to Asheville?"

"And you didn't want me back?"

"I still loved you, Katelyn, but I had to protect Maisie."

"It was a good call." She wiped her eyes with the back of her hand. The black makeup smudged. "I wasn't fit to be her mother. After I came out of the hospital, I could barely be a sister. I lost another year to my illness, but with Delaney's help, I pasted myself back together. Five years ago, we moved to Durham so I could work with an artist called Ben Holt, not reclaim my old life. It's unlikely Maisie and I would have reconnected but for the docent program."

Callum turned his new wedding ring around his finger.

"I will love our daughter until my last breath," Katelyn said, "but I haven't earned the right to be part of her life. I hope Lilah has."

He tensed. "Please keep Lilah out of the conversation."

"I'm not a threat to your new family, and Maisie need never know who I am. But maybe I have one last shot at being her mother, by giving you information that can help her. That's all I want, Cal. For you to help her. And I wish, with all my heart, that what I'm about to say wasn't true." She drew a deep breath. "I think Maisie has OCD. And don't freak out, but I think Mom had it, too. That means there could be a genetic link."

"You said it was postpartum. I heard you say 'postpartum.'"

"Since reconnecting with Maisie, I've started looking back. Questioning odd behavior—mine and my mother's. I think the OCD was there, dormant but with a wick, and Maisie's birth was the match. As a child, I couldn't handle spontaneity. I had this overwhelming fear Mom would die, and . . . And remember how I couldn't cope with traffic delays, and how everything had to be just so? That was OCD building its strength."

"This is ridiculous. After limited interaction with our daughter, you're diagnosing her like an armchair psychologist? Maisie is a confident, happy child." His breathing sped up; he was panting hard. "She doesn't wash her hands until they bleed. She's not a neat freak."

"There's nothing *neat* about obsessive-compulsive disorder, Cal. It means getting kicked to the ground by an invisible force that won't stop, no matter how much you plead. And even if you find the strength to drag yourself up onto all fours to think, hope, pray you can keep going, it pummels you over and over."

"Don't go there, Katelyn." He struggled to stand, to get up from the stupid futon that was so damn low. He needed to get out of this white room filled with the heat of the afternoon before he vomited.

Katelyn kept talking, her voice a distant echo. "I don't expect you to understand how it feels to be paralyzed by fear. But OCD is a hardcore news cycle that runs on a twenty-four-hour schedule of horror."

"I understand better than you think." He swallowed the taste of puke. *I know what real monsters look like. Not the invisible kind.*

"Does she have night terrors, nightmares, disturbed sleep patterns?"

"Every kid has—"

"The bastard can find her even in sleep. I've watched her, Cal. I've talked with her. And I'm telling you, she has OCD."

"You've talked to her about this?"

"When Maisie and I met at CAM, I had an anxiety attack. I told her I have a voice inside my head. She told me she has one, too. That's OCD."

On the other side of the window, a black helicopter buzzed low in the cloudless sky. Callum hugged himself.

"You shared. Intimate details. Of your mental illness. With a young girl. Who thinks Katie Mack. Is a superhero." If he spoke in bite-size pieces, maybe rage wouldn't tear him apart. "Did you consider she might be eager to impress?"

"Jake agrees with me," Katelyn said.

"You think Maisie told Jake something she hasn't told me? She tells me everything."

"No, I'm saying he suspects, which is why he agreed to mediate this meeting." She stood up and handed him the envelope. When he refused to take it, she slipped it into his bag. "In there you'll find a list of local child psychologists who are experts in the field. Please, for Maisie's sake, contact one of them."

"Maisie is a mentally healthy child. She's not vulnerable in any way. She doesn't have disturbing thoughts. She makes up ghost stories, for goodness' sake."

"If she's hardwired for full-blown OCD, Maisie has two big triggers looming—end of elementary school and a new sibling. What if they're enough to wake up the beast the way pregnancy did with me?"

"I don't have to listen to this." He glanced at his watch. "I need to get back to campus. You are not to meet with her again unsupervised. Do you understand?"

"I'll do whatever you ask if you'll agree to contact one of those doctors. And I can help, if you'll let me."

"I haven't needed your help in nine years, Katelyn. What I do need is for you to stay away from my family."

He walked toward the door. As he reached for the doorknob, she spoke.

"This is my world, Cal. And I promise you, it's going to get worse."

He slammed the door and found himself on the metal landing, alone. This time there was no misreading her words. Katelyn had issued a clear threat.

FIFTEEN

LILAH

The witching hour brought moonlight in through wooden blinds that had been another decorating miss. Wasn't it hard enough to stay asleep through the heat of pregnancy? But now—at three o'clock in the friggin' morning—she had to contend with her husband cracking his knuckles? Lilah kicked off the sheet. Callum, naked but for a pair of boxer briefs, collapsed in the floral armchair that screamed, *The first wife chose me.*

"Couldn't sleep again?" she said.

"Sorry." He jolted up, a sheen of sweat on his chest. The ceiling fan ruffled his hair. "Did I wake you?"

"No," she lied. "Baby MacD seems to think it's time for spring training. Come back to bed. I miss you." She reached over to pat the empty space.

Callum walked to his side of the bed and spooned behind her. While she wrestled with the body pillow he'd given her, one arm circled her mountainous belly.

"I love you so much." He brushed her hair aside and rested his chin on her shoulder.

But you don't have to keep chanting it like a spell. Great, now her inner chatter had become catty. Sleep deprivation was turning her into a harridan.

"I love you, too, but I wish you'd talk to me." She raised his palm to her mouth.

His muscles tensed under her lips. "About?"

"Whatever has you prowling around our bedroom for a third night in a row. Is it Maisie?"

"Everyone thinks I'm a good dad."

"With excellent reason. You're the most competent parent in the history of parenting. You know when to be silly, when to be serious. You have endless patience, set clear boundaries, on it goes. If they handed out dad-of-the-year rosettes at the state fair, you'd have ten, lined up in a neat row on the mantelpiece."

His breath tickled her skin. "But I make it up as I go along."

"I was hoping that was the definition of parenting. If it isn't, I'm screwed."

Callum covered her neck with butterfly kisses. "You're going to be such a great mom."

Going to be, not are. A fact that she couldn't debate, and Lilah was all about facts. At least she used to be, before hurtling into Callum and Maisie's life as if she were an arrow that couldn't fly straight.

"In case you haven't noticed, my attempts to parent your daughter have not been successful."

"Our daughter. Yours and mine."

"Your daughter, my stepdaughter. Those four extra letters will always spell out *exotic other.* Or in my case, *not the real mother.*" Letting out an "Oof," she managed a three-step roll to face him, despite the maternity sleep shirt that fought against her. Could Callum see the big white letters stretched across her ginormous boobs that read *You Did This to Me?*

"She's never really had a mother. You're her first and only."

"Repeating something doesn't make it true. And much as I appreciate the vote of confidence, Maisie talks about her real mom nonstop. And Jake talks about Katelyn as if she were a paragon of motherly virtue."

"Jake did that for Maisie's benefit when she was little. Now we're stuck with the myth." Callum flopped onto his back. "I loved Katelyn, but something happened to her after Maisie was born, and neither of us understood. At least not back then. With hindsight I realize she had serious emotional problems."

"Did you try and help?"

"Of course I did, but everything fell apart too quickly. I couldn't get traction." He paused. "I want you to be happy. And suddenly I can't reconcile everything, can't keep everyone happy."

"Who's 'everyone'?"

"You. You and Maisie."

"I'm ridiculously happy. Look at me, I'm living the Disney World happy—the wonder of us. The realization that *you*, my adored prof, fell in love with *me*. That still blows my mind."

"What blows my mind is that you fell in love with me." He reached out and eased her down onto his chest. His heart beat in frantic claps. No wonder he couldn't sleep. "I used to watch guys watching you in class and wonder if I was a creep."

She kissed the dip between his pecs that made her want to swoon. Until pregnancy hormones kicked in, she had vowed to never read a romance novel. Now she was living one.

"I don't want to screw this up," Callum said. "And I'm terrified of waking up tomorrow to discover it's a cruel joke and you don't love me."

The overhead fan hummed and shifted air, but failed to cool the room. Outside in the Carolina night, a chorus of frogs and insects croaked and chirped. An owl hooted in the forest behind their house. "Callum, I'm not going anywhere. You need to start believing that."

"I do, but"—his arms wrapped around her—"I want us to be perfect."

"Perfect doesn't exist. It's an impossible dream, baby. An illusion."

"I'm petrified," he said. "Of losing you."

He didn't have to add *too*.

"I know we hit fast forward and this happened quickly, but—"

"Too quickly?" His heart rate picked up again.

"Faster than we might have chosen, but everything we wanted to happen, happened. It's as if we won the love lottery."

"You would tell me, if you were struggling?"

"You mean other than being a pregnant Heffalump who is hardly the laid-back 'I've got this, yo' epitome of blooming mother with child?"

His laugh was soft as he rested his cheek on top of her head. "I love that you make me laugh, I love that you remind me to stop being so serious. I love calling you my wife."

His breathing returned to normal, and she drew circles on his chest with her index finger. The security lights flicked on over the front porch. Were the deer munching on the remains of his first wife's garden?

"Callum, can I ask you a question about Katelyn, just one? Did she commit suicide?"

He reached out to stop her hand. "I can't go there."

"Maybe you should talk to someone about what happened. Clean the slate before Baby MacD bounces onto the scene. I'm concerned that we're making Maisie anxious."

Callum eased her off his chest and sat up. "What do you mean?"

"The printout of child psychologists on your desk?" She sat up next to him. "If you want me to be Maisie's mother, you need to give me facts I can work with. Even as a kid I didn't get 'let's pretend.'"

"I haven't made a decision about hiring a therapist, which is why I didn't consult you. But if I decide to follow through—if—the sessions would be private."

"This *private* would exclude me?"

"I would need to talk about Katelyn, and I don't want to upset you."

"That's total crap. I'm not upset." Lilah rolled to one side and dangled her legs off the bed. "I mean, of course I am. I'm pregnant and my emotions are tumbling around on the maximum-heat cycle. But I'm tired of sneaking around Katelyn's memory. She's everywhere in this house, everywhere in Maisie's mind, and the source of everything that's troubling you. You would never expect your students to turn in a paper without their sources, without a bibliography. How is this any different? Tell me what really happened."

"And risk that you'll hate me? I don't want my past failures to overshadow what we have. Before I met you, all that mattered was Maisie. Now all that matters is our new story—yours, mine, Maisie's, and the baby's. There's no room in our lives for my past. My past is irrelevant. Katelyn is irrelevant."

"Right, then." She grabbed her body pillow.

"What are you doing?" He got up and moved toward her.

"I'm angry, and I don't like it. And need I remind you that we study the past, you dingbat?" *Dingbat?* "If the past didn't matter, you'd be out of a job. I'm going to sleep in the guest bedroom."

"No, please. I'm sorry. I don't mean to be a jerk, but I'm not ready to share that part of my life."

"How about you get ready before the sun comes up so I can start being a mother with more tools than guesswork. I'm lost in the dark here, Callum."

He said nothing.

"Until then I'll be in the guest bedroom. Let me know when you decide I can be"—she created bunny ears with her fingers—"part of that life."

"No. I'll go to the guest bedroom." And he left her alone with no idea of what had happened, except that she and Callum appeared to have had their first fight. Rather, she had her first fight with him. In typical Callum style, he didn't even raise his voice.

✳

Half an hour later, Lilah, the person who had once slept through a hurricane, was still wide awake. Their marriage bed was too big without Callum, the moonlight too bright, and her back ached. Her brain filled up with everything that had been nagging since their wedding night, when she joked, "I guess it's official, I'm the second Mrs. MacDonald," and Callum walked away. But enough of this ridiculous notion that she couldn't handle her new family history. *Enough.*

Lilah punched her body pillow into submission between her legs. Callum had insisted it would help with the backache. He was wrong about that, too.

The baby kicked, and she smiled. *Are you an Ethan?* In the book of baby names that Callum refused to open, Ethan was defined as strong. *Or are you an Edmond?* After Uncle Ed, the other member of the Tremblay family who'd migrated south for college and never left. Callum might not want to know their baby's sex, but she knew. She'd always known. Did this mean she actually had a mother's intuition, or was it another example of how she and Callum were moving apart?

"Daddy?" Maisie said from the doorway.

Lilah sat up. "What's wrong, sweetie?"

"I—I had a nightmare. Where's my dad?"

What was going on in the house tonight? Was there a full moon? "He had an idea for that paper he's been struggling with. You know how it is when the writing inspiration hits." Terrific, now she was lying to a child. "But I have this huge bed all to myself, and I'd love for you to keep me company."

Maisie glanced down the hall and then leaped in.

"Need a hug?" Lilah said.

"Will it hurt the baby?"

"Nothing can hurt this guy. He's already shooting hoops."

Maisie nestled against Lilah's chest and slowly tucked her legs under Lilah's belly. Lilah smiled.

"You think I'm going to have a brother?"

Through the far wall, a toilet flushed in the guest bathroom.

"I think so. Although, your dad wants to be surprised, so let's keep that our secret."

"I'm a very good secret keeper."

"I know, in the same way I know you'll be an outstanding big sister. When you're not bossing Baby MacD around as big sisters do. Take it from someone who has four."

Maisie made a little noise that could have been a laugh. "I was hoping for a sister."

"I'm hoping for a healthy baby."

"Oh, me too. You think the baby's healthy?"

"Definitely, and the way he kicks? He's going to need a big sister to set limits. Do you want to talk about the nightmare?"

Maisie shook her head. "Do you have nightmares Lil—sorry, sorry—Mom?"

"I don't even remember my dreams." She paused. "You know, I've been thinking about your special name for me. How about Evil Stepmom?"

"But you're not evil. That is a very inaccurate name!"

"And you're laughing, which seems a good cure for nightmares. You know what? I need a nickname for you, and all the good ones have been taken. What should I call you? Something sweet and chocolatey, since you're good enough to eat."

Lilah pretended to nibble on Maisie's neck, and she giggled. "I know! How about my little M&M?"

"I like M&M's." Maisie yawned.

"Good, that's settled."

"But I don't have a name for you."

"One thing at a time, and right now, you need sleep before school."

"Why do you think my dad never talks about my real mom?"

A door opened and closed downstairs. Was Callum going into his office?

"I don't know, sweetie, but it's probably too painful. I'm not sure you ever get over the death of a spouse. He must have loved her very much."

"As much as he loves you?"

"More, because she brought you into the world."

"I wish I'd known her."

"Maisie, I can never replace your biological mom, but I hope you'll come to think of me as an okay substitute."

"Gosh, yes. You're a very good substitute. And thank you," Maisie said in that polite, oddly formal voice of hers. "My dad refuses to talk about my mom, and that makes me sad."

So, we share something after all.

Within minutes, her stepdaughter fell asleep. Finally, she'd gotten something right—without Callum interfering, without Callum forcing them to be friends. And all she'd had to do was let Maisie talk about the one topic Callum wouldn't discuss: Katelyn.

SIXTEEN
KATIE

Katie opened her door and spilled vodka tonic over her bare feet. "Seriously? You're making a house call at nine on a Thursday night?"

"Your phone kept going to voicemail." Jake pushed past and stopped two paces inside her apartment, face-to-face with Delaney.

"Lookie here. If it isn't my favorite fuck buddy."

"Delaney!" Katie stared at her younger sister.

"But you were, weren't you, *darlin*?" Delaney raised her glass and then downed what was left of her tap water as if it were whisky. "And you're fully dressed. It's a Christmas miracle on September first."

Jake slipped his hands into his jeans pockets and cocked his head for a smile, but not the full-beam, money-making version. "Well, I never. Long time no see. How's it going, Delaney?"

"I hate to break up this reunion," Katie said, "but could one of you hand me a paper towel?"

Jake shot into the kitchen, unraveled multiple sheets of paper towels, and yanked. Then he shoved a fistful at Katie.

Delaney stepped around him to put her glass in the sink. "Is this a first for you, Jake? Someone not answering *your* messages?"

Jake stared at Delaney's back. "It wasn't me who stopped answering."

"And when exactly was that?" Katie looked from one of them to the other.

Jake said nothing. Delaney turned slowly, but gripped the sink behind her with both hands. "Not sure I remember. It's been years since I answered a booty call."

"I thought you guys hadn't seen each other since the christening?" Katie said.

Nobody answered her.

"You doing alright?" Jake said casually.

"Peachy. Better than peachy. And about to go home." Delaney pulled her keys from her purse and rattled them.

"Don't leave on my account," Jake said.

"Oh, I always leave on your account, sugar."

Jake stretched his neck. His expression started to soften, and the Jake Vaughan smile crept out, the one with a patina of charm. "You getting your panties in a wad because I didn't send you a dozen roses after our last tryst? Well, bless ya heart." True to form, his accent had turned country.

Katie dried her toes and blotted at the vodka spill on the wood floor. As she tossed the wad of paper towels in the trash can, Jake stayed in the hall and Delaney stayed in the kitchen.

"Am I missing something here?" Katie said.

"I don't know. Let me see." Delaney walked into the hall and frowned at Jake's groin. Slowly, she moved her head from side to side, as if considering the merchandise.

"Nope. I guess no one's missing anything. Time to get home to my brilliant lawyer. A passionate Irishman who came to Yale on a scholarship. Now Irish guys, they understand sex. And commitment. What a novel combination—sex and commitment. You should try it sometime, Jake."

Delaney leaned in to hug her sister. "If you need us, we can be here in ten minutes."

Head held high, Delaney left, but it was several moments before her footsteps rattled on the metal stairs.

"You okay, Jake?"

His head snapped around and he scowled at her. "Of course I am. Why wouldn't I be?"

She sighed. "Why're you here?"

"Not to listen to your sister rail on me, that's for sure. Got any tequila?"

Katie finished what remained of her vodka tonic and breathed on him. "No." Anger hummed in her gut, looking for a target. Either Cal or Jake would do, and the latter was in her crosshairs.

"Can I have one of what you're having?"

"Be my guest. You know where the kitchen is."

"Seems southern hospitality's a lost art around here. Nice place, Katelyn."

"It's Katie now." Ben had been right to choose Katie. Katelyn had hidden matches in the garbage can along with the knives; Katie controlled fire. "I don't go by Katelyn anymore." She walked into the front room, sat on one of her stools, and slid the glass across the breakfast bar toward him. "Here. Give me a refill since most of mine is soaking through the floorboards."

Jake opened and closed cabinets. "Want to give me a hint about where to find a glass?"

"Next one over. And the ice maker's broken, so you'll have to reach in and grab the ice." Jake's hands, covered in who knew what, in her ice. Good thing she didn't have contamination fears.

She sprawled across the breakfast bar. That first vodka—the half she'd drunk—had gone down way too fast.

"And you—doing okay?" Jake said.

She propped herself up on an elbow. "Want an honest answer?"

"Up to you. I'm just being polite. You asked me, so I'm returning the favor." Jake took an interest in the poster mock-up centered on the fridge door. "'Do you have unwanted thoughts and/or mental images of causing harm, or being responsible for harming others?'" he read. "'Are these thoughts upsetting to you?'" He looked at her. "You fixin' to start a support group?"

The anger fled, which was a pity. Dealing with Jake was so much easier when she was in a pissy mood. "It's a distant goal."

"Your sister looks good. She serious about this Patrick guy?"

He dropped a couple of ice cubes, swore, and grabbed a paper towel.

Katie leaned over the breakfast bar. Jake was on his hands and knees on her kitchen floor. "Yes, she's serious about him, and I don't remember anyone mentioning his name."

"You don't?" He gave a little "Huh," stood up, and tossed the ice cubes in the sink. The paper towel went in the trash can. "Tell me more about this group. Not sure I can imagine sharing personal shit with strangers."

"Not much to tell. I don't have experience working with support, except from my sister. I'm mostly self-taught in the art of therapy."

"How does that work—therapy for OCD?"

"Painfully."

He raised his eyebrows.

"I'll show you. Do me a favor? Unstraighten the poster. Tilt it a bit."

He did, and the need to get up and move it prickled. Katie scratched her arm. "I'm now incredibly uncomfortable because that thing's crooked, which means I get to boss back the OCD and ride out the discomfort. Thanks for the free therapy. If you want to up the ante, open the cabinet behind you and leave it open."

"Nah, I'm not a masochist. Even I like closet doors to stay closed."

As Jake struggled to unscrew the tonic bottle, a memory floated by of Cal asking why she always turned everything so tight. The bottle gave a little *fizz* when it finally opened.

"Lemon's in the bottom drawer of the fridge. Knives are in the drawer to your left." *Yes, Jake. I now have a knife drawer.*

He poured two vodka tonics, both strong. Clearly he wasn't planning on driving home anytime soon. Picking up the glasses, he came out of the kitchen and handed one to her. Then he walked across the living room, pausing for a slug of vodka before settling in the same spot Cal had chosen. Unlike her ex, Jake spread out and flung an arm over the back of the futon. One leg rested casually on top of the other in an archetypal Jake pose.

"You and Callum never made sense to me," Jake said. "He didn't date much, and then he lost his heart to you, a pretty young woman who was piss-poor needy. I tried to talk him out of the marriage."

"This is fun. I'm glad you stopped by to insult me while drinking my liquor." She stared at the white lights outlining her window.

"Acting," Jake said, "is all about figuring out what makes people tick."

"Nice way to avoid dealing with your own shortcomings."

"Quite the opposite. Taking on another persona leads to a lot of soul searching. You have to figure out what parts of you are like the character. I watched you a whole lot in college, and I recognized someone who was also trying to bury a rough childhood."

Katie got off the stool and walked toward him. "I'm already hunting for a therapist, thank you. I don't need you to weigh in."

"You were always so anxious, and Callum fed off that. Like he was terrified of getting it wrong."

"And this is where you tell me wife number two is a vastly improved model?"

"For Callum? Yeah."

"Gee, I'm so sorry my mother was crazier than a shithouse rat and I wasn't Ms. Perfect Wife who wanted world peace and a good manicure."

Jake grinned. "This is going downhill fast, isn't it?"

"Yes, and I can't wait to see what you throw at me next."

"Cute fairy garden."

"Seriously?"

He sipped his drink and, with a swipe of his middle finger, brushed a piece of lemon pulp from his bottom lip. "I looked up those violent thoughts you mentioned," he said. "Did my homework."

"Gold star for you."

He leaned forward, legs splayed, arms on his thighs, hands around the glass. "I found something called harm OCD. I'm guessing that's what you have?"

She blew out a sigh and settled opposite him, curling up her legs. "Some people brand us predators, abusers, psychos. Other people think we're merely certifiable. And you know what? It's hard to discount those attitudes. I mean, if your brain was capable of imagining something horrific, you wouldn't think too highly of yourself, would you?"

Jake swirled his drink, then raised his glass and took a long gulp. She watched his Adam's apple bob. He put down the glass and threw himself back against the futon. "And you think Maisie has this harm OCD, too?"

"I don't know how hers manifests, but it's irrelevant. OCD is OCD. We all use the subcategories, but they don't mean anything. Religious OCD is no different than contamination OCD. It's all about the feeling, the sense, that something's not as it should be. Then we overreact as our fight-or-flight response goes haywire. For example, I see images of me deliberately running people over with my truck, even though I would never do that. But those thoughts are terrifying even if you know how to deal with them, which Maisie doesn't. Jake, what's going on?"

"Callum's having second thoughts about seeing a child psychologist."

She smacked her glass down on the coffee table. "You're kidding."

I failed her. I failed her then, and I'm failing her now. I should never have left her. I should never have run away. What have I done?

Katie folded her arms over her head. *Breathe in, breathe out.*

"You should follow through with the support group. Mentoring gives you a different perspective on your own"—Jake grinned—"shortcomings. Assuming your idea gets off the ground, y'all going to have a code of confidentiality?"

"Of course." Katie lowered her arms. "How is that relevant?"

"If we talk about something, here and now, will it stay in confidence?"

"Yes, if it's about helping Maisie."

Liar. I'm a liar. What if I don't want to help Maisie? What if I don't have OCD and I really want to hurt her? What if I'm a psycho?

A thought is just a thought; it has no power.

A siren roared through downtown Durham, and in the distance, cars raced along the Durham Freeway. Jake stood and walked over to the window, where a luna moth had settled.

"Callum has a problem with the concept of therapy."

"I know, Jake. This isn't news to me."

"I can talk him around, but it could take a while. In the meantime, I don't want things getting worse for Maisie. Coming to you wouldn't have been my first choice, but I don't have too many options."

"Wait. You're asking for my help? But you don't trust me."

"No offense, darlin'. I don't trust anyone." He placed his hand on the glass, covering the huge green moth.

"Jake, are you bisexual?"

"Do what?" He swung round, his mouth open, his expression, for once, unedited.

"This thing between you and Cal. Are you—"

"I heard you fine the first time. You think I'm in love with the guy who's the closest thing I have to a brother? Are you itchin' to get me riled up? Act like you got some sense." He shook his head and muttered something.

"Sorry, but I'm on my second vodka—you make them strong, by the way—and you're talking in riddles."

"No. I'm not bisexual. Can we move on? Good." Jake turned back to stare out the window. The luna moth hadn't budged. "I was hoping you could help Maisie while I try and help Callum."

"Are you setting me up? Cal will never let me take the lead on this."

"He isn't asking. I am."

SEVENTEEN

JAKE

Saturday morning, and Jake was sitting on the concrete steps outside Durham Sculpture Workshop, sweating like a whore in church and lying to his best friend. Shielding the screen of his phone from the noontime glare, he reread the text, swallowed his own steaming pile of horseshit, and hit "Send." Did it count as lying if you were acting for the higher good—Lord have mercy on my dumb soul and all that?

To keep things real simple, he'd wrapped up the lies in a big bow of truth, and everyone had fallen for it. Callum believed that Jake was covering for Maisie, who was making a secret present for her daddy; Maisie—now this was the toughest piece of gristle to force down his gullet—thought she and Katie were designing a surprise gift to give Lilah after the baby was born; and Katie believed she was spinning a cover story so that Maisie didn't rat anyone out. For now the plan worked, and that was all Jake needed to know. Worrying too far ahead was as pointless as inviting a vegetarian to a pig pickin'.

He laid his phone on the concrete, rested back on his elbows, and, closing his eyes, raised his face to the sun. Giving up one of his last Saturdays at the pool sucked, but the sun was doing a fine job of baking him and the blacktop. Five minutes and he'd scoot on over to the shade. The last thing he needed was to alarm Maisie with a sunburn.

Hopefully things were progressing well in the building behind him. He should thank Katelyn—Katie—one day. After all, her sinkhole of a marriage had led to everything good in his life: helping to raise Maisie, getting to see more of Delaney—okay, that part hadn't worked out too well—and meeting Gus, the founder of Kids Act, right after Gus was diagnosed with stage four lung cancer. He went to his grave believing Jake was the answer to his prayers, although truthfully it was the other way around. Jake had expanded the program to include the twelve-week moviemaking sessions, added the summer camps, and changed the name to Kids on Film.

The idea was simple. Campers and students did everything: wrote, acted, directed, and dealt with the props, hair, and makeup. It appealed to boys and girls with all kinds of skills, but the acting classes were still his favorite part. Some of those kids had been with him since day one. He taught them life skills and helped them figure out how to be confident, how to take charge, and how to be vulnerable. Vulnerability was a strength—not that he could ever convince Callum.

Was that Katie's idea behind the support group, to break down those walls? Things had been easier when he could evaluate her by one action. Threatening your baby was wrong. No debate necessary there. But now things weren't quite so clear-cut, and he knew—*oh, he knew*—that regret could yank you backward worse than a fender bender ending in whiplash.

In the distance a motorbike revved and drew closer. Much closer. Jake opened one eye as Ben pulled into the space in front of him, then tugged off his helmet and shook back a mess of hair. Did the guy not own a comb? Ben slid off his bike with a grace that contradicted his height. Jake sat up, both eyes open now. Good old Ben, the boyfriend, was an easy read. Confident, a little intense, and seriously ripped.

"Morning." Ben pushed at the long sleeves of his tee, even though they were already jammed over his elbows, and glanced at his macho black watch. "Or rather, afternoon."

"Nice wheels," Jake said. "Vintage?" Like he knew or cared.

"Seventies. BMW/5, a toaster tank. All original, even the paint."

Clearly the bike was an issue of pride. Why people invested energy in possessions made less sense than domesticating a raccoon. Jake had a good bicycle because he worked it hard and he needed to be safe on rural roads; he had a Honda Fit because he needed a versatile compact. His car was bright blue because the dealer didn't have another color.

"You're not hanging out with the girls?" Ben said.

"Not sure I'd describe Katie as a girl." Playing the jerk was the easiest method of self-defense, as easy as blocking a scene for the camera.

"Really? I would." Ben gave a smile that seemed to say *Like me, don't like me; I don't give a shit.*

Jake stood and brushed off his butt.

"This is a miserable place to wait unless you wanted an excuse to admire my sculptures," Ben said.

"Those are yours?" Jake pointed with his thumb. Who knew steel could curve that way, could look so fluid, so elegant? And they had to be, what, twelve feet tall? Funny thing, though, the more he looked at the closest one, the less he could identify the shape. At first glance, he'd taken it to be a contemporary flower, but now the movement suggested a belly dancer or a ballerina.

"I could see that one as a centerpiece in a garden," Jake said. "A big public one."

"Her sister? She's in a botanical garden in Maryland."

"How d'ya know it's a sister?" Jake turned back to Ben.

"I hated to split them up. Seemed they should stick together—same as Katie and Delaney."

The way he emphasized Delaney's name told Jake all he needed to know. Clearly Katie didn't keep secrets from Ben. Not that she knew all the secrets. Maybe he'd play along, see where this ended up. "You gonna take me behind the studio and whup my ass for something I did a lifetime ago when I was drunker than Cooter Brown?" The dumb southerner was always his favorite role.

"I'm not judging you." That quiet smile again. "Well, I am. Delaney's someone I care about."

Cute, loyal, and talented—Katie'd snagged herself the Triple Crown of boyfriends.

Jake sighed. "Guess we share something."

Ben appeared to be grappling with a decision. The guy should definitely work harder at concealing his thought process. "Want to grab a coffee?"

"In this heat?"

"Iced tea?"

"Make it sweetened and you're talking my language."

"We'll have to take my truck." Ben nodded at a piece of rusty junk on four wheels. "I don't have my spare helmet with me."

"Sure. Why not?"

They walked across the parking lot in silence, and Jake opened the unlocked door and hopped up onto the passenger seat. Darn plastic was hot enough to grill steak. Jake made a mental note to not touch anything on the inside until they'd gotten a nice cross-breeze going.

"Sorry." Ben joined him several minutes later. "I was texting Katie so she knows where we are in case Maisie needs you."

"Thanks, man." He was seriously off his game. Hadn't even thought twice about leaving Katie alone with Maisie. Callum would skin him alive if he ever found out.

They rattled off, and a breeze did, indeed, blow through the open windows. Not exactly a cooldown, but preferable to AC.

"I'm guessing you know how my past intersects with Katie's," Jake said. He wasn't about to blurt out everything. It was likely Ben knew plenty, but no good ever came from telling on others.

"I know her side of the story, which is all the information I need."

Ben braked hard to let a little old lady cross the road, and his arm shot in front of Jake. Good reflexes. He probably held up traffic to rescue stranded turtles, too.

"Her ex-husband and I go way back. *Way* back."

Ben drove with one elbow leaning on the open window. "Blood brothers, right?"

"A little cheesy, but yeah. Let me ask you a question." Jake raised his face, and the breeze caressed his cheek, his chin, his neck. "Why're you being nice to me?"

"How do you know I'm being nice?"

Jake gave a laugh. He may have met his match in Ben Holt, the guy with blackened fingernails, steel-gray eyes, and the slightest hint of attitude.

"I look out for my friends," Ben said, "and if I'm going to have a conflict of interest with someone, I like to know up front. My turn for a question: Why do you hate Katie?"

"I don't."

A young brunette walked up to the light and stopped. Bit too skinny for him—nothing to hold on to—but she was hot enough. Durham was a captivating city. Cosmopolitan. He should hang out here more. Check out the nightlife.

"All those years Katie was with Callum . . . ," Jake continued, watching the brunette. *Cute ass.* "I'm not sure I knew her. I didn't take the time. She seems different now, different from the woman I—"

"Didn't know?"

Jake turned toward Ben, who was squished into his seat. Life had to come with more than a few challenges when you were that tall, although

Ben appeared to be the kind of guy who was always at ease. "She seems to be someone I could admire—if we didn't have all that history. But we do, and I need to make sure her intentions are aboveboard. There's a lot at stake here. Maisie's happiness is—"

"As important to Katie as it is to you."

They fell back into silence. The truck rolled to a halt at a red stoplight, making a god-awful vibrating noise.

"Do you know how she became a welder?" Ben said.

Jake shrugged.

"I was doing this show up in Asheville, and Katie walked in. Marched right up to me and asked if I ever took on interns." Ben spoke as if tripping on a memory. "I was going to say no when she started talking about why she took up welding—to overcome her fear of fire. I was intrigued, so I told her to look me up if she ever came to Durham. Three months later, she was on my doorstep. She'd dragged Delaney here so they could both start over. Katie was passionate, eager, and determined. For her, I changed my rules." Ben glanced sideways.

"You got something against interns?" Jake couldn't run his business without them.

"My process is solitary. I don't want to be in someone else's head-space when I'm working. I certainly don't want to be explaining what I do."

"It wasn't that way with Katie?"

"Wasn't, isn't. She learned from observing."

"Like a good actor."

"I wouldn't know," Ben said. "When I took her on, she revealed nothing of herself, and that made me even more curious. I figured she had some dark secret and she'd tell me when she was ready. It took her five years. My baby sister was an addict," he said. "Mental illness isn't a joke, and Katie's suffered enough. She's worked hard to get where she is, and I won't have anyone hurting her."

"Are you warning me off?"

"Yup."

Jake smiled. "I like you, man."

"Thanks. Let's keep it civil, shall we?"

"You've got to know Callum's a mess over this."

"Maybe he should have considered the implications of locking his wife out before he acted on that particular impulse."

"He had his reasons."

"No doubt he did. As I said, that doesn't interest me." Ben flicked on his turn signal. "Having Maisie in the studio is incredibly hard for Katie. She sees danger everywhere—a thousand ways Maisie could get hurt. But Katie's making today happen, because nothing is more important to her than helping her daughter. And I think she deserves respect for what she's doing. Which means if you take that for granted and mess with her, you'll get me plus everyone else in the studio on your case, and Trent has a dubious past that includes jail time."

"For what?" Jake asked. "Armed robbery? Drug activity?"

"Gay rights parade. He attacked a guy who made homophobic comments about his boyfriend. The point is, the studio looks after its own."

Through the rusted-out crack in his footwell, pavement rushed by in slashes of gray. Jake kept his eyes lowered. "Do you believe people can change?"

"I guess."

"Katie's not the only one who used to be someone else." Jake looked up at the dashboard. "I used to be *that* guy. An asshole I didn't expected anyone to like, least of all me. Sex was my drug of choice. Still is, if I'm being entirely honest. When I slept with Delaney at Callum's wedding, I needed a quick fix. Problem was, stone-cold sober the next morning, I realized I liked her. I liked her a lot, man. And that scared the shit out of me because that feeling? It wouldn't go away. No matter how far I ran."

Ben nodded slowly, as if he understood, but how could he? Even Jake wasn't entirely sure what had happened that first time with Delaney—other than him living up to expectations. Being the lowlife who decided to nail the girl all the other guys wanted. Man, she was hot in that bridesmaid dress. A blind monk would've noticed. And then that dark mood settled, the one that used to fill him with an overdose of self—self-loathing, self-pity—and finally fear. Delaney was supposed to be one night of escape. She wasn't supposed to haunt him for years. Years now in the past, or so he had believed until two days ago.

EIGHTEEN
MAISIE

Maisie glanced at the *Star Wars* tattoos on her arm. Uncle J had put them on yesterday, right before he drove her home from Ms. Katie's studio, and already they were wearing off, but in a crazy bad way. They were ruined. Ruined like everything else in her life.

Her dad and Lilah were arguing, and their words made her head hurt and her tummy ache. But she had to be brave, she had to listen. Uncle J always said if you slowed the world down, you could hear your next move. "Never jump in, fists swinging," he would say as he pretended to be a boxer. "Think with your head first, then your heart."

Holding Lulabelle across her mouth and nose, Maisie tiptoed down the stairs and tried to think with her head first. 'Cept it was full of those awful thoughts speeding around, and her heart was going so fast it could explode, and oh, gosh, now Lilah was yelling. Yelling!

Her dad had been so happy when Lilah became his girlfriend. On their wedding day, when Uncle J was trying to pin the flowers on her dad's jacket, and she was hopping from foot to foot because her dress was super scratchy, Uncle J said, "You're one lucky bastard." And instead of telling Uncle J off for using a bad word, her dad brushed at his eyes, and she ran up to him and threw her arms around him and said, "Don't be sad, Daddy," and her dad laughed and said, "I'm not, peanut. I'm happy. This is a new beginning for us." Which was super confusing because Maisie didn't want a new beginning. She wanted everything to stay the way it had always been. The three musketeers: her, Uncle J, and her dad. And everyone told her she must be so happy to finally have a mom, and she wasn't, but if she had been happy, maybe her parents wouldn't need to argue. What if it was all her fault?

Stop, please, stop. I'll be good, I'll call Lilah Mom. I'm sorry, I'm sorry. Please stop arguing.

But nothing would stop, and it was all her fault. She rocked back and forth to hold in her screams. Maisie reached up and grabbed her hair. Yanked hard and—*Ow. Ow!* She looked at her hand. Uncle J called her hair her crowning glory, and now she'd pulled out a fistful.

Stop, please, stop.

Her dad never got this upset, not even when she broke the window while she was training for the softball team and he stood on a piece of glass, and there was so much blood she'd been afraid he would bleed to death. But right now Daddy was very, very upset, and even though he was shushing Lilah, one word was very, very clear: *Maisie.* They were being so mean to each other and she was to blame. She was a bad kid, the worst, and her dad and Lilah didn't love each other anymore and it was all her fault. And her dad and Lilah would become another divorce statistic like Ellie's mom and dad. And they would have to move like Ellie and her mom did because there wasn't enough money for two houses, and she really, *really* didn't want to go poor. And she really, *really* didn't want to move, because she'd lived in this house her whole life. Her whole life! And if she moved she wouldn't be near Ava Grace.

No. No. She had to be brave, had to be strong. If they were arguing because of her, she was the magic solution. She could fix this if she listened the way Uncle J had taught her.

I can be strong enough for both of us, Daddy.

Maisie took a deep breath, tiptoed across the hall, and leaned against the study door.

"If you leave, Lilah, it will kill me."

Daddy's going to die.

No, no, he didn't mean that.

But what if he did? What if he's going to die because of me? What if, what if?

Maisie's hand shot to her mouth. This was the worst of the worst. This was end-of-the-world worst. She turned and ran, out through the kitchen, across the yard, and onto the street.

No, can't have that thought in my head. Not about Daddy.

The voice told her he was going to die and maybe Lilah would die, too, and if Lilah died the baby would die, and it would all be her fault, and she would be an orphan. And if Daddy died because of her, because she'd been naughty, because she hadn't called Lilah Mom, Uncle J wouldn't love her anymore. Maisie kept running and crying. Running and crying. But she couldn't do both! Oh, this was too much.

The gate to the playground squeaked as she pushed it open and ran inside. Empty swings, empty slide, empty play structure, empty bench where the mommies sat and giggled. She was alone in a place built for families to have fun, to be happy. To be together. Maisie jumped on one of the swings, tucked Lulabelle up in her lap, and went around and around in a circle. Tighter and tighter. She was alone and no one could understand except . . . A name, one name. Maisie stopped moving and the swing spun in the opposite direction. *Ms. Katie.* Ben Holt had said, "You can text her anytime."

Yes! Yes! Maisie sniffed. She had no tissues and she couldn't wipe her nose with her arm because *ewww. Gross-oid.* She sniffed harder.

"Call me if the voice gets loud. If you need help," Ms. Katie had said. Yes! She needed help like never before. And yes, it was loud, and telling her over and over she was a vile person and Daddy would die because she hadn't called Lilah Mom, and Lilah and the baby would die and everyone would die. They would all be dead, dead like her real mom. Maisie pulled out her phone, but her hand was shaking too much to type, and she was crying harder than she had ever, ever cried before. Even harder than when Rose died on *Doctor Who*.

Maisie glanced up and down the street. No one was around. No one could hear her, because she was entirely, completely, one hundred percent alone. She hit "Call," and Ms. Katie picked up straightaway.

"Maisie, honey. What a lovely surprise."

"You"—Maisie hiccuped—"said I could call you if, if . . ."

"Ah. Is the voice being super stinky?"

"Gosh, *yyyes*! Stinkier than a thousand stinky butts. My dad and Lilah are fighting because I'm a bad kid, and I'm worried Daddy's going to die, and—"

"The voice is telling you it's all your fault?"

"I knew you'd understand."

"Sweetheart, I know it's distressing when parents argue, but the voice is lying to you. It's a liar and a bully. And bullies are the absolute worst, and we always stand up to them, right?"

"Uh-huh."

"Let me teach you about something super cool. It's called a fear thermometer, and we're going to use it to figure out how high your fear is so we can lower it. Does that sound good?"

"I guess."

"If you could grade your fear on a scale of one to ten, ten being the highest, how high would it be?"

"Eight and a half and rising! What if they both hate me? What if they both die? Where will I go? Who will I live with?"

"Parents argue all the time, honey, and it rarely has anything to do with the kids. Mine used to fight over whose turn it was to do the dishes."

"But they're arguing about me. Lilah insists I need help and my dad says it's not her call to make and I can't take it. I can't." More tears built up behind her eyes—like she could have even more—and now her nose was blocked. "I don't want to be the causation of fights."

"Honey, can you do something for me?"

"What?" Maisie gulped.

"Take a deep breath. A nice big, deep breath. We're going to do nothing right now except breathe, okay? We're going to slow everything down and breathe. You're going to inhale through your nose, hold that breath, and exhale slowly through your mouth. All to the count of four. Come on. Let's do it together."

"I can't, Ms. Katie. I can't breathe through my nose."

"Can you blow it really loudly?"

"I don't have a tissue."

"Can you give a humongous sniff?"

She did.

"Bigger?" Ms. Katie said.

She did.

"Perfect! You sound like a skunk with a cold."

Maisie stopped crying. "How does a skunk with a cold sound?"

"Like you?" Ms. Katie laughed, and her laugh was awesome. "You were talking about stinky butts, and I pictured a skunk, and . . . How high's the fear thermometer now?"

"I don't know. I was imagining your skunk."

"Good, and now I want you to repeat this as loud as you can: 'This is just a stinky skunk thought. Thoughts aren't real. They can't hurt me or anyone else.'"

She did, and did it several times more because Ms. Katie kept saying, "Louder, louder!"

And then she started breathing through her nose again.

"When we went to the Chocolate Factory," Ms. Katie said, "you told me you were good at debating, right? So we're going to debate with that stinky voice. What can you say to the voice to prove it wrong?"

"I don't know, Ms. Katie."

"Okay, how about some logic. I'm sure your parents have argued before. And no one ever died, right?"

"No! They never argue. And Ellie's dad is a doctor and he once said stress kills people. Did you know most car accidents happen when people are angry?"

"Hmm. That was helpful of him," Ms. Katie said, but it didn't sound like she meant it. "You're being very brave right now, Maisie, and I need you to keep being brave."

"I don't feel brave."

"How about next time you come to the studio, we make medals? For heroic actions when dealing with the stinky voice. Like Purple Hearts, except not purple. What's your favorite color? Please don't tell me pink."

"Oh, no, Uncle J would *neeever* forgive me. My favorite color is teal, Ms. Katie."

"Let's drop the 'Ms.,' okay?"

"Sorry, sorry. I know you told me that before, and I don't mean to be disrespectful but—"

"*Shhh*, honey. Slow everything down. Teal it is. That's an easy patina. Now, take a deep breath and start from the beginning. Tell me what happened so I can pick this whole thing apart like a giant jigsaw puzzle and help you put it back together. But with facts, not unwanted thoughts."

"I like puzzles."

"I had a feeling you did. Now, let's figure out what's really going on. Take it from the top, Maisie!"

"Well"—big sigh—"I was upstairs finishing my homework so I can go to Ava Grace's this afternoon, and my dad and Lilah were arguing in my dad's office. My bedroom is over the office, so I heard them. Lilah was getting angry because my dad doesn't want me to see a therapist"— big gulp of air—"and then she said something about my real mom but I couldn't hear properly so I came downstairs"—another gulp—"and that's when Daddy said that if Lilah left it would kill him and if he dies I'll be an orphan. An orphan!"

Katie seemed to be doing some deep breathing of her own. Then she said, "Where are you, honey?"

"I ran away. If I'm not there maybe my dad and Lilah won't argue and no one will die. But I didn't think to pack a suitcase or even a snack bag. Not even a water bottle and that was very, very silly. The high is going to be eighty-eight degrees today, and I could get dehydrated. It's already very hot on the playground."

"This playground, is it the one near your house?"

"*Yyyes.* How did you know?"

"A wild guess." Katie went quiet again.

Maisie's heart got super loud. Oh, gosh, had Ms. Katie—Katie—hung up?

"Honey, you have to call your dad and let him come fetch you. Can you do that for me?"

"I can't! Daddy and Lilah hate each other and Lilah said she's going to leave and if she does it'll kill Daddy, and Daddy will be dead like my real mom, and Lilah will be gone and it will all be my fault. My fault! And I don't know what to do." Maisie stopped talking, because she couldn't squeeze out any more words now that she was crying again.

"Okay, I'm going to come and help you, Maisie, but you have to promise you'll stay put." Katie's voice sounded all jumpy. Was she running? "You're not to go out near the road or talk to anyone except your father. Do we have a deal?"

"I promise." Maisie hiccuped a sob.

"I'm in my truck and starting the engine. There's never any traffic on Sunday morning, so I can be there in half an hour. Do you know what we're going to do in that half hour? We're going to make up a story. I hear you're pretty good at that."

"B-but you d-don't know w-where I live."

"Uncle Jake told me, which makes me the best person to call. And I want you to imagine that noise in your head is a train fueled by stinky thoughts. But the brakes on the train are broken, so it's picking up speed, and together we're going to slow it down and bring it safely into the station."

"I—I don't like trains."

"You don't? I do. They carry you from one place to the next, and all you have to do is sleep and read. Or make up stories about the passengers."

Maisie sniffed. "What passengers?"

"Gross ones."

Maisie stopped crying. "How gross?"

"Last time I was on a train there was a nose picker. Let's call him Mr. Nose Picker."

"Ewww."

"Very *ewww.*" Katie paused. "I'm heading to the Durham Freeway, but we're going to keep talking, okay?"

"Daddy says you shouldn't talk on the phone and drive."

"Quite right, but this is a special circumstance, and it's Sunday morning so there won't be much traffic. And besides, you're going to do the talking. I'm going to listen. Can you picture Mr. Nose Picker and laugh at him?"

"That's not very nice, to laugh at someone."

"No, it's not, but laughing at the voice is the same as declaring, 'I won't hide from you. You don't scare me!'"

"You mean like calling Parker out for his very atrocious behavior?"

"Exactly. I knew you were smart."

It was super kind of Katie to call her smart, but right now she didn't deserve compliments.

"This story of yours is going to need a plot. I want a beginning, a middle, an end, and lots of conflict. Did I mention Mr. Nose Picker is with Mrs. Nose Picker and their two sons, Booger and Snot? It's a Roald Dahl story!"

A giggle snuck out. A tiny giggle, and she didn't feel quite so anxious. *"The Twits!"*

"I love Roald Dahl."

"Me too. My real mom bought all his books for me before I was born. Or so—"

"Uncle Jake said?"

"How did you know I was going to say that?"

"Another lucky guess. But back to the Nose Pickers. Mr. Nose Picker and Mrs. Nose Picker are on their way to Ohio, when—"

"Why Ohio?"

"Why not?" Ms. Katie gave a giggle, too.

"Ms. Katie—I mean, Katie? I'm super glad we're friends."

"Me too, honey. And guess what? Five minutes have gone by. There's no traffic on the Durham Freeway, and I'll be there soon. But if I enter a black hole and lose the connection, I'm still on my way and I want you to keep working on the story so you can tell me the ending when I get there."

"Katie"—Maisie's hand shot to her mouth and she chewed on her thumbnail, even though there was nothing left to chew on and it was pretty sore and Uncle J was trying to get her to stop—"how do I know nothing bad's going to happen to *you* on the Durham Freeway?"

"Because nothing's going to prevent me from coming home."

Maisie stopped chewing her nail. What did Ms. Katie mean by *coming home*?

NINETEEN
LILAH

Attempting to make a dignified exit without the proper tools was not the smartest course of action. Lilah sat in the car with the envelope, her purse, and no car key. A truck pulling a trailer of lawn mowers rattled to a stop between their mailbox and the neighbor's. Two men got out and began unloading, but Callum didn't move. He was standing barefoot on their porch, as he had been five minutes earlier.

Sighing, she heaved herself out of the car. Callum walked down the front steps, not with the movements of a guy who could pour himself into spandex and bike the hundred-mile Assault on Mount Mitchell, but as if he were walking on razor blades. She stooped down to pick up the *New York Times* and held out international news as a peace offering.

"I tried to make a getaway without the car key."

He stopped in front of her but didn't take the paper. "Where were you heading?"

"Around the corner to cool off. Do you think Maisie heard us behaving badly?"

He shook his head and reached for her. Lilah stepped into his arms as she always did. She let the paper drop.

"Tell me you love me," Callum said.

"Love isn't our problem." Lilah stared up at him. "When we got married, I also vowed to be Maisie's mother, and you're withholding information I need to be that person. I'm here because I forgot my car key, not because I'm backing down. I won't be the kind of parent who runs from problems."

His arms slipped to his sides, and he stared at her, jaw set. Once again, she'd pushed a button without understanding how.

"I'm not the one who ran away," he said.

"I wasn't running away. I was attempting to calm down. I want to discuss this as parents, not rant at you in full banshee mode. But you won't listen, Callum, and you need to hear me out." He didn't say anything, so she continued. "Maisie's become needy in the last few months, and it's getting worse. And exhibit A"—she held up the envelope—"is a suicide note. I think there's a correlation between what happened to your first wife and your determination to protect Maisie from something a therapist could expose."

"Maisie's not needy."

"Wrong word, then. A worrywart. The other day she asked me if a freckle was skin cancer."

"Good, she's being sensible."

"Not good. She should be doing something fun and kiddie, not worrying about cancer. And you're not being straight with me. If that doesn't change, we'll be seeing a therapist together. It's called marriage counseling."

"How did you even find that letter? It was hidden in the bottom drawer of my desk."

"I snooped because you kept stonewalling. So I'm going to ask you again: Did your first wife commit suicide after the divorce? Did she suffer from depression, anxiety, something that Maisie might have inherited?"

He reached up and dragged his hands through his hair. His T-shirt rose to expose the flat stomach, the trail of dark coppery hair that disappeared under the waistband of his boxer briefs. His ratty weekend sweatpants hung lower than usual.

"Katelyn tried to commit suicide and didn't succeed," he said. "And I've been protecting Maisie from what happened. Everything I've done has been to protect Maisie."

A rusty black truck pulled up in front of the house, and a woman got out. The passenger door slammed and Maisie appeared, her face red and blotchy, Lulabelle clutched to her chest.

"Maisie!" Callum ran across the grass. "I thought you were upstairs in your room."

"I heard you two arguing about me, and I ran away and called Katie." Maisie moved closer to the woman. Katie? Katie Mack the artist?

"She was on the playground down the street when she called. Needing a friend." Katie looked directly at Callum. "We talked, and I persuaded her to let me bring her home."

"How did she get your phone number?" Callum said.

"I gave it to her. That's what friends do. Exchange phone numbers. You must be Maisie's mom. I'm Katie Mack." The woman pressed her thumb into her palm, forcing her hand back at what had to be a painful angle. "Strange way for us to meet."

Lilah looked from Katie to Callum and back to Katie. Did they know each other?

"Thank you for bringing her home. Maisie—" Lilah held out her hand, but Maisie didn't react. "I'm sorry you overheard us fighting, sweetie. Pregnancy's making me witchy."

"Maisie." Callum's voice was low. "Come here."

"I can't, Daddy. Katie understands."

"What does Katie understand?" Lilah said.

Katie looked down at Maisie. Maisie gave a nod, and Katie looked back up. "Your daughter's very brave, Mrs. MacDonald."

Maisie stood up straight. "I've been scared to tell you, Daddy, so scared. I didn't want to be the causation of more worry, because I know you have a lot to deal with right now. But you taught me to tell the truth." She stepped toward her dad. "And Katie says it's time to be honest with you, so I'm going to try."

Callum dropped to his knees. "I've been scared, too. But it's okay, peanut. It's okay."

"Any chance one of you could fill me in?" Lilah said.

"I have a voice inside my head," Maisie said. "Not really a voice. I mean, it's part of me, but not a part I want. These horrid thoughts come from nowhere. Nowhere! And they feel very alien and scary. They got super loud when you and my dad were arguing, and told me you hated each other and it was my fault. And that awful things were going to happen, but Katie explained the voice is an in-*tru*-sive thought and I should tell you both. So I am. And I feel a bit better. Telling you. Are you mad at me?"

"Of course not." Lilah wrapped her left arm around her belly. Maisie was hearing voices?

"I have the same thing." Katie smiled. "That's why Maisie contacted me. It's called obsessive-compulsive disorder, and it's treatable. But Maisie's had a rough time." Katie turned to Callum. "Go easy on her, Cal."

Cal? Why was Katie calling Callum . . . ? Lilah held up the envelope. Katie's hand shot to her throat and she gasped.

Callum stood up and tugged Maisie to him. He crossed his arms over her. "Leave," he said to Katie. "Now."

Lilah looked down at the envelope addressed to Maisie, care of Cal MacDonald. The return address read *K. M.*, followed by the name of a homeless shelter in Asheville, North Carolina. K. M.—Katelyn MacDonald, but also Katie Mack.

"Is that for me?" Maisie said. "It's addressed to me. Why do you have it, Lilah?"

Lilah raised her eyes slowly; her mouth opened, but no sound came out.

Katie knelt down in front of Callum and took Maisie's hands. "That puzzle we talked about? I know how to put it back together, honey. Your parents aren't arguing because of you. They're arguing because of me." Katie glanced up at Callum. "You want to tell her?"

"I don't understand," Maisie said, but Lilah understood all too well.

She finally had her answers, her conclusion. This wasn't her family and never had been. She wasn't Maisie's mother. Maybe she wasn't even Callum's wife. Had everything been a lie?

"When you were born after ten hours of labor, you were black and blue," Katie said. "A forceps baby. You were six pounds, seven ounces, and so quiet. You slept a lot because you were jaundiced. But then you got well, put on weight, and learned how to cry. You were the most beautiful baby in the world."

"How do you know?" Maisie said.

"Because she's your mother," Callum said, and released his hold on Maisie.

"Mommy? You're my mommy? You're alive?"

Katie nodded, and Maisie threw her arms around her mother's neck. Lilah staggered and hit the railing of the front steps. *No, I'm her mommy. Me.*

"Uncle J was right! You're beautiful and awesome and we can make art together and—" Maisie pulled back. "Why? Why did everyone tell me you're dead?"

"Your dad and I agreed it would be better that way."

"I was going to tell you, Lilah, but so much happened so fast, and I couldn't keep up. I'm sorry." Callum tossed out a shaky smile. Lilah contemplated tossing a thing or two back, until Maisie spoke.

"Didn't you want me?" Maisie's little voice said.

171

Groping behind for something solid, Lilah sat heavily on the steps and tilted her head up to the sky. How could a mother—or a father—do this to a child?

"Honey. There was only one thing I wanted more," Maisie's mother—her real mother—answered. "For you to be happy. The truth is . . . I ran away when you were a baby, because my voice was too loud. It told me I wanted to hurt you, which was the biggest lie of all. But I believed its lies, and I had to keep you safe, Maisie. And your dad was trying to do the same."

"But why didn't you come back for me?"

"I'm not as brave as you. I was scared to get help, and by the time I did, I couldn't look after myself, much less you. I grew up worrying about a mommy who couldn't cope, and I never wanted to put you through that. You deserved the best, and that wasn't me. It was the right decision for everyone, Maisie. Especially for you."

Think, Lilah, where are your car keys? She should get up, go inside, pack a bag, and drive home to her own mother.

"But you could have come back after you got well," Maisie said.

"I think she just did," Lilah mumbled.

"It was too late, Maisie. You thought I was dead, and you had your dad and Uncle J. And now you have Lilah and a baby brother or sister."

"But I wanted *you*. You! And you didn't want *me*."

"Sweetheart, I wanted you more than anything, but I had nothing to offer. And you deserved better. You have better."

Maisie twisted around and flew at Callum, arms flailing. She hit him in the stomach; he didn't react. "You always told me to be honest, but you lied to me, Daddy. You're the biggest cheater of all."

"I second that," Lilah said. She pushed herself up. *Enough.* She was leaving—in earnest this time. If she couldn't find her car keys, she'd take Callum's.

"I love you, Maisie," Callum said. "And I needed you to be safe. To have the best childhood, the happiest childhood. I wanted that for you more than anything."

"I just wanted my mommy!" Maisie yelled.

Callum said something, but his voice drifted away. Everything became fuzzy. The world was tipping over, and she was sliding off.

"I hate to go all Victorian heroine," Lilah said. "But I think I'm about to—"

TWENTY

JAKE

Whistling a Taylor Swift song stuck in his brain—*Thanks, Maisie*—Jake glanced at the crew mowing the lawn next door to Callum's house. The push mower hit something, the machine bucked, but the guy kept going. Shit job, cutting grass on a Sunday. He should know, since he'd been a subcontractor for a Mexican landscaper before moving to LA. Poor dude didn't speak much English, so Jake functioned as a translator, too. Spanish, now that was one subject he'd aced in school, thanks to all that extracurricular activity with Rosalita and—*darn*, what was her friend's name, the one with the best ass in high school?

Jake stopped whistling and maneuvered around a truck parked with all the finesse of a crashed Fourth of July float. The truck looked kinda familiar, and why was the door of the house flung open? Callum saw an open front door as an invitation for danger to stroll on in. *Danger.* Jumping out of his car, Jake ran toward the house, calling for Maisie and Callum. No one answered, but there were voices coming from the living room.

Lilah Rose was lying on the sofa, pushing Callum away. Drained of color, Callum looked worse than he did after cycling a century on a warm day.

"You okay, man?"

"Lilah fainted," Callum said in little more than a whisper.

Maisie was huddled in the alcove, crying, and Katie had an arm around her. Katie mouthed, *She knows.*

"Baby?" He rushed to Maisie.

"You knew, too?" Maisie said.

"That your mama's alive? Yeah, I knew."

"You lied to me!" Maisie shouted. "All of you lied to me."

He sank to his knees and held out his arms for a Maisie hug, but she dodged as he'd taught her. *A boy you don't like starts making moves on you, this is what you do.* Would she also kick him in the nuts? His brain stated fact: *Far worse things have happened to you.* But his heart screamed otherwise.

"Lilah didn't lie to you," Katie said softly. "Your stepmom clearly knew nothing."

He stood up and nodded at Katie. His mama's words came to mind: "You done real good, sugar."

Maisie seemed to pivot on the spot before flinging herself across Lilah Rose's chest.

"Shhh." She brushed back Maisie's hair. "I'm fine, you're fine, the baby's fine. Everything's fine." Lilah Rose gave a high-pitched laugh. "Actually it's far from fine, but we'll get through this together, my little M&M."

"Maisie, I'm sorry," Katie said. "I never meant for you to find out."

"You think that makes me feel better?" Maisie sobbed.

Callum sank into the nearest armchair and hung his head in his hands. Jake looked to the nearest window and focused on a large black-and-yellow spider that had built an intricate web on the outside of the screen and decorated it with zigzags of silk. He would not cry. He would not.

"You're—" Maisie sucked in a huge sob, and Jake struggled to not ram his fingers in his ears. "You're my real mom and you didn't want me to know? Never. Wanted. Me"—another sob—"to know?"

"I never stopped loving you, honey. Not for one second." How could Katie stay so calm, while his insides were being ripped out through his belly button?

"When we met at CAM," Katie continued in that damn steady voice, "I saw the amazing young lady you'd become, and I knew I'd been right to stay away. But the anxiety, Maisie. I can help with that."

Maisie clung to Lilah Rose—not Callum, not him—as if she were a flotation device. "So now you only want me because I'm faulty?"

"Hush, sweetie," Lilah Rose said. "You're not faulty, you're brilliant and kind and we all love you. You're 'Mazing Maisie."

That's my name for her. But the realization caught in his craw. He'd stolen 'Mazing Maisie from Katelyn. Deliberately. With malice.

"No!" Maisie darted away. "I hate all of you. Leave me alone." And then she ran up the stairs and slammed her door.

Jake inhaled sharply.

"I should leave," Katie said.

"Now you say this?" Callum said. "It wasn't enough to take a wrecking ball to my life once? We had a deal, Katelyn. Why couldn't you have stayed—"

"Dead?" Lilah Rose sat up. "And you, Callum, you confided in Jake, but not me?"

Jake stepped forward. "The deal the four of us made—"

"Four of you?" Lilah Rose said.

"Maisie's aunt," Katie said. "My sister."

"Are there any more of you I should know about?"

"Lilah Rose, it was my plan from the get-go." Jake turned to Katie. "I'm guessing you knew that."

Katie bit into her lip.

"I appreciate you covering for him," Lilah Rose said, "but Callum's a big boy. He could have explained the truth to me at any point in the last year that he's been fucking me."

Callum winced. "I was going to tell you after the baby was born. How could I risk upsetting you when you're pregnant?"

"You just did, you bastard."

"Don't!" Callum shot up. "Don't look at me as if I'm contagious. Don't talk as if you hate me. Yes, I messed up. Don't you think I know that? But we can move beyond this, we can."

"I'd like this back so I can destroy it." Katie picked up the letter from the floor and shoved it in her pocket. "Suppose Maisie had found it? Why did you keep it, Cal?"

Callum laughed in a creepy-as-shit way. "Why did you send it to her?"

"Guys," Jake said. "Our priority here is Maisie."

"Oh, yeah. I forgot," Katie said. "I can't talk to Cal without you in the middle."

"Katelyn, you need to leave my house," Callum said.

"The house I found, the house I chose, the house I decided was ours? No. I'm not leaving. I've changed my mind. I'm going to sit outside our daughter's bedroom door until she talks to me. Until she talks to us." She looked at Callum. "For once, we're going to deal with something as a family."

"We're not a family." Callum spat out his words. "We haven't been *a family* since the day you left us."

"Since the day you locked me out."

"You"—Callum walked toward her, pointing—"need to leave so I can deal with my daughter."

"Enough, you guys," Lilah Rose snapped. "I have an unborn baby to think about, and you two are turning my air toxic. The only person who's going to be dealing with Maisie is me, since I'm the only person who hasn't lied to her. All of you, scram."

"You're throwing me out of my own house?" Callum yelled.

What about me? Jake wanted to say. *But yeah, what about me? I'm the one person here who isn't her parent.* He'd never needed a label to tell him what his heart knew. But standing here, he wanted that label.

"Our house." Lilah Rose glared, briefly, at Katie. "And yes. Slink off with Jake and think about what you want to say to me and your daughter, because at this precise moment, I want nothing to do with the father of my child."

"You want me to leave when Maisie's this upset?"

"I don't think she's upset, Callum. I think she's devastated. Thanks to you, you"—Lilah Rose nodded at Katie—"and you." She nodded at Jake. "Nice job, the three of you. Now get out, so I can be the parent this kid needs."

"I am not leaving. I'm the one constant in her life," Callum screamed. Jake glanced toward the stairs. "Her father, you hear me? Her father!"

"I think half the street heard you." Lilah Rose rubbed her stomach. Jake put a hand on Callum's shoulder, but he shrugged it off.

"I'm not going," Callum said, although his tone suggested otherwise.

"Yes," Lilah Rose said, "you are."

Jake wanted to speak up, be the bigger person. Do the right thing. Leave and take Callum with him, but he couldn't.

"Her anxiety's going to ramp up," Katie said to Lilah. "If you need help—"

"I have a friend who's a psychologist. I'll call him the moment you leave."

"Tell him we think she has OCD, that her mother does, and her grandmother was an alcoholic prone to angry outbursts. Lilah," Katie said, "I'm sorry."

"I'm a little tired of apologies right now. All of you need to leave while I tend to a ten-year-old girl who's entitled to better parents." Lilah Rose pushed herself up—belly first—using the arm of the sofa.

In another situation, Jake would have applauded, would have congratulated Lilah Rose on becoming the mama he'd always hoped she'd be. But he was having a hard time thinking beyond his own pain. Even if Maisie forgave him, this moment would remain. Maisie didn't hold grudges, but her moral compass swung only two ways, and he was stranded in the middle.

"Come on, y'all," he said. "It's best we do as Lilah Rose suggests."

Katie nodded and left the room. He followed, but Callum lagged behind, grabbing his keys and wallet from the hall table and fumbling through the pile of shoes. Katie headed to her truck, and with a sigh, Jake followed.

"You okay to drive?" He wasn't sure *he* should be driving.

Katie stopped with her hand on the door handle but didn't turn. "Maisie hates me," she said.

"You and me both." He couldn't even pretend, as Lilah Rose had done, that it would all be fine. "Don't drive home. Give me your phone and I'll call Ben. Ask him to come get you."

"No. He's working on a big commission. Besides, I do my best work alone." She stared straight ahead, her eyes dry. "Once you know how rock bottom feels, you're always waiting for it to return. And when it does, it's almost a relief. And it's comforting because it's what you know. And expect. And deserve."

They both jumped when the front door slammed.

"Revenge as sweet as you'd imagined?" Callum stalked toward his car.

Katie touched Jake's arm. "Maisie will forgive you. When she agrees to see you, please tell her I love her."

"Ignore her, Jake."

Jake swung round. "Back off, Callum. We've all been through enough."

For once he wanted to be the person who fell apart. The difference between him and Katie was that he didn't want to do it alone. As Katie closed her truck door and Callum slammed his car door, Jake pulled out his phone and typed a text.

Maisie emergency.

Wondered when I'd hear from you, Delaney replied.

TWENTY-ONE
KATIE

Katie had lied to Jake.

She sure as hell shouldn't be behind the wheel of a truck, a vehicle that could use size and weight to cause death, but if she didn't drive back to Durham, alone, the voice would win. Looking over her shoulder, Katie backed up at a snail's pace to avoid taking out the mailbox. Jake stood at the end of the driveway, staring at his phone.

How high's the fear thermometer, Katie? How high? Six? Am I safe to drive? No, no, I'm not. I'm going to cause an accident, kill a child. What kind of a mother pretends she's dead, lets her child believe she's dead? I'm the angel of death. Death. Heart's racing, can't breathe, shouldn't be driving. Fear thermometer's seven. Got to be seven. That mom on the sidewalk, holding her little girl's hand? I could run up onto the grass and hit them both. Kill them. Cal's right, I destroyed his life, and now I'm going to destroy another husband's life. Take a stranger's family. Kill his family.

No, this is the voice. I'm in control of my actions. I'm not going to jump the curb. Have I ever caused an accident? Been in one? No.

Her hands, perfectly spaced on the steering wheel the way they showed you in Drivers' Ed, grew slick with sweat. Too slick? Would she lose control of the vehicle and jump the curb? Did her hands want to tug the steering wheel to the right? That could happen, couldn't it? Her mind played the answer: a bloody movie running on a broken projector to a broken soundtrack.

Katie drove past and glanced in the rearview mirror. The little girl, she couldn't see her. Did that mean she'd hit her? *Hands, Katie, watch your hands, make sure they don't slip.* Oh, God, had she—hit the child? *I killed a child. I have to stop right now. Put both feet on the brake and engage the parking brake.* She leaned forward, her back rigid. *No.*

A feeling isn't an action. Panic is nothing but panic. It comes from OCD, not fact. What can I see in the real world? What are the facts? Look, there's a man walking his dog. That's real. So's the squirrel darting across the road. Good, good. Heart rate's coming down. I can do this, I can do this. Eyes ahead, Katie, read the road. Keep to the speed limit, watch for cars pulling out. You've got this.

Music, she needed music. The National. Yes, that was a good choice, always calming. But that meant stopping to find a CD, and if she stopped, she might never start again.

Look ahead, Katie, read the road. Keep to the speed limit, watch for cars pulling out. You've got this. No, no, I haven't. That little girl back there? What if I killed her, and I'm fleeing the scene of a crime? That makes me a criminal as well as an unfit mother. I need to go back and check. Check I didn't kill her. Go back and check check check check.

A thought is just a thought; it has no power.

What if I hit that little girl, and I don't go back? What if that dark stain on my window is blood, her blood?

Thoughts are nothing more than ones and zeros. My mind is running what-if math problems like a possessed calculator. And I hate math. Are you listening, OCD? I hate math.

I control fire; I am strong.

Katie flicked on the turn signal—*flicked it on with purpose, with strength, with control, OCD*—and entered the maze of residential streets that led out of the subdivision. She turned right, then left. The road widened, and a median planted with burning bushes—still green—stretched out on her left. To her right was the lake with the fountain. Behind it sat the clubhouse and the entrance to the pool. Ahead was the exit from her old neighborhood. The city street that would take her to Falls of Neuse Road and back to I-540, the road that looped around the capital. But a fast road, a multilane racetrack. How many high-speed accidents were fatal? What were the statistics? What if she caused a wreck on I-540? How many people would die because of her? And what about the little girl?

I need to turn around, go back and check. Make sure she's okay. Go back and check. If I don't, I'm a criminal. What if I left the scene of an accident?

I-540 would take her to the interstate, which would take her to the Durham Freeway, which would lead to her quiet, sunlit apartment. To her big white bed. To a place where she could be alone and not hurt anyone.

I should turn around and go back. What if I ran over that little girl? What if she's bleeding to death in the gutter? What if her mom can't help her? What if I hit her, too? Killed them both . . .

Katie kept going; so did the voice. She pulled onto I-540 and settled into a middle lane. So many lanes, so many cars passing on both sides. Everyone driving too fast. Was that a siren in the distance, getting closer and closer? *Yes, and it's gaining.* She had killed the little girl, the cops were coming for her, and she was going to jail. She'd left the scene of an accident. Why, why hadn't she turned around?

She glanced up at her rearview mirror. Not a cop car, but an ambulance. She needed to pull over, but she was hemmed in. How, how did you pull over when there was nowhere to go? She hit the brakes; the car behind honked; the ambulance dodged in front and sped away. By some miracle, she was still driving. She was still on the road. She hadn't caused a pileup. But who was in the ambulance?

The little girl I killed. I should be in jail.

A bead of sweat snaked toward her right eye, and she raised her hand to—*No. Two hands on the wheel, Katie. Two hands.* Quickly, she moved her hands back into position. Everything was better with two, but not right now. Once she got home, she would crawl into bed and stay there. Isolate.

It all came back to truth. Undeniable truth: *What if I'm capable of doing the things my mind sees? What if I'm no different from a person who thinks twice before committing murder?*

TWENTY-TWO
LILAH

Amazing how you could devote your adult life to finding new knowledge, new understanding, and then fall back on a hackneyed mantra: *It's all fine.*

Lilah gave her mom one more "fine" and hung up the phone after their weekly Sunday-afternoon chat. With seven grandchildren under her belt, the novelty of a new baby joining the family had worn off, but her mother took maternal duties seriously. And at the top of her current worry list was whether Baby MacD's lack of name meant that her own baby was in denial. Lilah had assured her mother everything was fine, because the last thing Maisie needed was stepgranny on the doorstep with a bulging suitcase of concern.

The paddles of the living room ceiling fan turned slowly, and the air conditioner kicked on with an efficient click. That new compressor was the bomb, which it should be, given the price tag. Callum's half-drunk cup of coffee stared at her from the coffee table. Lilah turned her back on it and headed into the kitchen. Once she reached for his *Doctor Who* mug and put it in the dishwasher, she would be entering the first stage of her new life: dumping his leftovers. Would his clothes follow?

A squirrel launched itself from the railing of the back deck onto the big oak and chased another squirrel. The hands of the kitchen clock moved steadily, marking out her *before* moment. Before friends and family knew. Before she owed anyone an explanation. Before she had to answer to the curiosity of others. Her sparkly new secret was hers and hers alone: *I kicked my husband to the curb.* The clock also reminded her that another thirty minutes had ticked away.

Lilah rubbed her belly. "You doing okay in there, sprout? Let's go check on your sister again." And this time she wasn't taking "Leave me alone" as a rejection.

Lilah opened the freezer and pulled out the unopened pint of Ben & Jerry's Phish Food. She moved around the kitchen on autopilot: two spoons from the drawer next to the dishwasher, check; two paper napkins from the napkin holder on the middle of the table, check. Leave the kitchen and mount the stairs. Check and check. She knocked on Maisie's door.

"Sweetie? Evil Stepmom is here to feed you an obscene amount of Phish Food."

No answer.

"Ice cream for lunch is a pretty sweet deal. If three o'clock counts as lunchtime."

The door creaked open, and then Maisie scurried away and threw herself on top of the rumpled covers. It was suffocatingly hot inside, given that Maisie had stopped using the ceiling fan after it had developed "an annoying clunk." The electrician was supposed to fix it later in the week. Maybe he could fix everything else while he was at it.

Lilah sat on the edge of Maisie's bed, which was tucked against a wall painted midnight-blue to cover up some mural that no other color could erase. Everything in Maisie's room had its place. No one was allowed to touch anything, including the cleaning lady. Until this moment, Lilah had never questioned that as odd. Then again, she'd questioned so little in her ready-made family.

She put the ice cream down on the floor and rubbed Maisie's back.

"Where's my dad?" Maisie mumbled into her comforter.

"I sent everyone away. There's no one here but you and me, kiddo."

Maisie sat up and crossed her legs. Tucking her thumb under her palm, she brushed her hair twice on one side, twice on the other—a nervous habit that had snuck in during the last few weeks, along with Katie Mack.

"What happens next?" Maisie said.

"For starters, I plan to eat my weight in ice cream. And given how large I am, that could take a while." Lilah picked up the ice cream and handed over a spoon and a napkin. She wouldn't have bothered with the napkin, but Maisie wasn't big on food in her bedroom.

Lilah popped the top of the ice cream container and excavated a fudge fish. "And then serious retail therapy on your dad's credit card. It's definitely time you designed a pair of Converse high-tops."

"Those are super expensive. Ellie's dad bought her a pair, and her mom was *fur*-ious." Maisie scowled. "I don't think my dad would approve."

"Good. You want to get your ears pierced, too? We could get matching earrings as part of a new, exclusive mother-daughter group I'm calling Girls with Attitude."

"Thank you, but I've decided I'm not getting my ears pierced. Ava Grace's big sister got an in-*fection* when she had hers done last week. She said it was very painful." Maisie went quiet and ate a miniscule scoop of ice cream. "I feel super bad about using the *h*-word. That was mean."

"No, it wasn't. You were expressing anger that your dad and Uncle Jake needed to hear. Anger is an important part of grieving, and you and I have lots of grieving to do."

"Why? I don't understand."

"You grew up with certain facts about your family. Turns out those facts were wrong. Now you and I have to find ways to make sense of this new information so we can adapt and encompass the change."

Maisie did the thing with her hair again. "I don't like change."

"That's why we're going to meet a friend of mine for lunch tomorrow. He's a psychologist at Duke, and I hope you'll talk to him. It's healthy to talk about your feelings, even negative ones."

"Am I a bad kid for using the *h*-word?" Maisie whispered.

"No. I wanted to use it, too."

"But you didn't."

"Only because you got the jump on me. You've had a lot to process today, my little M&M. Too much for any person, even an adult. And I think talking to a professional would be a good idea. Maybe we can get a price break on family therapy."

"Is that what he is, a therapist? I heard my dad saying he didn't want me to see one."

"He doesn't, but your . . . other mom does. And so does Uncle Jake, and so do I."

"You mean, my dad's wrong?"

"No. I think he's scared." Lilah dug deep into the ice cream.

"When we were all outside, he did say he was scared." Maisie frowned. "But scared of what? I still don't understand."

"Who does your father love more than anyone?"

Maisie looked at her spoon. "Before he met you, I used to think it was me."

"Sweetie, it still is. The first thing I learned about your father was that nothing was ever more important than you. It was stated as fact in our department: 'Professor MacDonald's great to work with, but he'll insist on Skyping in to your thesis defense if his little girl gets sick.' My guess is that he wants so desperately to be the best daddy in the world that he can't admit he might need help." Lilah popped her spoon into her mouth and giggled. "Brain freeze!"

Maisie smiled, but the smile didn't stay in place.

"And one thing I learned from growing up with four siblings is that family life is an obstacle course. This feels huge—an epic crisis—and we're going to wallow. But then we're going to figure out how to move forward. Together, with all of us heading in the same direction. That's what family does when the road ahead gets bumpy."

Wow. For one whole minute she'd convinced herself that she no longer wanted to castrate her husband or do unspeakable things to his wingman. "And I hope you'll talk to my psychologist friend about your voice."

"No, no." Maisie shook her head and kept shaking it. "I can't! Look what happened when I spoke about it outside! Those things . . . I can't talk about them, because what if—what if I say them out loud and they come true and that proves that I'm a bad person and it's all my fault?"

"I see your problem."

Maisie stopped shaking. "You do?"

"Damned if you do, damned if you don't."

"That's a very bad word, Lilah. You shouldn't use it. Awful things could happen, and—"

"*Damned?* It's just a word. Words can't hurt you."

"Kat—" Maisie covered her mouth.

"It's okay to use her name, sweetie."

Maisie shook her head again; outside, car doors slammed.

"Is it frightening, having a voice?"

"I can't talk about it. My fear thermometer is very high right now."

Fear thermometer? That must be something Katie had taught her. Clearly Katie and Maisie had been spending time together. Clearly Callum had not shared that fact, either.

"*Ohhh,*" Lilah said as heartburn cramped in her chest and throat.

"Is something wrong with the baby? Do you need me to call Daddy?" Maisie tugged on the hem of her T-shirt.

"Not on my account." Lilah patted her chest. "Heartburn. Best-kept secret in pregnancy."

"Would you like me to tell you where Daddy keeps his Zantac?"

"I'm not big on taking meds, especially not"—Lilah blew out a long, slow breath—"while pregnant. Hey, stop looking at me as if I've sprouted three heads."

"Four. Can you make it four?"

"If you'll smile for me."

"Promise me you're okay."

"Sweetie, I'm fine. I'm way tougher than I look. Despite my four heads."

"Promise me again. If anything happens to you, I'll, I'll—"

"Hey, stop before you hyperventilate." Lilah held up the Phish Food. "I think you're suffering from a severe case of empty tummy. Ice cream is the cure. Eat up."

Maisie threw herself back down on her pillows. "I'm so angry, it hurts, and I want to go back to before this *ever* happened. I want it to be before."

"Me too, sweetie." Lilah stroked Maisie's hair. "But that's not possible, so we need a new train of thought."

"Why did this happen? Why did any of it have to happen?"

"Because adults have lived longer than kids, which gives us more chances to screw up."

"What am I supposed to think about Katie? What if I'm like her, and what if—"

"Forget she's your mom for a moment. What did you think about Katie Mack when you met her?"

"That she was super awesome. And when she told me about her voice, I was happy because it was a secret we shared. But that was before I knew who she really is *and* that she'd worried about doing wicked things to me."

"I did some homework on this voice. Got to love Google." Lilah smiled. "One thing I've learned already is that OCD focuses on whatever frightens you most. For a new mom, that would be someone harming her baby."

"And she did have a funny turn when we met."

"There you go. Additional evidence. Imagine how she must have felt seeing you again."

"You're not acting like Evil Stepmom." Maisie paused. "Are you going to leave me, too?"

"Never. You're stuck with me and your brother or sister for the rest of your life. I love cold, hard facts, don't you?" Lilah spooned out more ice cream, which had softened quickly in the heat of Maisie's room.

"Do you feel as if you got smashed apart and put back together all upside down and inside out?" Maisie said.

"Unfortunately, yes. And I'm pretty sure my heart's stitched to the outside of my body."

"Does that mean you don't love my dad anymore?"

"Love isn't that fickle, sweetie. Right now my anger's sucking up everything inside me. The love I have for your father is hiding behind it, but that's okay. Today I need to be mad at him, and I'll figure out everything else tomorrow."

"Daddy taught me to tell the truth. He told me that as long as I was honest with him, he could never be mad at me. And then he lied about everything." Maisie heaved out a sigh.

"Tell me what you need, Maisie, and I'll follow your lead."

"I can't be part of the docent program."

Lilah waved it away. "Consider it gone. First thing tomorrow I'll call the director and say we have a family emergency."

"Thank you."

The landline rang, and the answering machine kicked in. "I need to know you're both okay." Callum's voice filled the house. "Please, Lilah. I love you. Let me come home."

"It's your call, Maisie. Are you ready to talk to your dad?"

Maisie threw herself into Lilah's arms and sobbed as the remainder of the ice cream melted into the carpet.

TWENTY-THREE
JAKE

Delaney pushed past him the moment he opened the door to Studio C, one of the three buildings that housed Kids on Film. She'd refused to meet him anywhere with a bed, and Studio C was empty except for a stack of chairs. Since his short-term goal was shit-faced oblivion, tonight he'd likely be sleeping in Studio B, the old shed that now housed the props. Or maybe he could curl up in a corner of the boys' changing room in Studio A. One of the many pluses of being single: no one cared where you crashed.

"No problems finding this place, then?" He shut the door but not fast enough. A blue-tailed skink shot in and headed for the bathroom. Great. He'd have to catch that sucker and relocate it before he left. Why was he thinking about lizards? He turned. *Oh, yeah.*

The bottle of moonshine, full minus one swig, was serving its purpose as a prop. Keeping his right hand occupied while it was itching to pull her close. But his eyes found their target: Delaney's breasts, once a favorite place to lay his head. He had told himself he wouldn't look anywhere but at her face, the same way he told himself "This is the last time" whenever he sent a text that read *Maisie Emergency.*

"I know where you live, work, and play," she said. "How else do you think I've stayed out of your comfort zones for the last three years? You've been drinking?"

"What was your first clue?" He raised his eyes along with the bottle of moonshine.

Delaney was staring at the green screen. "Curious choice for a wall, bilious green."

"It's a color no one wears, which makes it ideal for filming."

"Is that a fact? Learn something every day."

She turned, and he stumbled backward until he was resting against the support beam in the middle of the space. Then he slid to the floor, bent his legs, and draped his arms across his knees. Created his very own island.

"So, it finally happened," she said. "The thing we both dreaded. Katie won't get out of bed. I had to let myself into her apartment."

"Callum won't answer his phone." He swallowed. "I wasn't sure you'd answer yours."

Delaney sat next to him, then shuffled aside until a respectable six inches fell between them. "I nearly didn't, but you never used our code unless there was a real Maisie emergency. The sex was always a bonus."

"Remind me again why we broke up."

"There wasn't anything to break up, Jake. We couldn't be alone without ripping off each other's clothes."

She crossed her legs and pulled at the frayed hem of her scarlet jeans. Did they have to be skintight?

"I hate to point out the obvious, but—"

"I'm spoken for."

"That doesn't normally stop me," he lied.

"Liar, liar, pants on fire." She took a deep breath and sat up straight. The chitchat was over. That was one of the many things he loved about Delaney. She always got to the point. Although mostly they were naked when she did.

"How the hell did Maisie find out? My sister won't say anything except 'She knows.'"

"Lilah Rose is one wily woman. She kept digging until she found the suicide letter."

"Please tell me Maisie didn't read it. Please."

"No, thank God." The skink fled from one side of the studio to the other. "Katie isn't suicidal again, is she?"

"I'm hoping not, but Patrick's my backup plan. He's watching over her until I return. And before you ask, yes, he knows where I am. And who I'm with."

Jake offered her the moonshine.

She shook her head. "We both know what happens when you and I mix with hard liquor, and I can't stay long. I just needed to put eyes on you, make sure you weren't doing anything stupid."

"No, ma'am." He placed the bottle on the floor, pushed it away, and told her everything.

When he was done, he hung his head. "I want to punch through drywall, hit something solid. It's been years since I've felt this outta control."

"Is this worse than when Maisie stopped sleeping through the night and you wanted to throttle her?"

He nodded.

"Worse than when she broke her arm and you felt responsible?"

He nodded again.

"Worse than when I told you we were done?"

"That one was earned. I have, as you so kindly pointed out, commitment issues. But this? I can't even articulate the fear swallowing my sorry ass right now."

A sinister thought slithered into play: Had he lost Maisie? Ten years ago he would have sworn on his parents' grave that kids weren't part of his future and neither was the picket fence. Maisie had changed that. Well, not the picket fence part. Owning the business was bad enough.

The idea of not being tied down, of being able to pick up and leave anytime he wanted, had always anchored him. But being needed was a powerful drug. Delaney had never needed him, but Callum did. And until today, so had Maisie.

"I guess you finally understand what Katie and I went through. Pretty sad this had to happen first." She stood, he didn't. "I have to get back to my sister. Jake, you can and will hold it together. That's what you do best, and it's what Maisie will always need from you. We both know Callum's too fragile in a crisis."

"I'm sorry," he said. "For my part in—"

"Well, bless your heart, darlin'. I know that." She grinned down at him.

"I shouldn't have asked you to come, but I'm sure glad you did. Thank you."

"Let's not make a habit of it, okay?"

She walked toward the door, then stopped. "Remember that night you snuck me into the house when Callum was out of town, and Maisie woke up screaming? She wasn't calling for her dad. She was calling for you."

Then she left, and Jake pulled out his phone to try Callum again. Weird, the things a mind could remember. Like how Delaney never, ever said goodbye.

TWENTY-FOUR
CALLUM

One by one, lights turned on in his leafy neighborhood, and a herd of deer slid silently between gardens. In his mind, Callum was not sitting in his car, spying on his family: he was walking into his house; he was kissing his wife; he was hugging his daughter; he was saying, "I love you both. Tell me about your day."

Tell me about your day.

You failed us.

The car doors were locked, but noises of the night tapped for entry. Bugs dive-bombed his windshield. *Splat.* Frogs, crickets, probably even a few rabid bats were out in force. Temperatures had cooled somewhat with the beginning of September, but not substantially. Could he suffocate if he didn't crack open a window? Would it matter if he did?

The persistent ache in his lower back ramped up to actual pain, and hunger became nausea. His hands were clammy; his T-shirt had sweated into his skin. An owl hooted, fell silent, hooted again, and one of the neighborhood dogs barked. He pictured Ringo. That poor creature used to shake if anyone but Katelyn came close. Once, Ringo had lashed out with a warning bite that shocked both of them—man and dog.

Callum never told Katelyn. He hadn't respected the dog's boundaries; the mistake had been his.

The mistake is always mine. I'm pathetic. A second-rate father, a worthless husband, a deplorable human being. Maisie would be better off if I did suffocate and Lilah raised her without me.

Another text popped up on his phone. A variation on a theme.

I'm going to keep bugging you until you tell me where you are, Jake had texted.

Raleigh. I'll call you in the morning. I'm fine.

Like hell you are.

Night.

Then he muted his phone and tossed it onto the passenger seat.

Were the raccoons on the back deck, foraging through his recycling bins, dragging empty yogurt containers down into the creek? Last week he'd found tiny paw prints on the outside of the sliding glass doors, as if the raccoons had been begging to come inside. Maybe tonight they'd come and sniff around him. Chances were high he smelled of human garbage.

In the house that used to be his, Lilah lowered the blinds, starting with those in Maisie's bedroom. Finally his girls had joined the same team, but he wasn't even benched. He'd been evicted from the stadium.

Twiddling his wedding ring, Callum replayed the scene in the living room. How could Maisie use that word to describe herself? *Faulty?* She was strong, confident, and adventurous. Could swing a baseball bat as well as any boy—he'd made sure of that. She was 'Mazing Maisie, the little girl who stood up to bullies. The child who would never be a victim.

And Katelyn had ripped it away. Callum tugged on the back of his neck. No, *he* had ripped it away. He could be mad at Katelyn for moving back to the Triangle; he could be mad at Lilah for kicking him out. But there was no one to blame for today's events other than himself. If he needed additional proof of being a lousy father, Maisie had snuck out of the house in broad daylight, and he didn't even hear the stairs creak. Suppose she hadn't had the phone Jake insisted she carry at all times? Suppose she hadn't called Katelyn?

A van pulled into his driveway, and the porch light came on. Lilah opened the door and smiled at the pizza delivery kid. Then the door closed and she was gone. Did she not see his car, or had he already become invisible?

Evening wore on; lights turned off. Callum relieved himself in the forest, not caring if the neighbors saw him marking out territory like a tomcat. He returned to his station wagon. A sensible car, a family car. The car a good father would drive. Not a father who'd been banished.

Callum closed his eyes and remembered.

∗

He's happy.

The flight landed twenty minutes early. There was no traffic; he's home to his girls. And he's made a decision. He's going to cancel classes and take time off to help Katelyn. Maybe she's on the wrong antidepressant. Maybe she needs a different psychologist. Maybe he needs to go with her; maybe tonight they'll make love. It's been months.

Studying up on PTSD was harder than he'd imagined, but he wanted to understand her diagnosis. What he discovered was a revelation. Information that could help both of them. Never before had he considered she wasn't the only one still running from her childhood. He's pumped, he's primed. He's no longer afraid. They're going to pick their lives apart to put them back together. Together. They're going to tackle this together. Unlike Katelyn, he's not religious, but he's been thinking about Ecclesiastes. There is a time for everything.

It's time. Time to tell her what happened to him.

He puts the key in the lock and opens the front door. The words "Darling, I'm home!" die in his throat. The house is too dark, too hot, too quiet. His shoes are too loud on the hall floor. Tensing, he puts down his bags, turns on the hall light. The living room is empty. His heart pumps a one-word beat: danger. *Maisie screams. Breathing hard, he runs. Two stairs at a time.*

There she is in her crib! Safe. He reaches for Maisie. Holds her, rocks her, protects her. She smells of baby powder and everything he finally got right. She will giggle through her childhood. She will never know the darkness.

He fiddles with the Winnie-the-Pooh lamp—clearly the bulb is going—smiles, and turns.

Why is his wife huddled on the floor with the dog? Why didn't she pick up the baby? Why is she crying? Hair greasy and matted, clothes loose and dirty, huge bags under her eyes, Katelyn looks half-wild.

He pulls Maisie closer. Katelyn rants about setting the house on fire. Instinct tightens like a trip wire. Has to get away from the dog he can't trust, away from the woman who is threatening to burn down his house, burn his family alive. There is danger here. Danger for Maisie. Danger for him.

The devil breathes, "You're mine."

✳

Callum jolted awake, heart racing, clothes damp from sweat, and cracked his knee on the steering wheel. He was safe; he was inside his car. And Lilah was standing outside, knocking on the window, wearing one of his T-shirts and a deep scowl. She leaned against the door, preventing him from opening it.

He turned on the ignition and lowered the window.

"You've been here all night?" She handed him the paper, as she did every morning.

"Yes." He scrubbed his hands over his face. "I didn't like the idea of the two of you here alone."

"We weren't alone. We had each other."

"Please, let me come in. I need to talk to Maisie. I need to explain to you both."

"No, you don't. Maisie doesn't want to listen, and neither do I. Stew in your own juices for a while. I'm keeping her home from school today so we can meet Ian for lunch and then hit the mall for serious retail therapy. On your credit card."

"But you can't—"

"Can't what? Take her shopping, take her to see my psychologist friend, or be the only parent who hasn't let her down? And shouldn't you be prepping for class?"

"I handed it off to my TA." He swallowed the dry fuzz in his mouth and reached for the door handle. "If you move, I can get out and explain this to you face-to-face."

"We are face-to-face, and I'm not moving. I do have a question for you, though: Is our marriage legal?"

"Of course it is. Katelyn and I are divorced. What do you take me for?"

"A stranger who lied to me. So think carefully before you answer this: Do you still love her?"

"No."

Back in the forest, a hawk cried and another hawk answered. A pair of hawks. Mates. The new neighbor from the end of the block walked by with her sandy-colored Labradoodle and called out, "Morning!" Lilah waved.

Callum watched the woman and her dog disappear. "Did I love Katelyn? Yes. She's the mother of my child. *Was* the mother of my child. *Was.* But the crack that opened up between us after Maisie's birth kept widening until she ran away. And yes, when she resurfaced in a mental hospital after a year and a half, I left her to her sister and hired a lawyer. He warned me she could return at any time and demand full custody or snatch Maisie. He suggested I go after her parental rights, and I listened because I was terrified."

Grabbing the sides of his head, he collapsed into his seat, forgetting he'd tilted it back.

"Let me get this right. Your first wife had a breakdown, and your response was to strip her of motherhood?" Lilah was far too composed.

He jerked back up.

"The night she ran away, she was someone I'd never seen before. Half-wild, half-mad." He shook away the remnants of the nightmare. "I didn't want to believe the woman I loved was capable of the stuff she told me, but the facts? You want facts? Both her parents were crazy. Her mother stabbed her father in front of Katelyn when she was a child. A child. And then he vanished. Abandoned his family. What was I supposed to think when she talked about burning our house down, ran away, and didn't contact us again until she sent Maisie a suicide letter nearly two years later? Life is about tough choices. Did I put my daughter's well-being first? Absolutely, and so did Katelyn.

"She didn't contest the terms of the divorce, because she knew they were in Maisie's best interests. And we agreed that when Maisie was old enough to ask, I would tell her Katelyn was dead. What was the alternative? To tell Maisie that her mother had threatened to kill her and attempted suicide?"

"From the letter it didn't sound as if she'd threatened anyone."

"You're taking her side?"

"Callum, I'm about to have our baby, and what does this tell me? That if I get postpartum depression, you'll dump me and trade up for a newer model?"

"That's ridiculous."

"Go back to Jake's."

"No—" He reached through the window and grabbed her arm.

"Take your hands off me or I will scream."

He let go, and, rubbing the small of her back, she waddled toward their house, disappeared inside, and closed the front door.

Callum turned the key in the ignition. He would park out of sight, and the moment Lilah and Maisie left for lunch, go home to shower and pack a bag. Then check into the nearest motel and figure out how to win his family back.

This time he was not going to be passive; this time he was not going to accept defeat.

This time he was going to fight.

TWENTY-FIVE
KATIE

Wrapped in sweat-stained sheets, Katie opened her eyes and stared at nothing.

Despair creeps, crawls, slithers. It starts out small, a nugget you can't quite define in the pit of your stomach. Slowly, steadily, it rises until it settles in your face, in your jaw. In the way it solders your teeth together. In the way it steals your appetite, your oxygen, your hope, and finally time itself.

What day was it, Wednesday? Morning or afternoon? The light across the cracked photo on her nightstand told Katie it was daytime, but there was no sun. Her world had shrunk to this room, to this bed, to the faded baby picture that was her only possession worth an emotional dime.

She should have died that night on the overpass. It would've been better for Maisie. Saved her from the biggest trigger of all: abandonment. *What if Maisie didn't have OCD before, but does now, thanks to me? What if I don't love her? How can I, after all I've done?*

The searing pain above her right eye had flatlined into the dull residue of a migraine. Her stomach was hollowed out, scraped clean, but her mind kept churning. A mental ticker tape spat out images of her daughter's bedroom as she'd last seen it: the red metal crib, the mural of the cow jumping over the moon, the Winnie-the-Pooh lamp.

Grief the first time around had almost killed her. Only working alongside Ben had lugged her back into the world of maybe-I-give-a-damn. But how could anyone survive losing the same child twice?

Katie scratched a bug bite on her leg. A mosquito must have come in during the night. She pulled her hand away. Blood. There was blood under her fingernail.

What if it's Maisie's? What if I stabbed her and didn't realize? What if it's not Maisie's blood? What if I hurt someone on the drive back from the house, a drive I barely remember? What if the police are on the way to arrest me?

If she huddled here, alone, if she didn't go out, if she reverted to her "stay in the tent" philosophy, she couldn't hurt anyone. The experts told you avoidance was bad, very bad, but they never sat on the other side of therapy. They didn't know how it felt to open your veins and say, "This is the color of my blood; watch me bleed." They didn't know how hard you had to cling to the dream of recovery. How many times you had to gaze up at Mount Everest and think, *I have to climb that without oxygen, in a blizzard, and I'm terrified of everything that stands between me and the summit.* Because it came back. That's what they didn't tell you. The monster always came back.

Her phone rang. Ignoring it, she pulled the damp sheet and blanket over her head. The phone rang again, stopped. Rang again.

Singing. Muffled singing. Was she hallucinating? She lowered her bedclothes and listened.

"Katie, you are my sunshine," a chorus sang down in the street.

Dragging herself out of bed, she forced up the lower half of her window, one of the few in the apartment that opened. Ben and Delaney were below, and so were Trent and a few others from the studio. Delaney had her phone in her right hand, and her left arm was looped through

Ben's. He stood still, staring up with a slight frown. He didn't get it, but why should he? She'd let him in only to slam the door in his face.

Why couldn't Delaney leave her alone? Wasn't the oath sworn on their mother's Bible enough to convince her sister she wasn't suicidal? The gray sky was impossibly low; the clouds impossibly heavy. A storm was coming. She could smell it—sharp and slightly sweet.

"Rapunzel, Rapunzel," Trent called up, "let down your hair before we get swept away in a gully washer." He glanced at Delaney. "Heard that one in the barbershop. Gully washer. Isn't it wild? I *luuuv* me some good Southernisms."

Katie tugged up a few greasy strands. "I chopped off my locks after I graduated from a mental hospital. Why are you guys here?"

"For an intervention of love," Delaney said. "Plus we both know it ends badly when you isolate, Sis. Hell is for sharing."

"I'm not in the mood for company. Certainly not in a pair of boxer shorts and a camisole." Katie glanced at the clouds. "And you guys are going to get soaked in about five minutes."

"Yup. Flash flood warning until three o'clock," Delaney said. "You'd better let us up before we drown."

Another surge of grief sucked her down. "Please, guys, leave me alone."

"No can do, babe." Trent smiled like a mischievous elf in a too-small T-shirt. "You once said I could come to you anytime I need help. And I do! I think I might be, you know, gay." He giggled. Delaney joined in; Ben didn't.

"We've each pledged to tell you one thing that we love about you," Delaney continued. "And if you let us in, we won't have to do it out here and risk being either swept away in a raging torrent or arrested for causing a public nuisance."

"Or both," Trent said. "And I'm only on lunch break for another thirty minutes, which means I could get fired if you make us wait much longer."

"See?" Delaney said. "In addition to forcing us to risk life and limb during a weather advisory, you're wasting our precious working hours."

"Fine, I'll unlock the door."

She closed the window, grabbed her thrift store cardigan—the closest thing she had to a robe—and walked to the door. What followed was a receiving line of hugs and casseroles, as if she were presiding over her own funeral. Maybe, Katie thought as Ben came in last, she was.

Outside, it began to hail.

*

After everyone had left, Ben hovered in the kitchen. The microwave door slammed, and the apartment filled with warm, buttery smells. Corn kernels popped as rain bombarded the window. A flash of lightning lit up the living room, and thunder cracked overhead.

Ben appeared with a large bowl of popcorn and a bag from the Apple Store.

"Don't you have somewhere you need to be?"

"Yes. Here." He put the bowl down on the coffee table, slid off his work shoes, and stretched out on the futon.

"Are you angry?"

"No."

"Disappointed?"

"I'm concerned, but that's my problem." He opened the bag and held up a box. "Think of this as an early birthday present. I remembered you and Delaney talking about problems streaming movies on your laptop, and Delaney told me *Love Actually* is your favorite movie." He put the box down next to the popcorn and pulled a DVD case from the bag.

"Ben, I can't accept that. It's too much."

"It's a portable USB SuperDrive and one movie. It didn't exactly break the bank. If it makes you feel better, it can be a belated graduation gift for my favorite intern."

"I don't have the energy to fight."

"Good. Then I'll pretend you thanked me."

"Thank you," she whispered.

A truck rattled up the street; a car honked. Rain splashed the ordinary world full of ordinary minds cluttered with mundane trivia such as what to cook for dinner. Minds not worrying about how to drive down the street without running people over like bowling pins.

"The OCD's winning," she said. "I can't leave the apartment."

"Did you call your new therapist?"

She shook her head.

"Why?"

"Because I don't have one."

"Damnit, you told me you would deal with this." He put the DVD case down and raked his hands through his hair. "Katie, you need help."

"How? How do I get help when I have no money and a four-thousand-dollar deductible?" She waited for Ben to object, to get up and leave. "Sorry, sorry, I don't mean to snap, but none of the therapists in my network specialize in OCD. And besides, once I've met the deductible, I still have to pay fifteen percent, and sometimes insurance barely covers enough visits to make it worthwhile. Therapy takes time and work, Ben. Why start out with a new person who knows less than I do? By the time I've brought him or her up to speed, we'll be out of appointments." She looked down at her bare feet. Nail polish was the only nonessential left to cut. She glanced up. "I've been doing okay on my own. Keeping up with the techniques."

"You haven't left your apartment in days. Whatever you're doing isn't working."

Crossing her arms, she hugged her shoulders. "Ben?"

"Yes?"

"I don't want to talk."

He tried to smile. "What do you need? Tell me, and I'll do it."

"A hug, but I haven't showered in a while."

He moved over to create a gap and opened his arms to her. "Come here, you."

She didn't hesitate. This was all she wanted: her favorite movie and her favorite person. *What do I need? You, Ben. You.* Such a simple thought, but one she couldn't keep, because her mind would twist it into torment. Curling up tightly, she grabbed fistfuls of his T-shirt and inhaled his energy, his calm, the scent of his Moroccan oil shampoo.

"Thank you." She rose and fell to the tempo of his breath. "Thank you for not asking anything of me."

TWENTY-SIX

CALLUM

Right hand supporting the weight of his head, Callum sat on the polyester bedspread used by strangers doing God only knew what, and watched Jake. Before Lilah, Callum had often caught himself wishing he could be more like his friend, who lived in the moment and took what he wanted. Except at the end of the day, Jake lived alone in a rented cottage. Callum sighed. At the end of the day, *he* lived alone in a rented motel room.

"I can't believe it's been three days."

"I can't believe I ate all your hush puppies." Jake belched. "I haven't eaten that much since sixth grade."

"How can you stay so positive?"

Jake tossed his plastic fork onto what remained of his pulled pork, mac 'n' cheese, and fried okra, and tried to push his take-out container across the table. It caught on the peeling fake-wood laminate.

"Binge eating has nothing to do with staying positive." Jake glanced out of the window covered in streaks and splatters left from the dinnertime monsoon. "Since the frog strangler seems to have passed, I vote for an emergency run to the nearest ABC store. Tequila should not only hit but eradicate the spot. Or I could be talked into moonshine."

Callum shook his head. "I need to stay sober in case Lilah calls and says come over."

"Not gonna happen, man. Too close to Maisie's bedtime."

"Thanks for the reminder." Callum picked up his phone, typed a quick good-night text, and added a row of silly emojis. Maisie loved emojis.

"No answer?" Jake said after a few minutes.

"You think she'll ever forgive me?" Callum tossed the phone aside.

"*Us*, and damn right she will. Our Maisie doesn't have a mean bone in her body, but you've always been the rule setter with high standards. Now she gets to relearn you as flawed. Welcome to the human race, Dad."

"If that's supposed to make me feel better, it isn't working."

The air-conditioning unit rattled like a clunky old jet trying to barrel down the runway.

"Can we hold this pity party in a Marriott Courtyard?" Jake said. "That roach I saw scuttle under your bed was bigger than a baby possum."

"A flea pit suits my mood." Callum got up and walked to the window, avoiding the wet patch under that noisy air conditioner. The room was beginning to stink of damp carpet. If he could be bothered, he would complain. In the parking lot, covered in puddles and lit by harsh overhead lights, a couple hurled accusations with jabbing fingers. Maybe they had kids; maybe they, too, were trying to decide who was the worse parent. He turned back to Jake.

"Every day since Katelyn left, I've worried something bad could happen to Maisie."

"I think it just did," Jake said.

"But I never imagined I'd be the cause. I worried about classroom bullies, accidents on field trips, Katelyn grabbing her and disappearing." Callum walked the two strides it took to get back to the bed and threw himself, facedown, on the bedspread. To hell with strangers' stains.

"Why didn't I move across the country? Why did I stay in Raleigh with a target painted on my back?"

"That would be my fault since I encouraged you to stay close to the grandparents."

"Christ. What am I going to tell Mom and Dad? Guess what, I failed at marriage a second time, and this one didn't make the six-month mark?" Callum rolled onto his back and stared up at the ceiling tiles. One of them was cracked.

"Blame me. Your mama's opinion of me never recovered after I taught Maisie to burp the alphabet."

Callum turned his head and smiled. "And encouraged her to show off her newly acquired skill at my parents' Hogmanay festivities."

"That was classic, man." Jake cleared up their dinner, grinning as he dealt with the aftermath of one man's inability to cope with his own life. Again. "But you're missing the obvious as you stare into that glass half-empty. If you guys had moved, you'd never have met Lilah Rose."

"Who hates me."

"*Hate*'s a bit strong. She'll come around once she accepts that you were putting Maisie first. As she is now. As Katelyn would have done if roles were reversed."

"Admit it, I'm screwed. Lilah solves problems as effectively as the Enigma machine cracked the German code."

"You talking about that movie, *The Imitation Game*?"

"World War Two history, not Hollywood." Callum sighed. Again. "Sorry, didn't mean to be snide. My point is, when she hits a wall, Lilah won't stop until she's figured out how to tunnel underneath or climb over the top. She's never going to forgive me. And Katelyn would never have done what we did. She takes in strays, remember? The more broken, the better."

"Her boyfriend isn't exactly broken. Although he did threaten me."

"She has a boyfriend?"

"You skimmed right over that part about him threatening me. And he's, like, six foot six with serious muscles. Younger too. Guess you both—"

"Enough, okay? Christ. How did things get so screwed up? How did I become such a contemptible parent?"

"Whoa, stop acting like you're one fry short of a Happy Meal. You, Mr. A-Plus Dad, have raised an exceptional human being."

"Who, according to all of you, is intensely anxious."

"Not because of bad parenting."

"I doubt bad parenting has helped." Callum pulled off his glasses and pinched the bridge of his nose. "If you could go back, change things, would you?"

"Hell, no." Jake picked at his teeth. "For years your friendship was all I had. I'm never gonna forget the debt I owe you, and why on God's holy earth would I regret being part of Maisie's life? If either of us had acted differently, I'd be the godfather who mails birthday cards with crisp twenties shoved inside, and Maisie would be asking why some guy called Jake was sending her money."

A crack rang out in the parking lot. A car backfiring, a shot?

Callum bolted upright. Specks of light burst in front of his eyes. He started to shake, shake as if some giant had snatched him by the ankle and swung him upside down. Pumped him upside down. Up and down, up and down, up and down.

Stop, stop, stop!

He tugged his T-shirt over his head. Had to crawl inside himself. Had to hide. Couldn't. Couldn't ever hide. His heart boomed like fists on a drum. Forget the drumsticks, forget pace, forget melody. Fists. Nothing but fists. Pain squeezed his chest. He was dying. Dying without holding his baby, without kissing Maisie and Lilah one last time. Dying in a cheap motel room.

Mouth dry, he gasped for air and the devil laughed.

Throat clamped shut. Couldn't get oxygen.

In the distance, Jake's voice. "You know the drill. Breathe with me."

He gulped. A clog of air hit his lungs. Gulped again, and again. Started breathing.

The mattress sank and an arm rested across his shoulders. Pushed down with an even weight. "That's it. Release the T-shirt and breathe with me—in, out. That's it. In and out. Slow everything down and listen to me. You're having another panic attack. Feels like shit, I know, but you're not dying and no one's hurting you. You gonna throw up this time? Need me to fetch the garbage can?"

Callum shook his head and kept breathing, kept finding the oxygen, kept telling himself he was not dying. He blew out one long breath, and then another, and another. Gradually the world slowed down.

Jake squeezed his shoulder and then disappeared. Water ran in the bathroom, and Jake returned. "Drink this."

Callum emptied the plastic cup and handed it back, but the world remained off-kilter, and his eyes watered. Blinking, he grappled for his glasses.

"That the first one you've had in a while?" Jake said.

Callum shook his head slowly. Pain had moved up from his chest to lodge in his temples.

"Didn't think so. It doesn't have to be this hard, man. You can get help."

"It's not something I can talk about, even with a shrink."

"I know, I—damn, that's it! I could leap around like a June bug at a porch light." Jake grabbed the only chair in the room, flipped it round, and straddled it. "Lilah Rose thinks you mistreated your first wife. Prove her wrong by joining forces with Katelyn."

"And Lilah will assume we want our child back so we can play happy family in the burbs. I was her teacher, for God's sake. I understand how her brain works."

"Legally she can't keep you from Maisie. And if you and Katelyn are acting sane and unified, how can Lilah Rose turn you down?"

"You think Katelyn will agree to be in a room with me at this point?"

Jake yanked his phone from his back jeans pocket and held it out. "Call her. She'll pick up 'cause she'll think it's me. Tell her you guys need to talk, and if it would make her feel better, she can bring the hunk."

"You want me to do this with an audience?"

Jake gave his trademark smile. "Everything's better with an audience. Besides, this keeps it from becoming a he said, she said situation if things turn ugly and end up in court."

Callum stood. "I am not dragging my daughter through a legal battle."

"Good. Keep that righteous indignation. Now act on it and broker a peace treaty."

"And how, exactly, do I do that?"

"Tell Katelyn everything." Jake swept his tongue over his front teeth, sucked, and swallowed. "Marginally edited version of everything."

TWENTY-SEVEN

KATIE

Why choose Chapel Hill for a meeting? Was Cal nostalgic for their undergrad days, or avoiding chance encounters with friends and colleagues? Confrontations were out of character, but so was being late. And so was asking her to meet him at the UNC botanical gardens.

In the trees on the edge of the parking lot, fall was making an early appearance with the occasional red leaf. The voice insinuated that winter, a season she dreaded, was a breath away; handed her another blank check of fear for things yet to come. This, not happiness, was her natural state of being. Happiness had never been more than a collage of treasured moments: a husband's kiss, the sweet-and-sour smell of a baby's bedroom, the softness of a child's cheek, the first redbud blossom in the forest behind her old house.

Under the watch of an intense September sky, a tufted titmouse hopped through a puddle. Would Cal find a parking space? The beautiful Friday weather had brought Chapel Hillians out in droves and filled the lot with every color of Prius on the market.

The heaviness crept back in. Yes, she was out of bed and functioning, but only because Ben refused to give up on her, and compliance was less exhausting than resistance. After raving about the steel-and-concrete oak leaf arch by the side of the parking lot, he had disappeared toward the arboretum in search of inspiration. Ben was now her crutch. Correction, she had let him become her crutch. Let the OCD demand his constant reassurance, which he provided since he was a decent guy. If you wanted to take OCD on a date, you should pick an asshole.

Thoughts spun in a whirligig of dysfunction. The sun, a blistering fireball, hung in the middle of the sky; the light was bright, harsh, unforgiving. Her brain filled with gray fog.

I can't do this anymore. Why am I even here? Why do I think I can still help Maisie? I should text Ben, ask him to drive me home.

Leaning back against Ben's truck, Katie closed her eyes and gave in to her thoughts.

A car pulled out of the space next to her; another one pulled in. The sun warmed her face as a door slammed. His shadow fell over her. She'd always felt Cal before she'd seen him.

"Hey," he said.

For a moment she saw only his outline while memory shaded in the details. She almost smiled, remembering the *Hot Dudes* coloring book Delaney had given her one Christmas. Cal and Jake had always been a stunning pair, generating glances and whispers. Some women were drawn to Cal's pale Celtic beauty; others couldn't resist the hint of darkness that Jake carried so effortlessly.

She snuck a glance at Cal's car. A Volvo wagon with no dents and no bumper stickers. A family car. He probably drove it through the car wash once a week.

"Hey, yourself," she said, and used her bottom to push off the truck.

He gave a hesitant smile, and for a long, empty moment they watched each other. Abandoning her baby would always eclipse a lifetime of bad decisions, but standing an arm's length away was proof that she had also run from the man she loved. Katie shoved her hands deep inside her pockets and put on her outside face, the one she showed to the world. "How's Maisie?"

"I don't know. She won't talk to me, and I'm living in a motel. Lilah kicked me out."

"Sorry to hear that." Katie squinted at him in the bright sunlight. Behind his glasses, his eyes were red and watery; his hair looked unbrushed and unwashed. His body was slightly rank. "So it was Lilah, not you, who pulled Maisie from the docent program?"

Cal frowned at her.

"You didn't know?"

He shook his head. "Would you mind if we followed one of the trails? I need fresh air and exercise."

"I'm not sure eighty-five degrees counts as fresh, but sure. Why not?" A mosquito landed on the back of her arm. She swatted and missed. The OCD warned her about tainted blood and disease; Katie didn't counter.

Cal slipped back into his car and retrieved a can of bug spray. "You need some?"

She nodded and held out her hand. He watched as she rubbed DEET onto her arms, her legs, and the back of her neck. Then he did the same, and it was her turn to watch him. Was his body also remembering what his mind longed to forget?

He tossed the can inside his car and grabbed a map and a baseball cap. She should have brought a cap, too, as protection against ticks dropping from low-hanging branches. Later she would ask Ben to check her scalp.

"Shall we?" he said, as he shoved on the cap.

They passed under the arch Ben had admired, and she paused to look up at the huge rusted leaves curled into an embrace. Cal consulted the map and took the lead. Without talking, they headed toward the wire gates, behind the back of the Education Center, and along the gravel path of the Streamside Trail. The forest rang with high-pitched squeals. A school group, no doubt. They passed a wooden information kiosk, crossed a meadow, and still Cal said nothing, which was fine. Her thoughts kept her busy enough.

What if I'd never run away? What if I'd come back? Would we still be together? Would Maisie be happy? What if she didn't have OCD until she met me? What if hearing her parents argue about me was the trigger?

The kids' voices faded and so did the rumble of traffic. A helicopter flew overhead and cicadas buzzed. Squirrels rustled through the undergrowth; pea gravel crunched under their footsteps. Cal stepped onto a small wooden bridge and paused to look into the water below, clear to the sandy bottom.

"I hate myself," he said.

"You get used to it."

He glanced at her and started walking again. His stride was long, his pace determined. Sweating hard, she struggled to keep up, but kept quiet. Katie understood the need to keep moving.

Passing a sign that warned them to watch their step, they entered deep shade and the sloping forest of hardwoods. The relief from the sun was short-lived as the path curved steeply over exposed tree roots and wooden steps built into the hillside. Katie slipped, and Cal grabbed her elbow.

"Are you okay?"

"Yeah." She brushed him off and kept her eyes lowered. "Should have paid more attention to the sign. I won't move away, you should know that's nonnegotiable. Even if Maisie never wants to see me again, she needs to know where I am. I'm done hiding."

"Katelyn, I wouldn't ask you to leave. I think we can both agree I've caused you enough pain. The only thing I want to do is make amends." He hesitated. "I might be the one who stayed, but I'm the one who's been running away."

Ten days ago she would have asked for an explanation, but her lifeboat was sinking fast enough without his baggage. "I have a silly question that's bugged me for years: What happened to my wedding dress?"

"I kept it for Maisie, but I learned about moth protection the hard way."

"And my books and the clothes Delaney didn't take?"

A hawk cried above them; the buzz of cicadas intensified.

"The PTA thrift store in Carrboro. I figured you'd approve."

The first Mrs. MacDonald had been packed away and recycled. At least she'd been donated to a good cause. "How did it go so wrong for us?"

Cal shoved his hands into his shorts' pockets. "I lost my footing in sleep deprivation and that ear infection that wouldn't quit."

"The pink antibiotic. What was it called?"

"Amoxicillin. Not a name I can easily forget," Cal said. "She had a lot of ear infections during those first three years."

A hiker came down the path and greeted them. He probably mistook them for a normal couple sharing a conversation about family life. Off to the right, the tail of a black snake disappeared into the undergrowth. They continued to climb, and Katie listened to her ragged breaths. He might be in prime physical shape, thanks to the religion of biking he presumably still practiced with Jake, but she wasn't. Up ahead, the path widened between two benches facing each other from concrete slabs.

"I need to sit," she said.

Cal joined her on the bench, but positioned himself as far away as possible.

"Want to put me out of my misery and tell me what this hike is really about?" she said.

He exhaled slowly, crossed his legs, and then placed his hands on his thigh. Folded one hand on top of the other as his fingers strummed in constant movement. "It's time you heard my side of the story. There are two different components, but . . . God, that sounded so clinical." His legs started jiggling a compulsive rhythm.

"Cal, why're you so anxious?"

"I need you to understand why I behaved the way I did, and this is fucking hard."

218

Cal never swore. Turning slightly, Katie watched the forest below. After nine years of waiting, she no longer wanted his explanation. Didn't want to make room for pity. Couldn't.

Shouts and giggles grew closer again. The school group must be on a lower trail. Were the children collecting leaves, identifying native ferns, hunting for salamanders under rocks? Hopefully the chaperones were watchful. Copperheads were out there, dozing in the midday heat, and if a kid should accidentally—she jerked up. Rustling surrounded them. Squirrels, please let it be squirrels, not venomous snakes, not while there were children on the trails.

"I want my family back," he said.

She didn't need to ask which one.

"And I'm hoping that we can reach a détente and present a united front to Lilah."

"I only want one thing, Cal. If you'll agree to take Maisie to a child psychologist who specializes in OCD, I'll stay away from both of you. For good. A bomb is waiting to detonate inside her brain, if it hasn't already. I'm not sure you get the urgency in all this."

"I'm trying to, Katelyn. But Lilah's shut me out."

A breeze rippled through the leaves.

"Was it bad for you," she said, "after I left?"

"I was devastated." He paused. "One year out, I was convinced you were dead. I couldn't imagine how you'd stayed away from Maisie for that long if you were alive. I wanted to grieve, but there was no closure. And I needed to protect Maisie. That was necessity, not choice."

"Getting Maisie help is also a necessity. You don't want her to keep hurting the way I do."

"You mean OCD doesn't go away?"

"It's a chronic illness. You learn to manage it, but it's always there, waiting to pounce when you're tired or overwhelmed." She looked at him. "It's flared up since our paths crossed."

"I'm sorry," he said.

"My OCD isn't your problem, but Maisie's is, and thanks to us, she's had a whopping trigger. So tell me what I need to know, and I'll promise not to freak out."

"I'm not going to hold you to that promise. You might want to slap me in a few minutes."

"In that case, bring it on."

He shot her a coy sideways smile that she remembered way too much. "Do you mind if we keep walking on the Oak Hickory Trail?" He pointed up to the crest of the hill.

"Please tell me it's not a ten-mile hike. I haven't so much as been on a treadmill in years."

Cal consulted his map. "We can take a connector route and cut back down to the creek. It wouldn't be as strenuous."

"Less strenuous gets my vote," she said.

Once again, they started walking. She nodded at an information sign. "Never knew we had flying squirrels. Did you?"

He shook his head.

"Are the local squirrels still digging up my old flower beds?"

"Yes, sorry. I gave up on the garden, and Lilah has no interest."

"My neglected garden," she said quietly. "Guess it'll never be finished."

They kept walking uphill through the forest, through the birdsong and the cicadas' buzz, and then down onto the connector trail. Without warning, the path flattened out, and they emerged in glaring sunlight. She blinked. Two long shadows led their way.

"Delaney was frantic after you left," he said. "When the police gave up looking, she persuaded me to hire a PI. He wasn't much help, either. Told us you'd gone off the grid."

"I know all this, Cal."

"Nothing for seventeen long months and then a suicide letter from a homeless shelter."

"I used the last of my panhandling coins to pay for the stamp."

He flinched. Had he never wondered what she'd done for money?

"My parents and Jake were at the house when the letter arrived. They were there for Maisie's second birthday."

She stopped; so did Cal. A partially submerged boulder rose out of the path ahead, threatening to block their way. Forest climbed sharply on one side; on the other, a steep slope disappeared toward the stream. Water trickled and ebbed. The sun beat down through every break in the canopy of green leaves.

"Silence for all that time. No word, no hope, but that letter proved you were alive. Or rather you had been a week earlier. Alive and four hours away. Mom agreed to stay with Maisie, so Jake and I drove to the mountains. I went to every ER with your photo, and we found you."

"You were in Asheville?" Her voice rose. "You saw me?"

"Not exactly. I knew you were being transported from the ER to the psych crisis unit. Instead of following, I called Delaney and told her where you were. And left."

"Without attempting to see me."

"I couldn't. You'd talked about killing our daughter, your mother stabbed your father. And I was—"

"I'm sorry. I can't do this, Cal. It's too painful." She started walking, following the tired descant of the stream, then stopped. "Was it real?" she said. "Was any of it real?"

"You know it was." Cal pulled alongside her. "I can't undo what happened after Maisie was born, but I can help you understand why I—"

"No, Cal. I'm going back to the parking lot."

"Katelyn, please. This is hard for me." He put a hand on her arm, and his eyes locked on hers. "Because of what happened when I was Maisie's age. When I was ten years old. And I've never spoken about it to anyone other than Jake."

A dog barked, leaves rustled, the creek gurgled. *Run, Katie. Run and don't stop.* But her legs wouldn't obey.

"I was raped."

She gasped. Unwanted images, sadistic images, crashed over her. "No." She waved her hands, kept waving them. "No." Her jaw was moving, but the scream refused to leave her mouth. Why couldn't she scream? "I can't have this in my head, Cal. Please, no." She screwed her eyes shut, squeezed hard, so hard. But the tears wouldn't stop. They rolled down her face, into her mouth. Her open mouth. She stumbled, he grabbed her. Helped her onto a bench.

"No, Cal, no."

He squatted in front of her, and she almost said, *Don't crouch, you'll get chiggers.*

"I'm sorry," he said.

She gulped for air. "Why are you apologizing?"

"Jake worked hard to teach me to say that phrase, *I was raped.* But I never realized how it would sound to someone who had loved me."

"No, you have nothing to be sorry for. You tell me this huge thing, and I—I fall apart. But I can see it, in my mind. And it's real. Oh, Cal. I'm so sorry. I'm so sorry." She rubbed her arms frantically. "Who? Who did it?"

"I was on a regional swim team."

She knew that; she knew that. "One of the older swimmers?"

"The coach."

She panted. "I'm a bit light-headed."

"It's the shock." He sat next to her. "You might want to put your head between your legs."

She slowed down her breath. "No. I've got this."

"Can you handle the rest?"

She nodded.

"The memories come back at weird times. The guilt. The disgust." He held his right palm in front of his face, and his fingers curled into a claw. "The shame."

Gently, she lowered his hand and held it in her lap. They were both shaking.

"It's the reason I lost it. That night, the night you left." His right foot started tapping the ground, and so did his left. He pulled his hand free, crumpled around the middle, and folded in half. She rubbed his back, her hand moving in ever-decreasing circles. Keeping his head down, he stayed motionless for several minutes and then slowly sat back upright.

"He threatened to set our house on fire if I ever told anyone. At night, while we were asleep." He swallowed. "He threatened my family, and I believed him—"

"Because you were a child and he was an adult you trusted."

"On the flight home from the conference"—he leaned against her—"I'd decided to tell you the truth. I'd been reading up about PTSD to help you, but I saw so much of myself, and I thought we could figure out everything together. How, I don't know, but I was hopeful. And then you talked about burning the house down, and I snapped. That's why I locked the door. Even now I don't know whether I was protecting me or Maisie, and it didn't matter. I could smell his breath, hear him whisper, 'You're mine.'" Cal slammed back against the bench. "During the attack, I had an out-of-body experience. Jake insists it was survival instinct, but I don't know. What if I secretly wanted it? What if I deserved it? Why didn't I fight back? Why didn't I tell my parents? Why me? Why? When the memories hit they're so—"

"Intrusive?"

"Yes. Intrusive. That's exactly the right word."

Like OCD, but worse. How could you out-reason reality?

"My mind goes in circles. Sometimes I feel as if the memories will kill me. Other times I feel utterly worthless." Cal took off his glasses, wiped the lenses on his T-shirt, slipped them back on. "I shut down after you left. Did what I had to do to look after Maisie and keep my job, but I was still glancing over my shoulder. My moods were unstable; I was easily provoked. Your sister and my mom assumed I was wired from lack of sleep. I started doing better and then your letter arrived,

and the nightmares and panic attacks returned. I saw danger everywhere. If Jake hadn't come with me, I would never have made the drive
to Asheville. I was falling apart, and all I could think about was what
would happen to Maisie with two unfit parents. Would she end up in
child protective services?"

He'd mentioned shame. They had both been defeated by shame.
Birds kept singing, and a woodpecker hammered into a tree. Her mind
showed her uncensored images of a beautiful boy trapped with a predator. The images played, and the sun continued to shine.

"Do you still think about suicide?" he said.

"I'm not sure I ever did. I wanted to come home, and I didn't know
how. I think that's why I wrote the letter and waited a week before going
to the overpass. But I was so screwed up back then. I guess we both
were." She stiffened. "Why? Do you think about suicide?"

"Heavens, no. I often feel as if I don't deserve to be alive, but I
would never take my own life. Now that you're back in Maisie's world,
however, I needed to ask the question. I'm sorry."

A man and a German shepherd walked past. "Afternoon!" he said.
They both ignored him.

"When you were pregnant," Cal said, "I was terrified. And I'm terrified now. The whole idea of therapy . . . I can't go there. I don't want
some stranger to say, 'You're not fit to be her dad.' Or to decide that
between us we've screwed up our daughter. Worse, call social services."

In a branch above, a pair of cardinals sang to each other. She looked
up through the leaves, through the dappled light. Turkey vultures circled, searching for a fresh kill. "Do you think there were other boys?"

"Definitely. He disappeared right after my assault. We were told it
was a family emergency, and the assistant coach took over. We never
saw him again."

Cal stood up and paced back and forth. "I'm wrecked. I need to walk."

She nodded and they started off downhill. The sounds of the kids
returned as they wove back down and came close to the road that led to

the UNC Hospitals. Sirens roared toward them and then disappeared. A fallen tree that should have blocked their path had been sliced perfectly with a chain saw.

"I'm sorry," he said, "that I didn't ask the right questions. That I wasn't strong enough to help you."

"I'm sorry that we weren't honest with each other."

At the top of the slope, against a vibrant backdrop of green and blue, black tree trunks stood out like iron bars in a prison cell.

"We both made poor decisions that night, but given the context, they make sense. And I know what you have to do next," she said.

"You do?" He didn't attempt to hide the eagerness in his voice. The eagerness to get his family back. His new family.

"Tell Lilah what you just told me."

"She's twenty-nine weeks pregnant with our son. She thinks I don't know our baby's sex, but I knew from the start. And knowing that I'll watch him grow up while remembering what happened to me? I had the same fears when you were pregnant, but this feels as if I'm watching myself in one of those distortion mirrors at a carnival."

"You have to see a therapist," she said.

"I can't."

"Not even if it's preventing you from helping our daughter? Healing's painful, but it gets you to the other side. Jake was smart to tell you to use the word I can't use right now. That was facing your monster. Now you have to take the next step and consult a professional. You have panic attacks, sleep issues . . . and some of what you're describing is catastrophizing. Cal, you're talking about anxiety."

"If you're about to suggest I have OCD, too, I can assure you I don't."

"Anxiety takes many forms—many. And trauma does weird things to the brain. Did you know dads and grandparents also get postpartum OCD? Anxiety's a strange beast."

They were back on flat ground, heading toward the parking lot.

"Look, I'm not trying to tell you how to live your life, and we both know some battles are solitary," Katie said. "But marriage is worth fighting for, and it's not too late for you and Lilah. Tell her. And together, you can do whatever it takes to help Maisie."

Cal wrenched off his baseball cap and clawed at his hair. "But Lilah won't see me! What can I do if she won't see me?"

A pair of squirrels played tag under a sign that warned of poison ivy. One stopped and barked like a pissed-off parrot, its tail flicking rapidly.

"Our meeting was Jake's idea, wasn't it?"

"Partially," he said. "He suggested I tell you about the coach."

"And yet you confessed more. Why did you tell me you'd come to Asheville? Delaney didn't know that. I would never have found out."

"I owed you the truth, Katelyn. You might never believe anything I ever tell you again, but believe this: I loved you once. And you and I will be forever linked through Maisie."

Years ago, she had waved him inside her private hell, with devastating results; today, he welcomed her into his, and it was her turn to take action. To dictate a new chain of events. She called up an image of Rosie the Riveter and held it in her mind.

"Jake was right about talking with Lilah, but it should be me. Alone. I won't tell her anything we've discussed today, but I can explain we've reached an understanding and agree that Maisie must see a therapist. And that for Maisie's sake, you need to move back home."

His face lit up with excitement, but it wasn't for her.

"We need to start making healthier decisions for our child. Not decisions that come from fear."

"Thank you," he said, placing his hands on her upper arms.

As he leaned in to kiss her cheek, she closed her eyes. He smelled of sweat and coffee and the life she had lost. *Happiness is a husband's kiss.*

Traffic began to drown out the harmonies of the forest. Only the chatter of cicadas continued. When she opened her eyes, Cal had started walking again, past another sign.

"Trail detour," it read. "Please allow the old trail to return back to nature."

Cal took the new path, but Katie hesitated. She pictured her books in boxes and her wedding dress full of moth holes, and despite everything, she wanted it back. All of it. And that was one truth she could never escape.

I never stopped loving either of you. I just learned to move on alone.

A text came through from Ben. When you're ready, I'm waiting for you by the truck.

Be there soon, she typed and hit "Send."

After pocketing her phone, Katie took the old path because someone had to walk it. Someone had to keep the imprint alive.

TWENTY-EIGHT
KATIE

Sitting cross-legged on her bed with a nest of soft white pillows behind her, Katie sipped peppermint tea and watched the red-throated male hummingbird hover at the window feeder and zip off. To the outside world it might be Sunday, when life moved to a different beat, but for her it was the beginning of a new stretch of identical days that would start at seven and end at eleven.

Unmoored hours could cast her adrift in anxiety, but the new week had gifted Katie two resolutions: cut the dependency cord with Ben, and regain her daily structure. The last decade had proved that she functioned best on a carefully orchestrated seven-day schedule of regular meals—*protein, protein!*—set periods of work both in the studio and in her apartment, and good sleep hygiene with no screen time after ten o'clock and a solid eight hours a night.

Restarting that schedule after a lapse often seemed as impossible as running a marathon through knee-deep mud, but it was no different from surviving a meds shift. The trick was to trust that eventually whichever doctor happened to be dishing out her drugs would hit on the right combination at the right dose. Of course, she hadn't been on meds—other than the odd Klonopin from her stockpile—in the last two years. That also needed to change.

So far so good, and yet still she had to wrestle the instinct to crawl between her cotton sheets and the layers of pain. Not *her* pain—an unpleasant colleague she'd grown used to—but her daughter's. She didn't have to be in the same room, the same house, the same city to know how Maisie was feeling: the cold knowledge that you hadn't been enough to stop your parent from leaving, the sharp fear that the fault had been yours. The torture of a mind spiraling smaller and smaller, shrinking into a pinprick of no return.

Keeping her eyes away from Maisie's baby photo, Katie put her mug down on the nightstand, next to the coiled chain she no longer wore, and opened her laptop. The screen jumped back to life as her phone announced a text from Cal.

Have you seen Lilah yet?

No.

Will you go today?

Later. I have to work first.

Katie put down her phone, took a few minutes to practice some rhythmic belly breathing, and reread the finished fourth-grade writing prompt on her screen.

Imagine you were playing outside and you found a magic rock. When you picked up the rock, it opened and you found something inside. Write a story about . . .

Her eyes skimmed down to the items she'd written underneath: the reminder to focus on what happened after the rock opened; the importance of making sure the story had a beginning, a middle, and an end; the necessity of using correct grammar, punctuation, capitalization, and spelling. If she found a magic rock, what would hers contain? The answer was easy: a wish for one whole day with Maisie. Even less than a day. Half a day? Four hours? One hour?

How would Maisie have tackled the assignment when she was in the fourth grade? Chewing on the skin around her finger, Katie pictured her daughter working on a story. Did Maisie have a desk? What kind of desk?

An old image took a swing. She saw herself pick up Maisie and throw her down a burning staircase.

A thought is just a thought; it has no power. And I can still help Maisie. I can make a difference in her life.

Another message popped up from Cal. Thank you, and sorry. Freaking out again.

Practice some belly breathing. Put one hand on your abdomen, one on your chest, and take a deep breath. Your abdomen should move, your chest shouldn't. Pause, exhale slowly, feel your abdomen go back down. Do it for fifteen minutes.

Okay.

"Oh, Cal," she said to her empty apartment.

Was he so desperate that he was taking advice from a woman he preferred to think of as dead? A woman who was pushing him to consider therapy when she couldn't afford her own? And what about Lilah? Did she have any idea that she'd married into the poster family for anxiety? And *ping*, the last thread of focus snapped.

What was Maisie doing right now? Was she eating enough, sleeping enough? Was Lilah keeping her busy? What if Lilah was merely handing out reassurance? What if Maisie's OCD was feeding on it? What if Maisie sank into a dark place where no one could reach her? After all, like mother, like daughter, right?

"No," Katie said out loud. She dug her hands into her hair. "No."

Hand shaking, she closed her Word doc, opened Mail, typed a new message, dragged the file over, and hit "Send." As her email shot through cyberspace, her phone honked with an emergency alert. An Amber Alert? Had she hit a child, killed a child, and not realized? What if she had? What if she'd left the scene of a crime? Yesterday there'd been a definite bump when she was coming back from the studio. Were the cops heading her way? Had they found the body? Bloody images played. She watched them, let them roll like movie credits.

"You're not real," she said and reached for the car keys.

✳

Katie slowed down for her exit.

Hope I didn't hit anyone on the freeway. Did I hit someone? One, two, three, four. Should I go back and check? I think I need to go back and check. One, two, three, four. Why am I doing this? I'm the worst mother. No, I'm not even a mother. One, two, three, four. Did I hit that green Subaru that was stopped on the hard shoulder? Maybe I did. I should go back and check. Go back and check. Is my heart racing? My heart's racing. Am I having a heart attack? Oh, God, I'm having a heart attack.

No, no, it's just the anxiety. Remember the breath, Katie, focus on the breath. I'm fine. I'm fine.

Humming along to Mumford & Sons, Katie narrowed her thoughts to one purpose: following the streets that led back to her old home. *I've got this.*

That strip mall was new. So was the Starbucks. How come she hadn't noticed on her mad dash to rescue Maisie from the playground? And the storage facility was now an apartment complex. Her old neighborhood had grown into an unknown landscape.

She flicked on the turn signal and pulled into Dogwood Drive. Her mouth was dry. No moisture. Why hadn't she brought a bottle of water? Was she getting sick? She could be getting sick. Maybe she shouldn't go near Lilah, a pregnant woman, in case she passed on germs, and Lilah got sick, and—

I control fire; I am strong. This is just the voice.

Katie turned from one residential street to the next, passing cookie-cutter homes built to similar blueprints. Fourteen years ago, had this land of SUVs, basketball hoops, and uninspired foundation plantings really spoken of her dreams? Home was such an odd concept. The studio was the closest she came to a home, although Ben had started neglecting his work to shadow her. And the moment she left, the texts started. The less she replied, the more he texted. Accountability was exhausting.

The truck bounced over the speed bump at the top of the street, and the house came into view. Something else she hadn't noticed before— the siding needed repainting. The trim too. Lilah's Honda Civic blocked the driveway.

Katie pulled up to the curb by the mailbox covered in the clematis she'd planted. Now huge, it was covered with a healthy mass of white floral starbursts. Thriving on neglect.

Her old mailbox; her old landscaping; her old house. And inside, her daughter.

I should turn around and go home before I make things worse. What if I go inside and accidentally push Lilah? I could hurt the baby.

The truck idled. Katie killed the engine and slowed her breath. Hands shaking, she grabbed her messenger bag off the passenger seat, slung it over her head, and climbed out. A rabbit hopped across the neighbor's lawn, where some kid had abandoned a brightly colored tricycle. An older couple used to live next door. Good people. What were their names? She walked toward the house, her feet keeping rhythm with the babble of her thoughts.

Halfway up the front steps, she grabbed the rail. Should she ring the bell or knock? Would Lilah look through the peephole before opening the door? Was she trespassing? The voice told her she was trespassing.

The door opened. "Hello," Lilah said.

"How did you know I was—"

"Saw your truck pull up." Lilah stepped onto the porch and eased the front door closed behind her.

Katie took two more steps so she was level with Lilah. Two steps, two wives, one daughter. Lilah was taller, by a good six inches, and—Katie glanced down—that was in bare feet. Tattooed calligraphy wound around one ankle. A strange thought: Had it hurt?

Katie raised her eyes. "You knew it was me and opened the door anyway?"

"I asked Maisie to run upstairs and find a cardigan in my closet. Only it's not there, so it could take a while. You realize that she doesn't want to see you or Callum?"

"How's she doing?"

"She's been better."

"Here." Katie opened her bag and handed Lilah the book she'd bought the day before.

When a Family Member Has OCD," Lilah read. "Thanks." She tucked the book under her arm and then folded her hands together as if waiting to take communion.

Below the porch rail, Katie's former sun garden contained deer-chewed perennials and Japanese stiltgrass. The hardwood mulch she used to special order and spread every February had been replaced by sunbaked clay.

"Was there anything else?" Lilah said.

"An apology," Katie said quickly. "For causing you both pain. You and Maisie. My mom was a drunk with angry outbursts, and—"

"You mentioned this before."

"Right. But the point is that I was the adult of the house at twelve. Which means I understand everything Maisie's going through. Not only the anxiety, but also the sense of abandonment. I guess what I'm trying to do is offer help."

Lilah said nothing, and Katie swallowed.

"So there's that. I mean, I'm willing to help. If you need me to. Or not."

Lilah's pale eyes stared without blinking.

"And weird as it sounds, I'm here on Cal's behalf. To ask you to let him come home, for Maisie's sake. Actually, he wanted me to beg."

A UPS truck clattered up the road and stopped several houses down.

"You've seen my husband?" Lilah said.

Katie nodded. "He told me his side of our story, and we decided to let it go. The past. And we agreed we're both committed to making sure Maisie sees a child psychologist, one who's an expert in treating OCD. I gave Cal a list a while ago."

"And Callum"—Lilah did a strange little thing with her lips—"he met with you more than once?" Her eyebrows went up. "The two of you were alone?"

"We met twice. The first time was in my apartment, but it was short and intensely uncomfortable. He warned me to stay away from you and Maisie. The second time he dragged me on a hike because he needed exercise. He looked emotionally hungover, and he'd given up on personal hygiene. To be honest, he smelled a tad ripe. He was not out to impress."

Lilah turned her head to the right and back again. "And were you out to impress him?"

"No. Neither Cal nor I have any interest in renewing our marriage, but we did need to reach an understanding of what happened. I think we've achieved that." Katie rubbed her neck and felt the loss of the chain that held her wedding ring. "Our moment is long gone, but it's obvious to me how much he loves you. Let him come home."

"Jake's behind this, isn't he?"

"More or less."

"I can't lie. I want to hate you," Lilah said.

"Join the club. You never find peace with giving up your child, even if you know you did the right thing. I set the bar pretty low for being a good mother, but you've outstripped me already. Kicking us all out was impressive."

Lilah put a hand on the small of her back and pushed her belly forward. "I'm so mad at him right now."

"I can imagine. The irony is that I'm not. Not anymore."

"Maisie worries about me dying," Lilah said. "All the time. It's a little freaky."

"I had similar fears at her age. My mom had self-destructive tendencies, including being a cutter. She didn't know, but I saw her do it once. That's the thing about irrational fear, it comes from a seed of fact: an offhand comment, a news story, something you glimpsed. But OCD takes that seed and blows it up into Armageddon. Given what Maisie thought had happened to me, it makes sense that her voice would sow similar doubts about you. And in some weird, twisted way, it's a compliment. Her fear comes from a place of mattering. If she didn't love you, the voice wouldn't latch on."

"What fun," Lilah said, the corner of her mouth hinting at a smile.

"Sorry. There's no way to make OCD pretty. It's total and absolute shit, twenty-four seven."

"Thanks," Lilah said, "for the book, the apology, and the honesty."

Katie turned to leave, then stopped. Next door a basketball bounced on concrete. With a *thud*, it hit the backboard of a basketball hoop. "Will you call Cal so he'll stop bugging me?"

"I guess."

"I should go before—"

"Evil Stepmom," a voice said as the front door flew open. "I can't find your cardig—"

Katie's breath sped up; a spike of pain jabbed under her ribs.

"Maisie," Lilah said, her voice even. "Your—"

"Katie. You don't have to call me anything else."

Maisie crossed her arms and pouted. "Why are you here?"

"I brought your mom a book to help her, and I came to plead your father's case."

"You've seen my dad?" Maisie said.

"He's desperate to see you and your mom. Please let him come home, Maisie. It's not his fault what happened. He loves you so much, as do I. Always have, always will. And I promise you this: I'll never change my phone number or leave the area. If you ever decide you want to see me again, you'll know where I am. The choice will always be yours. But you have to talk with your father."

"Why should I trust anything you tell me? You wanted me to think you were dead."

"No, Maisie. I wanted you to have a better mom. And now"—she looked at Lilah—"you do."

The UPS truck drove by and honked, and the driver waved at Lilah; she waved back.

"Katie, why don't you come in so we're not having this conversation on the street?"

"It's up to Maisie," Katie said. "Can I, Maisie? Can I come in?"

Maisie nodded, and for the second time in one week, Katie entered her former house and her old living room. She sank into a huge armchair that seemed intent on swallowing her, and shuffled forward to perch on the edge. Lilah sat elegantly on the overstuffed white couch like some idealized painting of a mother-to-be. Although, she would come to regret that decorating choice when the baby was a toddler with sticky fingers. White, really? And the glass-topped coffee table with angular edges? An accident waiting to happen. The voice showed her how. Katie cleared her throat.

Maisie threw herself down and scooted close to Lilah.

"I think it's good for the three of us to talk," Lilah said, and kissed the top of Maisie's head.

Could you hear a heart ripping? Did it make a sound?

On the mantelpiece, Katie's wedding picture had been replaced by a huge print in a silver frame. Maisie, in a white dress with a red rose pinned on her chest, smiled at the camera. Behind her, her new parents kissed: Cal in a dark suit with a red tie, and Lilah in a red lacy dress with sprays of white baby's breath woven into her hair.

Red and white. Blood and bandages. Katie tried to smile. Did that come across as a smile? Or was it a grimace? Was she grimacing at her daughter? The voice told her she was. "Maisie, what I did when you were a baby was inexcusable, and you have every reason to hate me."

"I don't hate anyone." Maisie snuggled up against Lilah. "*Hate* is a very bad word." Then Maisie glanced up. "How's my dad?"

"Missing you dreadfully. Please don't punish him. It's not his fault."

"Oh, I'm not punishing him. I'm not, am I?" Maisie looked up at Lilah.

I don't love her. I can't love her, not after I ran away and stayed away. I'm the worst kind of mother. How can I love her after the way I've behaved?

I control fire; I am strong. I love Maisie with all my heart. This is my truth.

"Adults, wow, we can really get things wrong, and all those years ago, I scared myself and your dad. He was simply trying to protect you, and now your mom is trying to do the same. Think how helpful it could be to both of them if the three of you could work together to get a handle on this before the baby comes. Babies bring a whole lot of disruption and change, and the voice doesn't like either of those things, does it?"

Maisie shook her head.

The phone rang and announced, "Caller unknown." After three rings, the answering machine kicked in and recorded nothing but a dial tone. Katie waited for silence before speaking.

"I know life's tough for you right now, Maisie, but you strike me as a fighter."

"Gosh, no. I dislike violence," Maisie said.

"I meant that you're strong. A stormtrooper with a heart."

Lilah twisted round to kiss Maisie. "Yes, you are, my little M&M. That's a good analogy, Kat—" Clasping her stomach, Lilah pulled back her lips in a contorted smile. *"Wooow."*

"What's wrong?" Maisie said. "Is something wrong? Are you sick?"

Katie rushed over to the sofa. "Braxton Hicks?"

Lilah grabbed Katie's arm and dug in. "Need. To pee." She wobbled onto her feet. "Oh—too late."

Katie glanced at Lilah's legs. A steady stream flowed down them, but it wasn't urine.

Maisie sprung off the sofa. "Mom, you're bleeding!"

"Lilah, I'm going to get you lying on the floor." Katie moved an arm around Lilah's waist. "Maisie, honey, please get me the phone. Now."

Maisie ran out of the room, and Lilah let out a groan. *"Shiiit,"* she said through her teeth.

"Is it a contraction?"

"Pain." Lilah looked up at the ceiling and panted. "Everywhere."

Katie kicked the white sofa with brute force. It refused to move.

"Damn," she muttered, then eased Lilah back to a sitting position. "Sorry about the sofa."

Lilah made a noise somewhere between a snort and a moan, as Katie pushed the coffee table aside. Then she hauled Lilah back up and eased her down onto the carpet. She grabbed a no-longer-white cushion off the sofa, threw it on the coffee table, and, wrapping her hands around Lilah's bloody ankles, lifted the other woman's legs onto the cushion. Lilah groaned again, stopping when Maisie sprinted toward them and held out the phone.

"Good girl." Katie wiped her hand on her cutoffs, took the phone, and punched in 911. "Now can you go fetch me some towels?"

"How many?" Maisie said.

"As many as you can carry. The biggest towels you can find."

Maisie nodded and disappeared again. Her footsteps thundered up the stairs.

"911. What's the address of your emergency?" the dispatcher said.

"1492 Dogwood Drive, Raleigh."

"Your name?"

"Katie Mack. And I'm with a pregnant mother who's bleeding heavily. Her name is Lilah MacDon—"

"Tremblay. My. Last name. Lilah Rose Tremblay."

"Lilah Rose Tremblay."

"The phone number you're calling from?"

Katie rattled off her old phone number as Lilah huffed out little breaths.

"Tell me exactly what happened, ma'am."

"Lilah was sitting on the sofa talking, nothing out of the ordinary, and she crumpled over in pain. We think it was a contraction. She said she needed to urinate, stood up, and started gushing blood." Katie glanced up to make sure Maisie hadn't returned. "She's bleeding heavily. Did I tell you that already?"

"How old is the patient?" the dispatcher said.

"I—I don't know. Lilah, how old are you?"

"Thirty."

"Thirty."

"And she's awake and talking. Is that correct?"

"Yes. Yes, she's conscious."

As Maisie reappeared, Katie leaned forward to cover the blood seeping out from under Lilah. She stretched her hand toward Maisie, took one of the towels, and dropped it over Lilah's lap. Then she put the other towels on the coffee table. Maisie glanced at the scarlet smudges on the sofa, dropped to her knees, and grabbed Lilah's hand.

"Squeeze my hand if it hurts," Maisie said. "Are you scared, Mom?"

"Nah." Lilah was horribly pale. "I'm a . . . *he-he-hoo* . . . tough Midwesterner."

"When's her due date?" the dispatcher said.

"Her due date?" Katie looked down at Lilah, who snatched the phone.

"November twenty-sixth . . . and I'm hemorrhaging . . . so get a goddamn ambulance." Lilah thrust the phone back at Katie. "Sorry, M&M." She paused for two more pants. "'Bout the bad language."

"Uncle J uses that word all the time when we're watching basketball." Lilah closed her eyes. "Don't. Tell. Your. Dad."

Katie grabbed a folded pale-yellow towel and pushed it under Lilah's legs in a grotesque mimicry of a giant sanitary napkin. A blood-stain spread instantly across the middle.

"Can you see or feel any part of the baby?" the dispatcher asked Katie.

"You want me to put my hand between her legs?"

Katie and Lilah stared at each other.

"Ma'am, I need to know if the baby's in the birth canal. Can you ask the mother?"

"Lilah, is the baby in the birth canal?"

"How the friggin' hell should I know?"

"Unclear."

"Then yes, you need to feel between her legs, ma'am."

"Lilah, I have to do this."

Lilah gave Katie a nod. "Maisie. Move up near my . . . *he-he-hoo* . . . head. We're way past . . . *he-he-hoo* . . . PG-13."

Reaching under Lilah's skirt, Katie balanced the phone on her shoulder and pushed aside the towel and Lilah's panties. A blood clot slid out, and willing herself to not gag, Katie felt around for any sign of the baby. She glanced up and mouthed, *Sorry*.

"Nothing. I don't feel him." Katie reached for another towel and threw it over the blood clot. Then she put the folded towel back in place. "And I have her lying on the floor with her legs elevated."

"That's not going to help, ma'am."

"Is there anything else I should be doing?"

"Let her rest as comfortably as possible and tell her my partner's dispatched the ambulance and first responders. Help is on the way."

"A whole battalion of help is coming." Katie held up her thumb to Maisie and then realized it was covered in blood. She cleaned it discreetly on the bottom of her T-shirt.

"Ma'am," the dispatcher said. "I'm going to stay on the phone with you as long as I can, and I need you to let me know if there are any complications, okay?"

"Lilah, do you feel the urge to push?"

She shook her head.

"Ma'am? Did something change?"

"Sorry, I was trying to figure out if the baby's on the move. I should probably call her husband, right?"

"No, ma'am. Stay on the line so you can keep me informed about what you're seeing."

Maisie kissed Lilah's cheek. "Please be okay, Mom. Please be okay."

"Honey"—Katie held the phone aside and spoke to Maisie—"you know what would be incredibly helpful? Can you stand out on the porch and watch for the ambulance? The house numbers are hard to read on the mailbox."

Maisie nodded. "What about Daddy?"

"Let's deal with your mom first, and then I'll call your dad. But right now, I need you to be my special helper and wait outside. Can you do that?"

"Got it!" Maisie said and jumped up.

The front door crashed open.

"Ma'am? Ma'am!" the dispatcher said. "Is everything okay?"

"Yes, sorry. We have a child here, and I was trying to keep her occupied." She gulped and looked down at the towels. They were no longer yellow. "Please tell the ambulance to hurry."

In the distance, a siren approached. As it got closer, so did the pool of blood.

TWENTY-NINE
KATIE

"Which hospital are you taking her to?" Katie kept an arm around Maisie.

"Raleigh Regional," the medic shouted through the open window. Then the ambulance shot into the street, sirens blaring.

"Come on, honey. Let's get inside and call your dad and Uncle Jake."

Maisie nodded but kept staring into the now-empty street. Katie eased her daughter around to face the house. As they started walking, Katie scrolled through the list of numbers programmed into the phone, found Cal's cell, and hit "Talk." He answered on the first ring.

"Darling?" he said.

"Sorry, no. It's Katie, and I'm here, at the house, with Maisie. Where are you?"

"On campus. Why? What's wrong? Where's Lilah? Did she leave us?"

With a glance at a bloody handprint on the frame of the front door, Katie shepherded Maisie into the hall. The siren retreated, and a mechanical click broke the silence in the house. Cold air descended on them from the vent above.

"Yes and no. Lilah's fine, but she had some bleeding. It came on suddenly, so we called an ambulance, didn't we, Maisie? And Lilah's on her way to Raleigh Regional."

"The baby?"

"We don't know." Katie guided Maisie past the arch that led into the living room.

"You said 'bleeding.' How much? You mean spotting?"

"Maisie's right here with me." Katie spoke loudly and slowly. "She's been incredibly brave."

"Understood. I'm leaving right now." His voice started jiggling as he ran. "Answer with a yes or no: Is Lilah suffering? Is she in pain?"

"Yes." Katie smiled at Maisie; on the other end of the phone line, Cal sucked in a breath. "And I'm about to call Jake, ask him to come over. I'll stay until he gets here."

"Can I talk to Maisie?"

As they walked into the kitchen, Katie handed over the phone.

"Daddy?" Maisie pushed up her glasses as she wiped her eyes. "Yes. Everything is fine here so please don't worry, but you need to get to the hospital super urgently." She paused. "And I'm sorry about—" Maisie plucked at her lip. This pause was longer. "I love you, too. And Daddy? Promise you'll call when you get to the hospital so I know Mom's okay."

She hung up and handed the phone back to Katie. "I didn't want my dad to worry about me."

"That was very brave of you, honey."

Maisie went quiet.

"What's on your mind?"

"Is it my fault?" Maisie glanced up, her eyes huge.

"I figured the OCD would tell you that, but know what I think?"

Maisie shook her head.

"I think it was a very good thing that both of us were here today."

"But suppose we caused it? I'm really, *really* worried I did something to cause this. Deliberately! What if I wanted this to happen, what if—"

"Aha! And that's how OCD tricks you. If you wanted this to happen, you wouldn't be upset, would you?"

"I guess."

"I know the fear seems real, honey, and I know a huge wave of emotion is crashing over you, but OCD lies. A thought has no power. Even the scariest of thoughts can't hurt you. In fact, we should take that stinky thought and put it in here." Katie tapped a large metal trash can shaped like a red bullet. It matched the coffee machine, toaster, and a cheery blind. Otherwise the kitchen hadn't changed. If she opened the cabinets, would she find her wedding china?

"I'm super big on recycling," Maisie said.

"Even better! Put stinky thoughts in the recycling bin."

Katie rested her hand on one of the four white-and-chrome chairs placed around the white-and-chrome table. This breakfast set had been out of their budget, but Cal caved because he never said no to her. All that devotion, and it hadn't been enough to save a marriage.

"You're very quiet," Maisie said. "Is your voice bad, too?"

"No. I'm lost in memories. I used to love this room. I think it was the view of the yard with the forest beyond. I put your high chair there, in the corner by the window." Katie smiled. "Once, you knocked a bowl of butternut squash over poor Ringo, who was sitting underneath. I had to hose him down, which didn't make him happy."

"Who's Ringo?"

"Your dad never told you we used to have a dog?"

"Oh, I don't think I would have liked that. I'm scared of dogs." Maisie chewed her lip. "I'm scared of lots of things."

"You mean the stinky voice tries to make you scared of lots of things. When I look at you, I see someone's who brave and strong. Which means the first thing we're going to do, even before we call Uncle Jake, is tell the voice to go to hell." Katie pulled out two chairs. She sat in one and patted the seat of the other.

"Really?"

"Yup. Shout it with me."

They did. Four times.

"And now, we'll boss back that stinky voice by lining up the facts of our case. Fact number one." Katie held up her thumb. "The voice is a cheater. Fact number two"—Katie tapped her temple—"trust what your eyes saw, not what the voice tells you. What was the last thing that your mom did before the pain hit?"

"I don't know."

"Think hard, sweetheart."

Maisie frowned. "She kissed me!"

"Exactly. So our conclusion is . . . that she wasn't angry?"

"But you can't always tell. It's very hard to tell with my dad."

"True, but we're not talking about your dad. Does your mom tell you when she's upset?"

"Oh, yes! She's been so mad, we went shopping on my dad's credit card." Maisie slotted her hands under her legs and swung her heels out and in, out and in. "He's not going to be very happy when he gets the bill, but she said that was the point."

"Good for her. And here's something else I want you to think about. You were calm today. That was the real you. Not the poopy voice that screeches with alarm bells."

"I didn't feel very calm inside."

"But you didn't panic, which must have been really helpful to your mom."

"I'm very confused," Maisie said.

"About what, honey?"

"Don't you want me to call you Mom?"

"I want nothing more. But I haven't done a great deal to earn the honor. And with the baby coming, it might be easier for everyone if you call Lilah Mom."

"That's what my dad says."

"Well, there you have it. Your biological parents are in agreement, so it must be right."

"Is the baby going to die? The voice is telling me—"

Katie help up her hand. "The voice is telling you the worst thing you can imagine, because that's what it does. It's called catastrophizing. Isn't that a great word?'

Maisie nodded.

"But you and I are going to stay positive and bring in Uncle J!" She scrolled through the phone to find Jake's number. "You know, Maisie, you have four grown-ups who want to parent you. That says something about the kind of person you are."

"I guess . . . it's almost like I have three moms, but three's a very bad number."

"Jake isn't a dad?"

"I'm not?" the voice at the end of the phone said.

"Hi, Jake. Katie here. And Maisie! Everyone's fine, but we've had a bit of a situation. Can you hang on a minute?"

"Ssssure," Jake said.

"Maisie, can you run up to your room and find some colored pencils and paper? We're going to color through our fear. Create some art."

"Oh, that is an awesome plan!" Maisie said, and disappeared.

Then Katie told Jake everything, in more detail than she'd told Cal.

"Holy shit," Jake said when she'd finished.

Maisie tore back down the stairs.

"Put her on." Unlike Cal, Jake didn't ask.

"I love you, baby." Maisie must have hit "Speaker," because Jake's voice filled the kitchen. "Hang tight. I'm on my way."

"We're going to make art and think positive thoughts," Maisie said.

"Yes, we are!" Katie said.

"Well, you two ladies barely need me, do you?" Jake paused. "I'm sure Lilah's going to be fine. So don't you worry. Right, Katie?"

"Right." They had reassured Maisie, but triage moments demanded triage tactics.

"You look after each other till I get there, okay?" Jake said.

"I love you, Uncle J. I'm sorry I got so mad before."

"Love you, too, 'Mazing Maisie. That's all that counts."

Katie hung up the phone and slotted it back in its cradle. When she turned around, Maisie was huddled by the table, arms crossed over her stomach, hair flopped forward.

"Your mom strikes me as a strong woman." Katie sat down.

Maisie lifted her head. "Oh, she is."

"And she's going to an excellent hospital."

"But the baby's not due for—"

"Babies are born early all the time. You were three weeks early. Shall I tell you about the day you were born?"

"Oh, yes, please," Maisie said. "I've never heard that story."

Without thinking, Katie held out her arms, and Maisie was in her lap. *Maisie.* Her daughter—

so tiny, so huggable—smelled of strawberries and summer.

Swallowing hard, Katie began to relive the best day of her life. A day when she surprised herself with her own level of calm. Cal, however, had been all over the place. He even left her in the car twice while he ran back into the house to grab things. Right there was a missed warning sign: she packed her hospital bag at the end of her first trimester as Cal retreated more and more into his own world. He told her he was trying to get ahead on two papers, but every time she went into his study, he was staring at a dark screen. Even then they hadn't been on the same journey.

Before long Maisie's breathing evened out into a pattern of sleep. She twitched once, but Katie kept talking, kept filling the kitchen with the story that belonged to no one but her, Cal, and Maisie.

*

Jake didn't knock. She heard a low "Fucking A" as he walked through the hall, and then he was in the kitchen. Eyes only for Maisie. Katie held her baby tighter, pulled her against her heart, but Maisie stirred and raised her head.

"Uncle J? That was quick."

"Hey." Jake crouched down in front of them. "Next time use the bat signal, and I'll be quicker. How're you doin', baby?"

"I was super scared, but I tried to be brave even though there was *sooo* much blood. Even more blood than when Ava Grace cut her head open."

"That so?"

Maisie nodded once, and Jake uttered a solemn "Hmm." How many more memories did they share?

"But Katie was awesome and didn't panic once. She stayed as levelheaded as Ms. Black did when Parker ran out into the road that time at school pickup. Have you heard from Daddy? Is there any news?"

Maisie thinks I'm awesome. Or does she? Did she say that? Maybe she didn't and I imagined it. Did I, did I imagine it?

"Not yet, but give a guy a chance. He's got to park, find the right ward, talk to the docs. It could take a while. C'mere."

Maisie launched forward and he caught her. In one swift movement her limbs fastened around Jake, the keeper of all the missing childhood milestones. He stood, taking Maisie with him, and Katie looked down at her empty lap, her empty arms, her empty hands. One puff and she would evaporate. Disappear.

"I'm sorry I was so mad at you," Maisie mumbled into Jake's neck.

"Now, now, 'Mazing Maisie. You had every reason to be, but remember two things are never variables in your life: one, I will always love you; and two, I'm always here for my number-one girl. Even if we're mad at each other."

Maisie pulled back. "You get mad at me?"

"I'm projecting into the future. When you're a teenager with a boyfriend who thinks your dad and I are stupid."

"Uncle J! I would never have a boyfriend who didn't like you or Daddy. And besides, no one is smarter than my dad. He has a PhD, and you're very clever, Uncle J."

He looked at Katie. "There you have it. Out of the mouths of babes." Then Jake started singing "My Girl," his voice deep and gritty and slightly off-key, but strangely pacifying.

Katie stood and pretended to clear up the art supplies, still in a neat pile. A small plane rumbled overhead, and she closed her eyes and prayed, prayed that Lilah and her baby would live. Then Katie opened the door to the closet where she had once kept cleaning supplies. And so, evidently, did Cal and Lilah. Reaching up, she found the spray bottle of carpet cleaner. And a scrubbing brush. And a bucket that was—Katie scratched her wrist—exactly like the one she'd bought ten years ago. Towels, more towels would be good. Paper towels would be useless on such a large stain, would create more mess, would—

"Katie?" Maisie said.

Katie turned in a flash. "Yes, sweetheart?"

"You're not leaving, are you?"

"Not unless you and Uncle Jake are tossing me out."

"Would you like her to stay?" Jake said.

"Yes, please."

Swallowing, Katie grabbed a trash bag. "Okay, then. I'm going to clean up the living room."

She marched out of the kitchen. Maisie wanted her around; Maisie wanted her to stay. This should be the happiest moment of her life. Instead, the voice kicked into high gear:

What if Lilah dies? What if the baby dies? The ambulance would have gotten here quicker if not for the clematis I planted, obscuring the house numbers. That cost the medics precious seconds. And Cal should've been here; he would have been here but for me. He never used to go to campus on weekends.

If something happened to Lilah and her baby before Cal got to the hospital, Katie wouldn't ask for forgiveness—from Cal, Maisie, or God. No, she would accept her guilt. Guilt beyond a reasonable doubt. And finally the OCD would have what it craved: certainty.

THIRTY
LILAH

Razor-sharp sounds sliced into her brain. Words snapped, metal clanged on metal, footsteps ricocheted like gunfire. Why so many people in the room? Why such chaos, such noise? Something hit the floor with a clunk and a clatter. Shouldn't hospitals be quiet?

Voices echoed; someone swore. People yelled in words that didn't make sense.

Can we try that again in a language I understand?

Had anyone called her parents? Was Maisie okay? Why were people rushing around? There was no pain. She just needed sleep, but sleep was impossible if they couldn't muzzle it. She tried to open her mouth. Maybe they'd given her hardcore drugs. The world, wrapped in cotton wool, was white and soft. She could get used to this—except for the noise.

Lilah stood next to Callum and tried to take his hand, but her arms refused to work. Nothing worked. Why couldn't he see her?

I'm right here, baby.

Baby. The baby . . .

You and I are fine, sprout. Don't let all these grown-ups in scrubs scare you. We'll get you a doctor's outfit when you're a toddler.

The pain in her womb had dulled. The spasms had vanished, but the noises deafened. Why could the staff not be quiet? Callum leaned over to kiss the person lying on the gurney. Wasn't her, though. She was everywhere and nowhere. Could see all around. Three hundred and sixty degrees.

"Don't leave me," he whispered. "I can't do this without you. I love you."

Why the tears?

Machines beeped. She was sliding down a smooth slope. Warm, wet, peaceful. The beeping disappeared off into the distance. The person in charge—a beautiful Asian woman in a white coat—pushed Callum aside. Why was she shouting?

"No! Don't you dare, Lilah. Do you hear me, Lilah? Don't you dare!"

The doctor pounded on the patient's chest. Kept pounding.

Lilah started falling, falling . . . falling into white noise. Muffled noise. Silence.

Serenity.

THIRTY-ONE
KATIE

After concocting a hundred excuses to circumvent her birthday, Katie had given up when Delaney proposed a no-gifts rule. And now she was paying the price for her weak-willed mistake. In the last two hours, everyone from the studio had partied on the Durham Hotel rooftop bar, unaware that the birthday girl stalled out on the first round. Trent wanted to go for pizza afterward; Ben had stepped up and said no. Then everyone left, except for Ben.

He raised his beer. "Here's to turning forty-one."

She clinked her glass against his and turned back to admire the view. The city sprawled, but in a contained way. The air was warm but not humid, and cool enough to make the half-hour walk home pleasant. The Art Deco building opposite was decorated with a vertical line of square purple lights. White floodlights illuminated the top layer of the skyscraper. The effect hinted at Gotham. Jake would likely tell Maisie the rays of light were the bat signal. Night had barely fallen, so it couldn't be much past eight o'clock. Was he reading to Maisie? Were they watching a movie? Was Maisie crying again? Jake had shrunk Maisie's world to him and him alone, which Katie understood and applauded. And hated.

The voice volleyed back with fact, told her she was jealous, which she was. *It should be me. It would be me if I'd been a better mother.*

Above, the sky was solid and starless; below, the downtown streets were artificially lit. Not with holiday lights, but even so, the city seemed to taunt her with Halloween, Thanksgiving, and Christmas: family celebrations from a defunct timeline.

For the last two days, the voice had launched unarmed missiles: she'd failed Maisie, irritated Jake—*Since when do I care what Jake thinks?*—was an ungrateful friend, and Ben hated her. Or she hated him. *Toss a coin, Katie, see where the thoughts land.* On the upside, less focus from the voice meant OCD had yet to settle on a target, hit, and detonate.

"The architect who designed that also designed the Empire State Building," Ben said, with a hitch in his smile.

"I know." She glanced at the cocktail in her left hand. Mainly melted ice, it was called the Undeniable Truth. Trent and Delaney had insisted the birthday girl be adventurous and try something new. It mattered to them, it didn't matter to her, and the name had been appropriate.

"You're awfully quiet," Ben said.

"Not in a celebratory mood."

The woman at the next table laughed too loudly and put a hand on her male companion's knee. Her fingers inched upward; his smile dared her higher. Katie looked away.

"I feel useless." Ben sighed. "I know you're suffering, and all I want is to help. Why won't you let me help?"

"This is how I survive. Alone." She glanced back at the man and the woman. Were they a new couple, not yet disillusioned? "I'm sorry."

"I wish you'd trust me."

"This has nothing to do with trust, and it's better this way. For both of us."

Ben shook his head slowly. "Can I at least drive you home?"

She stood. "I prefer to walk."

He stood too.

"Besides"—she pulled his wrist toward her and glanced at his watch—"I need to call and check on Maisie before it gets much later. Don't worry about me."

"I always worry about you."

"Well, don't. I'm used to city streets at night."

"That's not what I meant," he said, "and you know it."

As they waited for the elevator, he dipped forward for the birthday kiss she'd been avoiding all evening. She stopped him with her hand flattened against his chest. "I'm sorry, but it's taking all my strength to battle what's going on in my head. There isn't room for anyone else. Please don't take it personally. This is me, Ben. The real me."

"I've told you countless times, you don't need to explain."

"But you also want me to feel better about myself," Katie said. "And I can't."

"No, I want to look after you. Big brother with two younger sisters, remember?"

She didn't answer.

"You can't fight instinct, Katie," he murmured.

The elevator door opened, and they stepped in. Ben cracked his knuckles—first one hand, then the other. Katie leaned against the far side, hidden behind him and his all-black outfit: black T-shirt, black jeans, black canvas Dr. Martens. Black mood.

He hates me.

She stared at the floor, and the door closed. Trapped her in a small space with Ben and a tumble of dark thoughts. Around and around those thoughts went, landing on Ben, the baby, Lilah, and Maisie. Always Maisie. Was Jake coping? Did he really know what he was doing?

When they stepped out into the lobby, Ben drew in a breath and released it. "Happy birthday, Katie. I'll see you around."

"Yeah. See you around."

Ben pushed the glass entrance door open, said "Night" to the concierge, and crossed the street toward the parking deck. He didn't look back.

He deserves the best, and that's not me. I'm a fool to expect anything else. Was that OCD or a real thought? She could no longer tell the difference.

*

Katie strode away from the downtown lights and the couples arm in arm. Traffic thinned, the energy of a Saturday night pulsed behind her, and the symphony of cicadas and katydids played on an endless loop. A lone firefly sparked in a patch of long grass under an empty child's swing set, its frame a ghostly shape looming out of the darkness. Her mind shot to chemical warfare, to bombs, to dead children, to abandoned playgrounds.

Stop, stop. But the thoughts kept spinning, stuck on an imaginary record player.

Sleep, she needed sleep.

A thought is just a thought. It has no power.

She turned onto a dark, tree-lined street with a thousand places a predator could lurk. The voice whispered that she'd screwed up big time, that she should have let Ben drive her home. Should call him and say, "Come get me. I'm not safe." But she knew how to protect herself, didn't she? *No, it was Ringo who kept me alive on the streets, who guarded me.*

Katie slowed her breath and kept walking. Feeling at risk didn't put her at risk; feelings were not facts. Yes, a woman alone on a dark street should be vigilant, but she didn't need to listen to OCD warning bells. She could keep herself safe; she knew how. With her phone in one hand, Katie used the other to create a makeshift brass knuckle by curling her fingers over her keys. Then she lengthened her stride.

She was about to hang up when Jake answered his cell.

"Sorry—" He was breathless. "It was hard getting Maisie to sleep tonight."

Katie cleared her throat loudly. "Any news?"

"No change."

Lilah was still on the vent, still heavily sedated. Jake was staying with Maisie, Cal was camped out in the hospital, and Katie was alone.

She glanced over her shoulder. "The baby?"

"No longer lavender colored. Callum says he touched him, through the incubator."

Three pounds, four ounces, and holding his own, despite being born with an Apgar score of one, which basically meant Baby MacDonald had a heartbeat and nothing else. And the poor little guy continued to be nameless. Of everything that had happened, that bothered her the most.

"And Maisie?" Katie increased her pace. "How's her anxiety? You're not letting her sit around, right? She must keep busy, otherwise—"

"Yes, ma'am. I'm following your advice to a T."

Not a comment she'd ever expected to hear from Jake.

"She's eating? Sleeping?"

"Would you stop sounding as nervous as a jerked-off cat? I've been looking after Maisie since she was two. I know what I'm doing." He paused. "Mostly."

Not with OCD, you don't.

"By the way," Katie said, "I've narrowed that list of child psychologists I gave Cal. Chosen two. Assuming he still has the same health insurance, both are in network. If Cal would pick one, I'd be willing to take—"

"He's pretty much shut down, which is standard for our boy. It's how he handles trauma. And he knows Maisie is fine with me. Let's not give him more to worry about."

"But she's not fine, Jake. She can't be."

"Thor still looking after you?"

"Stop changing the subject."

"Stop interfering and go spend the evening with your boyfriend. Isn't your birthday around now?"

How did he remember that? "I haven't seen much of Ben in the last few days."

"Well, there's your mistake right there, darlin'. I'm sure he could keep you distracted through many a night."

"Ben needs a break from me. I rely on him too much."

"Isn't that for him to decide?"

Two cars raced down the street, tailgating and speeding. Dear God, they could hit each other. They could hit a pedestrian. *I should hang up and call the cops. What if I don't and they hit someone? I'll be culpable, and—*

"It's complicated," she said loudly.

"Not to me. You avoidin' him?"

"I appreciate the advice, but I need to keep things simple."

"Ben seems like a simple kind of guy." Jake paused. "Darn, that came out wrong. Lack of sleep and adult interaction, sorry."

Now he was apologizing to her?

"But I wouldn't let that guy slip through your fingers. He's got *keeper* stamped all over him."

Katie glanced toward an unlit house, its front yard obscured by a massive magnolia tree. "You're giving me love advice, Jake?"

"I reckon so." He blew out a sigh. "Guess we're not in Kansas anymore."

"For once you and I agree."

"Don't get used to it," he said. "You can go back to giving me shit tomorrow."

And Katie gave her first smile as a forty-one-year-old.

THIRTY-TWO
LILAH

"She's fighting the vent!"

"You mean she's awake?" The voice belonged in her dreams, where it spoke of love.

"It means she's breathing on her own, sir."

The noises were back but louder: the bells, the beeps, the footsteps. Tubes snaked into her body, pumping her full of drugs. *No. Drugs were bad for the baby. Her baby. Where was her baby? Not in her womb! Her womb was empty. There was no flutter of life, no movement. Nothing.*

Lilah tried to swallow, tried to breathe. Couldn't. Couldn't breathe, couldn't swallow, was choking on silent gagging. She reached up, grabbed the plastic tube blocking her throat. Tried to snatch it away, pull it free, get it out. *Get it out.*

An arm restrained her; another voice spoke. "I know it's uncomfortable, honey, but try to stay calm. You're okay, your baby's okay, and your husband's right here. Can you squeeze my hand?"

Lilah squeezed. *My baby, my baby.*

"Good job. We're going to send for the doctor and see if we can get you weaned off the ventilator and get that tube out, okay?"

No, not okay. *Get it out now. Now!* She tried to wrestle free. Why the noise, why the pain? Why couldn't she feel her baby? She kicked; she thrashed. *Must get free.*

Where's my baby, where?

A woman said something about more sedation. Serenity returned.

＊

Lilah woke up coughing, with burning in her throat and pain in her womb.

"Welcome back, Mommy," a female voice said. "Take some slow, deep breaths. The tube's out, and you're doing great." A nurse was leaning over the bed. She smelled of soap, and a gold crucifix swung between her breasts.

Lilah tugged the oxygen mask down. "My baby?" The words cut like broken glass.

"Upstairs in the neonatal ICU." The nurse smiled. "With all his fingers and toes. And you're in the ICU. He's doing great."

"A boy?"

"Yes. And your husband's here. He's barely left your side." The nurse pulled back to glance up at the monitors.

"Need to see him." Lilah shivered. The room was cold, too cold.

"He's in the bathroom."

"No." She ran her tongue over her teeth and swallowed. "My baby."

"Mama and baby will be reunited soon, but first we've got to get you well. How're you feeling?"

A toilet flushed and a door opened.

"Darling, you're awake!" Callum rushed at her and leaned in for a kiss.

She turned her head away, and his stubble grazed the side of her mouth. "Please"—she spoke to the nurse—"take me to see him."

"Soon. Real soon. Do you have any pain?" the nurse said.

Yes. Everywhere. Lilah shook her head. "Let me see him."

Callum fussed at her hair. "I can't believe you're awake."

"Stop." Forming words hurt. She batted his hand away. "I need to see my baby."

"He's fine, darling. He's in the NICU."

"And I'm not. Get me out of here."

"The NICU nurses are amazing, and they're taking excellent care of him. And your mom and sisters are camped out in the family room, comparing baby stories. I gather you never cried."

"I'll do more than cry if you don't get me a wheelchair." She tried to sit up and flopped back, biting into her lip as a burst of pain shot through her belly.

"You are not going anywhere. It's not up for discussion," Callum said in a tone she'd only ever heard when a student asked, "Is this going to be on the test?"

An aftershock of pain hit. She closed her eyes, held her breath, and willed it away. Willed Callum away. *My baby. I want my baby.*

"I need you to get well, Lilah." Callum took her hand, but she kept her eyes closed. "Please, do whatever the nurse says."

The pain subsided and she started breathing again. Lilah opened her eyes and focused on his face, searching those blue eyes for the truth. They stared at each other. "Promise me he's okay. Promise me. Because if you're lying again—"

"You're both going to be fine," Callum said.

"How big is he?"

"Three pounds, four ounces."

A call came through on the device hung around the nurse's neck. Lilah's ears rang as the nurse talked with a disembodied voice.

"What happened?" Lilah asked Callum.

"You had an abruption and an emergency C-section."

The nurse finished her phone conversation and checked the computer. "Your placenta tore away from the uterine wall," she said, "which obviously isn't ideal, but you're healing up nicely."

"It happened so fast," Lilah said. "I didn't feel anything until one big contraction."

"Abruptions can happen without warning or symptoms." The nurse paused her typing. "The bleeding must have been frightening for you and your family, but it alerted everyone to what was going on." She sighed. "That isn't always the case."

"Maisie. She saw everything." Lilah grabbed Callum's arm. "Is she okay?"

"Bit shaken, but she handled it well." Callum smiled the smile that had once shrunk the world to the two of them, and the pain returned. Lilah let go of his arm and stared toward the window, covered in an opaque shade. A nondescript beige, it matched everything else in the room.

"Everyone's looking forward to meeting Maisie," the nurse said. "Your husband talks about her all the time. One proud daddy, huh?"

"He needs a name," Lilah said. "Our baby."

"Luke was at the top of Maisie's list for a boy. As in Skywalker," Callum explained to the nurse.

Top of Maisie's list for a girl was Theodosia, which she had explained meant "God's gift." Lilah turned back to face Callum. "How about Theo? I think Maisie would like Theo."

"I think so, too. I held him last night, next to my heart. Your mother shot a video." Callum was messing with his phone. Then he passed it to her.

Lilah watched a jittery video of Callum, naked from the waist up. No sound. He sat in a purple chair, and a pair of blue latex-gloved hands placed their baby on his chest. She touched the screen. He was so tiny, her baby, so wrinkly; his diaper so small. His eyes were covered with a blue mask, and the rest of his face was obscured by a ventilator. Tubes and wires trailed from his body, from the IV in his arm, from sticky pads on his chest. Callum kissed the top of his head, and then the latex hands covered Theo with a small blanket. *Theo.* Childbirth wasn't meant to be this way: silence, medical equipment, and a mother's heartbreak. She hadn't been the first to hold him.

The video ended, and Callum closed up his phone. Lilah blinked, her sight misty.

"It looks worse than it is," he said.

"When's his birthday?"

"September eleventh. Three days ago."

Lilah sniffed. "Three days?"

"That's why you need to rest and get your strength back. Theo," Callum said as if trying the name on for size, "isn't going anywhere, and neither are you. Dr. Eliot says you could be here for a while."

The nurse slid the oxygen mask up, but Lilah lowered it. "Who's with Maisie?"

"Jake. Mom's flying back next weekend to help out after you come home." Callum pulled the oxygen mask back into place.

Lilah pushed it aside. "Next weekend?"

With a look that said, *You're trying my patience,* he stayed silent until she fixed the mask. "Jake's living at the house and keeping her close. So far they've had a *Star Wars* movie marathon, including *Revenge of the Sith,* and eaten the state out of Phish Food. Plus he's teaching her to cook. I dread to imagine the state of our kitchen after days of Jake's experimental meals."

Our. He might be ready to use that word; she wasn't.

"Katelyn gave him the name of two child psychologists, and I have an emergency appointment with one of them on Monday. Your mother's volunteered to sit with you that day."

She shifted to get more comfortable and winced.

"Lilah, this isn't helping. If you don't cooperate, you'll be in here longer than a week. Are you in pain?"

She closed her eyes and nodded.

"Can you give her something for that?" Callum asked the nurse.

"Sure thing. I'll be right back."

Lilah lowered the mask again. "Maisie, can she visit?"

He peered over his glasses until she tugged the mask back up.

"Let's wait a few days. You look like the best thing on the planet to me right now, but Maisie might be a little shocked." Callum paused. "I should have been there when it happened. If I hadn't lied to you . . ."

But he had, and she lacked the energy for a discussion about broken trust. She blinked. The tears were coming back. Callum pulled a tissue from the box on the table over her bed and dabbed under her eyes.

"You used to look at me with such wonder, but every day I worried that you'd find someone better, younger, less damaged. On our wedding day, when you asked if I was getting sick? I was shaking and sweating out of fear that you'd say no." Callum slipped the tissue into his pocket. "I've nearly told you the truth a thousand times, but I didn't want to drag you into the deception. Ask you to lie to Maisie. And yes, I was selfish and wanted to keep the halcyon days of our marriage. But I love you so much, Lilah. I couldn't sully us with what I'd done, with the mistakes I've made." He threw back his head. "With the person I really am."

Lilah closed her eyes. She didn't understand what he was saying. And nor did she want to. All she wanted was to hold her baby.

✳

Next time she woke up, it was dark and the oxygen mask had gone. Callum was asleep in the plastic recliner, his eyes moving rapidly behind closed eyelids. She watched him, this man she had never doubted despite the speed at which things unfolded between them. And now, after a crash course on the real Callum MacDonald, she had to sift through her knowledge to reevaluate the facts. Fact number one: he lied.

Their kids were counting on two parents, which meant that if she couldn't do this, a clean break would be best. After all, she'd never believed in peeling off a Band-Aid. One yank and then you dumped it in the trash.

Callum stirred, opened his eyes, and held her gaze. This was the Callum she saw when they were alone in bed, when they were making love, when they were sharing a shower. Callum without his glasses; Callum stripped bare. He pulled forward and rested his head on her arm. With the other hand she reached over to muss his hair.

"I'm a disgusting person," he said.

"No, you're not. But protecting your loved ones by omission doesn't work for me, Callum. I come from a big family. We have no secrets, and I like it that way." She sighed. "I'm giving you one hall pass, and if you ever lie to me again, we're done."

He sat up. "If Katelyn hadn't called 911 straightaway, if we didn't live so close to Raleigh Regional, you and Theo wouldn't be here. You had massive blood loss." He swallowed. "Technically, you bled to death. You were dead for three minutes."

She sucked in her lip.

"Theo's Apgar score was one. He had a heartbeat and that was all. He was resuscitated once, and the doctors got the score up to seven in a few minutes."

"And you swear to me on Maisie's life that he's okay?"

"You know what one of the NICU nurses told me today? That three pounds, four ounces, isn't that small. He'll probably stay in the hospital until his due date, but we *will* be bringing him home."

"Is there anything else you've kept from me? Anything?"

"Yes." He closed his eyes.

The only surprise was that she wasn't surprised. They'd jumped into a relationship, a marriage, a family, without the benefit of research. "Is this worse than lying about your first wife being dead?"

He reached for his glasses, laid out on the table next to her bed with the water pitcher, the tissues, part of the newspaper, two plastic cups, and their matching phones. "Yes."

"Tell me everything, Callum. I need to know."

And in the twilight of the hospital room, with light streaming under the door and night on the other side of the blind, Callum talked and she listened. He told her things, in graphic detail, that she would never be able to erase. She didn't cry, she didn't speak, and when he stopped, she opened her arms and held him against her chest.

THIRTY-THREE

KATIE

Outside on the old loading dock, sparks flew toward Katie's leather apron. Grinding was never as much fun as welding, but today the slow process worked as effectively as an extra half tablet of Klonopin. It dulled the edges of her anxiety. Smoothed them out.

I am calm; I am calm.

She finished cleaning up the edges of the steel frame and leaned in to blow off the filings. Noises intruded from inside the studio—banging and screeching. It was inevitable that people would start trickling in. No day jobs to mess with the muse on a Saturday, but the old warehouse had been hers since five o'clock.

I am calm; I am calm.

Sighing, she unplugged the grinder, unscrewed the vise, pulled out the frame, and left the bright morning behind. As she stepped into the dark, windowless space full of artists at work, anxiety hitched a ride. Bored into her body: nibbling, gnawing, and feasting with pointy fangs.

I control fire; I am strong.

Repeating her mantra, over and over, she kept moving: put away her tools and the frame, slotted her right-angled jig back where it belonged, and double-checked the welder was switched off. The WhatNot that Maisie had admired caught her eye. *Maisie.*

The night before had been the show's opening at CAM. Would Ben walk over the moment he arrived to give her the highlights? Hopefully not. She didn't want to know who had been her docent.

Katie picked up the WhatNot and examined the weirdest piece she'd ever created, a piece that had spoken to Maisie. What if she took it to Maisie, as a consolation gift for missing opening night at CAM? Jake could hardly object if there was a legitimate reason for intruding. Katie was trying to not bug him, trying to limit herself to contact four times a day, but trying was exhausting. Everything was exhausting.

Why would she want a gift from me? I'm not her mother. I'm nothing to her. And that WhatNot could kill the baby. Fall on his head and crush his skull. It has no place in the house.

A thought is just a thought; it has no power.

I control fire; I am strong.

WhatNot in hand, she turned around as Ben walked in with a pretty blond Amazon. They made a striking couple. He had a new haircut, a serious haircut that said, *I mean business.* The crop had taken off the sun-bleached tips. His hair was darker, spiky, and if she was being honest, sexy. And what was with the stubble? Ben stopped by the box of safety glasses and moved closer to the woman. He touched her shoulder and said something. She smiled up at him. Had he taken the woman to opening night? Was this a date still playing out?

Katie turned her back on them.

I am calm; I am calm.

I am not calm.

She could feel Ben's presence; she could feel his absence. Had he come on his bike, with the woman astride the back, arms locked around Ben? Katie tapped the WhatNot four times. Four to keep him safe.

I don't deserve his friendship, I'm a shit person. What if I've been using him for the last five years? If I answer the final text he sent—four days ago—he'll crash his bike and die.

The voice kept churning, kept sucking up thoughts into a vacuum of fear and doubt. Reason vanished. Toward Ben's corner of the studio, a woman laughed. Katie pulled off her apron and sent Jake a text.

How's Maisie?

Ok, he replied.

Something wrong?

Bad morning.

Anything I can do?

No.

She stared at the phone. Another laugh came from Ben's corner, and an image hijacked her brain. Him slamming the woman against the wall, covering her mouth with one hand so she couldn't scream, unzipping her jeans with the other, and . . . Tapping her teeth together, Katie replaced the image with one of Ben and the woman kissing. But that one played out with a cold suspicion that settled in the lining of her stomach: *You've lost him.*

Pathetic. It was none of her business who Ben dated. So why this sudden sense of ownership that told her to dash across the studio, put herself between him and the woman, and say, "I need you"?

What if he falls in love and gets married and has a whole houseful of babies? What if I never see him again? What if he hates me? What if I've lost him?

Grabbing the WhatNot, she headed for the exit and then bolted across the parking lot. Rain had started to fall despite the sunlight. A sun shower. Ben's truck was parked next to hers. It would be open; it always was. She could crawl inside, lie across the seats, and wait for him to find her, to pick her up and carry her back inside.

I need you.

Instead she unlocked her driver's side door. His hand squeezed her shoulder—how did he learn to be so quiet?—and her mind rewound to show his hand on another shoulder, touching another woman. A woman smiling up at him. A woman not her.

"Are they bad, the intrusive thoughts?" Ben said. "If you talk to me, it might help. It did before."

She didn't turn.

Tell him. But what if I'm playing with him? What if I'm jealous and selfish?

"I'm sorry, Ben. I can't—" *Tell him, otherwise he's going to crash on the way home and die and I'll be responsible.*

She put the WhatNot down on the passenger seat and climbed into her truck. Then she slammed the door, jammed the stick into reverse, and, watching over her shoulder, pulled out. That was a bump, right? What if she'd driven over someone? Katie slammed her foot on the brake. What if she'd hit Ben?

Daylight fled as the wind picked up, battering the puny crepe myrtles planted around the lot like unarmed border patrol guards. Rain pinged against her roof. She flicked on the wipers, but silent images pelted her brain: Ben's lifeless body, bloody and broken after she'd run him down.

It's not real, I didn't hit him. Don't go back. It's not real. Don't turn around. Don't—

She turned around. Ben was standing where she'd left him. The rain became a downpour and pounded on her hood. It drenched him, but he didn't move. Katie collapsed over the steering wheel. The monster nudged her in the ribs, whispered of failures past, present, and yet to come.

I can't do this anymore; I can't.

A knock on her window. She sat up and rolled it down. Rain dripped from the edge of his jaw and flattened his hair against his skull. Resting his arms on the lowered window, he leaned into the cab. Instinctively she looked for the scar left by fifty stitches—the reminder of sitting up with him all night, trying to rediscover her belief in prayer. At one point, drugged and loopy, eyes closed, he had mumbled something about love. She never called him on it. Why now, as rain came in through the open window to soak her jeans, did she wish that she had?

"Maybe between us we can push back the voice," Ben said. He watched her, his mouth slightly open, his eyes half-closed. He blinked, and the rain kept coming.

He's in pain and it's my fault. I'm playing with his feelings. Messing with him because I'm a terrible person. He's too good for me.

She shook her head.

"Katie, please. I know you're in a bad place. Come back inside before we both catch pneumonia."

"You have company. I don't want to intrude, and I have to go see Maisie."

"Do you need us to drive you?"

Us. "I'm not an invalid," she snapped. Imagine that—the voice had been right; she was a shit person. And no, she didn't care. A negative became a positive, anger brought strength, and he should return to his girlfriend.

"I'm not suggesting you are," Ben said. "I'm merely offering to help."

"Yeah, well, last time a man offered to help it didn't work out so well." She began to roll up the window. Stupid thing was stuck. She gave it a jolt.

He took a step back. "You know where I am, if you want to talk."

"Yeah. Yeah, of course." What she meant was no.

Katie inched forward, unable to make out shapes through the sheets of rain. Pressing the brake slowly—*No hydroplaning, no hydroplaning*—she glanced in her rearview mirror. There was nothing behind her except for the deluge flowing down her rear window. To drive in these conditions had nothing to do with fighting OCD and everything to do with reckless behavior.

She would wait in the parking lot until the rain eased up. And then she would drive to her old house and give Maisie the WhatNot. And as she drove, she would focus on reading the traffic so she didn't accidentally run anyone over.

Sometimes you had to listen to fear.

THIRTY-FOUR
JAKE

Anger reverberating worse than the bass in his car stereo, Jake glanced up the stairs to the recently slammed door. Was a shot of tequila at noon on a Saturday bad form? He'd been the walking, talking definition of *delinquency*, which meant he could defuse any hissy fit in the making. And yet, right before his eyes, Maisie had acted like he'd maced her with demon kid hallucinogenic.

Could be he was to blame. After all, he'd made Maisie the center of his world for the last eight years. Could be she was jealous of all the attention her baby brother was getting. Who knew, but he had to get a handle on the situation, fast.

Jake turned and gave himself a prime view of the bloodstain. Even though he'd dragged the coffee table over the top, that thing lit up brighter than Venus on a clear night. He needed air, activity, something to do other than babysit a tantrum or stare at dried blood. An expanse of free time was never welcome. A shrink could charge a fortune to trace that back to the formative years he'd been labeled a *slack-ass* by teachers and his aunt. But every day, he got further behind on editing the movies from the last of the summer camps. Would that mean postponing the VIP screening—the post-camp highlight? Disappointing kids was a shitty option however you justified it, especially when they'd been excited little rascals about reuniting for their red carpet moment. Hell, he loved that part, too.

Well, he would work his ass off when Maisie went back to school next week. Callum had made two good decisions recently: Maisie was going to see a child psychologist, and she'd skipped enough school. Amen and hallelujah.

September sunlight blazed through the panels of glass in the foyer, calling his name. With one final glance up the stairs, Jake opened the front door and stepped from the bubble of overeffective central air into warm sunlight. In deference to Maisie, who liked to be cold, he was keeping the AC lower than he should. Callum would go apeshit when the electric bill arrived.

Jake stretched and surveyed the yard. A storm had moved through earlier, making the grass too wet to cut. And the deer had eaten what remained of the once-thriving garden, except for the clematis and Katelyn's chocolate vine, which had grown over the porch railing and up into the gutter. He could definitely spend an hour taming that into submission. Yes, ma'am, yard work might be just the ticket.

A truck appeared at the top of the road, driving slowly over the speed bumps. Thank God he didn't live in a subdivision with speed bumps. A fine idea for little kids, but it screamed *PC neighborhood*. Everything was so falsely jolly around here: basketball hoops came in two heights—full-size and child-friendly—all the minivans had stick-figure decals on the back windows, and every other house hung banners of cardinals or dogwood blooms. He never did figure out why Callum and Katelyn had chosen to live in a community that organized meet 'n' greet block parties. Had they both been that desperate to belong?

The truck slowed as it negotiated the next speed bump. Imagine that. Think of the devil and there she was. Katelyn—Katie—pulled into the driveway like an old lady in need of a stronger glasses prescription.

Jake crossed his arms and braced his legs. She wasn't getting past him. Last thing Maisie needed was a misplaced mama fussing in her face. And man, could that woman fuss. If she texted him one more time . . .

Katie climbed out of her beaten-up old truck, then reached in to retrieve a metal orb with more than a few identity issues. A half-melted lip ran around the middle, and whereas one side was smooth, the other was studded with bits of iron. Interesting color: rusty on the outside, bright red on the inside. Sci-fi helmet meets medieval weapon, if he had to guess.

"I'm not here to intrude. I thought this"—she held out the thing—"might console Maisie for missing opening night at CAM. She commented on it when you guys visited the studio."

"That is ridiculously weird and strangely beautiful." Truly, it was. "Like a planet that can't decide whether to smile or eat itself. Or some weapon that belongs in the future and the past. What is it?"

"A mistake?" Katie shrugged. "I'm calling it a WhatNot. How's the baby?"

"Holding his own."

"Lilah?"

"Getting her strength back."

"And Maisie?" Katie raised her eyebrows.

A car revved out of the driveway opposite. Jake imagined he was sitting across from another actor, responding back and forth through a repeated phrase: *You look like you don't trust me right now.* The point of the exercise was to figure out what was happening in the moment, to access genuine emotion, to stop thinking about what to say and respond freely and spontaneously. Good acting, he'd been taught, came from an authentic reaction to your partner's behavior. Katie was offering concern. Maybe even a dollop of compassion.

Jake unfolded his arms. "She's being a pain in the ass. Callum wants me to take her to the hospital, and she won't go."

Katie settled the WhatNot on her hip. "Did you ask her why?"

"I tried, and she ran up to her room and slammed the door." He nodded in the general direction of Maisie's bedroom. "I half expect her to be up there decapitating Beanie Babies. Which wouldn't be a bad thing in my opinion."

"You don't like Beanie Babies?"

"I favored G.I. Joe. Your ex-husband went soft on me."

Katie watched him, and for one god-awful moment, he saw Delaney.

"Hospitals can be overwhelming," Katie said. "The noise, the fear, the smells. The knowledge that inside, people are sick and dying. Lots for an anxious person to absorb."

"But hospitals are also full of people healing."

"The OCD brain doesn't work that way. We run straight to the worst-case scenario. Going to the hospital might not be something Maisie can handle right now."

Jake threaded his thumbs through his belt loops. "You mean this could be OCD?"

Katie nodded. "And she might not be able to articulate it. Maisie's ten years old and unable to understand her brain."

"So she hasn't been abducted by demons?"

"I can probably figure out if anxiety's responsible. If it is, I can give her some tools that might help both of you."

"You'd be willing to help me?" he said.

"Why do you have such a hard time believing that I'm capable of a selfless act?"

"Poor little orphan boy raised by vicious aunt? Not a whole lot of trust where I come from." He gave Katie the grin that seemed to charm the pants off everyone but her. True to form, she didn't even crack a smile.

Katie put a hand on the white railing that ran up the side of the steps. "Let me talk to her."

He stepped backward to block her way. "Could you make it worse?"

"I know what I'm doing."

A female cardinal flitted in and out of Katie's chocolate vine as Jake pretended to consider his options. All zero of them.

"Fine, but I want to listen. And stop staring at me that way. This isn't about keeping an eye on you. If you must know, I'm hoping to learn from a pro." He smiled. "So don't disappoint me, Katie Mack."

THIRTY-FIVE
KATIE

Driving to Raleigh to meet the docents had not been the ultimate expo-sure. Could not begin to compare to retracing her steps through the memory imprint of the night she ran: tearing down these stairs with Ringo; the suffocating conviction that she was insane; the fire in her mind screaming, *Run, Katie, run*; the nausea, the urgency, the fight for each breath; the heat in the bedroom; the cold that Cal had allowed into the hall.

With her line of sight fixed on Maisie's bedroom, and sweating despite the ferocious air-conditioning, Katie passed her stained glass window. Jake followed, stalking her like prey. Stalking her like the voice.

Why did I run away? Why didn't I stay and fight? If I'd stayed, that bedroom on the right would still be mine. I made a terrible mistake I can never fix. Why am I even trying?

I control fire; I am strong. For Maisie, I am strong.

As she knocked on Maisie's door, Katie's mind saw the red metal crib, the Winnie-the-Pooh lamp, the mural of the cow jumping over the moon. The Winnie-the-Pooh lamp. Always the Winnie-the-Pooh lamp.

When Maisie didn't respond, Katie knocked more forcefully.

"Please respect my privacy, Uncle J."

"It's Katie, honey. I've brought you a gift." She glanced at Jake. With one hand resting on the wall, he loomed over her. For once he wasn't wearing aftershave.

The door opened slowly, and Maisie's tearstained face appeared. It would be so easy to wrap her in a maternal hug. But Katie had given up that right nine years ago. Jake moved silently into place beside her.

"Can we come in?" Katie held out the WhatNot.

"*Ohhh,*" Maisie said, and her big hazel eyes grew even bigger. "For me? Really?"

"It's in need of a loving home, and I picture it standing guard by the front door. A sort of good luck charm to ward off bad things. Shall I leave it here?" Katie stepped into the room and put the WhatNot on the white dresser that had replaced the small white bookcase where the Winnie-the-Pooh lamp used to sit.

You could take that WhatNot and bash in her head.

So the OCD keeps saying, but it's not true. A thought is just a thought; it has no power.

"Thank you," Maisie said. "I do love it." Then, with her thumb tucked underneath her splayed fingers, she stroked her hair twice on one side, twice on the other, and looked at Jake.

"C'mere," he said, and Maisie ran to him.

"I am sorry, Uncle J. I love you. You know that, don't you?"

"Love you, too." Jake guided Maisie down to sit on the end of her bed. He kept his arm around her, and she glued herself to his side. The bed was where the red metal crib had stood, but the mural had disappeared under a wall of dark-blue paint. Katie's mind ran a marathon of doubt—*Why did I run? I should never have run*—as she lowered herself onto a psychedelic beanbag.

I control fire; I am strong. For Maisie, I am strong.

Katie scratched her legs, dug deeper and deeper with her nails, raked at her skin until it burned. Until her anxiety dipped. Was this why her mother had sliced open the inside of her thigh with a razor?

"I'm sorry, so sorry," Maisie said. "I don't mean to be a bad kid, but I feel as if I could explode. Explode, Uncle J! And I want everything gone—these feelings, these thoughts. And I—I want Daddy. I want my daddy."

"*Shhh.* Everything's okay, baby. I know it's the situation, not you."

As Jake started rocking and singing, Katie blocked the memory of Cal soothing Maisie in the same spot nine years earlier, but another memory tumbled in to fill its place.

Katie was twelve and standing in the kitchen in Boston, screaming at her mother, "It's your fault Dad left. I hate you." A rush of guilt started behind her eyes and shot down to her stomach. It had been so easy to blame her mother for everything. After all, her father was the handsome charmer; her mother was needy and temperamental. And Katie translated everything through a black-and-white prism. Always had. Had chosen to see her father as the wronged party even though she'd heard her mother yell about "the other woman" before grabbing the steak knife. Maybe that was the reason she struggled to trust Jake. He reminded her too much of the first man who broke her heart.

"Your anxiety's pretty high," Katie said. "Isn't it?"

Maisie started bashing the crown of her head with her open palms, a gesture that made a world of sense to Katie. *Bash it out, God. Bash it out.*

I did this to my daughter. Me.

No, if it's genetic, it's not my fault.

"Hey." Jake eased Maisie's hands down and held them.

"And the anxiety ramped up when Uncle J mentioned taking you to the hospital," Katie said. "Am I right?"

Head lowered, Maisie nodded.

"But here's the thing. You don't have to go."

Maisie pushed herself up and glanced at Jake. "I don't?"

"She doesn't?" Jake repeated.

"No. You don't. Is your fear thermometer so high that the idea of going to the hospital makes you feel as if you could shoot into the sky and orbit Pluto?"

"Yes! I can't do it, I simply can't." Maisie burrowed back into Jake. "Other people go to the hospital all the time. I should be able to go, but I can't. Ava Grace went after her grammy got a new hip."

"But Ava Grace doesn't have a stinky voice, does she?"

Maisie shook her head multiple times.

"Honey, OCD loves to tell us we *should* or *must* be able to do something, but that's baloney. Human beings are not robots, programmed to behave or feel the same way. We're gloriously messy thinkers." Katie swallowed. "And we're not fortune-tellers or psychics, even though OCD loves to warn us about the danger lurking around every corner. Driving here, my voice told me that I'd run someone over, and I needed to turn around and check to prove that I wasn't a criminal. OCD wants proof and certainty all the time. But that's not how life works."

"Gosh, that's awful." Maisie twizzled the ends of her hair. "How did you keep driving?"

"I reminded myself that a thought isn't a call to action. It's nothing but a powerless thought. Brains are very complicated, especially when they malfunction, but we can learn how to retrain them."

"That sounds hard." Maisie scratched her arm.

"Like everything, honey, it gets easier with practice."

Maisie sat up and turned to Jake. "Do you forgive me? Do you?"

"Of course I do, 'Mazing Maisie."

"Really forgive me?"

"Once is enough," Katie said gently.

Jake glared at her; Katie ignored him. "Once is you asking, twice is OCD. The voice is telling you that if you don't keep apologizing, something awful will happen to Uncle Jake, right?"

Maisie nodded.

"Wrong. Checking is a nasty trick OCD plays on you, and eventually you and Uncle J will need to come to an agreement on how many times a day you can check. Your ultimate goal will be zero, but that could take a while."

"How's that helpful?" Jake asked.

"Obsessive-compulsive disorder is sneaky, and checking is a well-disguised compulsion. So is reassurance seeking. Both send you spinning around on the worry wheel." Katie patted her chest and cleared her throat theatrically. "Checking is bad," she said in her best Darth Vader voice.

Maisie giggled.

"Avoidance creates problems, too," Katie said. Ben's face flashed through her mind.

"But if we don't go to the hospital, isn't that—"

Katie cut Jake off with a flick of her hand. "Maisie, have you read Harry Potter?"

"Gosh, *yyyes*! Uncle J does the different characters very well. He's especially good at Snape."

"My favorite character. I knew all along Snape was Harry's protector."

Maisie smiled, and Katie continued. "You know how Harry insists on using Voldemort's name, not saying 'He-Who-Must-Not-Be-Named'?"

Maisie nodded again.

"To tackle anxiety, you have to be as fearless as Harry. You have to name your fear and face it. That's how you take away its power. But some fears are *sooo* big they take a long time to tackle. Going to the hospital might be one of those fears—until you've met with a psychologist and learned how to out-debate the OCD monster."

"I don't like failing," Maisie said.

"This isn't about failing, sweetheart. It's like trying to do calculus before you've learned your times table."

"Learning the times table was super annoying."

"Fear is super annoying, too, but you have to follow certain steps to reach the good stuff."

"I really, *really* want to see Daddy. I miss him very badly." Maisie paused. "Did you feel like a failure, when you ran away from us?"

"Yes. And that's something I'll always struggle with." The images started up. Katie let them come, let them go. Just ones and zeros in her head. "Honey, nothing mattered to me more than you and your dad, and my voice knew that in the same way your voice knows nothing matters more than seeing your parents and meeting your new brother."

"I don't want to run away."

"Then you won't. You control your behavior, Maisie. I made the decision to run away, because I believed I had no other options. I didn't understand what was going on in my brain. But you've been smart enough to tell your family, and you're surrounded by people who will do anything to help."

In the street, a car pulled up and the mailbox flap squeaked open. Ten years ago, the mail used to come late. Often not until six o'clock. Small changes in her old neighborhood were oddly gratifying. They proved this world was no longer hers; they proved change could be good. OCD buzzed but couldn't get a foothold.

Katie relaxed into the beanbag, and it molded around her with a soothing squishy sound.

"Didn't Daddy want to help you?" Maisie blinked.

"I wasn't honest with your dad. I didn't explain what was happening until it was too late. And then it came out wrong, and I scared him. But I'm glad you found Lilah and Baby MacD."

"Theo," Maisie said. "My brother's called Theo."

"Great name." Katie kneaded her right shoulder where Ben had touched her, and a tension knot crunched. "And you also have Uncle Jake and me. Think of it this way: most cars have one spare tire stowed in the trunk. Not a real tire, but good enough for emergencies. And you have not one but two—Uncle Jake and me. That means you can never get stuck on a deserted road, late at night, by yourself."

"I've been called many things before," Jake said, "but never a spare tire."

Maisie giggled.

"See how good Uncle J's going to be at helping you with this? It's pretty hard to be anxious when you're laughing, right?"

"*Rrright,*" Maisie said.

"That's your new job, Jake. Make Maisie laugh when she's anxious. Are you up for the challenge?"

"Uncle J is very good at being funny," Maisie said. "He performed magnificently as a Minion in my second-grade parents-come-to-school day."

"You went into an elementary classroom dressed as a small yellow creature that served history's villains?" Katie said.

"My interpretation of one. I'm impressed you got the reference." Jake hefted Maisie onto his lap. "Callum was out of town and—"

"I needed cheering up because I was missing my dad," Maisie said. "My friends thought Uncle J was awesome."

"That's because I am." Jake grinned.

What would she have done for parents-come-to-school day? Something forgettable that involved baking too many cupcakes.

"Feel up to talking about going to the hospital?" Katie said.

"I can't. I can't because the voice is saying I can't go and I shouldn't go because I hate baby Theo, which I don't, I don't! I don't hate him." Maisie swung round to face Jake. "I don't hate baby Theo."

"Is this one of those times when I say once is enough?" Jake peered around Maisie.

"You're a quick study, Jake."

"Why, thank you, ma'am."

"Let's pick up that stinky voice"—Katie mimed picking up a box—"and put it aside for a moment. What do *you* want to do, Maisie? Not the voice, but you? Do you want to see your dad?"

"More than anything!" Maisie pumped her forearms for emphasis. "I want to see Daddy so badly it hurts, and I want to meet Theo. My family's happening without me."

"Good, those are the thoughts to hang on to, in the same way that I hung on to thoughts of you to drive here. As you learn to deal with the poopy OCD, you have to make a decision. Probably the hardest one you'll ever have to make."

"What's that?" Maisie whispered.

"Whether or not you're going to let the OCD behave worse than your class bully and make decisions for you."

"No way." Maisie slashed her hand through the air. "No way."

"Excellent. That's a no, then," Katie said. "Have you ever been to a hospital?"

"She broke her arm when she was six," Jake said quietly.

"It was super painful, and when we were in the emergency room this big man came in, and he was covered in blood and"—Maisie's hazel eyes grew wide again—"a policeman was with him. The man—not the policeman, the other man—was wearing handcuffs. And he couldn't stand up straight. And he smelled funny. It was very distressing."

"He was drunk and swearing," Jake said.

"I'd never seen a drunk man before," Maisie said.

Katie glanced at Jake. As if reading her mind, he gave her a long, cold stare.

"ERs can be chaotic. But your mom's staying in a quiet part of the hospital where people go to heal. I bet, at this very moment, she's cozied up in bed watching a large flat-screen TV. And your dad's there. And he's going to be so happy to see you."

"Do you think he likes the baby better than me?"

"Is that OCD asking?"

Maisie nodded; Jake stayed quiet.

"I have a suggestion, honey. And that's all it is: a suggestion. I could take you to the hospital and arrange for your dad to meet us there. And I would promise that if, at any point, you decided you couldn't do it, I would drive you straight home. What do you think? Do you want to try?"

"I don't know if I can."

"But that doesn't matter. What matters is that you tried, that you didn't let a bully win."

"Score one for Maisie, zero for the voice?" Jake said.

"Exactly." Katie smiled. "But trying to see both your baby brother and your mom might be too much. That's a huge exposure, and you have to warm up for the big ones."

"It would be easier if Daddy came home," Maisie said.

"I know, sweetheart, and I'm sure he wants that, too. But he needs to be with your mom right now, and he can leave you here because you're with Uncle Jake. One thing I know about your dad, he trusts Uncle Jake more than anyone else." Katie sensed Jake's eyes on her.

Maisie sat up straight. "I'll go for Daddy. But you'll be with me the whole time, Katie?"

"Until you're safely delivered to your dad. How does that sound?"

"Okay, I guess."

"And we don't have to go today. We could go tomorrow, or the next day. You set the pace."

"No." Maisie leaped up and put her hands on her hips. "I don't think I can put it off."

"Now or never?" Jake said.

Biting her lip, Maisie gave a single, exaggerated nod.

"In that case, we'll need to think up a fun treat for afterward," Katie said. "A reward. How about we go get your nails painted at the mall?"

"Gosh, no. My dad says I can't wear nail polish until I'm twelve."

"If you can find the courage to go inside the hospital and visit your mom, that proves you have the heart of a twelve-year-old. And Uncle Jake and I will petition your dad for nail polish. How does that sound?"

"You're on." Maisie disappeared to find her shoes.

"Impressive," Jake said.

"What Maisie's about to do is harder than bungee jumping off a cliff without the cord. Maybe all we do today is drive into the parking lot and walk to the main entrance. And then the next day, we go back and get inside the lobby. And we keep doing that every day until we get to Lilah's room."

"I see how this works," Jake said. "Baby steps. You need me to ride shotgun?"

She shook her head. "I've got this, and I think you need a break. OCD isn't for sissies."

"You calling me a sissy?"

"No, I'm giving you another lesson: take breaks when you can."

"Thanks. 'Cause I feel as if I've been skinny-dipping with snapping turtles. And oh, Lordy"—he tossed out an expression that reminded her of Robin Williams playing Mrs. Doubtfire—"you know how much I value my body parts."

With a twinkle in his eye, Jake cupped his groin, and Katie started to laugh.

THIRTY-SIX

MAISIE

Maisie's chest was tight and fizzy and full of bubbles. If she had X-ray vision and could see inside herself, would her chest look like a bubbly science experiment? Not bubbly in a good way, with bubble bath or bubbles that caught rainbows. Bubbly like that video she'd seen once of acid. Why did Katie always tell her she was brave? She was only brave for other people, like Ava Grace and Ellie and Daddy. She couldn't be brave for herself. What if her legs gave out and her heart stopped beating right here in the hospital parking deck?

She inched closer to Katie, who was checking her phone. It was so hot and so dark and she felt all tingly and shaky and her clothes were too tight and, gosh, the concrete ceiling was far too low. Would it collapse on her and Katie and flatten them? Did they have earthquakes in Raleigh? She grabbed Katie's hand. What if the voice was right and Theo and Lilah would die because she'd come to the hospital, and what if—

"Your dad says he can't wait to see you." Katie frowned as she read the text. "And . . . he's typing something else." Katie looked up with a grin. "He loves you."

Why wasn't he here in the parking deck? Why did they have to go inside? Why couldn't he come out here and take her home? "W-where's he going to meet us?"

"In your mom's room. I've already figured out the route, so we can't get lost; but right now, we have a simple goal. We're going to walk through the parking deck and out into the sunshine. Does that sound like a good plan—to get out of this place that's making me claustrophobic?"

Claustrophobic! That was the word she'd been trying to remember. As they walked toward the daylight, Maisie repeated *claustrophobic* again and again in her head.

A shuttle came toward them going very slowly. It was like the shuttles that helped old and sick people get to their gates inside an airport. Sick people. There would be lots of sick people inside a hospital. Lots of germs. Would she catch Zika and die? Had there been any cases of Zika in Raleigh? What exactly had Ellie's dad said about that?

A car alarm went off behind them, and Maisie jumped.

"The alarm will stop in a minute," Katie said. It did. "You're doing great, Maisie, and look. We're out of that horrible structure." Katie's voice was as tranquil—*Such a good word!*—as the water in the pool when it opened every Saturday, right before people started splashing and making waves. Uncle J said sunlight made him tranquil.

Maisie raised her face to the sun, eyes tightly shut. Even Parker knew that looking at the sun could make you go blind. Everything was orange and warm. Did this make her feel better? Not really. She opened her eyes and turned to the huge building opposite. A sleeping giant made of concrete and glass. If she didn't go inside the hospital, she would let her daddy down, but she couldn't do it. She couldn't.

"Can I tell you a secret?" Katie said.

Maisie nodded.

"When I was your age, I hated hospitals. I'm still not crazy about them, but who is?" Katie had the best smile. "Do you know what helps me get inside a hospital?"

Maisie shook her head.

"I practice magical breathing. Shall we do that? Slow everything down and breathe. Can you do that for me, sweetheart?"

Maisie chewed her lip. Why hadn't she brought Lulabelle? She watched the woman who had named her stuffed rabbit. It was one of the few things her dad had ever told her about her real mom. Now, her real mom was here and breathing funny and using her finger to count beats like the conductor in the school band. You had to learn an instrument in fifth grade, so she had chosen the trumpet because Uncle J once played the trumpet and he said it was cool and she really, *really* wanted to be in the school band, and maybe she'd do band in sixth grade out of choice, and—

"Maisie, honey, are you with me?"

Maisie shook her head hard, hard enough for it to fall off, if she were silly enough to believe a head could fall off from shaking, but you never knew, because they said bad things happened to babies when you shook them and—oh, gosh, Theo. Was something bad going to happen to Theo?

"Can we go home now?"

"How about we try this magical breathing once. Once is easy peasy. You've done so well to get this far. Slow everything down and breathe. Nothing else matters but the breath. Take a nice big breath in through your nose, hold, out through your mouth. Let's do it together. On the count of—"

Don't say three, don't say—

"Four. I'm quite partial to the number four."

"Me too!"

"CAM high five!" Katie said and held up her hand.

The voice, that big, fat bully, told her she was a failure for pulling out of the docent program. But did the CAM show count, since she couldn't have gone anyway, with Lilah and Theo in the hospital?

"Let's do this breathing," Katie said. "You've got to pay attention, though, and clear your mind of everything but the breathing. Can you do that?"

"I'm not sure." But she tried to focus and listen and follow Katie's lead.

They stayed put for a very long time.

"Great job," Katie said. "And now we're going to take the pedestrian crossing to the other side of the road and keep doing the breathing. That's all. Breathe and walk. That doesn't sound so bad, does it?"

"*Nooo.* Not so bad."

Breathe and walk; breathe and walk. Over the pedestrian crossing and up the hill. Maisie kept her eyes on her feet, on the concrete slabs, on avoiding the cracks.

"Ta-da!" Katie said. "We've made it to the entrance. That's four whole things off our list: we left home, we drove here, we parked, we arrived at the entrance. The number four rocks!"

The huge glass door in front of them moved in a slow circle. People came out and went in, and Maisie clung tighter to Katie's hand. Katie sighed, but it seemed to be a happy sigh.

"Together, we've got this." Katie leaned in to whisper. "And I'm right here. Now we're going inside the lobby, which is big and bright. There's even a little garden we can go and sit in, if you want to."

A garden sounded quite nice actually.

The moving door seemed to swallow them, but Katie was right. The lobby was very light. The ceiling was super high and made of glass, so the sun streamed in. And it created a nice, even pattern of shadows on the floor, but the smell? *Eeek.* The smell was worse than the disinfectant in the school bathrooms on a Monday morning. And there were so many people, but none of them looked very happy. Even the man carrying the *humongous* bunch of balloons looked sad.

Katie glanced up, checking signs. Didn't she know where they were going? If she didn't, they would get lost. And lost was very, very bad. What if Katie didn't know where they were going and they got lost and she never saw her dad again?

Please don't let me cry, please let me be strong for Daddy.

Lilah and Theo are going to die, die because I didn't bring them balloons.

She stopped, and so did Katie. "Maybe we should leave and come back with balloons. Do you think we should? Get them balloons?"

"Is this a voice thing?" Katie said.

"Yes."

An announcement filled the space. A very loud announcement that hurt her ears. "Adult rapid response team for oncology. Cancer Center. Room 4841."

The message repeated. Paused. Repeated. Maisie let go of Katie's hand. *No!* Maisie covered her ears. Too loud, too loud. Someone was sick, very sick. A medical emergency in the cancer hospital. Where was that—nearby? Were people dying right now, in this place? Would she get cancer and die?

Katie wrapped her in a huge, warm hug. She smelled of shampoo and buttery croissants. Chocolate croissants were the best. Maisie hid her face in Katie's super soft top.

"*Blah, blah, blah, blah,*" Katie said. "Every time you hear an announcement, sing, '*Blah, blah, blah, blah,* I'm not listening.'"

Katie's phone vibrated against Maisie's back, and Katie wiggled around to read it.

"That was your dad. He's waiting for us by the elevator."

Elevator? No one had mentioned an elevator. Maisie pulled back. "I prefer not to use elevators. They get stuck."

"Do you know that hospital elevators are the safest?"

"Why?"

"They don't want sick people getting stuck."

But how did Katie know that? Did she one-hundred-percent-to-infinity-and-beyond know that? Could Katie prove her argument, as Daddy always did?

Katie slipped her phone into her pocket and took Maisie's hand again.

Another announcement filled the lobby. "Code medic to the terrace café, first floor, Children's Hospital." Pause. "Code medic to the terrace café, first floor, Children's Hospital."

"I want Daddy."

Katie pointed at the elevator. "He's on the other side. Only two floors up."

"Can't do this, can't."

"What if your dad came down here?"

Yes, Daddy! Maisie nodded.

Katie pulled back her hand and typed fast. They both stared at the screen.

"He's on his way!" Katie said. "He'll be here in two secs."

Maisie rubbed her eye. She didn't want her dad to see her cry. She wanted to be strong, show him how strong she could be. But they'd never been apart this long and she really, *really* wanted her daddy. She chewed her lip.

The elevator doors opened and—"Daddy! Daddy! You have a beard!" She giggled and he rubbed his face against hers. "It's all prickly. And you smell like the hospital!"

"I love you, Maisie. I love you so much," her dad said, but his eyes were red and watery.

"Don't cry, Daddy. Please don't cry. I can be strong enough to protect both of us."

293

He took off his glasses and wiped his eyes. "I know you can, peanut, but you don't have to be. And you shouldn't be. That's my role—to be strong enough for both of us. Thank you, Katelyn."

"You're welcome. What she did today was pretty amazing. Keep things light, Cal—stress can be contagious."

"Wait!" Maisie grabbed Katie's arm. "You're leaving?"

"You don't need me anymore, sweetheart. Your dad's here, and he's going to take you to your mom. And you, Ms. Maisie, should be very proud of yourself."

"Will you come up with us in the elevator? You're so calm and you make me feel stronger and with both of you, I think I can do it."

Her dad and Katie looked at each other.

"Of course," Katie said.

They stepped into the elevator. The door closed, and she clung to her parents' hands. *Her parents.* Her dad pushed the button. Was the elevator moving? It didn't seem to be. Should she panic? Was something wrong? Was it stuck? If it was stuck, why didn't the door open?

"Remember to keep breathing, Maisie," Katie said, and then she started humming "My Girl" as Uncle J would do.

Her dad kissed her head, and Katie rubbed her back. If one word could describe all her jumbled-up feelings, what would it be? *Loved.*

The elevator doors slid open, and they walked out together. They were in a quiet corridor with a super shiny floor.

"This way," her dad said.

Two men dressed in black pushed a woman on a hospital bed. Her eyes were closed, and her skin was gray. Wheels squeaked as they went down the corridor, and Maisie read the white letters on the backs of the men's shirts: *Critical Care Transport.*

People die here. Lilah and Theo will die, and it'll be my fault.

"I should leave," Katie said. "I'll wait in the car, and you can text me when Maisie's ready."

"Please don't go." Maisie tightened her hold on Katie's hand.

"Okay, sweetheart. Okay."

They stopped in front of a pair of big black doors. Her dad pushed a buzzer and spoke into it. A nurse appeared and let them in, and the doors closed behind them. It was quieter here, and there weren't so many people. Two nurses were talking behind a long counter. One of them laughed.

"Do you want to meet Theo afterward?" her dad said.

"*Yyyes*, please," Maisie said. "But does it involve more elevators?"

Her dad laughed. "You don't have to wait for her," he said to Katie. "I'll drive her home when she's ready."

"You're coming home, Daddy?"

"Your mom insists. Apparently we all need to get maximum shut-eye before Theo comes home and no one sleeps."

They followed the corridor into another corridor, and it was a bit confusing because there were lots of doors—some open but with big white curtains across, and some closed. Gosh, thank goodness her dad was here to steer them in the right direction. A nurse walked by and smiled. "Good afternoon, Callum," she said. "You must be Maisie. Nice to meet you at last."

"You too," Maisie said. When the nurse had gone, she whispered to her dad, "How does she know me?"

"I've told everyone all about you." Her dad grinned and looked super proud.

And suddenly she was super proud. She had done it! Done something she didn't think she could do. If Uncle J were here, he'd be celebrating with his happy dance, which he only did on very special occasions. He called it the moonwalk.

Maisie bounced on the spot—higher than Tigger! "Katie promised me nail polish."

"Did she indeed?" Her dad looked at Katie with that half smile he had sometimes.

"I mostly definitely did, and she's earned it."

"Yes, I did!" She and Katie slapped their hands together in an awesome high five, which also stung a bit.

"Out-gunned. I guess we could stop at the mall on the way home."

"We can? Oh my gosh, you're the best, Daddy."

"Isn't nail polish girlie girl?" her dad said.

"According to Uncle J, not if I get black. Isn't that right, Katie?"

Her dad smiled again. "I need to have a talk with your uncle Jake."

They stopped by an open door, but she couldn't see around the huge curtain.

Katie let go of her hand and said, "Follow her lead, Cal." Then she kissed Maisie's cheek. "Never forget how awesome you are, Maisie. You are brave, you are a fearless warrior, and when the voice insists you're a failure, that's your answer. Repeat it back to me."

"I am brave, I am a fearless warrior. And I'm getting nail polish even though I'm not twelve!"

Katie laughed and motioned her forward with a finger. "I'm leaving now, but I'm only ever a text or a phone call away. And tell your dad," she said in a stage whisper, "it has to be at least two colors of nail polish."

"Thank you for helping me." Maisie grinned. "I think you're pretty awesome, too."

Behind her, a curtain whooshed open, and Maisie spun around. The room was big and white with lots of high-tech stuff. And filled with flowers, and even a balloon saying, *Get well soon*. And Katie had been right! There was a flat-screen TV, and *Star Wars* was playing!

"Hey, there's my little M&M," a pale figure said from the bed.

"Mom!" Maisie ran toward her. When she turned, Katie had gone.

THIRTY-SEVEN
KATIE

Katie waited for the elevator to arrive along with grief, her old nemesis. Unlike an intrusive thought, grief wasn't something you could boss back, out-logic, and wave off. Grief was no place you wanted to be and no place you could leave.

A slideshow of random snapshots played in her mind: the last Valentine's Day dinner with Cal, the tug of Maisie nursing, the three of them sitting on the beach at Ocean Isle. Riding up in the elevator with Maisie and Cal. Watching Maisie run to Lilah.

The elevator arrived, and she stepped in with a stooped white-haired man. Had he also come from the ICU? Steadying himself with the handrail, he limped to the back of the elevator, taking with him the smell of mothballs.

"How's it goin'?" His greeting came with a tired smile. "Ground floor, please."

"Tough day?" She pushed the button, and the elevator door closed.

"Was visitin' the wife."

"I'm sorry to hear that."

"And you, tough day?"

They began a jerky descent. "Emotionally tough, but also . . . miraculous."

"Don't sound so surprised. Them miracles happen. My wife, she's the proof. Wasn't expected to live this long."

Katie shoved her hands in her pockets. "What's her name? I'll pray for her."

"Nora. And thank you kindly for the consideration."

The elevator stopped on the second floor, the doors opened, and no one got on. They rode the rest of the way in silent camaraderie. Hospitals had a way of doing that, of binding strangers through suffering. Or maybe this wasn't suffering. Maybe this was the hope of healing. Yes, she had walked away, but this time she had healed the family she'd broken. She had helped them reconcile.

The elevator doors dinged open, and she turned abruptly. "Want to grab a coffee and something in the café? Maybe we'll get lucky and they'll have chocolate chess pie."

"That's a mighty fine offer, but I need to go home and mind the cat. You have a blessed day, miss."

"You too. Take care."

He walked slowly through the revolving door and limped toward the bus stop. Did he have a neighbor to bring him dinner, a friend to offer him a hug?

She tugged out her phone to text Ben, a knee-jerk reaction. She had to stop doing this: yanking him into her world and then spitting him out. Thinking hard about what to say, Katie paused with her finger over the tiny keyboard, then typed:

Sorry for being a bitch earlier. Hope you dried out. Catch up soon?

The message was marked as delivered and read. He didn't respond, but he'd probably made dinner plans with the pretty blonde. Which made absolute sense: single guy, attractive woman, Saturday night. Consenting adults.

Katie slipped on her sunglasses and stepped out into late-afternoon air heavy with gas fumes and city heat. The old man had disappeared, but a long progression of people headed toward the parking deck. Visiting hours must be over. Katie dawdled, and why not? There was no one waiting on her. A pair of crows cawed, and she stopped to admire a huge concrete planter filled with Japanese blood grass, purple coleus, and a lime-green potato vine. The potato vine was peppered with slug holes.

A text came through, but not from Ben.

You done real good, sugar, Jake had typed. Thank you.

Katie replied with the thumbs-up emoji. Running away in the dark and staying hidden for nine years would never be okay, but leaving *had* been the right course of action. Her family was in a good place, and thanks to her, a new baby had joined the world. Theo.

Mother knows best after all.

Up ahead, a young couple walked slowly, hands entwined. The guy, who was carrying a diaper bag, had a loping gait that suggested a neurological problem; the woman was wearing a baby carrier. Hopefully they would make it as a family.

Katie joined the crowd heading toward the pedestrian crossing and reached the sidewalk outside the parking deck, now in the deep shade of a dying day. A day that spoke of miracles. She might have lost her Catholicism while living in a tent, but today she had found a different kind of faith: faith in herself. She would never be Maisie's real mom, not in everyday ways such as helping with homework, but she had finally behaved as a mother. And yes, she was proud, too. With a glance up at the Carolina sky, Katie thanked God silently.

A motorbike roared away from the traffic lights behind her, and she turned with a smile. But the bike was big and flashy, and the guy straddling it wasn't wearing a helmet. Ben never went anywhere without his helmet. He didn't take risks.

With a sigh, Katie entered the parking deck, where rows of vehicles greeted her, many of them black trucks. Why had she not paid attention when they arrived? She glanced over license plates and then bumper stickers until her eyes lingered on one that said *Coexist.*

Coexist. As she walked, she pictured the poster on her fridge, the mock-up she had created after Ben suggested she start a support group. She thought about the old man going home to no one but a cat. It was her choice to be alone, her choice to shut out Ben, but what if you had no choice? What if she could help others feel less alone?

Her phone rang, but yet again, it wasn't Ben.

"You doing okay?" Delaney said.

"I can't believe it, but I got Maisie inside the hospital."

"Duh. I knew you would. You're a total badass." Delaney giggled. "Sorry. Patrick's being inappropriate. Want to come over and celebrate? He's throwing together a hearty Irish stew that we're going to consume with a shitload of Merlot. You can eat yourself into a food coma and sleep over."

"Appealing offer, but no, thanks. I'm not up for playing third wheel."

Aha! There was the truck. Balancing her phone between her shoulder and her ear, Katie pulled out her keys. "Once I get home, I'm going to reflect on where I go from here. Double down on my search for a decent therapist I can afford, think more about this idea of starting a support group, and, first thing Monday, call my primary care physician. See what I have to do to get back on meds."

"You go, Sis." Delaney giggled again.

"Have fun with your wild Irishman."

"Oh, I will." Delaney paused. "Seriously, you okay?"

A woman and a little girl skipped by, swinging hands and singing. Not a worry between them. Katie closed her eyes and remembered Maisie's hand squeezing her own as they'd walked through the hospital lobby.

"Yeah, I am. I really am. Maybe I won't even need meds this time."
She hung up, and a text came through from Ben. One word, **Sure.**
Without thinking, she typed, **I miss our friendship,** and hit "Send."
He didn't reply, and the voice seized his silence. Snatched it up to
pummel her with a new cycle of worry. Stole the joy of all that she had
achieved, and found its new target: Ben.

THIRTY-EIGHT
CALLUM

"Not every day you see a Porta-John hanging from a crane," Jake said.

Callum followed Jake's gaze to the huge windows on the far wall of the psychologist's waiting room. They were on the third floor, but rather than a panorama of the city, the view was of a giant construction site. Nothing on the drive over had been familiar, although it must have been ten years since he'd visited the area around Duke University Hospital. In another ten years it would be unrecognizable again. Ten years. Theo would be ten. The age he was when . . . Tingling shot down his arm, his heart fluttered to a discordant vibration.

The vise tightened in his chest.

He reached for Maisie's hand. She was squashed between him and Jake on a surprisingly comfortable two-seater. Her feet didn't touch the carpeted floor.

"That fear thermometer you talked about in the car, is it still high?"

Maisie nodded and stared at her unopened library book. Her legs started swinging.

"Mine's in the red zone," Callum said.

"You're anxious, too, Daddy?" She looked up, and he wanted to scoop her into his arms and run.

The elevator dinged and another family headed toward the reception desk. Callum leaned closer. "Extremely."

"That's why I'm here." Jake took her other hand. "'Cause you both know I only get anxious when the Tar Heels are on the basketball court. I'm so relaxed right now, I don't even have a heartbeat."

Maisie frowned. "Uncle J! That does *not* make sense."

"Really?" Jake grinned.

A small, plump woman in purple glasses appeared in front of them, her outfit more visually confusing than his daughter's. "You must be Maisie. Hello, I'm Dr. Young." The woman's voice was high and chirpy.

Callum shot up and shoved his hands into his pockets. The tingling returned, intensified to live electricity. "Maisie's father, Callum." He yanked his right hand free and held it out for a handshake. "And this is Jake, Maisie's uncle. He's volunteered to stay with her while I bring you up to speed on our family drama. At least . . . the CliffsNotes."

"Fantastic plan. Maisie, I'll be back to fetch you shortly. Does that sound okay?"

"Yes, thank you." Maisie sat up straight and beamed. "I like your outfit very much."

"I like yours. See you in a few. Come on then, Dad." Dr. Young turned away, and Callum followed obediently.

She buzzed them through a heavy door and kept walking. His heart thumped in his throat, in his ears, behind his eyes. He imagined being trapped for all eternity in a never-ending white corridor that shrank into nothingness.

"Oopsy," Dr. Young said, and walked backward to grab a doorknob. "All the doors look the same, don't they? We're in here."

He noticed the smell first: stale and anonymous. Hundreds, maybe thousands, of people had passed through this artificially constructed family room—with a sofa, two armchairs, and a computer on top of a cubby. Would Maisie find it claustrophobic? She had a problem with small, windowless spaces. Although the huge mirror, dark at the edges, was large enough for a window. Large enough for observation. Was he being watched? There was no trash can. Where would he vomit? Since Dr. Young made straight for one of the chairs, he settled on the sofa. For sitting on, not vomiting in. Not that he was going to vomit. Or so he hoped.

"Thank you for fitting us in," he said. "On such short notice."

"Not at all. I had a cancellation."

Fiddling with the collar of his knit shirt, Callum glanced up at the camera in the corner.

"Used for training purposes only. And not currently switched on."

He nodded and grabbed a breath.

"What did you want to tell me?" she said.

"It's hard to know. Where to start."

She smiled and waited. Was this place always so quiet?

"There's Maisie's biological mother, who—" Callum swallowed the words *abandoned us*. Even in his head, they sounded disloyal. "Struggles with OCD and recently reentered Maisie's life. That was traumatic, for the whole family." Callum swallowed. "And Maisie's stepmother is in the hospital following a disturbing emergency that Maisie witnessed." Another breath, another swallow. "And there's the person who constructed a huge lie around her childhood to protect her from monsters when truthfully—" He stared down at his hands, clasped together. His knuckles gleamed white. "I was running from my own."

"That's a heavy load to unpack."

"And I think it might help Maisie if I saw someone independently. I was wondering if anyone in this clinic deals with adult anxiety related to intrusive memories." He glanced up; she smiled again. "Of childhood abuse. Sexual in nature."

"I know just the person. I'll find his card before you leave. You've never consulted a therapist?"

Callum shook his head. "And it's time to accept I'm not a victim." The tightness in his chest began to unwind; outside the door, a child giggled. "I'm a survivor."

THIRTY-NINE
KATIE

Katie stood on Jake's doorstep with a bottle of tequila and her phone, which she turned around and around in her hand. She had developed a new habit—*Be honest, Katie, a compulsion*—of checking umpteen times a day for text messages from Ben, who had been AWOL all week. Although, Trent had let slip that Ben was working late one night when he stopped by the studio.

New deal, Katie, no more checking for at least one hour.

She shoved the phone into her back jeans pocket and admired Jake's yard. Who knew he had hidden gardening skills? And the bottle tree with blue, red, orange, green, and purple glass was surprisingly whimsical. If she texted Ben about making her a bottle tree, that wasn't technically checking. Was it?

Jake opened the door in bare feet, worn jeans, and a T-shirt speckled with holes. Tempting cooking smells—barbeque, maybe?—drifted onto the porch as he stretched up to touch the top of the doorframe. His T-shirt rose to reveal a taut stomach and the black elastic waistband of his underwear.

"Well, well." He tossed out the signature Jake Vaughan smile, the one that should have made him a Hollywood star. And hadn't. "Reckon I'm not the only person in the Triangle without Friday-night plans."

She held up the tequila. "A future addition to the bottle tree?"

"Only if you help me empty it." Jake stood back and waved her inside.

"I didn't mean to interrupt dinner."

"Want to stay? You need fattening up, and I always fix enough to feed the whole town."

"Sure. I always overcater, too. Never adapted to cooking for one."

"Whereas I've never adapted to cooking for two." He grinned. "But luckily for you, I'm a leftovers guy."

Jake led her into a narrow hallway and disappeared through the doorway on the right. Katie glanced left into a simple white bedroom with an uneven wooden floor. Jake had a double bed—she would have expected a queen—a white dresser, and a single chair. There was a brightly colored throw draped over the end of the bed, and a small rug on the floor. No pictures, no books, no personal items except for the framed photos of Maisie on the nightstand.

"This is cozy," Katie called out and then joined Jake in the kitchen. "Oh."

She stared at the window seat. Or maybe it was a fairy hidey-hole. Gauzy fabric and strings of white lights hung down from a large hook. Inside the play tent were some books, a pile of cushions, and the Winnie-the-Pooh lamp.

"Maisie kept the lamp?"

"When she upgraded to a big girl's room, she struggled with tossing it." Jake closed the bathroom door, which was next to the oven.

Very cozy.

"I suggested the solution," Jake said. "A reading nook. She hangs out here when I'm doing yard work, which apparently is 'super boring.'"

306

"It's perfect, Jake." Katie clapped her hands together. "I always hoped she'd be a reader."

"That she is." Jake stirred a bubbling concoction and then lowered the gas. "And much as I love surprise gifts, how 'bout we establish the real reason for the booze?"

Katie put the tequila in the middle of the pine table. She stared at it for a moment before pulling back a chair and sitting down. "I owe you a belated thank-you for raising my daughter."

Jake reached up into a cabinet and took down two Mason jars. "I didn't do it for you."

"I know."

"Indulging in self-pity, are we?" He opened the tequila and poured one healthy shot.

"That was truth, not pity."

He started pouring a second shot, and she held up a hand. "Make it small. I'm driving."

Jake emptied his glass and refilled it; she clinked her own against his. "Cheers."

Tequila burned the back of her throat as she tried not to choke. Jake turned off the gas, put a lid on the pot, and joined her at the table.

"You know, I underestimated you for years," Katie said.

"Lots of people do, darlin'. But I've been rewriting my own narrative since I was seven. Sometimes even I can't keep up."

Katie glanced around the kitchen-cum-living-room. As with the bedroom, there was no personal clutter. "There's another reason I'm here. That support group idea I've been toying with? I didn't feel ready before. So many potential triggers. But I want to start reaching out to others, and that led me to you. It seems, Jake, that I'm worried about you. Came as quite a shock."

"Worried about me how?" He wrapped both hands around his Mason jar.

"I figured you might be feeling a little displaced. Might even need a friend. We both love the same little girl, we've both been mothers to her, and we both have next to no family. The pieces are there if we choose to put them together." Katie took another sip of tequila and almost gagged. Maybe it was less disgusting as a shot. "See, I don't think we're so different. Take out the womanizing, and your life's as solitary as mine."

He looked at the table. "I'm a more selective womanizer than I used to be. And you, you still in love with Callum? 'Cause if you are, get over it. This thing with Lilah's solid. I've watched them enough to know."

A thrush landed on the windowsill and serenaded them before flying off into light the color of a smoldering fire.

"I thought I was, but I was wrong." She took another sip of jet fuel. This time she didn't gag. "But back to you and me. We both ran away, and I got to wondering why. I mean, I knew why I did. And the more I thought about why you did, the more I circled the same answer—my sister."

Jake slugged back his drink and poured another shot. He held up the bottle to her, but Katie shook her head. After only a few sips, she was woozy.

"The code of confidentiality we talked about before," he said. "That still apply?"

She nodded.

"Sex used to be my version of self-harm. I hated it, I needed it, it numbed me. Your wedding was tough. I saw Callum pulling away to raise a family, and the old Jake kicked in. The one who was unloved, unwanted, and stupid. Your sister was collateral damage, but things didn't turn out quite the way I'd planned. And when I saw her again at Maisie's christening . . . She got to me, okay? But she plays for keeps, and I don't."

"And yet you didn't stay away from her, did you?"

Jake didn't answer.

"Because that vibe between you guys in my apartment didn't come from two random nights of sex and alcohol."

"Am I the test case for this support group, or you thinking about becoming a shrink?"

"Olive branch, Jake. That's all I'm offering."

"Yeah, well. I'd stay out of my head if I were you. It's not someplace you wanna be."

"Why's that?"

"You got some pit bull in you?"

"Since she met Patrick, Delaney's been in a good place. He makes her happy." She paused; Jake's chest began to rise and fall rapidly. "To quote what you told me, if you still have feelings for her, get over them. She and Patrick have the real deal."

Jake sat up straight. "It ended before Patrick. She was hungry for details of Maisie, and I used that to my advantage. It was a few random hookups over the years. Nothing more."

"Come on, Jake. This bad-guy act doesn't work with me anymore."

"Yeah? You forgettin' it was me who talked Callum into leaving you in a psych ward?"

"He didn't protest, though, did he? And he certainly let his lawyer bash me good and hard while I was a basket case."

"It wasn't that simple. Or maybe it was. We did it for Maisie. Take me back in time, I'd do it over."

"What, throw me under the bus for my daughter?"

"Hey. I stopped you from—" Jake downed his tequila and poured another shot.

"Stopped me from what?"

Jake said nothing.

Aftershave. Damnit, his aftershave. "It was you, wasn't it? On the overpass that night?"

"I don't know what you're talking about."

"Holy shit, Jake. It was you. I left the shelter where I'd been living after Ringo died and walked to the overpass. Climbed up on the railing, and someone grabbed me from behind. Next thing I knew, I was in an ambulance. It was you! You're the one who found me, not Cal. I smelled your aftershave right before you knocked me out. You were my Good Samaritan." She stood up, hesitated, and then collapsed back into the chair. "You saved my life to destroy it?"

"You might want to have a real shot." He pushed the tequila toward her. "I can always call you a cab."

She crossed her arms over her chest.

"Suit yourself." His chair scraped along the floor as he pulled it closer. "I understood, okay? I've considered it, suicide. Even know how I'd do it. Codeine. I have some stockpiled. Not saying I'd ever use it, but it gives me peace of mind. I also know that if I decided to do it, I wouldn't send advance notification."

He sighed. "I'm guessing you want the whole story, so here it is. I was working two jobs in LA and not making it. And then I got kicked off the soap for having a meltdown on set, which left me as an evening nanny for this director. Great kid, but it was part-time, and my career was officially in the shitter.

"Callum was worried about me. Suggested I come for Maisie's birthday and spend some time with him and his folks. And the idea of seeing Delaney again was a draw. Figured I'd take a mini vacation and have a rethink about where my life was heading. But your letter was waiting when we got back from the airport, and everything went to hell.

"We both assumed you were dead, given that the letter had been mailed days earlier, but we left right away. When we got to Asheville, we split up. Callum took the ERs, I went to the shelter you'd listed as your address. They wouldn't talk to me, wouldn't tell me anything. I was leaving when I saw you. I tackled you, you flailed around like a wild animal and hit your head. I dialed 911, and after the ambulance left, I called Callum. It was easy enough to check in on you at the hospital, and then Callum and I booked into a hotel and sat up all night. I convinced him to hire a lawyer, and we agreed Delaney would have to stay out of Maisie's life, too. A clean break. Persuading him to leave you behind was an easy decision. I assumed you were a drug addict, you'd gone to spectacular lengths to reel Callum back in, and the last words you'd ever spoken to him were a threat against Maisie's life."

"That's not true," she said. "The last thing I told him was that I loved them."

Jake twirled his empty Mason jar on the table. "You have no idea how hard he fought to hold things together after you disappeared, but when we found you in Asheville, he went to a dark place. I couldn't leave him, he couldn't cope without Delaney, and what did I have left in LA? So yeah, I threw you under the proverbial bus, along with the only real chance I had with your sister. But I was there for Callum and Maisie. The rest is window dressing."

"And overnight, you gave up everything for your best friend? No one does that."

"He offered me room and board, and I cast my eye to movie work in Wilmington, the Hollywood of the East."

He smiled; she glared. "Not buying it. There's more."

"You *really* might want to reconsider that shot." He stared at her. A penetrating look that told her nothing.

She topped up her glass. "Happy?"

"Did Callum ever tell you why he joined the swim team?"

Something malevolent clawed up her spine. She shook her head.

"It was my idea. I convinced him to join. And when I found him after the coach had . . . I made him a promise. That I would protect him. I've always protected him. It's"—he gave a weird smile—"my best role."

"I promised to protect Maisie when she was a baby, but we can't always live up to our promises, Jake. Life intrudes."

He threw back his tequila. "After my parents were killed in the car wreck, I didn't want to move to Chapel Hill. My aunt didn't want me any more than I wanted her, but there was no one else. The move was tough on both of us. I was acting out, she hated the disruption of me, and I was a disaster in school. I was teased for being dumb, for being an orphan, for being held back a year, for having a country accent. And on it went. But Callum, the class brainiac, was the other new kid. He always stood up for me. Looked out for me, and we became friends. Real friends. And thanks to him, I survived life as little orphan boy with auntie dearest. And how did I pay him back? I got him on the swim team."

"You can't blame yourself for what that bastard did to Cal."

"Yeah, I can, and if you ever go hootin' and hollerin' to him or anyone with what I'm about to tell you, you'll discover that I can be way nastier than you ever imagined. We agreed?"

She nodded, and Jake refilled his glass.

"Katie, please drink the shot. It'll help." His voice had softened. And when he looked up, his eyes were hooded.

She did as he asked, and the tequila burned.

"I could've stopped him." Jake refilled her Mason jar. "But I didn't say a word after it happened to me."

"No. Not both of you." Her hand flew to her mouth.

He watched, dry-eyed. How could he do that—not cry? She dug her thumb and index finger hard into her own eye sockets. When she finally lowered them to reach for her glass, her hand was shaking, her vision muddy.

"Rape doesn't define me," Jake said. "It's not who I am. And my life is pretty damn fine. Mentoring kids and living in a one-bedroom rental property might not be enough for some people, but it's my idea of heaven. Callum, though, I used to worry about him all the time. When you guys met, he was such an easy target. It's the reason I never allowed myself to trust you. What you did was a good thing, encouraging him to tell Lilah."

"How—how can you be okay with this?" She emptied her glass in one swallow. Burn, let tequila burn out the images.

"That meltdown I had on set? Turned out to be the best thing that happened to me apart from moving back here. I went to a therapist who diagnosed PTSD. He helped me put the abuse where it belongs. In my past. These days, I'm all about the present. I'd like to add the future, but I don't even have a savings account.

"First time that asshole shoved his hand down my trunks, I thought I'd earned it. Thought it was punishment for underperforming in some stupid swim meet. I never expected anything good to happen in my life, so why should it matter if he made me feel dirty? But the male body has a way of responding all by itself, and Lord, did he praise me. My coach, the only adult whose opinion mattered, told me I was good at it. Sex. It's always been the one thing I excelled at. So I let him do whatever he wanted. Again and again. Once, after I'd been bullied, I even sought him out." Jake poured another drink.

"I was a kid with behavior issues. I didn't think anyone would believe me, but if I'd spoken up, things might have been different for Callum. Different for you and Callum. But back then I was doing what I always did. Surviving. I started smoking weed, having outbursts. Punched a few walls, bashed my head into a school locker. The coach didn't need to use any mindfuck games to isolate me. I did that all by myself. But targeting Callum was his big mistake.

"Know why he moved on to Callum? I'd gotten too old. That one-year age gap between us made all the difference." Jake sneered. "When I found out he'd attacked Callum, I got mad. Real mad. I reckon anger's what saved me. Turned the tables and gave me a chance to care about someone other than myself. I meant that promise I made him. Meant it like I'd never meant anything before, because I knew it was my fault."

"You never confronted"—she struggled to get the words out—"the coach?"

"I got him fired. Went to the assistant coach and told him, in confidence, what had happened to me. I never mentioned Callum. Bastard didn't believe me, and I had no proof. No bruises, I hadn't fought back. All the classics. But I threatened to spread rumors, and the assistant coach had his eye on the top job. Didn't want a scandal rocking the team. Yeah, we were that good for his career." Jake's voice was full of venom. "He said if I stayed quiet, he'd deal with it. Next day, the coach was gone, and he never had the chance to touch Callum again." Jake reached out and began picking the label off the tequila bottle. "Callum and I quit the team a week later."

"Cal doesn't know any of this?"

"What, you think kids swap details? Sexual abuse doesn't work that way. What little Cal told me the night I found him, he never repeated. This isn't something you want to share, but my gut tells me you understand that. I'm hoping I'm right."

She nodded.

"When I was a kid, I pretended it hadn't happened. If I didn't talk about it, if I didn't own it, it wasn't real. I built a wall around it so I could get to the next day, and the day after that. One day at a time, that's how I made it, until I focused on helping Callum. Had he known, it wouldn't have made any difference. It sure wouldn't make a difference now. Watching out for him and Maisie, though, that was something I could do to make amends."

The alcohol buzzed through her brain. "Thank you for trusting me."

"Don't make me regret it, darlin'. I'm like your old mutt, Ringo. I don't behave too well when cornered." Jake stood up. "Come on, set the table. We need food if we're going to keep drinking."

Katie sat on her hands. "I'm struggling to make sense of all this."

"Drink enough of that tequila, and it'll be a helluva lot easier. Listen, I didn't tell you so you'd feel bad. I told you so you'd understand the last piece of our story and cut Callum some slack. Delaney too. Please don't ask your sister about us. We all have enough guilt, and you and I can make sure it ends here." He rubbed at his forehead as if trying to erase something. "What's impressive is that between us we haven't ruined Maisie."

"Or maybe she's the reason we're all still functioning."

He poured them both another drink. "I'm not set up for company, but if you don't want to catch a cab home, you're welcome to the bed. I'll take the window seat. I'm one of those misfits who can sleep sitting up."

She downed her third shot, which didn't burn as much as the first two. Jake was right: alcohol, at least tonight, was the answer.

After she'd set the table, Jake placed a steaming plate of what he called Jake Surprise in front of her, explaining it was his version of Brunswick stew. While they ate and cleaned up, he filled her in on the missing Maisie years. And then the question snuck out all on its own.

"Were you in love with my sister?"

"Now what's the point of that question? Things start, things end, and often things work out the way they should." He draped the tea towel over the oven handle. "She deserved better, that's the truth."

He deserves better. "So does Ben."

Katie pulled out her phone and checked. No new texts.

Jake shook his head. "Lordy, the two of you are lame. What's goin' on with you and the boyfriend?"

"He's not—"

"Don't be dense."

She put her phone down on the table. "I messed up. And now he has a girlfriend. And he won't answer my texts. And I want him back in my life."

"As a friend or something more?"

"I don't know, but I miss him so much it hurts, right here." She tried to slap her chest but missed and hit her shoulder. "I'm a lousy friend as well as a lousy mother."

"Wanna know what I think?"

Katie wobbled toward the bathroom door. "Hold that thought, 'cause I gotta pee."

When she came back, she half fell into her chair. And then she took another shot. Tequila after dinner made no sense, but that ache in her heart had crept back in.

"The only times I've seen you since your wedding have been as a mama," Jake said. "And you're good at it. You got Maisie to the hospital when I couldn't, and remember her christening? How she fussed?"

"Cried all the time." Katie pulled the bottle toward her and did another shot.

"Except when she was with you."

"Or you. I have a memory of her sleeping on your chest." Katie stared out through the kitchen window into the night. White lights had switched on in the magnolia tree. *Magical.* "Cal couldn't handle the crying. I kept telling him there was no right or wrong way, but every time he picked her up, he tensed, and she cried."

"You had this calm patience with her. I think that made it worse. Callum would watch you and think he was a failure."

"He never told me that." The room started to sway, but the pain of missing Ben, of missing Maisie, it all vanished. Poof! *Definitely magic.*

"Let's be honest, Katie. There's a lot you guys didn't tell each other."

"Maybe if we'd communicated better, things would have been different. He retreated, and I became new mommy on steroids. The irony is that I felt as much a failure as Cal did." Katie paused. "Is he going to be okay second time around—as a new dad?"

"Damn right."

"You ever wonder what if? What if I hadn't left? What if you'd stayed in LA?"

"Darlin', that idea ain't worth a crap. You take out the bad chapters of your life, and who knows what you'd have left? If my parents hadn't died when I was a kid, I'd probably still be in Podunk Nowhere, working at the seed and feed. I didn't want to move to Chapel Hill, but that put me square in Callum's path. Thanks to him and Ms. Jill, our middle school English teacher, I started chasing my dream. D'you have any idea how shitty it was being a moody kid in rural Carolina who fantasized about acting? And if I hadn't come back from LA, I might never have started working with kids. I love my job a whole lot. Would you have become a metal artist if you'd stayed put?"

"No, but I'd still have my family. And Maisie—"

"Will always be your daughter. You can't change biology. And I gotta say, I like this new, improved version of you. She's got a whole lot of potential." He refilled their glasses. "And now, we're going to dance. If I can find my iPod."

She downed another shot as Jake got up and fiddled with something on the dresser. Oh, yeah, blind drunk. This was da bomb.

"I suggest we start with . . . Got it!" Jake said. Bruce Springsteen's "Born to Run" came on.

"Bruce!" She giggled.

Jake pulled her up, and they danced around his kitchen table. One song led to another and another. Man, this was the way to do it! And she loved Uncle J, her new BFF! And the buzz and the music—all from that tiny speaker—and . . . *Whoa.* The room started to spin counterclockwise as someone banged on the front door.

Jake yelled, "Come in!"

Katie twirled into a chair, and there was Ben. Looking totally hot and totally pissed off.

"Bennie!" She lurched at him. "You look nice! Why're you here?"

"You texted me, remember?"

"Did not."

Ben glanced at Jake. "You're not in trouble?"

"No, silly." She giggled. "I'm drunk. Blind, stinking *druuunk.*"

"I hope you're not planning on driving."

"Course not." She tried to grab her car keys off the table, missed, and they fell to the floor. "I might be shit-faced, but I'm hyper res-res—"

"Responsible?" Jake lowered the music.

She pointed at Jake. "What he said. And it's okay 'cause I'm gonna have a sleepover with Uncle J. We're friends now. *Best* friends." She staggered toward Ben, which would be *sooo* much easier if he stopped moving.

"You are?" Ben scowled.

Angry Ben was *va-va-voom*. "We used to be *best* friends, but you don't like me anymore. And you have a girlfriend, and—wait. How'd you know where I was?" The words were hard to push out of her mouth. *Heavy*—she giggled again—*heavy words.*

"You texted me your address and said you needed help."

Katie hiccuped. "Did not, silly."

Now Ben was spinning, and she was . . . she was . . . "I'm going to be sick."

FORTY
JAKE

"Confession time." Jake tried not to listen to Katie barf in the next room. "Katie didn't send the text, I did. I don't deal with drunk women." The lie was smooth, as smooth as Katie's tequila. Shit, he was hammered. The guy with the serious biceps and huge gray eyes seemed to sway all over the place. "You scrub up nicely. Fingernails are still black, though."

"Hazard of the art. I was having dinner with a friend when *you* texted."

"Aha. The lady friend who isn't our Katie."

"What's that supposed to mean?"

Jake nodded at the bathroom door. "I wasn't lying, man. She needs you."

"Great. You get her drunk, and I get to clean up. This isn't something you can handle?"

"Nope."

Ben screwed the top on the tequila bottle. "What's your game, Jake?"

Jake tried to keep Ben in focus. "You change your hair? 'S cool. Suits you. Ya know, I get why she likes you."

Jake went to the sink, filled a glass with water, and downed it. On the other side of the closed bathroom door, the toilet flushed.

"What do you mean—she *likes* me?"

"You know the sexiest quality in a man?" Playing fairy godmother to these two was almost too easy. "Come on, not a tough question. Think about all those leading men who brood. You do the brooding thing, I've seen it."

Ben frowned. "The only thing I'm doing right now is wondering why someone tricked me into dumping my date."

"Aha! You were on a date."

"Get to the point, Jake."

Jake rolled his eyes. "Loyalty, man. You've got it in spades."

"What's that supposed to mean?"

"Take her home, look after her." Jake hiccuped. "Trust me. It'll work out in your favor. She doesn't want to wake up here to a massive hangover and m' handsome face. But I think she might want to wake up to you."

"And why would that be?"

Jake slapped his forehead. "How come you two don't get it? Any jackass can see you've got a thing for each other." Did people really make dating this hard? "You're the one person who's stood by her. Well, apart from her sister. That's a killer aphrodisiac, knowing someone wants to be with you even after you mess up big time."

"And how would you know?"

"Projecting, man." Jake took a deep breath. "It wasn't anyone's fault, you know, what happened in the past. Good people often make bad decisions for the right reasons."

Ben nodded. Clearly he thought they were still discussing Katie. Jake let that one slide, because he wasn't going to have a conversation about the deal they'd all made. The one he'd suggested and then broke when he used the last of the hemorrhoid commercial money to pay Katie's hospital bill. Delaney had applied for charity case status, but that was a long, slow process. One day Delaney called the house to demand Callum take care of it. Only Callum wasn't the one to answer the phone, and Jake used that call to get to Delaney. She was desperate for information about Maisie. He was desperate for Delaney. They arranged to meet in a hotel halfway between Asheville and Raleigh so he could give her a handful of Maisie's scribbles. No one knew those scribbles cost him $6,000, not even Callum, who was too out of it back then to take care of anything. But it worked out pretty darn well since Delaney and Katie thought Callum had been extremely benevolent. It was good to have a few secrets. Like how he managed to tell Maisie all that good shit about her mama. Although that one was pretty easy. He had been describing Delaney, not her sister.

"You know," Jake said. "Katie's got a helluva lot of spunk. She's one fine mama, and I think it's time she got herself a good man. You."

Ben glanced at the bathroom door. "I have feelings for her. Strong feelings."

Gotta love guy-speak. "Seriously? You don't think I figured out you're in love with her?"

"It's getting too hard, waiting for something that's never going to happen."

Yup. Couldn't argue with that one.

"I'm trying to cut the cord," Ben said.

Been there, failed at that. Mind you, he and Delaney had managed to be alone and not end up in bed. Progress was a fine thing. "And yet you ditched date night to deal with Ms. Vomiting."

Ben smiled. "I didn't say it was going well, my plan. In all fairness, I wouldn't have come if I'd known she was hugging a toilet."

"Yeah, you would have." Because it's exactly what he would do if Delaney sent him a text that said *I need you* followed by the address. Wouldn't even think twice. "She's had a lot to deal with. Give her time."

"I have. I'm trying to move on, you know?"

"And yet here we all are." Jake held up his hands. "Go. Deal with her. Be the guy she needs. Be warned, though. Treat her bad, and I'll beat the crap out of you." He went back to the sink and filled his glass with more water. "And drunk or sober? I fight dirty."

FORTY-ONE
KATIE

Katie opened her eyes to bright light. Sunlight. Where was she? Home, she was home. In her apartment, in her bed. *Oh, thank God.* How did she get here? She was at Jake's, and then she was throwing up and . . . The Durham Freeway was quieter than usual. Weekend quiet, which meant outside it was Saturday morning. Inside, it was . . . ? Swallowing through what could have been a throatful of thumbtacks and gasoline, she turned over and nearly collided with Ben. Fully clothed, sound-asleep Ben, lying on his side. Why, why had she drunk so much?

Because he hates me; because I've lost him. Maybe that wasn't an OCD thought. *Does he hate me? What if I hate him? No, no, I don't hate him, how could I? But what if I don't care about him? What if I want to ruin his life? Because that's what I do—ruin the lives of people I love and then blame OCD—isn't it?*

She pulled the blanket up to her chin and was about to sink into her bedding, never to resurface, when Ben opened those huge gray eyes.

"How're you feeling?"

"Humiliated, embarrassed, hungover, and incredibly sorry." Her voice was scratchy and thin. "You hate me, don't you? I'm sorry, so sorry."

He sat up and reached for a glass of water on the far nightstand. "Drink this. Do you need more aspirin? I made you take two around midnight."

She shook her head and pulled herself up on one elbow, drained the glass, and flopped back down. Then she covered her eyes with her forearm.

What if I don't care about him? What if I'm messing with him? I have the same thoughts as people who hurt children, right? Did Cal and Jake's swim coach have the same doubt as me? No, please no. Can't have that in my head. Really can't have that in my head. I am not this person. These thoughts are not me. Yes, yes they are.

"Do you remember throwing up in my truck?" he said.

"Sorry. Sorry. I'm not doing so well."

Her bed vibrated as he turned his back on her and swung his legs to the floor. "I'll make coffee while you shower. Then we should talk."

What if I'm an alcoholic like Mom? No, I'm not. I hardly drink. What if I'm about to change that? What if alcohol's my new coping mechanism? What if, what if?

She sat up quickly, too quickly, swallowed a surge of nausea, and glanced down. "Wait, you undressed me?" What panties was she wearing? Not the faded granny ones. *Please.*

"I removed your shoes and jeans. Closed my eyes at the first glimpse of black lace." There was an edge to his voice she hadn't heard before. "Shower and then we'll talk."

Leaning over, she grabbed his arm. "Don't."

"Don't what, Katie?" Still, he didn't turn.

"Do that. Talk to me as if I'm an errant child and then walk away."

He hates me, and why wouldn't he? It wasn't enough to push him to another woman, I had to vomit in his truck? He doesn't love me, he could never love me. He hates me. Ben hates me. And I hate him. I don't love him, I don't love anyone. I'm thoughtless and selfish and—

A thought. A single thought, so loud, so clear: *I could kill him.*

She gasped.

"You ruined my date and threw up in my truck. How should I sound?"

"I'm sorry, so sorry. I didn't deliberately ruin your date. At least I don't think I did. And I'll clean up the truck."

"Yeah, you will. I left it for you."

"How did you know where I was?"

"A text."

"I'm sorry, I didn't mean to text you."

"You didn't. Jake did."

Ben's only here because of Jake, because Jake asked for help, because no one wants to deal with me, because I'm unstable.

"Evidently he decided to play Cupid."

Cupid? His phone announced a message. Ben typed a reply and then glanced over his shoulder. His smile hit like a slap. "Luckily for you, she's cool with it."

"I guess you have feelings for her then"—Katie picked at a piece of peeling skin until blood oozed out—"the pretty blonde."

"How about you shower and—"

"Before I clean up my vomit?"

"I have a delivery of sheet metal coming at noon. If you want me to drive you back into Hillsborough to pick up your truck, we need to get moving. Take two showers if you want. Or don't. Do whatever you want, Katie." And with that, he left her bedroom.

After a long, hot shower, Katie towel dried her hair and stood, naked, in front of the full-length mirror. She wiped away the condensation and stared at her reflection. Her face was gray, her eyes red, and she'd lost too much weight. Her hands, where she'd gnawed and pulled at her skin, were a mess. She poked at her ribs. When had she done this to herself—stopped making smart decisions, stopped caring, stopped fighting for what she wanted? She reached up and twisted her hair. Where was the woman who had left Asheville with such purpose? The voice buzzed, louder and louder. Told her she deserved to lose Ben, told her she didn't care about him, told her she would hurt him. Wreck his life the way she'd almost wrecked Delaney's and Maisie's, break him the way she'd broken her family. The way she broke everything.

No, hope whispered. *I need him.*

I'm spiraling, I'm giving these thoughts power. Power they don't deserve.

"And you, OCD," Katie spoke to her reflection, "can't have him, too."

Ben knocked on the door, and she jumped. "I made coffee."

Turning away from her reflection, she grabbed a towel, secured it around her torso, and opened the door.

"Ben?" Panic rose. "Where are you?"

Don't leave me; I need you.

"I'm in the living room."

What if I don't need him, what if he hates me, what if . . . I love him?

He was sitting at the breakfast bar. "Feeling any better?" he said, without looking up.

"Yes, no. I'm sorry."

What if I don't love him but tell him I do? I could run away from him. I could break his heart. I could leave him. Leaving's what I do best.

Facts, Katie. What's real?

Ben. Sitting in her apartment, holding her favorite mug.

The man I love.

Grabbing his stool with both hands, she swiveled him around to face her. He jerked back as if she'd stuck him with a cattle prod, but he was pinned between her and the breakfast bar. "You didn't tell me how you feel about the blonde."

"I am not discussing my love life with you. Certainly not this morning."

She moved closer until her torso was touching his knees. "You wanted to talk after my shower? I'm here, let's talk." She put her hands on his thighs; his Adam's apple bobbed.

"I'm done, Katie. I'm moving out of the studio."

"What?" She pulled back. "Why?"

"I'm tired of people borrowing my equipment and breaking it." He sat up. "And I'm tired of being the safety monitor. And I want my own space."

"Why didn't you tell me?"

"Just did, in case you weren't paying attention." He never talked to her this way.

I should let him go. What if I don't love him? What if I make him fall in love with me, then run away again? See Katie run.

"I want out, Katie. From all of it."

No. Don't leave me. "Including me?" Katie swallowed more nausea.

"When I set my sights on something, it's all or nothing. I thought that if I was there for you, it was enough. That one day you might think of me differently. And my theory was working until your life imploded and you gave me nowhere to go except the nearest exit."

I need him.

"No." She tugged up her towel. "You can't move out of the studio, I won't let you."

He made a strange sound that could've been a laugh. "You can't stop me. The studio's too social. School groups come through, long-lost daughters show up. I don't even believe kids should be in that space. I get twitchy enough when Delaney drops by wearing flip-flops. And I want to get serious about my art, not follow every distraction."

"You don't get distracted. You have the focus of a rhinoceros."

"Rhinos have focus?"

"Who knows? Are you sleeping with the blonde?"

He blushed. "My sex life is none of your business."

"Yes, it is, because you brought up Cupid. And I need to know if it's too late to say I'm sorry. Sorry about everything. Sorry for last night. Sorry for every crappy thing I've ever done to you, but please. Don't do this. I know I screwed up, I know I've taken you for granted, I know I have no one to blame but myself. I know I've treated you badly, been self-absorbed. But I've lost so much, and I can't lose you, too—I can't. Please, please don't leave me. I *need* you."

"I'm not leaving you." He looked at the floor. "Just the studio."

"And us?"

He raised his eyes. His beautiful gray eyes. "There is no us. You made that clear."

"Who is she, the blonde?"

"A friend set us up. She's recovering from a bad breakup, and she's lonely. I am, too."

"Are you in a sexual relationship?"

He closed his eyes, breathed in and out, and opened them. "No. I had high hopes for last night, but—"

Act, don't think. Pushing down on his thighs again, she eased herself on top of him and straddled his lap. His arms moved quickly to secure her.

"Jesus, Katie. Now what are you doing?"

The towel started slipping, but he held her gaze.

"I'm making a move." She leaned forward, her breasts brushing against his chest. *I'm such a fraud. I don't know how to make a move.* "I ran away once when I should have stood my ground, and once is enough. Unless—" She pulled back and her finger shot to her mouth.

"Katie—" Laughter reflected in his eyes. "Stop chewing on your fingers."

"Sorry, sorry. Gross habit, I know, but I'm a mess right now. You don't want this? You hate me?"

"No. Any idiot can see that I'm . . . Damnit, Katie. That's not the problem." He leaned back against the breakfast bar again, but his arms stayed in place. "Please go and get dressed."

She pulled farther up his body, and he groaned.

"I thought you liked to be surprised by your works in progress," she said.

"Only if the conversation is flowing. You don't want this. Not in the way I do. Please, Katie. I'm trying to walk away. Let me go."

What if I hate him? What if I break his heart? "No."

"No?" A smile tugged at the corner of those lips. Those gorgeous full lips.

"Leaving Asheville wasn't about the welding. It was about working with you. It was about *you*." She ran her fingers through his hair and touched his scar. Then she looped her arms around his neck. *This, I want this.* "Because I think we could survive the throw test. I think that if we were welded together and thrown against the wall, we'd hold fast."

"You're comparing us to a basic weld?" With slow, stroking movements, his hands slid to the edges of her breasts. "That's the most bizarre thing a woman has ever said to me."

She stared at his lips and imagined kissing them. "How about this, then? When you came into the studio with the tall blonde, I was completely undone. You're the reason I got drunk last night, because when I think about you with her, about you not being in my life, the doubt that you hate me is real. I can't function without you, Ben. Not having you around this week, I've been drifting. I can't focus, I can't sleep, I can't eat. It's not just all the little things you do for me. It's you. Your presence, your energy, your laugh. Do you know I can tell when you're in the studio even if I can't see you? Do you know what it means to not have that? To not be able to look up and see your smile, to not be able to hear your voice, to not have the safety of knowing where you are?"

He raised his eyebrows. "So I'm a weld and your safety net?"

"No. You're the guy I can't live without. And this"—she looked around her living room—"isn't my home, and neither's the studio. You are. And I can't risk that you like the blonde enough to sleep with her. Because I really don't want that to happen."

"What do you want to happen?"

"You. All of it. With you. Also, I'm naked and we're still talking. And I haven't had sex in a very, very long time, and none of this is helping my self-esteem. Do you like her, the blonde?"

He brushed her lips with a kiss. She shivered, and he pulled up the towel to cover her shoulders.

"Nothing's happened between us. We talk about her ex and you. Do you really mean this, Katie, or are you going to break my heart?"

"You going to break mine?" She held out her arm. "Feel my pulse. It's racing to shutdown."

He kissed the inside of her wrist.

"My OCD's trying to drag me back into hell and using you to get me there. Telling me awful things could happen to you, showing me, and I can't fight back when it latches on to you because of how much you matter. That's what it does. Goes after whoever matters most."

"Would it help if I got naked, too? An exposure to prove I'm indestructible?"

Ben smiled a slow, intimate smile that landed in the middle of her chest. Aftershocks flickered through her body like a thousand trapped fireflies set free.

"I don't know when it happened or how," she said. "Or maybe it's always been there and I was too scared to drag it out into the daylight."

"It's daylight now." He placed her hand on his cheek.

"I love you. I love you fiercely, Ben Holt. Please love me back."

"Can I come with you next time you see Maisie?"

She nodded. *Tell me you love me.*

"No more shutting me out from the OCD?"

She shook her head. *Tell me you love me.*

"Will you come and see the house I've found? It's out in Orange County, about ten minutes from Jake's. There's an old barn with potential for a studio. We could create one together, from scratch."

"I thought you wanted out?"

"From the studio, not you." He brushed her hair behind her right ear. "I love you fiercely, too. Jesus, it's been driving me crazy—not allowing myself to hope for this moment."

"Why? Why do you love me?"

"Katie, you've bewitched me since you stormed into my world in skintight jeans and a Dead Sara T-shirt and said, 'Teach me how to make steel dance in the wind.' You were a fireball of determination, but the more time we spent together, the less I understood what drove you. You made it clear we'd never be anything more than friends, and I took what you offered. But I've always wanted to unlock the mystery of you, and when you told me about everything you've overcome, there was no turning back. I wanted in all the way."

"Will you"—she watched his lips again—"teach me how to do this right?"

"Let me show you."

"What happened to the steel delivery?"

"Us happened, and it's going to be huge."

"Text Trent, tell him to—"

But then he was kissing her and hoisting her up, and as he carried her back to the bedroom, she imagined dancing in the wind.

FORTY-TWO
KATIE

October and November came and went, bringing drought, burnished and rusty foliage, and patches of smoky fog from forest fires in the mountains. Thinking ahead to spring, Katie started to plan her new garden with Ben's bottle tree as the centerpiece.

Between them they had moved everything out to his new property: their work, their belongings, even the support group. The first meeting was small—four people plus Katie—held in front of the wood-burning stove at the heart of her new home.

The open-plan, solar-powered house understood cold weather. It closed around her and Ben, making it easy to huddle and stay put in their very own igloo created from wood and glass. She fell for the stained glass windows on the east side of the house; Ben fell for the wrought-iron staircase that wound up to the loft area they had turned into a shared office.

Every morning the house flooded with sunlight. Katie loved to pad out of their bedroom to make her tea, step down onto the tiled area with Ben's fifties dinette table and chairs, and look through the wall of glass to their deck with the forest beyond. In front of the tree line, rising from a small strip of grass, were the two sculptures they'd moved from outside the Durham Sculpture Workshop. Life should have been idyllic, and yet . . .

As the winter solstice approached, Katie curled in on herself. Darkness whispered, targeting her new relationship. The voice became a perpetrator of hate:

You're happy, are you? This matters to you, does it? Well, we can't have that, can we?

The OCD shouted that she was meant to be alone; taunted her about running away and told her if she didn't, she'd get pregnant and fail at motherhood a second time; demanded certainty about her feelings and his; showed her how she could hurt him. How she could make him bleed. When she retreated, Ben made no demands. One Sunday evening, after he found her lying on the bathroom floor in the fetal position, he picked her up—muttering she was easier to move than a twelve-foot steel sculpture—carried her to their bed, and spooned behind her. On their two-month anniversary, she asked why he stayed with her.

"I love you," Ben said. "Doubt isn't part of my equation."

He had enough certainty for two.

Ben also began putting aside money from his commissions so she could upgrade to weekly sessions with her new psychologist. When she tried to refuse, he insisted it was an investment in their future. *Our future*—she liked the sound of those two words.

Thanksgiving with Delaney and Patrick had been memorable. Delaney showed off the large sapphire on her fourth finger, and the four of them christened the new fire pit Ben had built as an early Christmas present. Sitting in lawn chairs around the bonfire of brush and old wood from the new studio, Katie watched sparks fly up to the stars and wondered if here—in this moment, in this house—she could find peace. When an owl hooted greetings from the forest, she had tried to believe the answer was yes—despite OCD. And now it was the third week of December. Whitmore was hosting a Christmas party fundraiser for the International OCD Foundation and auctioning off Katie's piece from the group show, the piece created from bullets and buckshot.

"Do we need to brainstorm coping strategies for tonight?" Ben said as he parked the truck outside the Chocolate Factory.

"You mean other than—" She started singing "I Got You Babe."

"Not really an answer, but I'll take it." He smiled his sexy little smirk and kissed her.

A long, gentle kiss that made her wish they were alone in his house. Their house. Every morning when she awoke to a tangle of limbs, she worried they'd become too insular. Even in sleep, they found each other. But everything about Ben surprised her. An adventurous lover, he treated her, his bike, and his art with meticulous care, insisted on absolute order in their new studio—which was still evolving—and yet his side of the bedroom said, *I'm a slob.* And when he cooked? A gargantuan disaster.

Ben leaned his forehead against hers. "FYI, I'll be mentally undressing you all night. You in that dress? The stuff of my fantasies."

"You mean this little ol' thing?" She opened her big black coat and tugged down on the cleavage of her red dress. With a low growl, he moved in for a quick kiss and a quick grope. She had found the dress at the PTA thrift store for five dollars. When she came home and modeled it for him, he reached for her and flicked up the short skirt, and they had made love on the rug in front of the wood-burning stove.

"Right." He pulled his jeans away from his groin. "Time to go and pretend we enjoy spending time with other people before we get arrested for indecent exposure."

After they clambered out of the truck, Katie buttoned up her coat against the temperature that had dipped in the last twenty-four hours, and Ben draped an arm over her shoulder. Even in four-inch wedges, she was lost in the sheer size of him. As they walked down the street toward CAM, someone gave a wolf whistle. Ben stopped and they turned together.

"How's it going, lovebirds?" Jake said.

"Hey, man." Keeping his left arm in place, Ben shook Jake's hand. "You still on for Christmas Eve dinner?"

"Sure thing."

"Where's our other star?" Ben said.

"Already inside. Callum texted me a while ago. Maisie insisted they get here ridiculously early, but I'm not sure how long he and Lilah will stay. Depends on Theo. I've been assigned the onerous task of driving 'Mazing Maisie home after the show."

"Gotcha." Ben squeezed her shoulder before she could say, *They could have asked us.*

When they reached CAM, Ben held open the huge yellow door. Warm air, laughter, and live music hit as they stepped inside. Ben helped her off with her coat, Jake complimented her on the dress, and, with his hand wrapped around hers, Ben led them into the main exhibition space.

A cluster of people surrounded her buckshot piece. Servers circulated with trays of appetizers and filled champagne flutes. On the floor below, a jazz band played in the spot where she had accidentally reunited with Maisie. Katie shook her head. She had come so close to backing out, to passing on the chance. Sometimes spontaneity was a gift, not a curse.

Whitmore came over, his eyes lingering on Jake for a second too long. A young woman, less subtle, sashayed over with a tray of canapés. Jake flashed his eyes at Katie as if to say, *So many choices, so little time.* Then he spotted Maisie and announced, "There's my number-one girl. Come on, y'all, let's go pay homage to Maisie MacDonald, the leading authority on Katie Mack."

Maisie, pad clasped to her chest, chatted away to her father. Next to him, in an ankle-length velvet dress, Lilah swayed, one hand under the baby snuggled in the sling. Her smile was bright, and her hair, loosely twisted off her face, was a mass of gleaming ringlets. Lilah wore motherhood well.

"I was telling Callum earlier"—Whitmore cast another glance at Jake—"that Maisie was the star of our docent program. I hope she'll consider returning in the spring."

"Oh, I would like that very much," Maisie said, and then bobbed up on tiptoe to kiss Theo gently. Theo slept on.

Cal turned to Lilah. "We can leave whenever you're ready, darling."

"As if," Lilah said. "I'm out of pj pants, and I'm having a grown-up conversation. I'm not leaving unless our little man starts bawling his head off."

"Mom," Maisie said, "my brother never bawls his head off."

Katie smiled. *Mom.* Now when Maisie used the word, it didn't feel as if someone were pulling her chest apart with rib spreaders. She and Ben had become a small but important part of Maisie's life, and nothing mattered more these days than gratitude.

The band stopped playing. "Katie," Lilah said. "Can I have a word in private?"

Cal glanced at his wife, and Ben gave Katie's hand a quick squeeze.

"Of course. Let's go over there." Katie indicated a quiet spot by a mixed-media sculpture of cement and rusted iron.

When they reached it, Katie nodded at Theo. "He's a good sleeper?"

"It appears so," Lilah said.

"Maisie had horrible sleep patterns." Katie searched for the server with the champagne, but he was trapped at the far end of the room.

"So I heard. You know, I was hoping you could teach me how to become Maisie's mother."

"What?" Katie stared at Lilah. "I—I don't understand. You *are* her mom."

"Not with the thing that counts most: her anxiety. Theo takes all my time, and I'm worried Maisie's needs will get lost. I was hoping the three of us could start a regular date. Maybe every Sunday afternoon at the house. Would you be game?"

"Lilah, I would do that in a heartbeat, but I'm not sure Cal will approve."

"I can handle Callum. It's amazing what happens after you come back from the dead. I could ask him for the moon right now, and it would be mine."

"That's a lot of power."

"Which I intend to use wisely to help Maisie."

Katie glanced toward Ben as a tic developed in her right eye.

We won't stay together. I don't love him enough; I was definitely checking out that cute guy at the supermarket last week. What if I break Ben's heart even though I promised I wouldn't? What if I'm lying? I should leave him tonight. Get it over with before I wreck his life.

A thought isn't a fact, and I won't assign meaning to this. I can't predict the future, but I know one fact: I need Ben. I'm going to love him the best I can and live with uncertainty.

"You okay?" Lilah touched her arm.

"OCD messing." Katie tried to smile. "It hates that I'm finally happy."

"He seems lovely, your Ben. I think Maisie has a bit of a crush on him. Having met him, I understand why."

"Our relationship's been a slow burn, but he's the love of my life."

Am I saying that for Lilah's benefit? What if I don't believe it? What if I don't love Ben? What if we argue in the truck driving home, and I distract him and we crash and he dies, dies because of me?

I control fire; I am strong.

"I'm not saying that for your benefit," Katie said. "He is. I've always had intimacy issues, but not with Ben."

Lilah nodded and swayed, looking down to check on Theo. "If you could give me one piece of advice on how to be a good mother to a kid with OCD, what would it be?"

"Are you the artist?" An older woman clutching a champagne flute lurched toward Katie.

"Yes, and bid high. The money's going to an excellent cause."

"You were saying?" Lilah spoke loudly, and Katie couldn't help but smile. Yes, Lilah could certainly handle Cal. In different circumstances, she and Lilah might have become friends.

The woman mumbled to her companion and tottered off.

"There's no single answer," Katie said. "Trying to support Maisie will be counterintuitive to everything your gut tells you. You'll want to make the hurt go away, but only she can do that. When she's struggling, the OCD will demand reassurance, which you mustn't provide. Often she'll seem self-centered, but you can't punish her for behavior that's a symptom of her illness, and you can't push too hard. Some days she won't have the strength to fight back, and on those days, hold her and love her. Remind her it's okay to fail, and that tomorrow's a do-over. That's what Ben does—loves me hardest on days I can't cope. I can recommend more books, too. If you'd like."

"On audio?" Lilah tossed back her hair. "I doubt I'll ever have time to read again."

"When's the maternity leave up?"

"It isn't. I've decided to be a full-time wife and mom for a while, give the family a chance to find its feet. There's been so much to absorb."

They exchanged a look.

"Now that's my ideal baby. Asleep." Delaney joined them, hand in hand with Patrick. The same height, both black haired, they balanced each other out. Patrick was wearing a dark three-button blazer, a bright-blue shirt, and his standard cashmere scarf knotted in a way that screamed European. On his wrist would, no doubt, be the *Sesame Street* watch that matched his nephew's. It was a family joke, and nothing mattered more to Patrick than family. When Delaney fell for him, that silly watch had told Katie all she needed to know: this man was good enough for her sister.

Katie handled the introductions, and the band started up again. It was only a matter of time before Cal and Jake appeared and Delaney and Cal came face-to-face. Cal might hate confrontations, but Delaney embraced them. Did he realize that Delaney had vowed to never forgive him? Katie's every muscle tightened. Pain spiked at the base of her skull; anxiety prickled under her skin and wormed into her gut. As if sensing she was going under, Ben strolled over.

"Hey." He kissed Delaney's cheek. "What's up?" he said to Patrick.

Patrick shook hands with Ben, oblivious to the two men who had moved into place behind him. Even if you didn't know, you would sense their connection. With similar sculpted physiques, they looked like brothers, and on some level they were.

Katie scratched her forearm.

"How interesting—seeing you again," Delaney said to Cal. She looked as if she was about to say more. Or maybe she was battling to stay quiet since she wanted his permission for Maisie to be her flower girl.

"Likewise," Cal said. He smiled; Delaney didn't.

"Patrick, this is my ex-brother-in-law." Delaney overenunciated *ex*. She made no reference to him being Maisie's dad, for which Katie was oddly grateful. "Callum, this is my fiancé, Patrick."

"Getting hitched, eh?" Jake said. "You're one lucky man."

Delaney had once complained that it was impossible to make Patrick jealous, but the look he gave Jake was, surely, reserved for muggers of little old ladies. "So, you're Jake."

"I've told him lots of Jake stories," Delaney said with a broad grin. "All bad."

"Then all true," Jake said to Patrick.

Maisie bounded over to join them. "I'm about to start my presentation. Would you please stop talking and come and listen?"

"Your wish is our command, darlin'," Jake said.

As Maisie began her docent spiel, a small crowd formed around them. She had inherited her father's public speaking skills, but as a teacher, Katie's hadn't been shoddy. Cal beamed at Maisie and then back at Lilah and the baby. Had he ever looked at her that way? It was hard to recall. The memories were fading faster than old photographs stored carelessly and eaten by mold.

Katie leaned back against Ben. His arms came around her, and she rested her own on top of his, rubbing her hands up and down his biceps. *I love you, Ben Holt. I love you fiercely.*

After Maisie had explained how the buckshot represented the artist's struggles to overcome fear, she swept her arm toward Katie. "And we're super lucky to have the artist here. She can tell you lots more about the piece than I can."

Katie smiled. "I have nothing to add."

Jake had been right: Maisie understood Katie Mack's work perfectly.

Raleigh, North Carolina

Katie glanced up at the Christmas tree created from live poinsettias. The third plant on the fourth row, the one in gold foil, needed water. It was crying out for attention, wilted enough to ruin the whole display. What if she didn't take action and it died? Dead holiday decor had to be a sign of something bad. Should she track down maintenance and tell them?

On the stage near photos with Santa, the middle school band stopped screeching through "Silent Night" and rustled sheet music. Parents applauded while Katie's ears continued to ring from the squeaky clarinet. Maisie, who had wanted to listen for comparison with her soon-to-be school band, didn't comment. In fact, Maisie had stopped talking. Did she wish she were home with her family? Did she want to be anywhere but here, in an overheated, overstuffed mall short on Christmas spirit? So far they'd been jostled, sworn at, and bashed by a woman who was yelling into her phone instead of watching where she was swinging her shopping bags.

"Let's go to Macy's," Katie said quickly. *Before the music starts up again; before I give in to the OCD and go find maintenance.*

After Maisie had mentioned that *Miracle on 34th Street*—the remake, not the black-and-white original—was her favorite Christmas movie, Katie offered to take her to Macy's to find Theo's Christmas present. That, however, was before she had realized her daughter hated shopping malls. Would it ever end, this struggle to create a three-dimensional oil painting out of a connect-the-dots worksheet?

Dodging shoppers, they walked away from the center of the mall, and the squawking of the clarinet in "Jingle Bells" receded.

"How are things going with Dr. Young?" Katie said.

"Quite well, thank you. I like her very much."

"Is she helping with the fear of middle school?"

"Oh, yes. It's still super scary, but I'm excited about trying out for the middle school band, and Ms. Lynn has been in contact with my dad and says she can't wait to get me in her classroom next year."

Katie glanced up at the mall clock. Their two hours were half-over, and there were still so many questions to ask. Why couldn't time slow down? Even better, why couldn't it stop and give them the gift of a never-ending afternoon?

"Thank you for helping me with my Christmas shopping," Maisie said. "Do you still have the twenty dollars my dad gave you?"

"Are you checking?"

Maisie smiled. "You've very good at this. My dad never asks about the checking."

"Sadly I have more experience than he does. But you're aware of it, which is huge. The less checking you can do, the better."

A security guard, walkie-talkie in his hand, dashed into a store up ahead, keys jangling on his belt. Was that a holstered gun at his waist? A gun, in a place with kids?

Does he think I stole something? Did I? What if I stole something and didn't realize? Is he going to shoot me in front of Maisie?

Feeling guilty is not the same as being guilty. This is OCD.

Katie pushed her hand deep into her pocket and scratched at the lining.

"Did Aunt Delaney buy nice sister gifts for you when she was my age?" Maisie said.

Why did it bother her that Delaney had reverted to aunt status, but she would never be anything other than Katie?

"We didn't do gifts when we were kids. To be honest, our Christmases were pretty small. Not much money to go around."

They reached the entrance to the department store, and Christmas Muzak blasted. Maisie fiddled with the strap of the *Star Wars* satchel Delaney had given her.

"I don't have much money, either. My coin bag only has four dollars and two quarters."

Katie glanced around for the store directory. So many people, too many people. "Your dad doesn't give you pocket money?"

"Oh, no. I don't like to wear things with pockets."

Katie looked at Maisie and started laughing.

"What's funny?" Maisie frowned.

"'Mazing Maisie, I love spending time with you. You say the best things."

Maisie beamed. "Did you have any Christmas traditions when you were a kid?" Maisie had started asking questions about the Sullivan side of her family. Not many, but a few dotted here and there. At first Katie gave vague answers, but then Maisie had explained she was collecting family stories for a scrapbook.

"We did have one tradition." Katie smiled. "Your grandmother was very religious, and she liked to go to Midnight Mass. When we were little, your aunt and I begged to go, but Mom was adamant that we were too young to stay up that late. Instead, she started this Christmas Eve tradition. We would have hot chocolate, brush our teeth, put out our stockings for Santa, and then snuggle in bed while she read the story of Jesus's birth. When she was done, she gave us each a special present. And she'd say, 'Don't tell Daddy.' I found out much later that she saved up her pennies all year long for those two gifts."

"Oh, she sounds lovely."

"She could be, yes. But she struggled to be happy."

"That's very sad."

"I know. But you know what isn't sad? Since meeting you again, I've realized your grandmother had a lot of problems."

"OCD problems?"

"I think so. With a few other things tossed in. She didn't get help, but she did the best she could."

"Why didn't she get help?"

"She believed mental illness is something to be ashamed of, which it isn't. And my dad wasn't supportive. Not like Ben is with me."

"Are you and Ben getting married?"

"One day, I hope. But I need life to find a boring rhythm for a while." Katie tried to not remember making love on the sofa the night before. "Do you need help choosing any more Christmas gifts while we're here?"

"No, thank you. I *always* make my own. Although, Theo's has to be age appropriate, which is the causation of my current problem. It was very nice of you to offer a solution. Thank you! It's super hard to find the right gift for a baby. Gosh—" Maisie started gnawing on her thumbnail. "There are lots of people in here, aren't there?"

"I'm sorry, I should have thought more about how busy a mall would be the weekend before Christmas. Sorry."

"Is OCD making you apologize?" Maisie looked up with huge hazel eyes.

"Busted!"

"I hate OCD. It's stinkier than a thousand stinky butts."

"A million."

"A trillion!"

Katie held up her fist for a knuckle touch, and they started walking again.

"Are you managing to boss back some of your worries?" Katie said.

"Yes, but it's super hard, isn't it?"

"Something only the bravest of the brave can handle. Are you using your mantra?"

"Oh, yes!" Maisie cleared her throat and pushed her arms back as if she were spearing snow with ski poles. "I am brave, I am a fearless warrior."

"Woot!" Katie pumped the air.

Maisie grinned. "My dad's hung a *huuuge* color-coded chart in his office called 'Maisie's Fears.' We're trying to be very systemic."

"Systematic?"

"That's the word!"

"And can you see the difference, after three months?"

"Oh, yes. We have *el-iminated* lots of smaller worries, but the exposures are very hard."

"I know, sweetheart. I'm doing them with my new therapist, and some days I think I'd rather pick up a large, hairy spider."

"Ewww," Maisie shrieked.

"But I'm learning a lot."

Like how everything goes back to uncertainty about my role. Of how becoming an actual mother recaptured the trauma of being a mom when I was still a child. And then the uncertainty of who I am to you, to Ben . . . One big cauldron of uncertainty.

"My dad says you've started a support group for adults with the really bad kind of OCD."

They reached the store directory and stopped. People streamed past on either side. "Honey, all OCD is bad. It's no different from hair color. Your hair can be the same exact shade as someone else's, but no one wears it quite the way you do. Aunt Delaney, for example, wears her hair long and mine is short, but we both have black hair." Katie smiled. "Goodness. That made more sense in my head."

"Oh, no, I understand." Maisie held up her own hair. "I only wore a ponytail to keep Ava Grace happy. I didn't want to offend her so she'd decide she liked Ellie more, and the voice told me she would. But now I say, 'Ava Grace. That is your choice, not mine. Only I get to decide how I want to wear my hair.' I like being a redhead. My dad always said my hair color was a sign of strength." Maisie pulled back her chin. "Forged in fire like Vulcan."

"Vulcan, the god of metalworking?"

"*Yyyes*. And how weird is that when we didn't know you were a metal artist?"

"Pretty weird. But everything about our blended family is unusual."

A young woman towed a screaming toddler toward the exit.

"I like weird. Weird means you're an *innn*dividual," Maisie said. "And I like that you and Uncle J have become friends."

"So do I. You, Vulcan Maisie, are very wise."

Maisie giggled. "My dad was telling me about this big conference that's held every summer for people with OCD. Mr. Whitmore told him all about it."

"It's my dream to go one year and give a workshop on how OCD can mess with new moms." Katie pointed at the escalator. "Maybe in the future. It's pretty expensive."

"Do they allow kids?" Maisie jumped on and Katie stood behind, arms spread-eagled so she could hold both handrails and create a barrier in case Maisie slipped and fell. But that wasn't OCD, right? That was normal mom impulse. Right?

"Yup. The kids' activities are meant to be the best part."

"That sounds super awesome." Maisie hopped off the escalator, and Katie followed. "Oh, gosh! I forgot to check in with my dad." Maisie pulled out her phone and typed quickly.

"All done!" Maisie said after a few minutes, and they headed toward shelves—and shelves—of baby paraphernalia.

"If we find something that's out of your budget, I'd be happy to kick in the extra. How would you feel about giving Theo a joint present, from both of us?"

"Oh, *yyyes*. After all, we did save his life."

"Wow. This is a bit overwhelming," Katie said. "I'm not a great decision maker. You?"

"My dad says I'm hopeless, but he also says I'm supernaturally observant. What did I like as a baby? Maybe if you give me some hints, I can find something appropriate."

"Honey, you have at least two years before Theo cares what you give him. And even then, he'll be more interested in the box than what's inside."

Maisie frowned. "What did you buy for me when I was born?"

"Lulabelle, books, and the Winnie-the-Pooh lamp because Pooh is one philosophical bear, and I loved the idea of him shining wisdom on you. The baby shower and your dad's parents took care of everything else. Your grandmother went a bit overboard, since you were her only grandchild."

"That's it!" Maisie pranced in place, her hands fluttering. "I know what to give Theo! I know what to give him!"

Katie laughed. It was impossible not to when Maisie was excited.

"My Winnie-the-Pooh lamp!"

The laughter died in her throat.

"I mean, I'm far too old for it, and I only still have it because I don't want to hurt Uncle J's feelings by telling him the Maisie Reading Nook needs an upgrade. I mean, I *am* in double digits. Not that you'd know it from listening to my dad and Uncle Jake."

Katie concentrated on a fake Christmas tree covered in fake snow and Disney ornaments. Maisie wanted to regift one of the few things her mother had given her?

"Yes!" Maisie sounded emphatic. "That is a very good idea! When I was a little kid, my Winnie-the-Pooh lamp was my protector and you lived inside. Remember, I believed you were, you know—"

"Dead," Katie said the word quickly so Maisie wouldn't have to.

"I was afraid of the dark, and my dad always left the lamp on. He told me that it would protect me because the light came from the strongest force in *alll* of nature—a mother's love."

Katie grabbed the hem of her jacket and balled it up, hand and fabric in a tight fist.

"Oh, this is perfect! I even created a story about the magical powers of the lamp. My dad paid to have it made into a book. He says it's one of his most treasured possessions. Not that it was like writing a real novel." Maisie held up both hands. "It was only a craft kit for little kids, but my dad keeps it on his nightstand. I suspect he'll move it when we start the babyproofing everyone keeps talking about. Would you like to see the book when you take me home?"

"I—"

Maisie's phone rang. "Hi, Daddy. Yes, we're having a very nice time, thank you." She turned and walked back to the glass balcony that looked down over the floor below.

Not too close, Maisie. Please, not too close.

Beyond the glass barrier, holiday shoppers moved up and down the escalators. The Muzak shifted to "Santa Claus Is Coming to Town."

Maisie swung around with her phone held out at arm's length. "My dad wants to say hi."

Katie took the phone. "We're not making a break for the Canadian border. Honest."

"That's not funny," Cal said.

"Did you tell Maisie the light from the old Winnie-the-Pooh lamp was me guarding her?"

"Yes. She wrote the sweetest story about it. She was terrified of the dark, so I told her that when she was born, you'd promised to keep her safe, and although God had other plans for you, that promise lived on in the light of the lamp. Why?"

"Nothing." Cal might have lived the experience with her, but only Ben understood the backstory. "So, what's up?"

"Maisie thinks we should give you a Christmas present."

"That's sweet, but unnecessary. I don't want to make things even more awkward."

"I was wondering if I could fund a three-day trip to the OCD conference next summer. I researched it after the fundraiser. The kid activities sound great."

Maisie grinned, her head to one side.

"Cal, that's incredibly generous, but—"

"With two bedrooms. One for you and Maisie, one for Jake."

"What?"

Maisie disappeared behind a row of shelves; Katie moved to keep her in view.

"Jake wants to learn more about OCD, and you and Jake are Maisie's second family."

"You would do that? Why?"

"As a long-overdue apology. A real one." He paused. "And as a thank-you for saving my family. And before you ask, no, it can't be four days. Think of three as a mother-daughter exposure."

"I don't know what to say."

"How about yes?"

Katie smiled. "Yes. Yes! Thank you, Cal. Thank you for giving me a second chance. I won't screw this one up. I swear on all that's sacred to me."

"You and Jake can handle a weekend without tequila?"

"Absolutely!"

In the background, Theo cried.

"Do you ever wonder how we ended up here?" Cal said.

"No. Because where we are right now, at this moment, is good. It's as if everything finally fits together—you and Lilah, me and Ben, Jake and Delaney. I mean, not Jake and Delaney as a couple, but as Maisie's aunt and uncle."

"I know what you mean . . ." Cal's voice trailed off.

What had Jake said, about potential? "And between us, we've got a lot of promise."

"I think so, too. Right, I'm on diaper duty. Bye, Katie. We'll see you in an hour." And he hung up.

Katie, he finally called me Katie.

Maisie walked toward her, carrying a box with pictures of Winnie-the-Pooh and Piglet on the side. "I've decided that I can never, *ever* part with my lamp. It's a very important part of my childhood. This lamp is forty dollars. Is that too much?" Maisie chewed on her lip. "If it is, we can pick something cheaper."

What if I snatch that box from her, pull out the lamp, plug it in, and cause a fire? What if I want to start a fire? What if I want to hurt her?

"Let's buy it. This is, without doubt"—*Without doubt, OCD*—"the most perfect baby gift ever."

"*Yyyes!*" Maisie said.

The sales assistant, who looked as if she should be home baking cookies for hordes of grandkids, not working a holiday cash register, smiled as Maisie handed over the box. "Would you like this gift wrapped, young lady?"

"Oh, yes, please. It's for my new baby brother. He's at home with my dad."

"Well, congratulations. And you, Mama, look pretty good for someone with a new baby at home." The woman smiled as Katie handed over the cash.

"Actually, he's my half brother." Maisie jiggled back and forth. "We have the same dad and different moms. This is my birth mom. We had to be apart for nine years because it was the only way she knew how to keep me safe, but she's back and she's never leaving again."

Katie stared.

"A long, long time ago, my mama gave me up for adoption," the woman said. "And she did it out of love. Way I see it, only the best kind of mamas can walk away so as to do right by their babies."

Maisie gave a little "Huh."

When the box with the new Winnie-the-Pooh lamp was covered in baby's-first-Christmas wrapping paper, Katie tucked it under her left arm and held her right hand out to Maisie. As they walked back toward the down escalator, one thought stuck. Only one.

I'm the best kind of mama.

ACKNOWLEDGMENTS

This story has been my constant companion through a year of incredible highs and unbearable lows. My father-in-law turned one hundred, my husband beat a major health scare, our son entered his senior year at Oberlin College, one of his poems was accepted for publication in the *Albion Review*, the family OCD surged, we navigated numerous aging-parent crises, and our hearts broke with a devastating phone call on Christmas night.

I know which lines I wrote alone in my bedroom before telling friends and family that my husband was in hospital, which dialogue I stole while eavesdropping in a surgical waiting room, which scene I crafted midair while returning from an emotionally exhausting trip to England. One day I wrote fourteen words. They were about grief.

Throughout, I struggled to move from my world of OCD to Katie's. If I've succeeded, it's because Zachariah Claypole White gently informed me that I'd written a sermon instead of a parable. My poet-musician-writer son also provided hours of brainstorming and drew a story map—I work better with visual aids—that he taped to my filing cabinet. Reading about OCD if you have OCD is a minefield, and I'm in awe of his bravery, honesty, and brilliance as a wordsmith and a storyteller. (Updated mama brag: he graduated Phi Beta Kappa.) Since he also found my story seed hiding in a different idea, I credit him with this novel's existence and hereby toast the former Beloved Teenage Delinquent.

An endless stream of gratitude goes to Nalini Akolekar and everyone at Spencerhill Associates. Nalini always has my back and never freaks out when I enlighten her on the latest family drama that could, quite possibly, wreck my deadline and prompt me to run for the horizon. To authors-in-waiting: the hell of querying is worth it to land the right agent.

I'm thrilled to complete another novel with my author team at Lake Union Publishing. Special thanks are reserved for my editors, Jodi Warshaw and Clete Barrett Smith, who continue to get my dark quirkiness, work around my personal crises, and push me to stretch for the next level with such enthusiasm. Even better, they make the process fun. Clete—I gulped when I got the five-page editorial letter, but your edits were brilliant.

A shout-out to Dennelle Catlett, Kathleen Carter Zrelak, Jeff Umbro, and Ann-Grace Martin for the PR push on *Echoes of Family*, and deepest thanks to web designer Adam Rottinghaus and author assistant Carolyn Ring. To Elizabeth Brown of Swift Edits, you are the queen of freelance editors and commas. Thank you for reading an early draft on a tight turnaround and posing tough questions in the nicest way. And to Sheryl Cornett, I'm sorry our schedules weren't in sync this time, but thank you for the emotional support and for letting me steal your cottage for Jake. And much gratitude to Margie Lawson, who took me aside at the Women's Fiction Writers Association (WFWA) retreat and forced me to pick apart the prologue, with incredible results.

Huge thanks to readers and bloggers—I wish I could list all of you—who keep me smiling with comments on social media and messages that make me say, "This is why I do it." To book clubs national and international, thank you for hours of engagement and fantastic questions; thank you to Readers Coffeehouse members for the daily fun; and thank you to everyone who weighs in on my mad Facebook research questions.

We have the best indie bookstores in the Piedmont area of North Carolina, and I am forever grateful for their support. Special thanks to Purple Crow Books, Flyleaf Books, McIntyre's Books, Page 158 Books (my new gin suppliers), the Country Bookshop, and Scuppernong Books. And thank you to writer pals who keep me sane: the Raleigh crew, BPers, my sistas and brothers at WFWA, Fiction Writers Co-Op, and the Ladies of the Lake (known on social media as Lake Union Authors).

Heartfelt thanks to the women who helped me understand the horrors of postpartum OCD, especially Angie Alexander—a sufferer and an advocate—and thank you to the people who continue to be part of my own journey through OCD: Family & Friend Support 4 OCD, and the two Dr. Gammons. To Nancy Young, Joy Ross Davis, Rosalyn Eves, and Judy Moticka, thank you for sharing powerful stories of placental abruption. For talking me through medical what-ifs, thank you to Melisa Holmes, Priscille Sibley, and Kerry Schafer.

Thank you to everyone at Liberty Arts Sculpture Studio & Foundry for allowing me to intrude on creative endeavors. I'm not sure what to say to metal artists Jackie MacLeod and Mike Roig, except thank you for giving me so much raw material. I left your interviews with a buzzing mind and that warm, fuzzy glow of fandom. Special thanks to Jackie for radiating calm when she handed me the welding torch.

For guiding me through the ins and outs of abandonment, divorce, and parental rights, thank you to Diana Ricketts and Cullen Cornett. Cullen also provided endless research on health care options for the less fortunate. It was, sadly, an eye-opener.

Thank you to Gab Smith of CAM and Raleigh art teacher Tonya Vinson for the scoop on the docent program. Thank you to Alison Taylor for explaining Delaney's job. For filling my head with the world of acting, thank you to Maddie Taylor, Grace Taylor, and Melissa Lozoff of Movie Makers and Studio A Acting Company. For helping me enter the world of ten-year-old girls, thank you to Beth Lundberg, Annabeth Lundberg, and Tasha Seegmiller.

Research takes a village, which is why I also need to thank the following: Trina Allen, Marcy Cohen, Cathy Davidson, Laura Drake (biker chick!), Peggy Loftus Finck, Carole Gillespie, Kathleen Gleiter, Tripp Javis, Ashley Johnson, Stephen Libby, Elena Mikalsen, Catherine Parker, Laurie Picillo, Melissa Roth, Laura Spinella, Jill Sugg (the original Ms. Jill), Damon Tweedy, Susan Walters Peterson, and 911 dispatcher Jessica Payne. Carol Boyer, the hummers are for you; and congratulations, Ed Tremblay, for winning a mention through the Independent Bookstore Day prize. Hugs to my son (again) and Danlee Gildersleeve, aka the Arcadian Project, for providing much of my writing soundtrack, and kisses to friends and family on both sides of the pond, especially the Grossbergs, the Roses, Anne Claypole White, Susan Rose, and Rev. Douglas Claypole White. (I visualize him puffing on a cigar in heaven.)

I've officially run out of ways to thank Leslie Gildersleeve, my beta reader. Leslie has critiqued everything I've ever written, helps me brainstorm over alcohol on Friday nights, lets me bug her with pesky research questions, and refuses thank-you gifts. I can no longer navigate writing, my reading stacks, or the crap of everyday life without her. Love ya, girl.

For Larry Grossberg, my raison d'être: Thank you for putting up with my imaginary friends and the chaos they bring to our lives. Thank you for letting me bounce ideas, titles, and character motivations off you (but you were *sooo* wrong about Jake). Thank you for keeping me watered and fed, and for buying the Botanist gin even though it's more expensive than Gordon's. Most of all, thank you for remembering that the woman who mumbles away in an upstairs office twenty-four seven is actually your wife.

To Stephen Whitney: love you lots. May the afterlife be a never-ending party with Leonard Cohen, Prince, David Bowie, and Princess Leia—and the occasional dance by the pool at the Paradise Island Beach Club.

BOOK CLUB DISCUSSION QUESTIONS

1. Katie and Callum both take extreme measures to protect
    Maisie from what they perceive as threats. Would you
    have acted as they did? Do you, or people around you,
    battle monsters? Does it make any difference whether
    those monsters are real or imaginary?
2. There are parallels between Katie's intrusive thoughts and
    Callum's intrusive memories. Katie's anxiety is genetic,
    but stays largely dormant until the postpartum period.
    Callum's is triggered—and retriggered—by trauma. Did
    their stories help you understand what it means to bat-
    tle anxiety? What did the novel teach you about anxiety
    disorders?
3. Shame and then lack of resources prevent Katie from seek-
    ing professional help. Do you think we've made any prog-
    ress in tackling the stigma that comes with mental illness?
    Does anyone close to you have experience in coping with

mental illness without access to good resources, including health care?

4. Hindsight can be a blessing and a curse. Often it's only after the death of a loved one that we can revisit the relationship with perspective and discover something that was hiding in plain sight. Have you ever reevaluated a relationship with someone in the way that Katie does with her mother? What did you learn?

5. Katie constantly reevaluates what it means to be a mom. What do you think defines a good mother? Can you imagine a situation in which you could give up your child and/or your parental rights as Katie did? Who do you think is Maisie's real mother, and why?

6. Might Katie and Callum's marriage have survived if they'd been honest and open with each other? Do you think they could have been? How does your family handle communication? Do you believe spouses should tell each other everything?

7. Callum is a tortured hero. Discuss his character arc. (Barbara would love to be part of any discussion about Callum, so don't forget she can Skype into your book club.)

8. Jake is another dark Barbara Claypole White character. What did you make of his journey? Did you feel empathy for him? Did your feelings about him change during the course of the novel?

9. Driven by guilt, loyalty, and a childhood promise, Jake packs up his life and moves across the country for his best friend. Is there a person for whom you would do that?

10. Katie's relationship with Jake is at the heart of this novel. How does it change and grow, and how do you see it evolving in the future?

11. In what ways do creative endeavors become therapy for the different characters? Have you ever used art as therapy?

12. The Winnie-the-Pooh lamp plays a significant role in the novel. Is there an object from your childhood that still carries meaning? If so, why do you think that is?

13. Barbara met her husband thirty years ago at JFK Airport. For this reason, she's drawn to the notion that people who need each other find each other and that quirks of fate can be life changing. How do both of these themes drive this story?

14. Did you spot the references to Barbara's other novels? Do you have a favorite character from her stories, and if so, who? Barbara writes stand-alone novels, but do you see continuities?

A CONVERSATION WITH
THE AUTHOR*

Spoiler Alert!

What was the inspiration for this novel?

As always, I found my characters' story through my own messy, organic process. I have vague ideas that lead to other vague ideas; I do tons of research, slap words on the page, and start looking for dark what-if moments. At some point a story emerges, but it goes through many transformations.

This time I started with two separate story seeds. The first was a heartbreaking incident in the OCD community. Many of us who are forced to share family life with OCD are active in confidential support groups. Someone in one of those groups had talked about her battles with pedophile OCD, and her comments were leaked to her employer. She was fired. That story haunted me for months and led me to think about the darkest corners of OCD, the ones that still carry crushing shame. Meanwhile, I was chewing on an idea about a single dad whose wife had run away when his daughter was a baby. His daughter, now a teen, hit a mental health crisis, and through her journey, he discovered his wife had struggled with the same illness. When I showed the synopsis to my brilliant creative writing major son, he highlighted one sentence—scratched out the rest—and said, "That's your story, Mom." I put the two threads together and found my premise: Can you be a good mother if you abandoned your baby?

Then the name Maisie MacDonald popped into my head and stuck, which meant her parents' heritage had to fit her surname. Other key elements came from strange places. At a Raleigh book club, one reader asked why I always write about UNC and Duke, but not NC State, which led to Callum. Jake was inspired by a photo of the actor Gabriel Byrne; Lilah came out of a conversation with a friend about the problems of being a stepmom; and I found Katie at the hairdresser's. I was admiring a piece of artwork in the salon when the wonderful stylist Angela Goldman said, "You should meet the artist, Jackie MacLeod. She's a girlie welder." That phrase did it: *girlie welder*. The next day I emailed Jackie and discovered the Liberty Arts Sculpture Studio & Foundry in Durham. Around the same time, I had a day to kill in Raleigh and went to CAM, where I discovered the docent program. (And the Videri Chocolate Factory.) Bingo!

The abuse angle came from an interview I watched with Gabriel Byrne, but I had no idea what part it should play. After brainstorming with freelance editor Elizabeth Brown and my son, I figured out that the abuse had triggered Jake's promise and Callum's anxiety, both of which drive the plot. As I researched abuse, I found fascinating parallels between the way Callum's brain processed his trauma and Katie's intrusive thoughts.

The final piece of the story came after my writing buddy Sheryl Cornett invited me to give a talk at her church. That evening three young people shared stories of struggling with mental illness without access to affordable health insurance, which triggered a new story angle.

I realized that while lack of money prevented Katie from seeing a therapist, shame achieved the same result for Callum. They had both tackled their problems the hard way: without professional help. Again, it was a similar issue viewed through a different lens.

The hero of your debut, *The Unfinished Garden*, also battled OCD. Why do you revisit OCD in your fifth novel?

I've always wanted to revisit OCD and anxiety. (James Nealy also suffered from generalized anxiety disorder, and if I were a shrink, I might consider that diagnosis for Callum.) I was also drawn to the idea of a story that delved deeper into the impact of OCD on relationships. OCD is so destructive, so twisted, so relentless, and yet there's a popular misconception it's about hand washing and the anal organization of sock drawers.

Even though I've been married to someone with OCD for nearly thirty years and our grown son has battled OCD since he was four, my learning curve continues. In fact, while working on this story, my son and I did some intense exposure response prevention (ERP) therapy—a refresher course we both needed. Like any chronic illness, OCD demands constant management. Lapses are common because stress and certain lifestyle choices can retrigger it. Ignore OCD, or get lazy with the techniques, and it rebuilds into a superstorm.

Much like Katie, I've also rethought my own mental health history through my child's. I never developed full-blown OCD, but I can identify two specific OCD fears I battled as a teenager. I never told anyone, and I dealt with them accidentally through repeated exposure. I've also been fascinated by harm OCD for years. Until recently I struggled with touching knives—anything bigger than a vegetable knife—because a little part of my brain would want to show me how I could stab someone. That's the real reason I wanted to create a character with postpartum OCD (which often manifests as violent images and thoughts): I can't imagine being a young mother trapped in horrific images of hurting her baby. To me that's a circle of hell.

Was it a challenge to fictionalize OCD in two different characters?

Given how much I know about life with OCD, it should have been easy. (A doddle, as we would say in England.) However, everything about OCD is intensely personal, and our family deals with OCD as an intruder—a separate entity—which isn't accurate. The OCD voice is not a third-person voice, as with schizophrenia. It's a relentless, unwanted thought, but it's still your thought. We all have intrusive thoughts, but most of us dismiss them. We don't assign them meaning. The OCD brain does the opposite: demands proof that, for example, you're not a bad person for entertaining unsettling thoughts. The hard part is learning how to process those thoughts without reacting to them. The thoughts are not the problem; it's how we deal with them.

As I excavated Katie's OCD, I was also riddled with my own intrusive doubts: Was I screwing up? Was it coming across as authentic? And why the hell did I think I could write a novel about anxiety and shame? After much angst and many conversations with my son, I treated the OCD differently from the way I did in *The Unfinished Garden*. I wanted it to present as accessible to readers, but I also wanted to remove the bumpers. To achieve that, I kept returning to something my son said: "If it's making you uncomfortable, you're on the right path." Because here's the truth: OCD is total and absolute shit twenty-four seven. Katie nailed it with that phrase.

What advice do you have for someone who is beginning his or her journey with OCD?

Go to the International OCD Foundation website before you do anything else. The IOCDF has a wealth of information and lists regional therapists who specialize in treating OCD, as well as local support groups. Therapy is painful for everyone in the family, and reaching out to others, especially for carers, can be lifesaving. My son's OCD returned full force in high school, and I could not have coped without my local support group. If you don't have a support group in your area, look online. Facebook is a wonderful resource.

Educate yourself and keep educating yourself, because OCD can adapt. Two books that have helped me enormously in the last year are *When a Family Member Has OCD* by Jon Hershfield and *The Mindfulness Workbook for OCD* by Jon Hershfield and Tom Corboy. I also recommend *The Imp of the Mind* by Lee Baer and the OCD page on the A2A Alliance website: http://a2aalliance.org/arc/ocd. *Dropping the Baby and Other Scary Thoughts* by Karen Kleiman (of the Postpartum Stress Center) and Amy Wenzel is a great resource for postpartum OCD, as is the group Postpartum Support International.

Tell us a little about the research for this novel, and the real people behind the story.

My characters are fictional, but I find them through interviews with real people. Obviously, there were many tough conversations behind this story. I remember talking to Angie Alexander about her journey with violent intrusive thoughts, and suddenly we were both in tears. Angie works tirelessly to reach out to other mothers who are suffering with anxiety, but her own story was hard to hear.

Other interviews were just plain fun. I had a blast learning about acting techniques from Melissa Lozoff of Movie Makers, and a riot discussing *Star Wars*, math, and sleepovers with a ten-year-old, Annabeth Lundberg. Maisie's favorite word, *causation*, came out of my interview with Annabeth, as did Maisie's line about pocket money. And my husband, the Prof, was an incredible resource for figuring out Callum's and

Lilah's academic lives. But the best part of working on this manuscript was entering the world of welding.

Jackie MacLeod and the other artists at Liberty Arts were so welcoming and gracious. I made three trips out to the studio to shadow Jackie as she worked, but she also answered endless questions via email and text, and insisted I experience welding firsthand. I'm a total wuss, so I tried to say no, but she persisted. Thank goodness! The moment that auto-darkening helmet came down and I saw the green light, everything in my head went quiet. I understood how and why welding had become Katie's therapy.

Interviewing local metal artist Mike Roig gave me a different perspective and helped me understand why welding is a cursing medium. If you check out Jackie and Mike's websites*, you'll see how much they inspired me. Jackie was working on a piece called *That Perfect Moment* when I interviewed her one day, and Mike creates huge, mesmerizing steel sculptures that dance in the wind. (I may also have stolen his motorbike for Ben.)

*http://www.mikeroig.com, http://jackiemacleod.com

What did this manuscript teach you?

I have good instincts as a person, but as a writer I second-guess everything, especially my ability to plot. My favorite freak-out follows the line of "Wait! My thing is crafting pretty sentences about flowers and light through the trees, and I don't have enough of those." But each manuscript has its own song, and I found this one by putting aside doubt and listening to instinct.

While working on the novel, I was slammed with a number of personal crises. Each crisis demanded my full attention, my emotional energy, and much of my writing time. As my deadline tightened around my neck, I allowed the story to flow the way it wanted to flow—through dialogue—and I became a ruthless editor.

I can't outline, but because I write to contract, I've trained myself to build road maps to avoid getting lost. These road maps are storyboards written to movie beats. I don't always stick to the details on the boards, but the framework—constructed around the beats—doesn't change. With this one, however, I veered way off course. Discombobulated, I started a second storyboard, which I abandoned halfway through. This novel, more than any of my others, took on a life of its own. What I learned was to let that happen.

For example, in the first and second drafts, I was convinced Katie's relationship with her support group was the B-story. But during one of my biannual trips to England to see my mother, I woke up early to write before breakfast and thought, *No. I don't want to work on the chapter with the support group. I want to stick with Katie and Jake.* Without a second thought, I bounced that chapter into the last act, and several months later, bounced it—plus a few other chapters—out completely. That gut instinct in England had told me the real B-story: Katie's relationship with Jake. It just took me a while to listen.

You often include a listening guide with your novels. Why is that, and can you tell us about the music behind *The Promise Between Us*?

I started building my writing career as a full-time mother in a high-maintenance family, and I'm part of the sandwich generation. That means something—or someone—is usually tugging at me for attention. Music has always been my escape from the stress of real life, and it allows me to block out everything beyond my characters' emotional lives. With music, I can write pretty much anywhere and through any distraction. My favorite writing retreat is on the direct flight home from London, which I take regularly. I remember pounding out one beloved scene while huddled in coach with my laptop, my iPod, and a glass of red wine. (Okay, so maybe it was two glasses.)

I can't feel my characters until I've found their music, and a soundtrack evolves naturally for each manuscript. I didn't publish the listening guide for *Echoes of Family*, because it followed Marianne's zany thought process and jumped all over the place. However, listening guides for all my other novels, including this one, are on my website.

My writing music has always included songs from the Airborne Toxic Event, My Chemical Romance, U2, and my son's band, the Arcadian Project, and this novel was no exception. However, I branched out in some unusual directions, including Marilyn Manson. Callum's song is "Creep" by Radiohead, Maisie's song is "Scarecrow" by My Chemical Romance (Jake introduced her to that one), and Katie's song is "Hourglass" by the Arcadian Project. Katie and Maisie's song is the amazing "Dear Alyssa," which my son wrote when he was sixteen as a prayer for anyone battling mental illness.

There's always one song that represents each novel for me, and for *The Promise Between Us*, that song is Mumford & Sons and Baaba Maal's "There Will Be Time."

Why do you tell this story from five viewpoints?

I had assumed I would be writing through the voices of Katie, Callum, and Lilah. But Jake's story drives much of the plot, and at some point it became obvious that Maisie needed a few chapters. When you strip everything away, this is a simple story about a small group of good people trapped in a bad situation. As with everything else in this novel, they're coming at the same problem from different angles. The writer and reader in me finds that intriguing.

What do you hope readers will take away from *The Promise Between Us*?

That motherhood, like most things in life, is not black and white; that OCD is a highly individualized anxiety disorder and can manifest in many different ways; that anxiety is a beast we should never under-estimate; and that our health insurance system often fails to provide access to mental health professionals. And, of course, that we all battle our own monsters and should never make assumptions about what goes on in another person's head. Phew. That's a lot, but here's the bottom line: I hope it's a good read. I certainly had fun writing it. Enjoy, y'all.

ABOUT THE AUTHOR

Photo © 2016 KM Photography

Bestselling author Barbara Claypole White creates hopeful family drama with a healthy dose of mental illness. Originally from England, she writes and gardens in the forests of North Carolina, where she lives with her beloved OCD family. Her previous novels include *The Unfinished Garden, The In-Between Hour, The Perfect Son,* and *Echoes of Family.* She is also an OCD Advocate for the A2A Alliance, a nonprofit group that promotes advocacy over adversity. To connect with Barbara, please visit www.barbaraclaypolewhite.com or follow her on Facebook. She's *always* on Facebook.